VICTORY

JULIAN STOCKWIN

VICTORY

HODDER &
STOUGHTON

First published in Great Britain in 2010 by Hodder & Stoughton
An Hachette UK company

1

Copyright © Julian Stockwin 2010

A CIP catalogue record for this title is available from the British Library.

Hardback ISBN 978 0 340 96119 3
Trade Paperback ISBN 978 0 340 96120 9

Maps drawn by Sandra Oakins

Typeset in Garamond MT by Palimpsest Book Production Limited,
Falkirk, Stirlingshire

Printed and bound by Clays Ltd, St Ives plc

Hodder & Stoughton policy is to use papers that are natural, renewable and
recyclable products and made from wood grown in sustainable forests.
The logging and manufacturing processes are expected to conform
to the environmental regulations of the country of origin.

Hodder & Stoughton Ltd
338 Euston Road
London NW1 3BH

www.hodder.co.uk

'The Royal Navy of England hath ever been its greatest defence and ornament. It is its ancient and natural strength – the floating bulwark of our island.'

Sir William Blackstone, Jurist,
Commentaries on the Laws of England

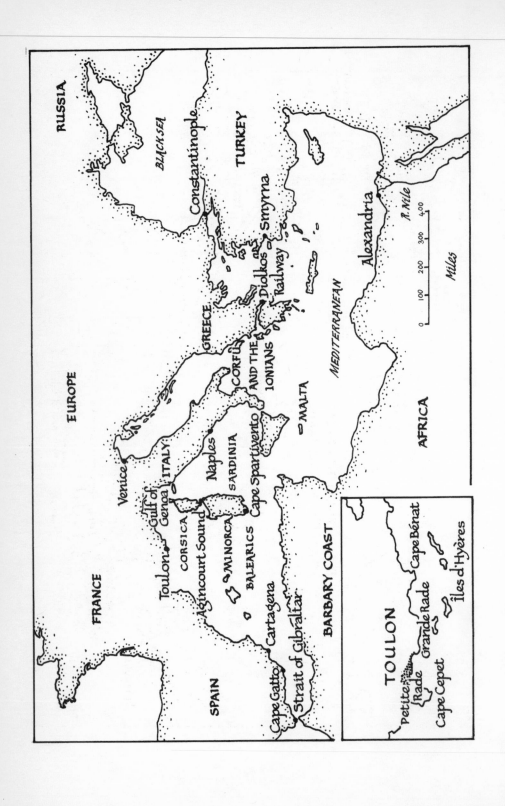

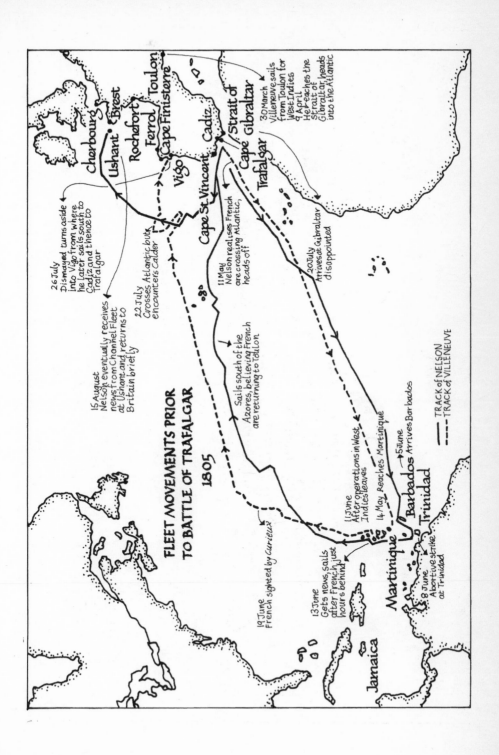

FLEET MOVEMENTS PRIOR
TO BATTLE OF TRAFALGAR
1805

30 March
Villeneuve sails
from Toulon for
West Indies
9 April
He reaches the
Strait of
Gibraltar, heads
into the Atlantic

26 July
Dismayed turns aside
into Vigo from where
he later sails south to
Cadiz and thence to
Trafalgar

15 August
Nelson eventually receives
news from Channel Fleet
at Ushant and returns to
Britain briefly

22 July
Crosses Atlantic but
encounters Calder

11 May
Nelson realises French
are crossing Atlantic,
heads off

20 July
Arrives at Gibraltar,
disappointed

Sails south of the
Azores, believing French
are returning to Toulon

19 June
French sighted by Curieux

13 June
Gets news, sails
after French, just
hours behind

1 June
After operations in West
Indies leaves

4 May Reaches Martinique

5 June
Barbados Arrives Barbados

8 June
Abortive strike
at Trinidad

Cherbourg
Ushant Brest
Rochefort
Ferrol
Toulon
Cape Finisterre
Vigo
Cape St Vincent
Cadiz
Strait of Gibraltar
Cape Gibraltar
Trafalgar

Jamaica
Martinique
Barbados
Trinidad

TRACK of NELSON
TRACK of VILLENEUVE

Chapter 1

At a hesitant knock on the cabin door Thomas Kydd's servant paused in shaving his master.

'Sir – Mr Hallum's duty an' Ushant is sighted to the nor'-east, eight miles,' blurted the duty midshipman, a little abashed at seeing his captain under the razor.

'Thank you, Mr Tawse,' Kydd grunted.

Nicholas Renzi looked up from the papers he was working on by the early morning light. He and Kydd were friends of many years. Both had achieved the quarterdeck from before the mast, but while Kydd had gained command of his own ship Renzi now pursued scholarly interests and acted as his clerk. Peering out of the stern windows of the little brig-sloop he said hopefully, 'And a fair wind for the Downs – I so yearn for a dish of Mistress Butterworth's haricot of mutton.'

Teazer had been taken from her patrol line along the French coast near the invasion ports and sent with dispatches, passengers and mail to the blockading battleships off Brest. A small ship had to expect such lowly employment but on her return, she would have a short spell in Deal, then be back on station, playing her part to thwart Napoleon Bonaparte's plans for the invasion of England.

It was the nightmare that haunted every man, woman and child – that the moat would be crossed and the staunch island nation must then taste the horrors of war. All it needed was for the emperor to wrest control from the Royal Navy for a few tides and, with half a million men under arms and two thousand vessels now in the invasion flotilla, he could flood the country with the armies that had conquered all Europe.

Kydd shifted restlessly. 'Thank you, Tysoe. A breakfast when it's ready.' The towel was expertly flicked away and he was released to take up his lieutenant's reworked quarters bill. They had lost two men to death and wounding and five to sickness; it had been made very clear that there would be no replacements, for the country had been stripped of trained seamen and *Teazer*'s humble station did not warrant special treatment.

He glanced at the paper irritably. Hallum had no doubt done his best but to rate up the pleasant but diffident Williams to full gun-captain was not the way to fill holes. Even now, after months in *Teazer*, his first lieutenant seemed not to know the men, their character, their individual strengths and weaknesses.

Kydd circled Bluett's name in the gun-crew and scrawled, 'to be GC' then realised that as a sail-trimmer the man could not be expected to absent himself just when his crew would need him. Damn. Very well, he'd make young Rawlings sail-trimmer. Barely more than a ship's boy, he was nevertheless agile and bright – he'd soon learn to swarm up to the tops with the best of them. But would he cope under savage enemy fire?

Imperceptibly the ship's angular rhythm of pitch and roll changed to a smoother rise and fall as she rounded Ushant, the lonely island that marked the north-west extremity of France. Now, with this fair south-westerly, it was a straight run up-Channel for home.

The masthead lookout's hail cut through Kydd's thoughts. '*Saaail hoooo!* Sail t' the larb'd quarter!'

He snatched up his grego against the autumn chill and joined the group on the quarterdeck. 'Mr Hallum?'

'Two points abaft the beam, sir, and steering towards us.'

Kydd nodded: the unknown ship was inward bound from the Atlantic Ocean. A lone merchantman? But every British merchant ship had by law to be a member of a convoy. Then was it a daring Frenchman breaking the blockade? If so, his luck had just run out . . .

'I'll take a peep, I believe,' he said, and swung easily up into the main-shrouds, mounting to the main-top. His pocket glass steadied on the speck of paleness away to the west. Smallish, but unmistakable with its tell-tale three masts, it was a *chasse marée*, a lugger, and the favoured vessel of the infamous Brittany privateers.

A smile of satisfaction spread across Kydd's face: he was perfectly placed to crowd the luckless corsair against the unfriendly Cornish coast, and in any chase the rising seas would favour the larger *Teazer*. He hailed the deck below, ordering the necessary course change to intercept.

Almost certainly the vessel was returning after a voyage of depredation from somewhere like St Malo, a notorious nest of privateers, but now it had found *Teazer* athwart its hawse. Suddenly the image foreshortened, then opened up again – it was putting about, back to the open ocean.

It would be to no avail: *Teazer* held it to advantage and

would converge well before it could escape. Kydd descended quickly and stood clear as the guns were cast loose and battle preparations made. The privateer was making a run for it. It was unlikely to take on a full-blooded man-o'-war but it was armed and dangerous with plenty of men so nothing could be left to chance.

The wind was veering and strengthening; there would be reefs in its soaring lugsails soon and, with the quartering fresh breeze as *Teazer*'s best point of sailing, he could rely on an interception before noon.

Within a few hours the sombre dark grey of the English coast lifted into view and they had gained appreciably on the privateer, which would soon be in range. Apart from a far-distant scatter of coastal sail there did not appear to be any other vessels and Kydd would shortly make his move.

'Bolderin' weather,' said Purchet, the boatswain, staring gloomily at the approaching change. Curtains of white hung vertically against sullen dark cloud banks. *Teazer*'s open main-deck in a line squall was not best placed for play with the guns; it was a challenge to try to keep the priming powder dry on heaving wet decks while rain hammered down.

The squall accelerated and then it was upon them, a hissing deluge of cold rain that blotted out everything beyond a hundred yards.

Suddenly Kydd snapped, 'Three points to starb'd!' The group about the helm looked at him in astonishment but hastily complied.

Teazer swung back before the wind, seeming to have abandoned the chase and wallowing in the temporary calm behind the line squall. But when the rain thinned and cleared, there was the privateer, not half a mile distant – and dead ahead.

Kydd had instinctively known that the captain would reverse course in the squall with the intention of slipping past him.

'Quarters, Mr Hallum,' Kydd ordered. 'We'll head him, I believe,' he added. 'And when—'

'Company, I think.' Renzi had come up beside him. While others were more interested in the unfolding action ahead, he had spotted a frigate emerging from the drifting curtains of mist a mile or two away in the wind's eye.

'T' blazes with 'im,' growled Purchet. Admiralty rules dictated that all on the scene would share equally in any prize-taking, no matter their contribution.

'Don't recognise she,' muttered *Teazer*'s coxswain, Poulden, at the wheel, his eyebrows raised.

'Private signal,' Kydd ordered Tawse.

Their flags soared up. After a short delay, fluttering colour mounted the frigate's mizzen, with what seemed very like the blue ensign of Admiral Keith's Downs Squadron accompanying it.

'Can't read 'em!' the youngster squeaked, training the signal telescope.

The flags were streaming end on towards them, but who else other than a roaming English frigate would be this side of the Channel?

The privateer had gone about once more in a desperate bid to evade capture but there was no chance for it now with a frigate coming up fast to join the fun. Kydd judged the distance to the privateer by eye and decided to make his lunge.

'A ball under his forefoot when within two cables,' he ordered, then glanced at the frigate. If it interfered, disregarding the unwritten rules of prize-taking that as Kydd was first on the scene it was his bird, the commander-in-chief would hear about it. He couldn't recollect ever coming across the vessel but it was not unknown for recent captures to be put into service without delay and this was clearly a frigate with distinct French lines.

The forward six-pounder cracked out: a plume arose not an oar's-length from the privateer's bows and precisely on range. The gunner straightened and glanced back to *Teazer*'s quarterdeck with a smirk of satisfaction. The lugger held on but it would not for long . . .

Then, in an instant, all changed. The frigate, now within just a few hundred yards, jerked down her ensign and hoisted another on the opposite halliard. After the barest pause it slewed to a parallel and guns opened up along its entire length, a shocking avalanche of destruction.

Aboard *Teazer* a man dropped, shrieking in agony, and one of the marines fell squealing. Kydd forced his mind into the iron calm of combat. The frigate had not achieved its goal: it had obviously aimed for their rigging, intent on disabling *Teazer*, so it could then range alongside and accept their surrender under the threat of overwhelming force. But *Teazer* sailed on obstinately, capable of fighting back, albeit with sails shot through and lines carried away aloft.

Kydd knew it was no dishonour to flee before such odds, and he would have to let the privateer go as his first duty was to preserve his ship. He looked around quickly. The frigate was in a dominating position to weather and he had noted her swift approach before the wind. Was she as fine a sailer close-hauled as *Teazer*?

'Down helm, as close as she'll lie, Poulden,' Kydd cracked out. *Teazer* surged nobly up to the wind. The frigate, taken by surprise, was forced to conform also. They'd established a precious lead on the larger ship.

It was taking them in a hard beat back out into the Atlantic but it couldn't be helped. Kydd bit his lip. If they were overcome, Napoleon's newspapers would make much of one of Britain's famed men-o'-war humbled, captured in glorious combat on the high seas and paraded into port for all to see, with no account taken of the odds. The frigate's captain would be well rewarded by his new emperor.

The frigate, trailing by barely a couple of hundred yards, had only to make up the distance and the guns would speak once more. At the moment the gap stayed. And the privateer had not fled: it had curved around and was beating resolutely after them. Then Kydd realised they were working together.

Straining every nerve his little ship thrashed away over the miles, out into the wastes of ocean, in a desperate race for life. Speed was being dissipated with the loss of wind through the rents in the sails but it would be suicide to pause to bend on new.

Slowly the privateer overhauled *Teazer* and took position on her defenceless quarter, confident she could not break off to deal with it.

Meanwhile Purchet, watching the frigate, said in a low voice, 'She's fore-reaching on us.' Out in the open seas the broad combers that rode on the lazy swell were meeting *Teazer*'s bow in solid explosions of white, each one a tiny brake on their progress, while the larger frigate was throwing them aside with ease.

Kydd felt the creeping chill of doubt. The privateer was easing closer under their lee, the masses of men it carried clearly visible. It had few guns – but on a slide on its foredeck there was a twelve-pounder, double the size of *Teazer*'s biggest carriage gun. Suddenly this crashed out with a heavy ball low over her quarterdeck. The vicious wind of its passage made Kydd stagger.

It was now deadly serious. With the privateer to leeward and the frigate coming up to windward, they would soon be trapped. Another shot sent powder-smoke up and away to leeward. The ball threw Dowse, the master, to his knees with a cry and smashed the forward davit. Their cutter hung suspended aft, splintering against *Teazer*'s pretty quarter gallery until it fell away.

Kydd saw it was the helm the lugger was aiming at. With that knocked out, the frigate would be up in a trice and it would all be over. But there *was* a card he could play.

'Ready about!' He was gambling their lives that the brig-rigged *Teazer* was handier in stays than the three-masted frigate, but if any fumbled his duty . . .

The privateer could do nothing to stop them, and the frigate must have thought their motions a bluff for it carried past as *Teazer* took up on the other tack. There was a price to pay, however – its other broadside thundered out at the sloop's stern-quarters as she made away. Two shot shattered *Teazer*'s ornate windows and erupted through her captain's cabin, slamming down the length of the vessel.

It was a stay of execution. Now on the opposite tack, *Teazer* was being forced back towards the French coast and would be lucky to weather Ushant. The privateer resumed its station off their ruined quarter and continued its slow but relentless fire as the frigate went about and took up the chase again.

There would not be another chance. They could only hope for the deliverance of a stray warship of the Brest blockading squadron having occasion to go north-about as they had done. *Teazer*'s luck had finally turned and there was every prospect that before the end of the day the tricolour of Napoleon's France would be floating aloft and Kydd's precious fighting sword would be in the proud possession of the unknown frigate captain.

Kydd's eyes stung. *Teazer* – his first and only command. To be taken from him so cruelly, without warning and on her way home. It was—

A twelve-pounder shot struck an upper dead-eye of the main-shrouds with shocking force, setting the lanyards to a wild unravelling. The heavy rope jerked away, then swung dangerously free to menace the quarterdeck. Poulden gripped the wheel-spokes defiantly – another ball had nearly taken his head off before chunking into the hammocks at the rail and sending them flying to the wind.

With the privateer now redoubling its efforts to destroy the helm, Poulden continued to stand fast, doing his duty. Kydd honoured him for it as he balled his own hands in frustration. Then he decided: there was one last scene to be played. He knew his men were behind him in whatever must be done.

'Mr Hallum,' he said, to his lieutenant, in a calm voice, 'I'm going to hazard a move at the privateer. If we can put him down, we've a chance – a small one – with the frigate. Post your men quickly now.'

The older man's face lengthened. For a moment Kydd felt for him: he should be quietly at home with his grown daughters, not at the extremity of peril out here in the wild ocean. Then he realised that, although the lieutenant had no deep understanding of his men, the stolid and unimaginative officer was determined to do *his* duty as well in England's time of trial. He added warmly, 'Never forget, sir, we've the better ship.'

'Ushant again,' Renzi murmured. The grey smudge gratifyingly to leeward was token of *Teazer*'s weatherliness, but they dared not ease away south towards the blockade, for the frigate had already shown her qualities before the wind. It was time for the final throw of the dice.

Warned off, the men hauled furiously on the lines as *Teazer* wheeled on her tormentor, her carronades crashing out – but the privateer was clearly waiting for such a move. Instantly it put down its tiller and bore away, the pert transom offering the smallest of targets.

Kydd saw that the move had failed and, alarmingly, he now felt the weight of the wind more squarely on the battle-damaged fore-topsail. Then it split from top to bottom, each side flapping uselessly.

'Ease sheets,' he said dully, conscious of the many pale faces looking aft, waiting to hear their fate. What could he offer them? Surrender tamely? Fight to the last? Think of some ingenious stratagem that would even the odds?

It was no good. The end was inevitable: why spill his men's blood just to make a point? He raised his eyes to the frigate coming up. It seemed in no rush – but, then, it had all the time in the world to finish them.

Should he haul down their colours before the broadside came? 'Mr Tawse . . .' but the order wouldn't come out. The frigate altered course and made to run down on them, the row of black gun muzzles along her side probably the last thing on earth many of his crew would see.

But the cannon remained mute. '*Ohé, du bateau!*' came a faint hail from the frigate's quarterdeck.

Kydd cupped his hand: '*Le navire de sa majesté* Teazer.'

'*À bas le pavillon!*' demanded the voice, in hectoring tones – Strike your colours!

Feeling flooded Kydd. This was not how it was going to end with his beloved ship. He would not let the French seize and despoil her. It would be like the violation of a loved one. Fierce anger clamped in.

'*Never!*' he roared back, and braced himself.

The shock of the expected broadside did not come. Instead there was a brief hesitation and the frigate's side slid smoothly towards *Teazer*'s.

'Stand by to repel boarders!' Kydd bawled urgently, drawing his sword.

It was crazy: a frigate carried several times their number and their own guns were charged with round-shot, not the merciless canister that would sweep their decks clear. It would all be over in minutes – one way or the other.

They closed. Now only yards separated them, the milling, shouting mass on the enemy deck jostling with naked steel amain in anticipation. Kydd heard a hoarse order in French and shrieked, '*Get down!*'

He flung himself to the deck just as the murderous blast of grape and canister lashed *Teazer*'s bulwarks. Choking on the swirling powder-smoke he heaved himself up. A swelling cheer rose about him as *Teazer*'s carronades smashed back, adding to the thick smoke-pall and screaming chaos. Then, through the clearing reek, Kydd saw the high side of the frigate bearing down.

'Stand t' your weapons!' he roared. Around him Teazers hefted cutlasses, pistols and boarding pikes. There was an almighty shudder as the two vessels touched and groaned in unison, the movement sending several to their knees.

The seas were high, producing a corkscrew effect on the two vessels that made them roll out of step with each other. The yells of triumph from the Frenchman's deck tailed off quickly at the sight of a dark chasm between the two ships and the boarders hesitated. Some stood on the bulwarks poised to leap and were hit by pistol shot and musket fire from *Teazer*'s marines. They dropped with shrieks between the grinding hulls; others held back at the sight of the lethal points of boarding pikes held by unflinching British seamen.

A swivel banged from *Teazer*'s rail, another from forward. The French boarders' hesitation was fatal for at that moment the frigate caught a wind flurry and surged ahead and away, snapping the grapnels that held the ships together and spilling three men into the sea.

A storm of cheers went up from the Teazers at the sight of the frigate sheering off, but Kydd didn't join in. As the frigate readied for another attempt the privateer was manoeuvring to close and it was obvious to him that this time there was the awful prospect of a boarding from both sides simultaneously.

He hastily summoned every man aboard to join the lines of defenders, sending some into the tops with grenadoes to hurl at the massing boarders, with swivels to mount that could bring fire down on them, but it was so little against such odds.

The frigate had backed its mizzen topsail and was slipping back in a stern-board to lay itself alongside *Teazer* – the privateer was cannily matching its movements on the other side, a crude gangway hoisted in readiness to lower over the void between them.

Kydd stood in the centre of the deck with drawn sword and turned to face the massing privateers. In seconds the screeching horde on the vessel would be flooding on to their deck – but dogged courage like a man-o'-war's man's would not be their style. If they met with too much resistance they would falter and break, the effort not worth any gain. If by naked courage the Teazers could sustain the fight until . . .

'I shall attend on the frigate side, brother.' It was Renzi, with a plain but serviceable sword that, since he had taken up his scholarly quest, he had sworn to draw only in the last extremity. Their eyes met, then the frigate bumped and ground into the hull as the privateer's gangway crashed down on *Teazer*'s bulwarks.

A roar of triumph went up and Kydd sprang forward to meet the rush across the improvised bridge. The first corsair had a scimitar and a pistol that he fired left-handed as he jumped – it brought down Seaman Timmins in a choking huddle but before Kydd could face him the man took a pike thrust to the chest and he had to kick the squealing body away to confront another with a tomahawk and cutlass.

There was no science in it: Kydd lunged viciously for the eyes and, when the man recoiled, turned the stroke to slash down at the wrist. The cutlass clattered to the deck, but before he could recover, a flailing body from behind catapulted him on to Kydd's blade, which did its work without mercy.

Beside him, Kydd was subliminally aware that Poulden was being overborne by a brutish black man and, without thought, swung his blade horizontally in a savage backhand slash that ended in a meaty crunch in the man's neck. With a wounded howl he turned on Kydd, but Poulden saw the opening and thrust pitilessly deep into the armpit.

Kydd turned back to fend off a frenzied stab from a wild-eyed man – the crude flailing had no chance against Kydd's skill and experience and, with one or two expert strokes, he had forced him to a terrified defensive. The man slipped and tried to ward off Kydd's straight-arm thrust to his throat, but in vain – he went down gurgling and writhing.

Suddenly there were no more opponents: he saw that the makeshift gangway had clattered down between the ships and many were left impotently on the wrong side. He whirled round. Renzi, in a practised fencer's crouch, lunged up at a frigate officer in a blur of motion. The man stood no chance.

Defenders from the privateer's side righted the gangway, then sprang across the deck. The smoke-wreathed chaotic mêlée, wreckage, stench of blood, groaning bodies and frayed cordage whipping about was a scene from hell.

The frigate was in heaving movement with the high seas, the vertical motion making it a trial for those dropping down on to *Teazer*'s deck from its higher bulwarks. The attackers had to time their move, unavoidably signalling this to the defenders, and when they landed, stumbling and off-balance, they were easy meat for the pikemen.

A trumpet bayed from within the frigate above the clash of battle – and then again. The retreat? With swelling exultation, Kydd saw the attackers left on *Teazer*'s deck fling down their weapons in despair, knowing the penalty for turning their backs to return to their ship.

It was incredible, glorious, and Kydd's blood sang. They had repelled the enemy and *Teazer* was made whole again. Inside, a cooler voice chided that in large part they owed their success to the restless seas.

The frigate pulled away and cheers were redoubled again and again from the smoke-grimed and bloodied Teazers. But in a cold wash of reality Kydd knew what was coming next.

'For y' lives! Hands to wear ship!' he bellowed, stumping up and down to get the men from their guns and to the ropes. *Teazer* began her swing – but was it too late? The frigate was wearing about as well, but Kydd was gambling that their own turning circle was less.

It was – but it was not enough to escape. The frigate now no longer saw *Teazer* as a prize but an enemy who must be crushed. And against the unrestrained broadsides of a frigate the little sloop had no chance.

When it came the punishment was hideous. Quartering across *Teazer*'s stern the bigger ship's cannon blows brought a cascade of ruin and devastation, a tempest of iron that smashed, splintered and gouged, brought down spars, turned boats to matchwood.

In the blink of an eye Purchet, who had been with the ship from the first, was disembowelled and flung across the deck, his entrails strung out into a bloody heap against the waterway. The inoffensive sailmaker, Clegg, huddled by the main-hatch, was frantically trying to stitch repairs when he simply dropped, his head dissolved into a spray of brain.

From all sides came shrieks of pain from cruel, skewering splinters.

Shaken by the destruction, Kydd shouted hoarsely for sail of any kind on the fore. If they could just . . .

The frigate completed her veering, but she had another broadside waiting on her opposite side and she took time to tack about, a manoeuvre that would end in her coming up alongside the wreck that would be *Teazer*.

He felt a cold wetness: a grey advance of drizzle brought a soft misery that seemed to shroud the scenes of dying and ruin from mortal eyes. It fell gently, dissolving the blood so that Englishman and Frenchman mingled in fraternal embrace before trickling together through the scuppers into the sea.

Kydd pulled himself together. There was now no alternative to yielding: he must therefore face— But, *no*, he saw one last move . . . As the frigate completed its turn and took up for its final run he wheeled the wounded sloop off the wind and steered straight for the privateer to leeward. By feinting at it and causing it to run directly from his ship, Kydd was bringing it into the line of fire from the frigate chasing *Teazer*. They would not fire on their own: for the moment *Teazer* was safe.

But they did.

The broadside erupted without warning. The storm of shot that broke over *Teazer* was cataclysmic, smashing into her with an intensity that numbed the senses. A series of unconnected images flashed in front of Kydd. The fore-hatch bursting upwards a split second before a ball ended its flight with a colossal clang against an opposite gun. A ship's boy snatched from the deck and flung like a bloody rag into the scuppers. Hallum's face turning towards him in horror and pain, his mouth working as the splinter transfixing his lower body turned in the wound. And then came the deafening timber-cracking of the main-mast as it fell in dignified but awful finality, taking what remained of the fore-mast with it in a tangle of cordage, ruined spars and canvas.

It had finished. It was defeat. The end of everything.

As if in a dream he watched men slowly emerge from under the wreckage, go to the wretched bodies, stare in haggard disbelief at the passing frigate – and then from forward came the single crash of a gun.

Squinting past the heaped ruin of spars and canvas he saw it was his gunner's mate, Stirk, dragging a foot behind him but going methodically from gun to gun, sighting carefully and banging off defiance at their nemesis – whatever else, *Teazer* would be seen to go down fighting.

Eyes pricking, Kydd had not the heart to stop him. The frigate began its final turn to take possession of them – and, extraordinarily, one of Stirk's shots told. At the precise point of the slings of its crossjack there was a sudden jerk, tiny pieces flew off and the spar dipped awkwardly, then fell, rending the mizzen topsail above it and engulfing the driver.

The frigate – name still unknown – fell back on its course. Disabled and unable to turn back, it eventually disappeared into the grey mists of rain. The privateer stayed with it and suddenly *Teazer* was alone and desperately wounded in the desolate expanse of the Atlantic.

Dizzy with reaction Kydd mustered the Teazers. They seemed dazed, the petty officers half-hearted in their actions, the men shuffling in a trance. Kydd didn't waste time on words: if they were to survive it needed every man to rally to the aid of their ship. The time of grieving would come later.

Teazer wallowed sickeningly broadside to the seas, her fore-mast a three-foot stump, her main a giant jagged splinter. It was a deeply forlorn experience to see nothing aloft but empty sky, and with the loss of steadying sails, the vessel lurched to the swell like a log.

The first urgency was for a party of men to find the wounded and carry them below. The dead were heaved over the side. Hallum was dragged with rough kindliness to the lee of the capstan where he died quietly. Another party was sent to find the few Frenchmen still aboard who had hidden in fear of their own ship's broadside.

But the main chore was to clear the deck and try by any means to get sail on. All hands turned to, including Renzi, who stood in for Purchet and led the fo'c'sle party to set a series of purchases on the main spars and haul them clear before starting work on a species of sheer-leg. Even a rag of sail set to the streaming oceanic winds would serve.

Kydd forced his mind to coolness as he reviewed their situation. There was just one thing in their favour: these

Atlantic winds were south-westerlies that blew directly for England. If they could keep sail on *Teazer* they would eventually make an English port, however long it took.

The carpenter brought welcome news. He had sounded the wells and made his rounds and could confidently say there was no hurt to *Teazer*'s stout Maltese hull that he could not deal with – in a jet of warmth, Kydd realised that it was more than possible his command would be able to lay her before long to the tender care of a dockyard, her grievous wounds to be healed.

'Pass the word for the purser's steward. He's to see every man shall get his double tot.' There would be inhuman effort required to cut through the maze of ropes and canvas and shift the heavy spars, and little enough time to do it for it was now well into the afternoon.

Other thoughts intruded. Would the frigate return? Their fallen crossjack would have torn down much of the mizzen's ropery and would not easily be mended, not this day – and by morning *Teazer* would be well away from the scene of the action. Kydd thrust away the possibility that the frigate captain could calculate their uncontrolled drift and lie in wait for them.

And where were they in this immensity of sea? Their desperate slant across the Channel and out into the Atlantic had been only hazily marked, the dead-reckoning tentative at best and their last frenzied moves not noted at all. The leaden sky offered no hope of a sextant sight – they were to all intents and purposes lost and adrift.

The day wore on. At three bells in the first dog-watch the young Seaman Palmer choked on blood and died. No longer in action, *Teazer* saw him buried at sea in the hallowed way. An early dusk put an end to their efforts to show sail and for the long hours of night they were left with their thoughts and weariness, awaiting the dawn and what it would bring.

With the tendrils of morning light spreading, there was hope. The sheer-legs took a boom lashed to the summit and a reefed fore-topgallant spread slowly below to the cheers of *Teazer*'s company. Poulden hurried aft and took the wheel again, feeling for the life that was now filling her.

A fore-and-aft staysail rigged from the jagged main gave control and purpose in their creeping progress – until a dreaded call came from a sharp-eyed seaman forward. The grey cloud-bank ahead had firmed. Ushant.

If their crazily lashed-up sail could not allow them to double the wicked northern headlands they would end driven by the same wind inexorably into the iron-hard cliffs.

Kydd tried everything: sweeps on the starboard side, scraps of sail everywhere they could be set, manhandling the guns aft – but it was not enough. In the dying light of day *Teazer* touched once, then again, before lurching to a stop on the dark, kelp-strewn Chaussée, a series of sub-sea reefs in the shadow of the ominous craggy heights of the Île de Keller.

Slewing sideways immediately, she lifted, then sagged, with a jarring, grinding finality, canted immovably over to larboard, the surf passing to end in hissing white rage on the further crags. It was so unfair! Nearly choked with emotion, Kydd fought against hopelessness and rage.

'Get forrard, y' chicken-hearted rabble,' he snarled, at a terrified crowd of seamen who were scrambling for the higher reaches of the after part of the crazily angled ship. But for a space his heart went out to them: this was how so many voyages ended for sailors, in terror and drowning on a hostile shore.

And Ushant was the worst: an appalling mass of rock flung

out into the Atlantic with surging ocean breakers and wild currents of ten knots or more, a place of nightmares for any mariner. The Bretons here had a saying, *'Qui voit Ouessant voit son sang!'* – He who sees Ushant, sees his blood!

Kydd crushed his desolation. 'Find the carpenter and send him below,' he snapped at the nearest seaman, who stared back at him in fear. 'Damn you, I'll do it m'self.' He pushed through the mass of men now on deck. The loss of the boatswain and his only lieutenant was a crippling blow: with just a single master's mate and the petty officers he had to take control of the fearful, milling men before they took it into their heads to break discipline and run wild.

He found the carpenter, broken at hearing of the loss of his friend Clegg. 'On y'r feet,' Kydd said brutally. 'Take a look around below, sound the wells an' report to me instantly. Now!' Without waiting for a response he stormed back to the wheel, collecting all the petty officers he could find.

'We've a chance,' he said urgently, shouting down the nervous cries from the back. 'Do your part, an' we'll swim again – don't and we'll be shakin' hands with Davy Jones afore nightfall.'

As if to add point to his words, a seething surf broke and thrust rudely past them, surging the hull further up with a deep, rumbling scrape that brought cries of terror from some.

But *if* they could get off the Chaussée and *if* they were not badly holed – there was hope.

'A strake near th' garboard forrard weepin' an' all, but nothin' the pumps can't clear,' the carpenter said woodenly, breathing heavily.

Kydd rounded on the haggard faces watching them: 'Hear that, y' lubbers? Next tide'll have us off! So clear this lumber and stand by!'

There was one thing he refused to think about: this was French territory. To his knowledge they had a form of military outpost, a signalling telegraph, on the western arm of Ushant, half a dozen miles to the south, probably tasked to report naval movements. If so, their situation would be known and . . .

'Get moving, y' shabs!' he roared, shoving men to their posts. The tide would return some time in the afternoon and they had to be ready. All wreckage overside, lighten the ship by any means – but not the guns. Not so much that they could defend their poor ship but to deny the enemy the opportunity of later grappling them to the surface.

A boat was lowered and fought to seaward, a small stream anchor slung under, the vessel rearing and plunging as it struggled out past the combers. When it was at a distance, the lashings were cut and the killick dropped away into the depths.

The tide receded hour by hour, leaving them still and silent on the wet rocks. 'They's come!' shrilled a voice, suddenly, and all eyes turned to the skyline above the black cliffs. Two figures stood looking down, and as they watched, others joined them.

'We ain't got a fuckin' prayer!' a young sailor blurted, eyes wild.

Stirk turned to him and scruffed his shirt. 'Shut y'r mouth, y' useless codshead. How're they goin' to come at us over that there?' He jerked his head at the sea-white cleft separating them from the cliff. 'They has t' come in a boat, an' when they do, we've guns as'll settle 'em.' He thrust the youth contemptuously away and turned to Kydd.

'Sir,' he said quietly, 'an' the carpenter wants a word. He's in th' hold.'

21

Kydd nodded. It was less than two hours to the top of the tide and then they could make their bid – pray heaven there was no problem.

They went down the fore-hatchway and Stirk, ignoring his leg wound, found the lanthorn. Without a word they went to a dark cavity at the after end of the ship. Moving awkwardly with the unnatural canting of the deck, Kydd dropped into the black void, filled with terrifying creaking and overpowering odours.

Stirk passed down the lanthorn and, bent double, they made their way to the lower side, where the carpenter and his mate stood with their own illumination.

No words were necessary. Evil and malignant, a wet blackness smelling powerfully of seaweed obscenely obtruded through the crushed and splintered hull for six feet or more, a fearful presence from the outside world breaking in on their precious home.

Kydd turned away that the others would not see the sting of the hot tears that threatened to overcome him at the unfairness of it all. 'Don't say anything o' this,' he said hoarsely. 'We'll – we'll fother, is all.' He nearly wept: for *Teazer*, to leave her bones in this break-heart place . . .

There was nothing the carpenter could do with a breach of such magnitude. There was a forlorn hope that fothering, dragging a sail over the outside, would give the pumps a chance.

Trusted men sat cross-legged in the gloom below, frenziedly sewing oakum and weaving matting into the sail, until it was obvious that the tide was ready to lift. It had to work: Kydd made sure the petty officers and others knew the stakes and personally selected the brawniest seamen to man the capstan that was to haul them off towards the anchor.

They had mounted the reef at about an hour before high water. Husbanding the strength of his men, Kydd waited until the ship shifted and moved restlessly, then drove them mercilessly.

Sobbing with the pain of the effort the men threw themselves at it, straining and heaving – and won. A sudden jerk, an odd wiggle like an eel, and *Teazer* was afloat and alive in the surging waters. Like a madman, Kydd roared his orders. Sail on the jury rig, the pumps manned instantly, parties ready at every conceivable point of trouble and the anchor cut loose just in time.

As they wallowed in clear water the fother sail was hastily produced, hauled into place and secured. Everything depended now on a clear run for England.

The wind was veering fitfully more westerly, fair to make an offing – but it would take them perilously close to that improbably named headland, Le Stiff. However, it was a bold coast, steep to with deep water, and in the brisk winds *Teazer* was making respectable way and within the hour had it laid astern.

Kydd had his two midshipmen positioned to relay any news from the hell below. He knew the chain pumps were beasts to drive, the rubbing of the many leather flaps of the watertight seal creating an inertia that was bone-breaking to overcome. It was not unknown in extreme circumstances for men to fall dead at the endless brutal exertion. 'Mr Tawse?'

'Holding, Mr Kydd.' The youngster was pale, his set face giving nothing away.

The hours stretched out. Kydd stood motionless on the quarterdeck, willing on his ship. After what she'd gone through . . . but they must be nearly halfway by now. In just hours more they would make landfall, say Plymouth or further on at Torbay. Rest for his sorely tried ship.

The carpenter broke into Kydd's thoughts: 'Sir, I'm truly sorry t' say, we're makin' water faster'n we can get rid of 'un.' Kydd could feel it now. A terrible weariness, no reaction to the bluster and boisterous play of the seas, a—

'*Saaail!*' Without tops to mount a lookout at a height, the stranger could not be far off.

'The Frenchy frigate,' Kydd said dully, as it smartly altered towards them. Fury slammed in on him – how could he give up his brave, his infinitely precious ship to the enemy after all this?

'No, it ain't!' Poulden said excitedly. 'That's *Harpy*, ship-sloop!' A friend! Glory be, they had help – they had a chance.

The sloop came alongside and hailed. In a whirl of feeling Kydd saw a tow-line passed and the men below on the pumps spelled. All the while, with a terrible intensity, he urged his wounded ship on.

With fresh men and new heart they laboured unceasingly, but the tow proved a difficult haul. At a little after one, a tiny blue-grey line was seen ahead: England. As if relenting, the seas and westerly began to ease and the unnatural wallowing softened as they struggled on.

But Kydd could feel in his heart that a mortal tiredness lay on *Teazer*. Like a dog in its last hour trying to lift its muzzle to lick its master's hand, she could no longer respond to please him. She was dying.

He hurried below in a frenzy of anguish. The men, in every stage of exhaustion, were fighting the pump to work amid as deadly a sign as the buboes on a plague victim: ankle-deep water, which was sloshing unchecked from side to side across the decks.

A lump in his throat threatened to choke him as he went back to the quarterdeck. The land was close enough to make out individual fields, the calm loveliness of Devon. And it was now so cruelly apparent that *Teazer* would not now make her rest. He could do no more for his love, his first command, she who had borne him on the ocean's bosom for so many leagues of both adventure and heartache.

It was time to part.

The tow was cast off, the men released from their Calvary and set to transferring their pitiful belongings to the boats. Such stores as could be retrieved were taken aboard and then, with the seas lapping her gunports, HMS *Teazer* was abandoned, her captain the last to leave with a final caress of her rail.

In mute sympathy, *Harpy* stood by as *Teazer* lay down and slipped away for ever from human ken.

Chapter 2

'Why, Miss Cecilia! We were not expecting you.'

'Is my brother at home, Tysoe?'

'I regret no, miss, but I'm sure Mr Renzi is at leisure to receive you. If you'll allow me to enquire . . .'

Renzi bowed politely as she was ushered into the drawing room.

'I did hear that Thomas took lodgings with you in London after . . .'

Renzi had no idea how she had, but he knew she was of all things a determined lady.

'Rather it is that *I* took lodgings with Thomas,' he chided gently. Her near presence was disturbing but he controlled his feelings. 'He's customarily engaged at the Admiralty at this hour but might be expected later this afternoon. May I – would you wish for some refreshment, my dear?'

'Should you tell of your recent . . . encounter, I would be much obliged.'

Renzi was aware of the control in her voice and understood what a shock it must have been for her to learn from

the lurid lines in the *Morning Chronicle* and the more measured but no less horrific account in the *Gazette* of the furious
action and later sinking of Kydd's ship.

'I shall not keep it from you. It was a bloody enough affair,
Cecilia. Er, might we sit at the fire? Tysoe, I know we have
a prime Bohea to offer our guest.'

Renzi felt Cecilia's steady gaze on him. He began to speak
of Kydd's cool courage, the noble *Teazer* taking her punishment, her company under Kydd's leadership achieving heroic
renown and then the final harrowing scenes ending in her
passing.

Cecilia sat quietly until he had finished. Then she dabbed
her eyes. 'So Thomas is at the Admiralty, these days. He's
making arrangements, no doubt, for his next ship. I wonder
what it will be.'

'I rather fear his prospects for another command are not
good, dear sister. You see, he's by way of being a commander,
not a post-captain, and there being a superfluity of such
gentlemen, there are many who will see it as their right to
be granted a ship before such as he.'

'You mean, he's not a proper captain? I find that hard to
credit, Nicholas.'

'It's the immutable way of the Service. A sloop may claim
a commander only as its captain, lesser breeds a lieutenant.
And beyond a sloop we find that a post-captain alone may
aspire to its command. Therefore Thomas is left on the beach
as we term it.'

'But he's famous! Did you not read of him in the newspaper? In our family Thomas is the only one ever to see his
name in the newspaper,' she said. 'They must give him a new
ship, surely.'

'Dear lady, the world is a wicked, thoughtless place, which

sets great store on today and has already forgotten yesterday. I rather fear they will not.'

She clapped her hands together at a sudden realisation. 'Then he must settle down on the land at last.'

Renzi said quietly, 'If you knew how much losing his *Teazer* has hurt him you would temper your joy. For a sailor his ship is his love and he has lost her.'

Cecilia dropped her eyes. 'Was he truly brave, do you think, Nicholas? I mean, all those men with swords and muskets climbing onto his ship – did he fight them himself or does he order his men to . . . to . . . ?'

'He must face them at the side of his men.'

Tysoe appeared with the tea accoutrements and set up on the small table. It was served in the Chinese style, delicate cups without handles and a cover on each.

'Then . . . he will— Do you mind, Nicholas, if I ask you a question concerning Thomas?'

'Why, if it is in my power to—'

'Killing a man: it is the last act, the final sanction of man upon man. I know his station in life demands he shall on occasion . . . do it, but can you conceive that over time the character might be . . . coarsened by the repeated experience?'

Renzi looked away, nearly overcome. This was the woman to whom he had lost his heart, but he had vowed never to disclose his feelings to her until he believed he was worthy enough to offer suit. And she had just revealed not only how far her own character had deepened, but her moral compass, the quality of mind that she would bring to any union . . .

At his hesitation she added quickly, 'Oh, Nicholas, I didn't mean to imply that you yourself have had to . . . are exposed to . . . in the same way . . .' She leaned forward in wide-eyed concern, her hand lightly on his arm – a touch like fire. 'You are so gentle, so fine a man, and to think I . . .'

A rush of warmth threatened to engulf him. An irresistible urge to let the dam free, to throw himself at her and declare— He thrust himself roughly to his feet and moved to the window. 'I'll have it known there's blood on my hands as must be for any other in a King's Ship!'

Cecilia bit her lip. Renzi collected himself and returned to his chair without meeting her eye again. 'If it were not so it would be to the hazard of my duty.' He stared for long moments at the fire and then said, 'The subject is not often broached at sea, you'll no doubt be surprised to know. Yet I believe I will tell you more.'

'Thank you, Nicholas,' she said.

He sipped his tea, then expounded to her the imperatives that, when all else failed, led to the resolution of differences between nations by open confrontation – that must logically result in coercion resisted by force, its ultimate expression violence, at first to the instruments of that force and then inexorably to its agents while they adhered to their purpose.

He touched on the singular but still logical principles of conduct that obtained in the act of taking life, that required the mortal hazard of one's body before that of an opposer, that in the act demanded dispatch without prejudice, and in the event of a yielding, compassion and protection.

It was an interesting paradox, yet explicable by known tenets of civilised behaviour if only as an outworking of—

Her face was set and pale. 'My dear, it was never my intention to fatigue you with such arcane matters,' he said gently. 'Rather it was to set you aright as to our motives when we face the enemy.'

She made no reply so he went on, 'You asked about Thomas.

And I'm to tell you that he's not a creature of blood and war, rather he's one of Neptune's children, glorying with a whole heart in his life on the briny deep. His duty is to destroy the King's enemies but we might say this only enables him to take to the waves and find his being on the ocean's bosom.'

'This is becoming clear to me, Nicholas, never fear. It seems that those whose business is in great waters are a tribe of man quite apart from all others.'

'Truly said, my dear. Should he be unsuccessful in his petition for a ship – which I fear must be so – he needs must find solace on the shore, and would, I believe, be much obliged for your sisterly understanding.'

'He shall get it, Nicholas,' she said seriously. 'I shall call tomorrow.'

'Dear sister, perhaps do give him a little time first.' Toying with his tea, Renzi added lightly, 'Would it be impertinent of me to enquire of your own circumstances, the marquess having left his position at the Peace?'

Cecilia had for several years now been a companion to Charlotte Stanhope when she travelled with her diplomat husband who had resigned in protest at the punitive terms of the armistice separating the War of the Revolution and the War of Napoleon.

'He is taken back by the prime minister to serve in the same capacity as before, and the marchioness is gracious enough to extend to me a welcome.' She smiled, her face lighting. 'You would laugh to see our antics, Nicholas, she so desirous to keep the megrims at bay while her husband is caught up in such desperate times.'

'So in London you would not lack for admirers, I'd hazard.'

Cecilia blushed and delicately took up her cup. 'But how then is your own situation, there being no place in a ship now available to you? Will you make application to another captain and sail away on more adventures, perhaps?'

There was not the slightest tinge of regret at the prospect that he could detect, and he answered coolly, 'This is not in contemplation at the moment.' Renzi knew only too well that an evident gentleman as he was would never find employment as a mere ship's clerk in any man-o'-war he was acquainted with. The situation with Kydd was unusual to say the least.

He went on in the same tone: 'When your brother is in better knowledge of his future, no doubt there will be an arrangement. Thomas, as you know, is in possession of a small but respectable fortune and is frugal in his habits. I'm sanguine he'll feel able to assist in the matter of respectable lodgings while I pursue my studies.'

Cecilia smiled encouragingly. 'Perhaps you would oblige me, Nicholas, by disclosing the progress in your great work.'

Renzi had sailed as a free settler to New South Wales, hoping to make his fortune there to lay before Cecilia, then ask for her hand in marriage. But his foray into crop-raising had ended in ruin and he had seized Kydd's suggestion of a project to enable him eventually to press his suit: he had embarked on an ambitious literary endeavour, a study of the varied cultural responses to the human experience. To enable this Kydd had promised to employ him as clerk aboard whichever ship he might captain and give him the opportunity to work on his studies in his free time.

Renzi put down his cup carefully and steepled his fingers. 'I own, my dear, it's been a harder beat to windward than ever I calculated when first taking up my pen. An overplus of facts, as who should say data, and a cacophony of opinions from even the most eminent.'

Cecilia listened attentively. 'And in this – dare I say it? – you shine above all others,' she said warmly, 'particularly in the art of untangling for us all the threads of the matter to its own true conclusion.'

Renzi took refuge in his tea, then went on, 'Nevertheless, I must achieve an order, a purpose to the volume, which I might modestly claim to have now laid down in its substance, it yet lacking the form.'

'Then it may be said that your travails are near crowned with success?' she said eagerly.

'Writing is a labour of love but a labour for all that,' Renzi admitted, 'yet the end cannot be far delayed.'

She straightened and, in a brisk voice that he recognised from long before, she said firmly, 'It does occur to me, Nicholas, that there is a course of action you may wish to pursue, given that you are now without means of any kind.'

'There is?'

'Have you considered the actual publishing of your work?'

'Um, not in so much detail,' Renzi said uncomfortably.

'Well, then, think on this. Do you not feel that if your work has its merits, then when published it will be bought in its scores – hundreds, even? Your publisher would stand to turn a pretty penny in his bookselling – why not approach one and offer that if he should convey to you now a proportion of this revenue for the purposes of keeping body and soul together, you would agree that he would be the only one with the honour to print it?'

'Oh, er, here we're speaking of a species of investment, of risk. I cannot imagine that one of your grand publishers would top it the moneylender, dear lady.'

'But it would not harm to enquire of one, to see which way the wind blows, as you sailors say. You will do this, Nicholas, won't you?'

'I really don't think—'

'Oh, please, Nicholas, to gratify me . . .'

'Er, well, I—'

'Thank you! Just think that very soon you shall hold in your hand the book that will make you famous.'

Kydd walked across the cobbled courtyard and mounted the steps through the noble portico of the Admiralty. He nodded familiarly to the door-keeper and turned left in the entrance hall for the Captains' Room.

'G' morning,' he said affably, as he strode in. Weary grunts came from the other unemployed commanders and Kydd crossed to his usual chair. He looked up quizzically at the bored porter, who in return shook his head. No news.

In a black humour he picked up an old newspaper but could not concentrate. The pain of his dear *Teazer*'s passing had now ebbed and he was coming to terms with it, but its further consequence was dire. He was once again in his career besieging the Admiralty for a ship – but this time with little hope.

The country was in deadly peril, which meant that every conceivable vessel – in reserve, dockyard hands, between commissions – was sent to sea as soon as possible at full stretch in the defence of the realm. There were, therefore, none that could in any way be termed surplus or otherwise available for even the most worthy of commanders. And in this room there were at least a dozen, all of them senior to him and some with a more glorious fighting record. What chance did he have?

One slid off his chair with a snore and awoke looking confused; there was tired laughter and the tedium descended again.

He rose irritably to pace down the room. Deep in black thoughts, he heard a polite cough from the doorway.

'Why, Mr Bowden! What do you here?' he said warmly.

'I was just passing, sir, visiting my uncle.' It brought a pang for Kydd to meet the midshipman he had seen grow from the raw and sensitive lad he had taken under his wing as a lieutenant in *Tenacious* to the intelligent and capable young man learning his trade under himself in *Teazer*. It had been his first command and they had grown together in different ways. They had parted in the Peace when *Teazer* had been laid up in ordinary, but after those years here was Bowden, strong and assured and clearly on his way to higher things.

'You've found a quarterdeck, I trust?' Kydd asked, trying to hide his own feelings.

'I have, sir – it's naught but a first-rate on blockade I'm to join. I'm sanguine the sport to be had in her cannot stand against our *Teazer*, sir.' Something made him hesitate. 'You're still in her, Mr Kydd?'

'No, I'm sorry to say. She's . . . no more. We took a quilting off the French coast and she foundered within sight o' home.' At Bowden's shocked look he hastened to say, 'Not much of a butcher's bill, thank God.'

The sense of unfairness had returned in a flood and made the answer rather more curt than he would have wished. 'So I'm to petition for another command, as you see.'

'I – I do hope you find success, sir,' Bowden said uncomfortably, aware of what this meant for Kydd. 'I'll take my leave now, if you will, sir, and – and do wish you well of the future.'

'Thank you,' Kydd said briefly, and lifted a hand in farewell as the young man left. It had been another time, another world, and different things had to be faced now.

In his waistcoat Kydd had a letter – a petition he had paid to have professionally drafted, addressed to the first lord himself and laying out in honeyed phrases all the reasons why he should be granted employment at this time.

It had to be faced that if this had no effect it would be a trial to know what to do next and he delayed, treasuring the moment while hope was still on the flood. Then, reluctantly, he drew it out: there was no point in wasting time.

It cost three guineas, an exorbitant bribe to the chief clerk, to ensure its insertion into the first lord's morning pack; when he turned to resume his chair he saw all eyes on him – they knew very well what was being done. Face burning, Kydd sat and buried his face in the newspaper, summoning patience.

He couldn't keep this up for ever: his means were sufficient but for a man used to an active life, with respon-sibility and the requirement at any time for instant decisions, a passive existence was hard to bear. What should he do if a command was not in prospect? A commander could not be un-promoted – he could not revert to being a lieu-tenant and take a menial post in another's ship – so what could he look forward to? His mind shied from the implications.

When the reply came he was quite unprepared. It had been less than three hours, and envious stares followed the porter crossing importantly to Kydd with a single folded sheet on his silver tray. After Kydd had taken it, the man bowed, turned and left – no reply expected therefore.

The room fell into a hush. Kydd nervously threw off a casual remark before he opened it, knowing that probably his entire future was about to be revealed.

It was a short but undoubtedly personal note and from

the great man himself – he recognised the energetic, sprawling hand. At first the words didn't register – he had to read it again to let their shocking burden penetrate.

> *Mr Kydd,*
>
> *I find it singular in the extreme that after this time you are still here demanding a sloop to command. For you this is not possible as well you should know. Your continued attendance here is neither welcome nor profitable to yourself and if you persist I shall regard it an insolence.*
>
> *Y^r obed^t serv^t etc*

In cold shock he stood staring down at it.

A portly commander from across the room called loudly, 'Well, old fellow, what did he say, then?'

'I – I'm not to trouble him with my presence any further,' Kydd said faintly. The note was snatched and handed about in consternation.

'Remember Bartholomew!' one red-faced officer blurted.

Pandemonium erupted. It had been only the previous year when an importunate officer begging a sea appointment right in these very rooms had tried the patience of Earl St Vincent too far. He had boomed, 'I'll serve ye a sea berth this very instant, y' villain!' and had him pressed there and then in the entrance hall.

The scandal had gone to Parliament and then to a Select Committee, which was still sitting on the case, but the last anyone knew of the unfortunate man was that he was still before the mast somewhere in the West Indies.

Kydd retrieved his note and, with pathetic dignity, took his leave.

*   *   *

Renzi heard the news with a sinking heart. Kydd handed over the note diffidently and he inspected it carefully. There was absolutely no questioning its authenticity. Neither was there any doubting the intent of its vigorous phrasing.

Thomas Kydd, it seemed, was going to remain ashore, a half-pay commander for the rest of his life.

'This is the end for me,' Kydd said, in a low voice.

'As a sea-going commander, perhaps – but there's always the Transport Service, the Fencibles, the um . . .'

'Thank you, Nicholas, for your concern,' Kydd said distantly. 'There's much to think on. I do believe I'll take some air.' He reached for his cloak, then thought better of it and left the room. He returned in mufti – plain civilian dress. 'Pray don't wait on my account. I may be gone some time.'

Heart wrung with pity, Renzi saw him to the door then turned back to his work.

It was no good – he couldn't concentrate. Too much had happened and what he had feared had come to pass. Could their friendship survive without the common thread of the sea? Each to his own retreat, seldom to meet?

Selfishly he must mourn the passing of the opportunity he had had to enrich and inform his studies of man in all his diversity from that most excellent of conveyances, the deck of a far-voyaging ship.

Now he would continue his study in some depressing room that would offer the same tedious prospect of the world every morning and—

It was much worse for Kydd. Where would he find a calling in life to equal the previous? What was there to occupy his talent for daring and quick-thinking in the world where he now found himself stranded? That he had come so far to this . . .

Kydd had left the note lying on the mantelpiece and he idly picked it up. It was quite clear what had driven the first lord to pen it and equally apparent that there would be no reprieve. But why had he been so peremptory with one of Kydd's recent fame? Surely a civil communication of inability was more to be expected.

Uneasiness stole over him. Was this a political act of some kind, perhaps instigated by Admiral Lockwood, whose daughter Kydd had spurned for a country girl? Very unlikely – that was now a while ago, and in any case, there was little to be gained in drawing attention to the incident.

In Guernsey there had been one officer so envious of Kydd's rise that he had contrived to bring about his dismissal from his ship but surely Kydd did not have any other enemy who would want to harm his career.

As he stared at the note one phrase stood out: *For you this is not possible as well you should know.*

The inability to find him a sloop-of-war was understandable but that it was necessary to deny Kydd a command if there was one was uncalled-for and did not fit, even in a burst of exasperation. It implied that there was in existence a real bar to an appointment – consistent, for example, with a scurrilous tale told against his reputation that was common currency and assumed to be true, and of which Kydd was aware.

But of all men Kydd's character was blameless of anything whatsoever that could be construed as morally reprehensible. If there were any alleging turpitude it would soon be discovered as false.

But what else? Renzi's brow furrowed. Then it dawned, a possible reason so fantastic he laughed out loud at its simplicity but nonetheless monumental implications. Admittedly it was a slim chance that he was correct but it was simple enough to test and he rang for Tysoe.

'Do call a messenger if you would,' he said, and scrawled a few lines, then sealed the paper firmly. 'For Somerset House,' he said to the man, when he appeared, 'and pray do not return without a reply.'

He was back within two hours. Renzi snatched up his message – and there, in a single line, was all he needed to know.

He took a deep breath and sat down slowly to consider. What happened next was entirely up to him. His first instinct was to lay it all before his friend immediately, but without proof – of the kind that could be held in the hand – it would not be a mercy.

'You, sir!' he barked to the waiting messenger, who started at Renzi's sudden energy. 'I desire you should take post-chaise to Guildford. There you will present an instruction to the person whose name will appear on the outside. You will then be entrusted with a package that you will guard with your life before you deliver it to me.'

Renzi gave a half-smile: within a day or two all would be made manifest.

Kydd returned in the evening, set-faced and quiet. They took dinner together and Renzi nearly weakened in his resolve but, knowing its grave importance to his friend's situation, he determined to follow it through to its end.

'A strange feeling, I tell you,' Kydd mused. 'Neither fish nor fowl. Never t' tread my quarterdeck again but not yet set m' course on land. What shall it be, Nicholas? Industry or commerce? Farming will never do – I'm terrified o' cows.' He looked moodily into the middle distance.

'Why, something will turn up, of that you can be sure,' Renzi said positively.

'How can you be certain?' Kydd said, nettled. 'I'm to find something soon or take rot in the headpiece.'

Renzi had a stab of conscience. Was delay until the proof arrived the right thing to do for his friend?

The next morning he presented his card at the stately mansion in Belgravia that was the London residence of the Marquess of Bloomsbury, diplomat and of the inner circle in Prime Minister Pitt's administration.

'Oh, Nicholas!' Cecilia gasped in anticipation. 'Tell me the news. You've been to the publisher and you have something to reveal.'

'Not, er, at the moment. This rather concerns your brother's unfortunate predicament for which I carry something of a – a bombshell, as it were, that exercises me as to its resolution.'

It took him a short time to convey the essence and even less for Cecilia to come to a solution. Despite Renzi's misgivings, she was adamant that her brother be told nothing yet.

When Renzi returned, Kydd was sprawled in a chair, staring listlessly into space. 'Tom, dear fellow – we're discovered!' he said urgently. This brought no more than a single raised eyebrow. 'I tell you, there's no escaping!'

Kydd turned his head idly towards him. 'Oh?'

'Your sister! She knows you're here, old chap!' It was lame enough but Renzi continued, 'She's asking that we do escort her tonight to the entertainments at Vauxhall, her friend having failed her. Clearly I cannot be permitted to do so on my own.'

* * *

None but the withered in heart could have failed to be swept away by the excitement and spectacle of Vauxhall Gardens in the early evening. Illuminations were beginning to appear around the exotic pavilions and temples and through the hubbub of the promenading came the elegant strains of Mr Handel's Water Music.

'Isn't it thrilling?' Cecilia exclaimed, squeezing Kydd's arm.

Renzi strolled on the other side. 'The nightingales sing in the groves of Elysium,' he murmured, eyeing a picturesque Grecian bust nestling in the shrubbery.

A passing exquisite in skin-tight pantaloons deigned to notice Cecilia with his quizzing glass; she inclined her head graciously, then impulsively reached out to take possession of Renzi's arm. 'There now! As I have the two most handsome men in London, I declare the world shall know of it.'

The walks took them by caves and waterfalls, grottoes and quantities of wondrous blooms and shrubbery, with discreet arbours and dark passageways between. Past the Druid's Walk they came to the Wilderness and from there to the Rural Downs, where a pleasing prospect of the river opened up. 'Milton,' said Renzi, admiring a glowering statue looking away to the south, 'and cast entirely in lead, of course.'

In the dusk more lamps wavered and took hold, suffusing the evening with a mysterious glamour. Individual faces appeared touched with gold and hidden players beguiled with soft melodies from the Musical Bushes.

'Shall we see your Hogarths in their original, do you think?' Cecilia said sweetly to Renzi, the softness of her expression touching him to the heart. She turned to Kydd. 'I've a fondness for the old rake, do let's go!'

They were indeed Hogarths, but rather than cutting satire

and acid commentary these were cheerful rustic murals and canvases displayed around the pillared walls of the elevated supper booths. '*The Milkmaid's Garland*,' Kydd grunted, peering at one. 'Not as it—'

'Do cheer up, Thomas.' Cecilia sighed. 'This is so enchanting – look, here's *Sliding on the Ice*, done with such wit!'

A roar of drollery came from the tables on the floor above. 'I find Mr Hogarth a mort *natural* for my taste,' Kydd said, with an effort. 'I'd think him to have had a hard time of it in his youth.'

'That's indeed the case,' Renzi said. 'He had the mortification of seeing his father imprisoned for debt in the Fleet. I rather think these works are payment in kind for long-gone pleasures.'

Kydd looked up. 'Oh? His father failed in business?'

'He did,' Renzi said. Then he added, 'In thinking to establish a coffee-house that would admit no patrons save they spoke only in Latin.'

Cecilia smothered her giggles but Kydd did not join in. She tried to engage him by asking sweetly, 'I'm more wondering what a sharp fellow Mr Vauxhall was to conceive the idea of this garden.'

At Kydd's silence, Renzi explained, 'My dear, "Vauxhall" refers more to the place than the gentleman concerned – probably from the vulgate "Foxhole" or similar.'

'Ah! There I have you, Renzi!' Kydd said exultantly. 'It's of another age, I'll grant – but back no further than the first James. I heard it when a younker – it was where the hall o' residence of the widow of Guy Fawkes was, Fawkes Hall!'

Cecilia laughed prettily to see Kydd's animation. 'There, Nicholas! You're to take instruction from Thomas in the article of antiquary.'

They strolled on past stately limes and sycamores, but Kydd's bleak expression returned. 'And we haven't seen the half of it,' Cecilia urged, playfully tugging him. 'There's the Rotunda, all properly done in King Louis the Fourteenth mode – and a Turkish Tent in the Chinese style, why you'll—'

Kydd broke free. 'I thank you, sis, for your entertainments,' he said sarcastically, 'but I have to say it's not t' my taste. See those strut-noddies an' fine-rigged dandy prats – just you hear 'em howl if I pressed 'em aboard. My fore-mast jacks could teach 'em their manners . . .'

He tailed off and stared away woodenly.

'Oh, er, Miss Cecilia,' Renzi said carefully, 'I rather think that following so close upon your brother's losing his ship this disporting is not to be countenanced. In lieu, I propose that we adjourn to an altogether more . . . róbust entertainment.'

'And what is that, pray?' she asked defiantly.

'Which being of a nature not becoming young females of delicacy, I fear.' Kydd looked up inquisitively. 'We shall take you home and he and I will step out together – as in times past, as it were.' He tried to ignore Cecilia's wounded look.

'As in times past?' Kydd asked, when they had settled back in the hackney carriage.

'Lincoln's Inn Fields,' Renzi instructed the jarvey, then replied mysteriously, 'Not as who might say *exactly* so.'

'But isn't that where your lawyer crew go to ground?' Kydd said, in puzzlement.

'Just so, but tonight you shall be entertained to a spectacle such as few have been privileged to witness.'

'Oh? I'll remind you we've seen some rum sights about this world in our voyaging.'

'Ah. This is different. Have you ever pondered the most singular philosophical line that separates a living creature from a dead?'

'No, never,' Kydd said.

'Then tonight your curiosity will be satisfied in full measure.'

'Nicholas, if this is your word-grubber's wrangling over some—' They had arrived at a discreet entrance to a dilapidated building along with numbers of others. Renzi was greeted by several distinguished-looking gentlemen and he and Kydd were shepherded inside where they were instantly assaulted by a repulsive, cloying fetor.

'My apologies – it seems their new building is not far from completing and we must make do with this,' Renzi said.

They went down the stairs into a peculiar basement. A deep central pit was surrounded by a series of observation galleries along which men gravely filed. When all were assembled the upper lights were doused and the pit readied. A single table in the centre equipped with straps was made to be bathed in light from reflected candles.

'Be damned! You've brought me to a dissection, haven't you, y' dog?' said Kydd, now recognising the sickly odour of new-dead corpses.

'Not at all,' Renzi soothed. 'This is now a scientifical experiment of the first importance. You will recall the celebrated Signor Luigi Galvani?'

'Frog's legs?'

'Quite so. Tonight his nephew, the most distinguished Professor Aldini, will demonstrate to us conclusively that his theories concerning the role of "animal electricity" in the sustaining of vitality is central to the meaning of life itself.'

'But what are we—'

'Sssh!' The polite murmuring around the galleries ceased

expectantly as a short man with a jet-black moustache and grand manner strode into the arena. Spontaneous applause broke out as he handed his hat and gloves to an assistant and bowed repeatedly until it had ceased.

'Tonight,' he began impressively, his barely accented English full and resonating, 'you are invited not as idle spectators but as witnesses! To the most profound experiment of its kind in all of history!'

There was an excited stirring. Aldini continued, 'I have invited you doctors and philosophers here tonight' – Renzi lowered his head guiltily – 'to attest to the world the truth of what you will shortly see occurring before you.'

He paused and looked about significantly. 'In proof of my theory of animal electricity as the conduit of all vitality, this night I will attempt, by means of a voltaic pile, the reanimation of a deceased body. I will, by the science of galvanism, revive a corpse!'

The commotion increased as the experiment was prepared but died away in breathless silence at the appearance of the subject, brought in and laid on the table under a white sheet. This was stripped back to reveal the naked cadaver of a man. In the absolute stillness of death, its chalky pallor was an obscene counterfeit of life.

The apparatus was connected. A peculiar tower of alternating copper and zinc discs inside a loose cage was produced, water oozing slowly from between each pair. A braided copper strap led from the bottom of the pile, another from the top. An assistant held them gingerly at arm's length.

Utter silence reigned.

'Splendid! We shall begin. This is Signor Volta's electric pile and it stands ready to deliver its vehemence on my command. Before we commence I must particularly ask that you do

45

observe most carefully and closely, as the vitalising effect is instant and dramatic.'

He bent to the body and inspected it for a moment, then straightened. 'I would now ask any who will to come forth to agree with me that life is entirely absent. Sir?'

An austere figure descended and, with practised skill, felt for a pulse and looked into the staring eyes. He pursed his lips and took out a speculum, which he held over the mouth. Then he pronounced, 'Life is extinct, gentlemen.'

'If you are ready, I shall proceed.' Aldini took the copper straps, each with a small disc at its end, and advanced on the corpse.

Kydd could hardly take it in. Was modern science about to tear down the last boundaries between death and life? To achieve on earth a mortal resurrection that defied the Church and all its teaching?

Aldini raised the discs and, after a slight pause, placed them firmly at each side of the lower skull.

Instantly there were jerking movements in the corpse – a tensing, then a wave of terrible contortions passed over the face and, as the discs continued their work, an eye flickered and the jaws quivered, as though in a desperate effort to speak.

The professor let it continue for a while longer, then withdrew the discs. The body slowly relaxed into the stillness of before. 'Disappointing,' he said briefly, inspecting the subject. 'Yet it might be said to be the clay I have to work with. A common murderer, I understand, but fresh hanged at Newgate and brought to me without delay.'

Kydd's mind flailed. That corpse had been a warm, living, breathing, despairing human so very recently. And now this.

A bluff gentleman next to him snorted. 'If he brings the wretch back, I shall demand he be re-executed. The law's insistent on the matter – hanged b' the neck until dead.' He turned back to the proceedings.

'Nevertheless,' Aldini continued, 'we shall continue. To increase the strength I will use another voltaic pile and this time for maximum effect I shall introduce the electricity directly into the interior of the body.'

He selected a slender silver probe. 'Via the rectum.'

Aldini then stood at the head of the table and carefully applied a disc to the nape of the corpse. The whole body trembled, then the back arched as if under intolerable pain, the legs kicked in a grotesque parody of desperate escape and the arms lifted in spasm. After a further minute one clenched fist suddenly punched the air in hopeless fury and hung in a tremor.

'A pity,' Aldini announced, after a space. 'I had hoped for a result this evening. My studies at Bologna were very promising...'

Faint and with an urgent need for air, Kydd endured until the good professor had concluded, then hurried out into the cold freshness of the night streets. 'Er, uncommon interesting,' he blurted, as they hastened to find a hackney.

'Quite. With refinement, who knows where it will lead?' said Renzi, but Kydd was gratified to note his distinctly pale face.

In the morning, Kydd was away with an attorney when the messenger returned from Guildford with a package.

Renzi hastened to open it. Yes! It contained a stout letter sealed with a cypher he knew only too well. He heated a thin knife over a candle and, with the utmost care, worked at the

47

seal. He read the letter with a smile of satisfaction. Exactly as he had surmised.

He reaffixed the seal carefully, then penned a quick note and gave it to the messenger. Now everything depended on the marchioness.

'A vexing, prating crew, your law-grinders,' Kydd said, flinging down his papers. 'Before you may even start in business there's first a memorandum of association an' then you must work up your articles. Only then are the books of account opened – it would tax the patience of Jove to see the matter squared away at last, shipshape and all a-taunto.'

He slouched into his chair and thrust out his boots towards the fire. 'Wind's in the sou'-east, I see,' he said, squinting through the low sun coming in the window. 'Johnny Crapaud'll sit up and take notice, I shouldn't wonder,' he added bitterly.

'It's accounted to be winter season now, brother,' Renzi said firmly. 'There's no prospect of a crossing, as well you know.'

He paused and went on in quite another tone. 'Dear fellow, I do feel we owe something to your sister, she having been abandoned so forlornly last night. Tonight there is to be a rout given by the marchioness, and it would delight Cecilia inordinately should you feel able to attend.'

At Kydd's expression he went on quickly, 'This is not to say she intends this by way of improving your spirits, rather the altogether understandable desire before her friends to show away her brother, hero of the seas.'

'Hmph. So this needs the marchioness as well?' Kydd said cuttingly.

'As it is her mansion, old trout. To show your face for an hour I would have thought no great imposition while you're, er, at leisure these days.'

'Do you lecture me on my duty to my sister, sir?' Kydd flared, then with an effort quietened. 'Very well, if it should please her.'

When carriages were announced he defiantly appeared in vivid bottle green and yellow, dress more in keeping with the colour and individuality of the last century than the increasingly plain and sober attire that was now the vogue. He glowered at Renzi, daring him to comment.

It took more than an hour to wind through the throng of evening traffic until they reached the imposing residence. The windows were ablaze with candlelight, and the strains of a small orchestra and laughter spilled out onto the street.

Kydd seemed cheered by the gaiety and strode forward to ring the bell. A well-dressed footman received him and announced his presence. Oddly, the entire room stopped and regarded him with looks of expectation as the orchestra tailed away. Eyes shining, Cecilia ran forward and took his arm possessively, turning to face the assembly.

Wondering what it was about, Kydd saw the marchioness moving to take position at the front. He bowed courteously.

She acknowledged graciously, then declaimed loudly to the gathering, 'My lords, ladies and gentlemen! Pray take your glasses if you will and drink with me to the brightest ornament in His Majesty's Navy – who I declare has come so far, yet bids fair to have before him the most shining prospects for fame and honour. A toast – to Captain Kydd, our newest sea hero!'

Cecilia's grip on his arm was so fierce it hurt, but Kydd's face was a picture of devastation as the throng gaily echoed the toast.

'Why, Captain, are you by chance out of sorts?' the marchioness said archly, handing him a glass. For some reason the room had quietened and everyone was watching them.

'Er, it's— I'm not really— That is t' say, I'm not a captain any more,' he stammered.

'Not a captain?' Her eyes twinkled. 'When all the world knows you to be made post by His Majesty's express command?'

Struck dumb, Kydd could only stare at her.

Renzi appeared and drew a stiff letter out from his waistcoat, sealed with the Admiralty cypher. 'I rather fancy this will prove the case.'

Kydd took it as in a dream and opened it out to its full grandeur. In words that had resounded down the centuries, he read of his being raised to the impossible honour of post-captain, Royal Navy, and signed thus by Melville himself, first lord of the Admiralty.

He turned to Renzi. 'Wha' . . . ?'

'A slight matter only. The letter was sent some weeks ago to your address, which is Guildford. There, your loyal mother has been zealously guarding it for you until your return.' He chuckled softly. 'As you may conceive, the first lord was put considerably out of temper at the spectacle of a post-captain demanding command of a mere sloop!'

In a wash of wonder and delight, Kydd clutched the precious paper and, seized in a delirium of happiness, looked up to see the gathering advancing to congratulate him. As the orchestra launched energetically into 'See the Conquering Hero Comes' the first to reach him was a beaming Captain Boyd. Kydd had met the elegantly dressed post-captain when, as a newly appointed officer of the Downs Squadron, he had been sent to London for briefing.

'Might I take your hand, Captain?' Boyd said sincerely. 'There was never a promotion more hard earned, sir.'

Kydd took a deep breath and stuttered, 'It was, well, I—'

'This is Captain Codrington of *Orion*, seventy-four, about

to join Admiral Nelson, and this, Harvey of *Temeraire*,' he added. The two men greeted him genially, both, Kydd knew, senior captains of a ship-of-the-line – and now he the same rank as they!

Cecilia tugged at his sleeve for him to notice an awed couple nearby. The lady curtsied nervously to him and the man bowed very respectfully. 'You must remember Jane Rodpole as was? In Jamaica I helped at her wedding to William Mullins here. And then we all met up in Plymouth that time . . .'

Kydd managed an amiable reply, then turned to a familiar face that had appeared. 'Sir?' the man said expectantly.

Kydd recognised, through a haze of feeling, Dyer, sloop commander of the Downs Squadron. 'Oh, so kind in you, Dyer,' he said, allowing his hand to be pumped energetically. He caught himself in time from saying he hoped to see him soon, for as a post-captain his was a higher destiny.

'We do take it as our own honour, your elevation, sir,' Dyer said breathlessly.

Others pressed forward to offer their sensibility of the occasion and then it was the marquess with another glass for him, taking him away by the arm to hear for himself the famous action that had resulted in the loss of the plucky brig-sloop *Teazer*.

Cecilia came up to Renzi and laid her arm on his. 'Nicholas, do look at him – I've never seen anyone in such transports of bliss!' she whispered, watching Kydd, his face red with pleasure, the centre of admiration, the man whose future had burst in upon him in a cloud of glory.

Chapter 3

As he had done for the previous several days, Kydd rose casually and went over to inspect the morning post placed on the sideboard. Suddenly he snatched up one particular letter. With a quick glance at Renzi, hidden behind his morning newspaper, he hurriedly stuffed it inside his waistcoat, but the movement was noticed. 'Oh, have we mail, dear fellow?'

'No. Er, that is to say, nothing to interest us,' Kydd said hastily.

Renzi lowered his newspaper. 'Are you not well, old horse? You seem a little agitated.'

Kydd hesitated. 'Um, I'll be back soon, Nicholas,' he said, and fled into the privacy of his bedroom. Feverishly he broke the seal. This *was* the letter he had yearned for – the impossible dream come true.

A ship. A frigate – newly captured and brought into the Navy, by name *L'Aurore d'Égalité* and he was, with all possible dispatch, to take on himself the charge and command of the said ship, now lying at Portsmouth dockyard.

His hand trembled as it held the precious paper, his mind spinning . . . A frigate! This was not simply a larger brig-sloop, it was in effect a minor ship-of-the-line, one-decked instead of two- or three-, but with everything from the three-masted ship rig to the make-up of her company simply proportioned down. A frigate was a major warship, an asset of significance in the fleet, and *L'Aurore d'Égalité* would be commanded by – Captain Kydd!

He took a deep breath. It had happened. Who knew what the future now held for him and his trusty frigate? Gulping with excitement, he tried to compose his features. Damn it – Renzi had made him suffer before he had told him the news. Now it was his turn.

'You're looking a mort flushed, Tom, are you sure—'

Kydd turned away quickly. 'I shall be fine presently, m' friend.' He nonchalantly resumed his chair and continued, in an odd voice, 'Er, shall you be going out this night?'

'Well, I did wish to see a gentleman who has promised to show me a curious artefact of the Eskimo people, which he—'

'God rot it!' Kydd exploded, and Renzi dropped his newspaper in alarm. 'An' I can't do it!'

'Er, do what, pray?'

'Nicholas – I have a frigate!' Kydd burst out. 'She's waiting for me in Portsmouth!' He jumped to his feet and thrust the letter at Renzi. 'Read!' he commanded.

Renzi admired it extravagantly. 'As I've always thought, your promotion to the select few was for a purpose,' he said.

'The devil with that!' Kydd spluttered happily. 'A ship! A frigate! I'm to post down tomorrow, I believe. With all dispatch, it says.'

'And your new uniform as yet still with the tailor?'

'Damn it, yes! I'll go in shore togs – she's not yet in commission, o' course.'

'Tomorrow?'

'At the earliest hour.'

Renzi paused. 'You'll have a great deal to do in a new-found man-o'-war, old friend. Certificating completions, books of account and similar. If you'd wish it, then I'll—'

'Nonsense!' Kydd chuckled. 'Clerking is not for a gentleman o' learning such as you now are. I'll soon find someone.'

'Er, I would not find it as insupportable as you suppose,' Renzi said carefully. 'And do recollect, this is a frigate and of no trivial complexity. If—'

'Never. Your studies must come before all,' Kydd said, with finality. 'Recollect – I will have some hundreds to command and there I will find my ship's clerk.'

With a set face, Renzi pressed, 'To have one to trust in such a post is of no small advantage, I'm persuaded. Should you—'

'No, sir! I will not have you top it the clerk at your eminence. In fine, the post is closed to you, Nicholas.'

Renzi bit his lip. 'Brother. I've no need to confide to you that the sea life is particularly congenial to me, ensuring as it does that a retreat to the scholarly recluse can never tempt, and each morning's prospect may be relied upon to be different. And the blessed regularity of the sea's daily round for the reflective is—'

'No.'

Renzi swallowed and continued in a low voice, 'It pains me to allude to it at this time but . . . but the attraction of a regular stipend, an income of my own . . .'

'Ah. Then you'll need an accommodation of sorts, a gentlemanly loan?'

Renzi drew himself up stiffly. 'That will not be necessary. I'm sanguine I shall find an employment to keep myself while you're at sea.'

'That's settled, then,' Kydd said cheerfully, and got up to pace about the room, ignoring Renzi's dejected expression. 'A frigate!' He laughed out loud. 'Who could conceive . . . ?'

'I wish you joy of it.'

'Thank you, Nicholas,' Kydd said. 'Tysoe must begin packing immediately. I wonder what I'll take? I'll stay at the George, I believe. Ship's accommodation won't be ready yet and there's much to be done.'

'Without a clerk?'

Kydd turned away suddenly as he was taken by a spasm that left his shoulders heaving. 'W-without a c-clerk,' he managed, then turned back, his eyes streaming with laughter.

'An' I had you gulled, Nicholas! Admit it – I had you trussed like a chicken!' he chortled.

'Th-then the post of ship's clerk . . . ?'

'You shall never have, as long as I'm captain!'

'But—'

Kydd pulled himself together and looked affectionately at his old friend. 'Nicholas. Do recollect – I'm now post-captain of a King's Ship, an officer of stature. It would certainly be remarked upon should I neglect to maintain a retinue. And in the first rank of these must stand . . . the captain's confidential secretary.'

Renzi looked dumbstruck.

'As must be a gentleman of some learning, one in whom the captain might need from time to time to confide matters of delicacy . . .'

At Renzi's expression, he continued, more strongly, 'You'll have the character of gentleman with a perfect right to the wardroom, Nicholas, your duties questioned by none. There'll be no more ship's books of account or your bo'sun's stores – this is a job for the ship's clerk, o' course.' He took a deep breath. 'Do accept, old fellow.'

For a moment Renzi did not reply. Then, with a sigh, he answered, 'And here I stand, my studies about to be crowned with the laurels of imminent publication. How could I desert my scholard's post at such a time . . . ?'

It was too much, and the friends roared with laughter as they shook hands on it.

'Tonight we shall wet your swab in bumpers!' Renzi laughed, then added, 'But if we're travelling south tomorrow . . . ?'

'No, Nicholas. I've a notion that all is sadly ahoo there at the moment. I will leave tomorrow, but pray do stay here until I'm able to send for you.'

The journey seemed never-ending, notwithstanding Kydd's travelling with all the speed of a costly post-chaise. At Guildford they changed horses at the Angel, and in the familiar surroundings of the Tudor hall set about with minstrel's galleries he took to wondering at the unreadable workings of Fate that had so quickly transformed him from the contemplation of a genteel retirement in the country to that of hastening to his destiny in command of a frigate.

He hugged the knowledge to himself yet again but ever more insistently came a thought. He had not been able to call on any 'interest' in his cause, no patron in high places who could speak for him, raise him to notice. To what did he owe his elevation, then? It was a deepening mystery for he knew that while his recent action had attracted favourable comment there were others, certainly, with equal or better claim to advancement.

He shrugged. No matter: he had achieved his transmo-grification and would join the tiny number of common seamen who had risen this far – Admiral Benbow, James Cook, even William Bligh, who was at this moment firmly set on course to fly his flag as admiral. The mystery would remain; he would probably never know why it had been him.

The rain had cleared by the time they made the Landport gate, Portsea and then the short distance to the George posting house. He had no wish to see his rooms – in a fever of excitement there was only one thing he wanted to set his eyes on, and she was lying somewhere in the dockyard past the Hard.

He paused at the dockyard gates and looked up at the pair of golden globes that surmounted the entrance. It brought him back to the time that seemed so distant, when he had passed through these gates as a young sailor to adventures that could fill a book. His eyes misted and he stood for a while, letting the feelings surge.

A moment later he stepped resolutely forward. The porter's lodge was just inside and he sought the man out. Nothing escaped the eye of the gate porter of a royal dockyard. 'Can you give me a steer for *L'Aurore d'Égalité*, frigate just caught?'

'*Le Roar*? Aye, I can. Past yon ropewalk an' th' basin and hard by y'r block mills. She's docked, havin' her lines taken off, y' knows.'

'Thank you.' Kydd smiled, leaving the man staring at the crown piece in his hand.

He strode off through the busy dockyard, past the mast ponds and ropewalk, between the steaming kilns and dock basins with their mastless hulls in all stages of fitting out and repair, and on to the new block mills, said to be the wonder of the age.

There was only one dry dock in front of them and Kydd knew that there he would find her. He hurried forward. His first sight was of three stumpy lower masts protruding above the dock edge. The docks were designed to take the mightiest first-rate battleships and the frigate was swallowed up in the space.

And then there she was! HMS *L'Aurore d'Égalité*, or whatever she would be named eventually. Sitting neatly, even primly, on keel-blocks was the naked hull of his new command. In the muddy depths of the dock, teams of men were at work and, on impulse, he found the chain-guarded stone steps leading down to the bottom and descended.

The gigantic immensity of the dark hull above him was awe-inspiring. Then his seaman's instincts translated what he saw into the actuality of a seaway. That fine entry forward and long, clean run aft spoke of speed but at the same time, no doubt, meant her being wet in anything of a head sea. Her unusually steep turn of bilge would help with leeway and the pronounced tumblehome might imply tender handling, but Kydd was left with one overriding impression: speed.

The work-gangs looked at him curiously as they plied their chains and plumb-bobs. It had long been Admiralty practice to take off the lines of captured ships such that if they showed exceptional qualities in service the quirks of their design would be adopted.

And this was what was going on: the distance of the hull out from the keel at different heights was being measured at regular intervals; later these points would be faired into the familiar sheer draught and half-breadth plans that shipbuilders had evolved down the centuries, and – who knew? – a new class of warship might be born.

Filled with new excitement, Kydd puffed his way back up the vertical side of the dock and turned to take in her length. There was no one on deck: the gangboard had been roped off. Disappointed, he had to be content with what he could see from the outside.

And there was much to admire. *L'Aurore d'Égalité* was in truth a full-blooded frigate and pierced for thirty-two carriage guns. He exulted at the discovery – she was a fifth-rate. He had skipped over the smaller sixth-rate and, apart from the despised fifty-gun fourth-rate, he was, in theory, next down from his old ship-of-the-line *Tenacious*.

Compared to *Teazer*, she seemed enormous, her unbroken deck-line stretching all the way from where he stood to the distant beakhead. Impulsively he began stepping out for the bows, counting the paces. Ten, twenty, thirty – fifty-six. A hundred and thirty or forty feet long at least!

She was not looking at her best without her topmasts, her top-hamper struck down and rigging laid along by uncaring dockyard workers, but he could still take in her modest, sheer, clean lines and somewhat old-fashioned trim.

Her stern-lights were lofty and spacious, however, the characteristic high arched curve of the French-style transom pleasing in its symmetry, the quarter-galleries noble and well proportioned. Her stern-piece was more vertical than a British shipwright would have it but it allowed a broader-bladed rudder and . . .

He ached to get aboard. It was the hallowed custom to allow captains a certain latitude when it came to the necessary conversion work for Royal Navy service and he was already forming ideas. The diminutive poop cabin must go, of course, and—

'Your business, sir?'

He swung round. An important-looking official, with two

attendants carrying plans, was eyeing him distrustfully. 'I'm appointed to be her captain,' Kydd said apologetically, knowing he was not in uniform.

'Well, now, Captain,' the man said, thawing. 'Hocking, master shipwright. You'd be wanting t' get aboard, I'll wager.' He chuckled drily.

'I would,' Kydd replied.

'Come wi' me, then,' Hocking said, and motioned to one of his assistants, who freed the barrier. They stepped across above the great pit to the dock floor and then Kydd was aboard his ship.

For a long moment his gaze took in the sweep of the deck-line, the rearing bowsprit, the pleasing square drop at the drift rail and he smothered a sigh. 'Mr Hocking – I see there's not so much action damage. Do you know aught of how we came by her?'

'Why, there's none t' be found, is all. She thought to make a break from Rochefort in the fog an' had the crass bad luck for it to lift – an' she finds herself in the middle o' our blockade squadron. With six o'-the-line sightin' down their guns, a decision wasn't hard t' make.'

Kydd felt a momentary sympathy with the unknown captain and crew, whose voyage and future had thus been settled in an instant. 'A pretty lady,' he murmured appreciatively, looking about him. 'I'd be beholden for your opinion, Mr Hocking.'

There was a fleeting smile and Kydd suspected that Hocking was not often consulted for his opinion by naval officers.

'I'm not taken wi' the Frenchy ways much, m'self – scantlings are too light an' that there fine-run hull'll mean a smaller hold an' that means her sea endurance won't be worth a spit.'

'That may be so,' Kydd said, 'but she's going to be a fast 'un, I'm thinking.'

'Aye, an' she'll be plunging into every comber God sends,' Hocking went on remorselessly.

'No sailor I know ever pines over a wet shirt,' Kydd replied defensively.

'And every Frenchy I know is crank and heels her lee gun-ports under in anythin' of a blow.'

'And so we bring in high sail as is needful.'

'Hmmph. Look, Mr Captain, survey's complete but we've work t' do. How's about you take yourself off for a look-see and come back in an hour. Then we'll have *your* opinion.'

Delighted, Kydd took his leave and began to make his acquaintance.

She was not a new ship. Over here were scores in the deck that could not be planed out, and there he noted smooth new timber scarphed into older. More clues of her maturity became evident: the shape of the knight-heads of a previous age, the pair of davits over the stern as an after-thought – she must be close to ten years old at least. She had therefore first kissed the waves at the time he had embarked on the voyage around the world that had changed him from a youth to a man and formed him as a seaman. In *Artemis* frigate he had sailed from this very port, the fear-some Captain 'Black Jack' Powlett in command. As clear as yesterday he recalled the pugnacious blue-black jaw, the terri-fying stare – and now he, the former Able Seaman Kydd, was in his shoes . . .

He returned his attention to *L'Aurore d'Égalité*. Like all frigates, the topmost deck was flush from bow to stern but this was deceptive. In reality there was a raised fo'c'sle forward and a poop aft; but these were joined into one by broad gang-ways each side. The open space in the middle was straddled by spare spars and on these would be nested the ship's boats.

He found the after ladderway down to the next level. This was their single gun-deck, and the frigate's main armament would be found arrayed all the way down each side. It was now deserted, all ordnance landed before docking, and the space seemed limitless, stretching away distantly to the bows.

Behind him were the cabin spaces – *his* living quarters. All other officers and men would berth below, in the perpetual gloom of the lower deck where, in the absence of ports or windows, no natural light could penetrate.

Turning aft, he moved towards a bulkhead: it spanned the ship right across in an intimidating show of exclusion – the captain's apartments. It was finished in polished red wood. The brass handles of the two doors still glowed with the efforts of her last sea-watch, now miserably under guard in a prison-hulk somewhere.

Feeling like a trespasser, he pushed on the larboard door. It opened into the coach, bare patches underfoot showing where items of furniture must have been, the fat girth of the mizzen-mast solidly to one side. A more elaborate door was at the far end. Tentatively he eased it open, walked in and stopped. This was the great cabin – and it was vast.

A blaze of light streamed in through the broad stern windows, bringing out rich colours of decoration that would not have been out of place in a fine country mansion. Oddly, an ornate little cast-iron charcoal stove still perched to one side; this had been a captain whose means and inclination had allowed him to consult his comfort above the ordinary.

However, what took his attention immediately was a substantial secretaire against the forward bulkhead. It was richly veneered and polished, and shaped to fit into the ship's structure, which was probably why it was still there. On impulse he pulled down the integral writing surface; inside was a perfect maze of compartments and miniature drawers – all empty, of course.

A discreet door led to his stateroom. It was sizeable, so much so that it sported not one but two gun-ports. A cot was still there, complete with an ingenious pulley system that allowed the lying occupant to raise and lower himself. At one end a cunningly contrived wash-place shared space with a dresser across the width of the compartment, and there was a fitted wardrobe opposite.

He stood back in awe. This was his kingdom and it was princely. In effect there was the splendour of a spacious great cabin right aft, then beyond the partition the coach to one side, private quarters the other, all his.

As he was about to leave, a ghostly sense of the last inhabitant's presence stole over him. He could picture the man – older, more careful, probably of the *ancien régime*, with a need for the certainties of gracious living and order in all things. He would not have been one to hazard his ship in valorous escapades or carry sail until the last moment.

He felt a rush of guilt that, here, he was an intruder, violating the little world that was the ship the unknown *capitaine de vaisseau* had shaped to his desires and satisfaction. He tried to shake it off as he left, closing the door softly behind him.

The lower deck was a hollow, echoing space, illuminated by the splashes of light coming through the gratings from above. Neat rows of tables, each with its rack against the ship's side, were spaced all along it for at this level, at or below the waterline, there were no guns, therefore no requirement to clear them for action.

He moved to the closest. Not unlike the familiar British domestic models, with the seamen's chests as seats, the tubs at the inner end for the ship's boys – and further down, canvas screens triced up to the deckhead. On impulse he unlaced one: it tumbled down to reveal a traditional scene of mermaids and King Neptune but done in a delicate and artistic manner rather than the hearty treatment of a British sailor. It was, of course, the demarcation of the petty officers' mess.

Aft was another excluding bulkhead, with two doors. This would be the place of the officers' cabins and wardroom – or gunroom, as it was called in a frigate. He went inside. It was shadowed and gloomy, with light entering only from the open door, but it was enough to see that it was as he had expected: there were cabins down each side, the two furthest the biggest. A long table occupied the centre, and in the far recesses there were lockers, probably stores or bread-rooms.

Here it was that his officers would have their being: the first and other lieutenants, sailing master, purser, officer of marines. This would be their unchanging home during whatever lay ahead for them all. He stepped out again; beyond the sanctity of the gunroom there were separate cabins for the warrant officers, the boatswain and gunner, carpenter and one other, making this particular after ladderway the unlikely intersection between the officers, warrant officers and the ship's company.

It was all he needed to see. There were no surprises with the layout; she appeared in good fettle and he felt he had her measure – older, without the brute strength of the latest English frigates but with a willing air, a desire to please. Only the open sea would search out her moods and delights and he could hardly wait to seek them.

'To y'r satisfaction, Captain?'

He hadn't noticed the master shipwright looking at him narrowly from beyond the main-mast and went to him. 'The poop cabin must go,' Kydd said briskly, 'and I will have the wheel forrard o' the mizzen.'

'O' course.'

'I'd like to see tougher bulwarks and the breast rail more in the way of a barricade. And what do you think of raising the bridle port to take a pair o' chase guns?'

'Ye know she's a twelve-pounder only?'

'Then we'll ship eighteens,' Kydd retorted. 'She's sound in her particulars?'

'She is,' Hocking admitted. 'Out of Nantes in 'ninety-four by Jacques Sané, one o' their best. An' you'll be wanting as much stowage below as we c'n give ye. Y' saw the middle part o' the hold as is your cable tier?'

He hadn't – and that a third of the space in his precious hold would be taken up with the anchor cable was not welcome news. 'I know you'll do your best for me, Mr Hocking,' Kydd said, with feeling. There would be a keg and spread waiting for him and his men tonight as an earnest for the future.

There would be other things, but they could take their turn – the Navy Board had its own ideas of what was meet and proper in a warship of the Royal Navy, and if it was not within the 'establishment' for this class of ship, he would need persuasive arguments to secure what he wanted.

He bade the master shipwright a good day and set out for the George. There was thinking to do.

The most pressing was the matter of the eighteen-pounders. There had not been any twelve-pounder frigates built for the British since as far back as he could remember, and the French had ceased constructing them in the last war. If he met another frigate in combat then almost certainly he would be facing eighteens and would be badly outclassed. It was as much a matter for the Board of Ordnance as the Navy Board and he was hazy as to the procedure.

Earlier he had been told that he should hold himself in readiness for an order to take the vessel into service – to commission her and thereby incur expense to the Crown in fitting her out. She would then formally exist and in all the signal books in the fleet her name would appear next to her unique pennant number. *L'Aurore d'Égalité*: the name could not be suffered to continue – but would a new one be as resonant?

And, of course, the standing officers would start arriving to stand by the fitting out: the boatswain, gunner, carpenter, cook – and, most importantly at this stage, the purser. He could open his books and life would begin.

That night Kydd found it difficult to sleep. The long history of the Royal Navy resounded with daring exploits in the face of impossible odds but none had gripped the public imagination so much as those of the famous frigate captains. Their names were known by every shepherd boy and mill-worker and some had returned home wildly rich to be fêted by their country.

Would he join their select company or be found wanting? A frigate was an entirely different creature from a sloop; he now held the equivalent rank to colonel of a regiment and had the management of the same number of guns as the whole of Napoleon's Horse Artillery – and twice their weight of metal. He was being given a serious and significant asset in Britain's survival and must not fail.

Chapter 4

By the time his ship had been moved from the dry dock to the water alongside, Kydd's orders had arrived, including his precious commission to take command of the ship. There for all to see, on crackling parchment, were the words that made him lord and master of a potent ship of war and several hundred souls:

> . . . *by virtue of the power and authority to us given, we do hereby constitute and appoint you captain of His Majesty's Ship* L'Aurore, *willing and requiring you the charge and command of her accordingly: strictly charging and commanding all the officers and company of the said ship with all due respect and obedience unto you, their said captain. . .*

So the frigate was to be known simply as *L'Aurore* and he now had the authority to incur expenditure and thus formalise arrangements with the dockyard to complete the conversions and render the ship in all respects ready for war.

The rest of the orders concerned the proper form for rendering accounts, while 'under the cheque' meant the dockyard was taking responsibility for payments on the Navy Office while fitting out.

It amused Kydd to note that, as a consequence of his elevation to a frigate command, the Admiralty clerks who had before signed themselves 'Your obedient servant . . .' were now punctiliously writing 'Your *humble* and obedient servant . . .'

Later there would be the ceremony of reading himself in as *L'Aurore*'s lawful captain, and in the eyes of the Admiralty and the world, the ship would, from that precise instant, begin its existence.

Tysoe arrived from London with Kydd's new uniform and an astonishing amount of gear that, it seemed, was absolutely essential to maintaining his new station in life. He had to be found accommodation until the ship was habitable but, aboard, matters were progressing apace.

The upperworks were duly strengthened and the bridle port seen to, then the small French oven on the lower deck was hoisted out and a respectable full Brodie galley stove was swayed on to a relaid hearth just beneath the fo'c'sle.

Kydd watched its installation – an amazing device, with smoke-jack driven spits, condensers for distilling water, range grates and all manner of cooking equipment, including an oven and monstrous boiler for the men's salt beef. It was just in time – a cheerful peg-leg cook had reported with the purser, a Welshman named Owen.

Taking the opportunity to get about the ship before her crew embarked, Kydd discovered that her ballast was now pig-iron rather than the shingle of before; this would require that the great leaguer water-barrels must be stowed on the flat of the foot-waling with wedges, three tiers high. Would it hold secure in raging gales?

Other oddities were revealed: the cat-tail was bolted under the lower-deck beams, a stronger fitting he had to admit, but it was disturbing that she had no figurehead – only a contemptible billet-head and scrollwork. This would not be looked on favourably by a traditionally minded British crew for her first voyage under a new flag.

The gunner appeared two days later. A ponderous individual, Redmond had definite views about the need for eighteen-pounders and went off to see what could be done about it.

As work progressed, Kydd could see no reason to delay so he and the warrant officers transferred aboard. He had just received a blunt letter from the Admiralty advising that as the ship was urgently required for service he should bend his best endeavours to that end. This was unusual to say the least: he had no influence over the dockyard, and until he had a ship's company, there was little he could do to help.

Time was pressing. In the next day or two the sheer-hulks would be alongside and the final stage would be reached, the frigate's rigging, but the most valuable standing officer at this point was missing: the boatswain.

Then the sailing master courteously reported. Kendall was soft-spoken and held himself with dignity; his was a seamed, weather-beaten face and instinctively Kydd trusted him – as he had his first master when he was a green officer: the equally quiet Hambly in *Tenacious*.

'Pleased to see you, Mr Kendall,' he said, with feeling.

'I did hear of y'r bo'sun, Captain Kydd,' he said levelly. 'Word's as how he's unable to sail wi' ye. It's not m' place but I do know the bo'sun o' *Actaeon*, now paid off, would admire for t' ship out in an active ship, he bein' at leisure, like.'

'It's an Admiralty matter, Mr Kendall, as you'd know,' Kydd

said, with regret. Any recommended by one of Kendall's calibre would be worth having but all standing officers were appointed direct and he had no authority to take one on.

'I knows, sir. He's willin' to present himself to ye now, hopin' you're able t' get him confirmed later.'

Kydd didn't hesitate. 'Very well. Where is he—'

'He'll be aboard wi' his dunnage within th' hour, sir.'

'I see. His name?'

'Oakley. Oh, an' savin' your presence, he can be a mort hasty in his speech, like, says things too quick he should've kept under hatches. Ben's rough-hearted but he's a ver' fine seaman, Mr Kydd,' Kendall went on earnestly. 'There's none o' the seven seas he don't know like Falmouth high street. An' he it was, in *Jupiter* gun-brig in the Caribbee, who—'

'Get him aboard, Mr Kendall.'

Oakley was big, red-headed and heavily tattooed, with hands that looked capable of bending a cutlass. 'Cap'n Kydd,' he said warily, touching his forehead.

'You've served as bo'sun before?' asked Kydd.

'Aye. Four years in *Actaeon* as was.'

'You know I can't take you unless the Admiralty gives me leave?'

'Sir.'

'And a berth in a frigate is no holiday.'

'I knows.'

'Then for *now* you're bo'sun o' *L'Aurore*, Mr Oakley.'

An enormous grin split his face, stretching his face into well-used laugh-lines that had Kydd hiding a smile. 'Why, an' that's right oragious in ye, Mr Kydd.'

'Tomorrow we'll have the sheer-hulk to work on the masting. We'll take measure of you then, I believe.'

*   *   *

Dismayed, Kydd watched the leisurely approach of the ugly barge with its sheer-legs. It was not so much the prospect of the hard work to follow but that the dockyard could spare only four riggers and a sorry-looking bunch of labourers. The work would get done – but it would stretch over weeks.

'Mr Oakley, come with me.' Kydd stalked across the dockyard to where *Spartiate*, a 74, was undergoing repair. A short time later he was talking with the officer-of-the-watch and a little after that he was in the berthing hulk alongside, calling for volunteers to help with the rigging.

It did not take much urging: these men were billeted out of their ship while it was in dockyard hands; they had nothing to do and had spent all their silver. Kydd had rightly guessed that they would welcome a change. Oakley took his pick and then the work could start.

The master rigger, however, insisted on a consultation first; it seemed that no good could come of a hasty commencing and Kydd sat dutifully as he learned that the ship was at the present in the style of the 'French Pyramid', a configuration of masts and spars that, with the logic of that nation, related everything to a ratio of spar to the beam of the ship. In proof, the main lower mast was pointed out to be at a ratio of 2.5 times the beam while the main yard crossed would therefore be in the region of 2.2. Might Kydd favour the broader British style?

He listened patiently but remained firm: if the original owners had seen fit to make it thus, then he would stay with it unless it proved inadequate. He did, however, compromise in the matter of the rake of the mizzen and allowed the master rigger his way that the bowsprit be steeved six degrees lower.

Oakley clearly knew his technicals and had a natural way

with men, always leading from the front, passing turns, the first to reeve the girtline, clapping on to lines with his huge strength to encourage and inspire. If he was not to be *L'Aurore*'s boatswain it would not be for want of Kydd's trying.

And the workmanlike lines of the standing rigging began to appear, the topmasts and then topgallant masts stretched skywards and in turn were crossed with yards, all proper stays and lifts, a soaring tracery of ropes criss-crossing aloft, while below the fitments of living were finally being put in place.

An astonishing mountain of stores appeared, requiring signature, and with the return of the gunner bearing the welcome news that a Board of Ordnance was shortly to inspect and put in hand their accession to eighteen-pounders, the end was suddenly in sight.

Tysoe had not been idle. Several times a day he would seek Kydd's views on this or that piece of furniture, whether the few small ornaments he had rescued from *Teazer* might now be retired in favour of a grander show and if the competence of his table in entertainment might profitably be brought forward.

In foreign parts *L'Aurore*'s entering port would be an occasion of some moment, and if Kydd failed to provide handsomely and creditably at table it would reflect not only on the ship but his flag. A dinner service edged in green and gilt from Mr Wedgwood was acquired for daily use and strategic items in silver were secured, but he hesitated over the grander pieces – a woman's touch would ensure the commensal subtleties were properly observed. He would talk to Cecilia.

The time had come – *L'Aurore* was ready for her company.

Her lieutenants must be summoned first, then, when they had made acquaintance with the ship, the senior petty officers and finally the rest. It was a significant step, for once men were aboard and consuming victuals, all at once the whole mechanism for managing a ship-of-war had to be in place and functioning.

A message to the port-admiral's office requesting his officers to report aboard was therefore dispatched. The first to show was Curzon, his third lieutenant, a young but confident individual with the languid drawl of birth and wealth. Kydd asked Kendall, who had little to do until orders were received specifying their station, to take him around the frigate.

The most important of the officers was close behind: Howlett, the first lieutenant. He, essentially, would run the ship for Kydd: make up the watch and station bill of the hands, their quarters, and designate special sea-duty personnel for evolutions such as unmooring and taking in sail. On a more subtle level his handling of discipline would be crucial: by the time matters reached Kydd's august notice only grave consequences could follow.

In the event his manner was all that could be desired. About the same age as Kydd, he was slighter in build but darker-featured and with a strong jaw. His speech was careful and he carried himself with a controlled energy, his eyes direct and appraising. Like Curzon, he was given Kendall's tour and the rest of the day to shift his gear aboard.

That left Gilbey, the second lieutenant. The man did not report until late in the afternoon, pleading business ashore. Kydd accepted his excuse and asked Curzon to take him around.

Three officers: it seemed few enough in a ship's company that would total 215 at full manning. Each one would be tested to the full when *L'Aurore* went to war.

And the men. When the purser advised that all books of account were ready, the first lieutenant was satisfied with his information on the ship's establishment of skilled hands, and the dockyard was near to finishing aloft, Kydd would notify the port-admiral's office. Howlett would then start the business of entering them in. After that sea trials could be made, probably in the sheltered waters around the Isle of Wight.

Kydd's pulse quickened. If all went well, within days he would have a ship full of life, a watch on deck, the settled order of an unchanging domestic naval routine. It was an intoxicating thought.

In the matter of a figurehead he was in luck: when Legge, their grey-haired carpenter, reported with his tools he had already noticed the absence of adornment at the bows and had an answer. Before the fashion for individually crafted figureheads had taken hold, the Navy had employed a standard design in the form of a lion and crown. The old carpenter knew of one that, in the distant past, had been removed in favour of the newer kind and was now gathering dust in an office.

He undertook to fit it and now *L'Aurore* proudly boasted a sturdy figurehead of an upright lion surmounted with a neat crown that offered enough scope for scarlet and gilding to gladden the heart of any true son of the sea.

Now they were ready.

Kydd took pen and paper and wrote three letters. The first was to the port-admiral, advising of the near completion of his vessel and thereby requesting men to be released into her. The second was a note to Renzi, inviting him to take post, and the last was to Calloway: he had been a young seaman in Kydd's day before the mast, and Kydd knew it would bring him the gladdest news. Now a midshipman without interest or patronage and of humble origins, it was unlikely he would find any quarterdeck open to him.

He sat back in satisfaction. In remarkably quick time he had brought the frigate to readiness. He had confidence in his ship and felt a growing respect and affection for her. She was not one of the new tribe of heavy frigates but she had breeding and promise.

She would never replace *Teazer* in his heart but that wasn't the point. He had now taken a major advance in his profession and necessarily had moved up to a grander ship. He would never forget his first command but it was in the future that destiny lay – for him and his new frigate.

Something of *Teazer* still continued, though: his Captain's Orders. They laid down his expectations of conduct for every officer and man, which he had evolved in his years in her. Now they would continue virtually unchanged in *L'Aurore*.

He smothered a sigh of contentment as the reality sank in. He would throw himself into the task of bringing his frigate to life and capability and it would be only a short time before he would set course south to play his part in the great battle that must come.

Mr Midshipman Bowden held his breath as topgallant sails beyond counting began lifting slowly above the far-distant hard line of the horizon. The dispatch cutter hardened in its sheets and altered towards the leading ships, slashing through the sullen grey seas in bursts of white, its canvas board-taut.

This was probably the greatest day in his life and he drank in the sensations avidly. In a very short time he would be joining his new ship on blockade duty, just as he had told his old captain, Commander Kydd, when he had met him in the Admiralty waiting room. What he had not mentioned, for pity of the situation, was that his uncle had secured for him the first prize: to be set on the quarterdeck as midshipman in the flagship of Admiral Lord Nelson, the famous *Victory*.

His heart bounded. This would be an experience few could boast of – service under the greatest fighting admiral of the age and at a time of desperate peril for the nation. Of one thing he was sure: he would do his duty to the utmost in whatever lay ahead, for everyone knew that Napoleon Bonaparte must make good his promise to destroy England by invasion, and it was the Royal Navy who would stand unflinchingly foursquare against him.

The ships of Nelson's battle-fleet were now hull-up and he took time to savour the grand spectacle of the Mediterranean Fleet standing away to the north-west in two columns, perfectly spaced at a cable-length apart, an unforgettable picture of splendour and warlike threat.

The crack of a signal gun from the cutter startled him. It was to draw attention to their signal hoist fluttering at the halliards: 'I have dispatches.' A grim-faced lieutenant stood aft with a satchel protectively under his arm, his gaze on the line of men-o'-war. He had travelled from the Admiralty to Gibraltar and now carried who knew what news, intelligence and orders from the greater world for his famed commander-in-chief.

Victory wasted no time in throwing out a signal to the fleet to heave to. As one, sails were backed and the stately progress of the warships was suspended.

The cutter passed under the lee of the great battleship, curious faces appearing along her high deck-line as they hooked on below the entry port. Bowden thrilled at the thought that very likely Nelson himself was looking down on them at this moment, anxious for the news they carried.

The lieutenant swung on to the slippery side-steps, expertly hauling himself up to disappear into the ornately decorated entry port. Bowden followed, careful to go the long way over the bulwarks. Later, as an officer, he would be entitled to board in the same way as the lieutenant.

He blinked. The space opened up was immense. Spotless decks stretched away to a distant fo'c'sle, and above, he had an impression of irresistible strength in the vast concourse of sails with their mighty yards and soaring lines.

He snatched off his hat and bowed to a frowning lieutenant with a telescope – he had to be the officer-of-the-watch. 'Midshipman Bowden, sir, come aboard to join.'

'Who? Speak up, man!'

'Bowden, sir.'

'I've heard nothing of you,' the officer said irritably, glaring at him. Distant shouts came from over the side.

'Ah, that'll be my sea-chest, sir.'

The lieutenant turned to another midshipman. 'Get it inboard, see him into the middies' berth and be sure to let Mr Quilliam know he's another damned reefer.' With a final glower at Bowden, he turned his back and paced away.

The midshipman called easily to a seaman, and while a whip was being rove he held out his hand. 'Bulkeley – Richard, t' my friends, Dick, t' the cockpit.'

'Bowden, Charles. You're American, er, Richard?'

'Born 'n' bred. You've seen some service, then?' he said, eyeing Bowden's sailorly build.

'Not as who might say. The Nile, Minorca before the peace, the Med in a brig-sloop,' he admitted, trying not to look open-mouthed at the sheer scale of *Victory*'s masts and guns.

'The Nile? As I thought. You're not to berth with the

77

reefers, it's the gunroom for you, m' friend. I'll square it later with the bo'sun.'

The largest ship Bowden had been in had been the old sixty-four-gun *Tenacious,* but this was altogether in another dimension. A first-rate, the largest type of battleship in the Navy, it was a floating city, teeming with men, crammed with guns and imbued with the irresistible arrogance of power.

The gunroom was on the lower deck, occupying the entire after end of the ship under the massive twenty-five-foot tiller. Far more capacious than any Bowden had seen, it was home for the warrant officers, boatswain, gunner and other senior men, together with the master's mates and privileged senior midshipmen.

'We sling our micks here. The bo'sun and so on have their cabins but we all mess at table in the gunroom.'

His sea-chest was given to the care of the gunroom servant and Bowden tried to thank his American friend, who brushed it aside. 'We've a right taut ship, Charles, an' under the eye of His Nibs at any time. Just be sure you measure up.'

Bowden nodded. 'I've heard Our Nel can be short with those who cross his hawse.'

'And he can be as nice as pie to those who try hard,' Bulkeley came back instantly. 'Now, I think it a wise thing right now to make your number with the first luff. This way . . .'

In his cabin the first lieutenant looked up from his work. 'Mr Bowden to join, sir. I have him ready berthed in the gunroom. Charles, this is Mr Quilliam.'

Victory swayed majestically – they must be under way once more. Quilliam efficiently noted details of Bowden's sea service and pulled down a large and well-creased diagram. 'Your watch – Mr Pasco, I believe. Station? Shall we say at the main-mast for now. Quarters? Something tells me you'll relish the lower-deck smashers – only a hop and step from your hammock in the gunroom, I'll point out.'

He looked up with a lop-sided smile. 'The sooner you've sheeted in the essentials the better. I rather think the best use of your time at this moment would be for Mr Bulkeley t' show you the ropes until we need not fear to trip over you.'

'Aye aye, sir,' Bulkeley said, and the pair left together.

'I rather think this must be one quick tour, Charles. Evening quarters are taken seriously and we don't want you adrift on your first day. Now, the fo'c'sle . . .'

Right forward, a hundred feet of bowsprit with its head-sails soaring up speared out, the elaborate beakhead just below. The roar and swash of the bow-wave made conversation difficult.

'You'll never see a main-mast s' taunt,' Bulkeley said, pointing up as they passed the tack of the fore-course. It was an awe-inspiring sight, mounting up beyond the fighting tops and cross-trees to the very heavens. 'Higher even than Westminster Abbey – should you fall afoul of the officer-of-the-watch and find yourself mastheaded.'

On past the big launches and barge and then Bowden saw a knot of officers on the quarterdeck deep in earnest conversation – and in the centre, unmistakable with his four stars and gold lace, was Lord Nelson.

They walked by respectfully, Bowden doffing his hat and taking his first look at the most famous admiral in the Royal Navy. There was an immediate impression of crushing care and worry, the lines in his face deep and set, but in the uncompromising quarterdeck brace there was resolute pugnacity.

'We carry nine lootenants,' Bulkeley said, breaking the spell, 'and a company of eight hundred and fifty – being short about thirty o' that.'

Getting on for a thousand men within the confines of one ship. 'Er, how many decks does she have?' Bowden asked, for something to say, as they mounted the poop ladder.

'Well, three gun-decks, o' course – twelves, twenty-fours and thirty-two-pounders – but if you're counting there's seven under us, including the hold platform.'

He went on to explain the layout of the carronades on the quarterdeck and fo'c'sle, and signal handling on the after end. Moving to the break of the poop, he leaned over to point out *Victory*'s great double wheel, taller than the men who steered her, and the near fifty-foot sweep of quarter-deck abaft the main-mast.

Bowden said in wonder, 'She's a grand lady, Richard – must be a few years old now?'

'Yes,' chuckled Bulkeley. 'Laid down for the Seven Years' War in 'fifty-nine. Seen a few admirals too since then – Keppel in your American war, poor old Kempenfelt later and, o' course, Jervis at St Vincent.'

Bowden blinked. She had started life in a very different age: halfway through the last century, before Captain Cook had charted the unknown regions, before Harrison's chronometers, before even copper bottoms for warships. And now she was the most famous flagship in the world.

They went below to discover vast gun-decks, the gloomy orlop and forward, giant bitts for the anchor cable. 'Twenty-four-inch cables, no less, so at a hundred and fifty pounds in every fathom and a four-ton anchor on the end, pity the capstan crew!'

Then it was up through the decks once more to the winter sky and dark complexity of rigging. The vast bellying main-course was the largest sail Bowden had ever seen – fully a hundred feet across and with an area on its own much the same as a respectable London townhouse. There were others and more, three masts in a towering pyramid of sea-darkened canvas, urgently drawing.

'Everything's on quite another scale,' Bulkeley admitted, 'and those grand sails are why we have near a thousand ton o' ballast – that's the weight of a whole frigate in our guts just to hold us upright.'

Pleased with Bowden's expression, he continued, 'The bo'sun says there's twenty-six miles of rigging and a thousand pulley-blocks to go with it. She's a hull nearly three feet thick at the waterline yet she's the sweetest sailer on a bowline, eight or nine knots and I've seen eleven going large. Why, when the fleet's at exercise—'

The visceral thunder of drums and the flat bray of a trumpet interrupted him.

'Quarters!' he said abruptly. 'You'd better go.'

Bowden flew down the broad stairways among racing men to find his place in the lower gun-deck. Already the gun-ports were open on the weather side and the guns had been cast loose. It seemed an impossible seething mass of people impatiently crowding into the low-beamed space, the sharp shouts of petty officers the only sound apart from the fearful rumbling of the huge iron beasts.

It settled as gun-crews were mustered, taking their implements and standing expectantly with handspike, ram-rod or tackle-fall to serve the three-ton monster. These were the smashers, the greatest guns in the fleet, which could send a ball as heavy as two men could lift through a yard of solid oak at a mile.

And this was his station in battle.

'Bowden, sir,' he said, to the lieutenant standing by the fat trunk of the mizzen-mast. 'I'm assigned here at quarters.'

81

The officer waited until the warlike bustle had subsided into disciplined silence, then said, 'Stand by me, Mr Bowden, and mark well how things are done. You may learn something.'

Falling back respectfully, Bowden watched as gun-crews limbered up, fourteen to each gun, all looking to their gun-captain, stripped to the waist and deadly serious. And there beyond each gun another and another – sixteen of the great guns on this one side alone. When they spoke in anger surely none could stand against them.

The practice began. Brute force and corded muscles to run out the chest-high black gun; quoin, crow and handspike to aim it; a ballet of movements to sponge, wad and charge it before the deadly ball was cradled to the muzzle.

It was precision work of a high order: wielding six-foot rammers, heavy handspikes and the sharp, curled worm in the narrow working space between the cannon, the sequence of powder, priming and shot exactly timed – a fumbled thirty-two-pound ball rolling around could cause chaos on a crowded gun-deck.

After the sweating gun-crews were stood down, Bowden reflected that if this was what it was like in drill, how would it be when *Victory* went into battle in earnest?

Lieutenant Pasco chalked on the watch slate and handed it to the oncoming quartermaster-of-the-watch, ignoring Bowden until the set of the sails was entirely to his satisfaction. At night it was difficult to see aloft to catch the angle of the yards and he had his night-glass up to inspect the results of the trim carefully.

To Bowden this small act spoke so powerfully of what the Navy had become with, at its core, a professionalism that was second nature to every officer and man. There was no one about on the upper deck besides the watch to appreciate it on this cold night, no admiring or critical audience, but at this moment *Victory* was trimmed to perfection, as though the eyes of the world were upon her.

The watch settled down, in time-honoured fashion finding a lee and engaging in swapping yarns that grew taller with every telling. The men at the wheel would be relieved every turn of the glass and join them for a few hours.

Lieutenant Pasco, as officer-of-the-watch, was now the supreme commander of the three-thousand-ton fighting ship. If he was awed by the notion he showed no sign of it. 'Right, then, young Bowden, tell me what you've been doing with yourself in His Majesty's finest.'

He understood what was going on: this was a long watch and he was a new face, hopefully with a repertoire of anecdotes to hand. He answered modestly, 'I started as a reefer in *Tenacious*, sixty-four, Captain Houghton . . .'

It was well received. All officers shared a common experience in aspiring to the quarterdeck and tales of the quirks and eccentricities of those set in authority were many. Later Bowden told at some length of his adventures in Minorca with an amusing account of one of their lieutenants a-spying with an improvised signalling system.

Pasco suddenly demanded, 'What was the name of that lieutenant again?'

'Kydd, sir.'

'Thomas Kydd?'

'That's right.'

'The same as was commander of *Teazer* brig-sloop, lately boarded both sides, fought 'em off but then foundered? We do hear of such in the Med,' he added sardonically.

'I was with him when he first commissioned her,' Bowden said proudly.

'Were you indeed? Then I'm to tell you he's been something of a hero to me, we both coming aft by the hawse as we did. A hard horse, at all?'

'We had our days,' Bowden admitted. 'Knows all the tricks, if you get my meaning. But I'll allow he's the very kind of officer I pray I'll be one day.'

'If we be spared. Now, look, where's your post at quarters, younker?'

'Lower deck, thirty-two-pounders aft.'

'The slaughter-house. I'm l'tenant of signals – would it grieve you much should you leave 'em and join me on the poop-deck as signal midshipman? I've a place for a quick thinker brought up in the right ways.'

'I'd be honoured, sir.'

Chapter 5

Renzi put down his book and got to his feet as Tysoe ushered Cecilia in. 'Why, sister – you've come to hear the news?'

Her face lit up. 'Yes! Do tell, Nicholas,' she said impulsively. 'Was it a grand office at all? Did you—'

'Office?'

'The publisher, you ninny!'

'Oh. Um . . . I was in fact to tell you that your brother has offered me the post of captain's confidential secretary in his frigate, a handsome gesture you'll agree.'

Cecilia sat slowly. 'Then you haven't been to a publisher?'

Renzi flushed. 'Er, I've been rather busy, you'll understand.'

She bit her lip. 'I shall ask the marquess for a letter of introduction to any publishing house you choose. He is not to be ignored you may believe, Nicholas.'

'Thank you, dear sister, but I can manage the affair myself,' Renzi replied quickly. 'A dish of tea with me? There's some superior China black we've been saving for—'

'Thank you, no,' Cecilia said coolly, standing and smoothing her dress. 'I find that I'm overborne with business. Good day, sir.'

Renzi glowered at the wall. She was right, of course. Sooner or later he must approach a publisher. The act of writing was the most gratifying and intellectually rewarding thing he had done in his life. The single-minded pursuit of meaning, its expression and, in fact, the entire act of creation placed his mind on a plane that lifted him above his mortal existence.

But what if he went to a publisher and was told that his first-born was not fit to see the light of day, that it was the mere vaporising of a dilettante amateur? His excuse for taking wings into the empyrean would be snatched from him and then he would be forced to return and . . . It couldn't be faced.

Therefore it could not be risked: he wouldn't go. The logic was simple.

Or was it? If he did not go he would never know if the work he had shaped so lovingly with his own hands might be valued by others – he would never see his scratchings on sheaves of paper transformed into a handsome leather-bound volume that would be launched into the far reaches of the world, or have gracious correspondence with enraptured readers, knowing his work delighted so many others.

And at last he would be able to lay before Cecilia his *magnum opus* to her wide-eyed delight, before falling to his knees and begging her hand in marriage. Dammit – it had to be done.

But how was he to approach a publisher and persuade them that his work was worthy enough to print? And, more to the point, was it that one put forward a sum in consideration to set them in motion or, much more improbably, was Cecilia right that they could be open to suggestions of some sort of body-and-soul advance against future sales?

Renzi was by no means a stranger to the warren of book-sellers in both Piccadilly and Paternoster Row as a book buyer, but for a would-be author it was a different matter. The latter was the haunt of the lower sort of hackery – as well as impoverished aspirants to letters eking out a living. The former, with St James's Street and Pall Mall, was where the better sort was to be found, where Samuel Johnson, Goldsmith, even Wilkes and Franklin had begun their ventures into print.

He dressed carefully, unsure of just what authors wore about town. He settled on his sober deep-brown but added a rather more flamboyant lace cravat and romantically raked hat to set the tone.

In his library there were works from all the publishers of note but he did not know enough about them to impel him from one to another. Then he recalled that John Murray, the 'doyen of *belles-lettres*', had himself seen service as an officer in the Navy during the Seven Years' War and presumably would be the more sympathetic.

The fly-leaf of a book, however, revealed that the publisher was in Fleet Street, rather nearer to Paternoster Row than he would have liked, but at least the right side of Blackfriars Bridge. Soon he was standing outside an undistinguished four-storey red-brick house with a well-polished brass plaque on the door simply proclaiming, 'Mr Murray'.

Through that door there might be a new future – or the ruin of a dream. The literary lions of society did not know he existed and he had no recognition from academia: by what right did he claim the attention of probably the most successful publisher in London?

In an agony of indecision he paced up and down until he'd summoned up courage to knock. He met with a quick impression of dark opulence, a discreet staircase and a kindly-looking gentleman in half-spectacles who stopped in surprise. 'May I help you, sir?'

'Is Mr Murray at liberty to see me, do you think? A – a private matter concerning any advice he might be able to provide.'

'Then it's an author you are, sir? If you'll kindly wait I'll see if I can secure an appointment for you.'

He was back promptly. 'Mr Murray would be pleased to receive you now. I do hope we shall be seeing more of you, sir.'

Ushered into a spacious and undeniably literary study, Renzi was taken aback by the youth of the individual who rose to meet him. 'Er, Nicholas Renzi. Do I address Mr John Murray?'

'You do, sir,' he answered, then smiled. 'I am the child of the father, so to speak.'

'Then you have no service in the Navy?'

His eyes narrowed. 'No, Mr Renzi, my father did. I have not, thank God. Might I enquire what it is you want of me?'

The gaze was confident and intelligent, and more than a little disconcerting, but Renzi pressed on: 'Mr Murray, you are a publisher of note and I would value your counsel exceedingly.'

'Yes?'

'Over these past few years I have laboured on a work that I flatter myself has its merit. It's close to completion and I'm now at a stand with regard to how I might proceed, er, to be published.'

'I would be honoured to advise, Mr Renzi. First, do tell me something of your origins.'

'My origins? If by that you are alluding to any academic or literary qualifications I might possess then I must—'

'No, sir. Your background of a personal nature – your upbringing, experiences of life, tragic circumstances, perhaps . . .'

'Sir, the book must speak for itself, surely.'

'Nonetheless, we publishers like to know something of our authors, sir.'

'Then I have to tell you that I come from a good family and was privately educated.'

'Go on.'

It would probably not be of advantage to bring up naval service again, Renzi decided. 'I've had the good fortune to travel a great deal, and to curious and remote lands upon which I gathered much first-hand data.'

'Ah. A travel piece! I can assure you, sir, that since the late Captain Cook's voyages to the South Seas the public are insatiable in their curiosity concerning outlandish and romantic parts.'

'Not, as you might say, a travel piece, Mr Murray.' He leaned forward. 'No, sir. Rather, from this data I have converged upon postulates of a causative nature that conjoins ethical imperatives with those of strictly economic concern.' Renzi drew a deep breath and confided, 'This work, sir, is in fact an exhaustive discourse in which I am in pursuit of an hypothesis of consequential response as mediated by culture.'

Murray sat back, blinking.

'Oh, I can assure you, sir,' Renzi went on hastily, 'that in my many appendices there will be sufficient evidence to persuade even the most doubting.'

'Not a travel book.'

'No, sir – yet of some interest to those who hold Rousseau to be—'

'Let me be frank, Mr Renzi.'

'Of course, sir.'

'I do believe you are more than you seem, sir. I'm a judge of character and in you I perceive one who has seen more of this world than most. Sir, in fine, you have a story to tell. Which is why I do not dismiss you summarily and am prepared to spend time on you.'

'Why, sir, I—'

'Consider. Our readership today values the novel before all else – in the Gothic fancy and tremulous with romance. These do sell in their thousands, and even with the barbarous margins booksellers demand, it affords us a flow of revenue sufficient to fund other authors.

'Your work, however, is of more interest to the scientificals and they will never pay more than a few shillings. Where, then, is the profit to be obtained from a run of just a hundred copies that will cover the printing outgoings?'

Murray leaned back and fiddled with a quill. 'There are those who will be published on a subscription basis but this I cannot advise unless your acquaintance with the literati is wider than I suspect it is. Others see salvation in a part-book treatment but this, I fear, is not to be contemplated in your case.'

He straightened in his chair. 'Could you conceive perhaps of a reworking, a different standpoint – say, to appeal more to the worthies of self-help and improvement? Or, better yet, a moral tome for children? Or, best of all, a tale of exotics and adventure such that—'

'I really cannot see that this will be possible, sir,' Renzi said, with a pained expression.

'Then it will be hard to see how you will succeed, Mr Renzi.' He paused for a moment. 'Of course, your chief difficulty is that you are as yet unknown to the world. Should your name be more before the public then it would be a different matter. Those in possession of a name may write whatever they will and be assured of an audience.

'I should start by placing one or two modest articles on your interest in the popular magazines – the *Agreeable and Instructive Repository* comes to mind.'

Renzi gave a half-smile and stood up. 'Thank you for your time, Mr Murray, and you have made your position abundantly clear. I shall not trouble you further.'

Murray offered his hand. 'I'm desolated to find that I'm unable to offer you any pecuniary encouragement, sir, but urge you not to abandon your endeavours on my account.'

'When the manuscript is finished—'

'Then perhaps we will look at it together. Good day to you, Mr Renzi.'

Cecilia stopped in the street and turned to Jane Mullins. 'My dear, as we're passing by, I think I'll pop in and see how my brother does. Do run along and take another look at that blue bonnet – I shall join you presently.'

It had been five days since last she had spoken to Nicholas. Had he news for her? Her heart beat faster as she tapped the door-knocker and waited for Tysoe to answer.

'Good morning, Miss Cecilia. I'm afraid Mr Kydd is not here.'

'Oh – then is Mr Renzi at home, perhaps?'

'Yes, miss. '

Renzi was stretched out in an armchair in the drawing room, moodily staring at the fire. He rose guiltily. 'Why, my dear . . .'

'Jane and I were passing and I just thought that I'd visit to see how Thomas is with his new ship. Have you heard from him at all, Nicholas?'

'Not – not recently.'

'No matter, he's probably very busy learning all about her. The frigate, that is.'

'Yes, I suppose so.'

She sat demurely. 'By the way, Nicholas, have you consulted your publisher yet?'

'I – er, no, not yet.'

Cecilia held back a wave of frustration. 'You mean to say you haven't been able to find an hour or two in all this time to see to your future as a writer? I really find this hard to credit in you, Nicholas.'

'I've been, um, busy.'

'This is not the way to see your book finally printed. You must make the effort and see an editor or somebody in charge and find out what has to be done. You *promised* me!'

'It's, er . . . I don't believe I'm quite ready to – to hand over my manuscript as yet.'

She caught her breath. 'Mr Renzi, if you find it so very difficult to accept the advice of your friends then there's nothing more to be said – is there?' Without waiting for a reply she stood and left the room.

Out on the street anger took hold. That he had the gall to refuse her perfectly reasonable request – her brother had told her in the strictest secrecy that Renzi had confessed to him an undying love for her, a confidence that she had since kept sacred. Was this, then, the man's conception of the word?

She knew, too, from Kydd that it was Renzi's plan to offer her marriage just as soon as he had in his hands the volumes that would provide him with the income to support a wife. Why then was he hesitating to conclude arrangements? A tear pricked as she hurried along to her rendezvous with Jane.

Her own feelings for Renzi were unchanged: no more upright and honourable man ever trod the earth and she felt that deep within him passions were held in check only by his formidable logic and moral strength. If they were to be married it would be . . . But he was doing everything to avoid the commitment. What did it mean?

She blinked furiously. Before too many more years she would cross that awful Rubicon – she would be thirty. How long should she be expected to wait?

A lump in her throat made her gulp. If she had been honest with herself she should have seen it long ago: Renzi was a born scholar, a gifted savant whose work the world would value. But it was transforming him. Into a hermit, a recluse. He didn't want to see a publisher because it was part of a world he despised. And history was full of those, like Isaac Newton and others, who had retired into their private world, had never married, never cared for a woman – who were lost to love.

She had to confront it. He was slipping away from her. No amount of patient waiting would bring him back. These last years had been wasted and if she didn't do something about it she would end up a sad and lonely figure on the fringe of someone else's happiness.

That stark prospect was now no longer a possibility – it was certain. The truth brought tears that could not be held back. She was still a handsome and desirable woman and had every right to look forward to marriage and a settled life, children. And – and with Renzi, this was no longer in prospect.

She crushed her anguish and dried her eyes. She had to

look to the future. Why, there was Captain Pakenham of the 95th – with only a very little encouragement, by this time next year she could be married into one of the foremost families in the north, chatelaine of her own estate and with a husband on an income of fifteen thousands.

He was twenty years her senior but there were others, too, younger, gayer – she would not lack for laughter and high living and would never have to open her purse with unease again. She must think long and hard about it.

She stopped. In her distraction she had gone right past the shop. Composing herself, she went back. 'Jane, my dear. The new bonnet, which then is it to be?'

The Board of Ordnance official leaned back with a tired expression while Kydd strove to make the master shipwright understand. 'It won't fadge, sir! In this age, a twelve-pounder frigate? Why, it's not to be borne! If there's an Admiralty order as will make us an eighteen-pounder, you must comply, sir.'

Hocking sat immovable. 'The Admiralty may order all it likes, Mr Kydd, an' it won't do a ha'porth o' good. This ship can't take 'em. I'm telling you an' I'll tell their lordships th' same. I've done m' tests – and there's two good reasons why, and these I'll tell ye.'

Kydd had seen him and his party with plumb-bobs and cryptic chalk marks deep in the hold while a single eighteen-pounder carriage gun was moved by degrees out from the centreline on the main-deck.

It seemed that with increased weight high on her decks an entity called the metacentre was being threatened by the upward advance of the centre of gravity, thereby reducing the righting arm available to *L'Aurore*. In graphic terms Hocking spelled

94

it out: in anything of a blow, as the ship lay over under assault by gale or wave, she would be reluctant to return to the vertical to the extent that her stability would vanish and she could then conceivably capsize.

When the man quoted the tons-per-inch immersion figure to show that, fully loaded with thirty-two eighteens, her gun-port sill would be barely four feet above the sea it became very clear that *L'Aurore* would remain a twelve-pounder.

After they left Kydd was in a foul mood. The loss of the guns was bad enough but when the surgeon, Peyton, reported, he was unprepared to put up with the supercilious young man and his airs. Readily admitting he was only filling in time before a Harley Street practice, the man had the hide to loudly protest the quality of his cabin. Kydd caustically reminded him that virtually all his patients were in somewhat harder living conditions.

His signature was being constantly required now; the sniffy ship's clerk, Erasmus Goffin, apparently saw it as his right to interrupt him at will, bearing the duly scratched-at paper back to the purser as though it were a holy relic.

It was a ray of sunshine when Calloway reported shyly. Kydd gratefully appointed him his keeper, and when two volunteers of the first class appeared he placed them in his charge – one eleven years old, the other twelve. Rated as captain's servants, they were in effect apprentice midshipmen, gaining sea-time and instruction in the best way possible. The ruddy older one was Potts; the more pale and serious lad was Searle. Kydd reflected that the wide-eyed youngsters were now about to start on a life that, for extremes of squalor and glory, could not be equalled. They would survive or not on their own, with little but their character and courage to help them.

At last the first batch of seamen arrived. Howlett set up court with a table at the main-mast, dispassionately disposing of their fates in accordance with their declared skills, Goffin duly inscribing beside him.

Kydd watched from the half-deck. As far as he could see, his first lieutenant was swift, efficient and sound in his judgements, and progress was made. He waited until the process was complete, then walked across.

'How goes it, Mr Howlett?' he asked pleasantly.

'A bare score or two of volunteers only, sir. The rest mainly the damned quod.'

The 'quod' was those men supplied by law from all the counties of England under the quota system. At best, they were guaranteed to be useless rural labourers and at worst, felons released to make up numbers.

'Any of value, do you think?' Kydd asked.

'Precious few. We've less'n fifty so far and no petty officers as I could see.' Kydd frowned – quite apart from being under a quarter manned, without a strong backbone of sea-experienced senior hands to train the others, how could they set sail, let alone fight?

He glanced up. The masts and rigging were full of men working and the shouts and cries of orders and curses sounded along the deck, as ignorant men were driven to menial tasking around the shipwrights, caulkers and artisans of all stripes hastening to finish their last jobs.

The noise was worse below-decks, the thuds and scrapes magnified and the empty spaces echoing with discordant noises. Kydd needed to think; he told Howlett he would be back and paced off through the dockyard, deep in thought.

He was being pushed to hurry completion for sea and the ultimate responsibility for manning *L'Aurore* was his.

There were authorities like the Impress Service but they were there only to assist. Attracting more volunteers was down to him. It wouldn't be difficult to get a press warrant and mount a raid, but in a notoriously man-hungry port like this their haul would be pathetic, of men with a grudge.

There had been stories told of ships swinging about a buoy for months waiting for men – the thought was too terrible to contemplate. What if—

Something cut through his dark musings. He had left the dockyard, yearning for the solitude of the open spaces of Southsea Common, but as he went through the gates he heard a man's voice, a pure, light tenor lifted in song:

> '*Life is chequer'd – toil and pleasure*
> *Fill up all the various measure;*
> *Hark! The crew with sunburnt faces*
> *Chanting Black-eyed Susan's graces . . .*'

It was issuing from within the old *Admiral Benbow*, hard by the dockyard gate. He stopped: he knew the voice and the air. The years fell away in an instant: his time of terror when first climbing aloft, that desperate open-boat voyage in the Caribbean – it had to be . . .

Without stopping to consider he hurried over and threw open the doors – and saw it *was* Ned Doud, songster and ship-mate from the old ninety-eight-gun *Duke William*, somewhat aged but still with the same open, laughing face and with his pot of ale as he sang.

The tavern fell still. Doud tailed off and the resentful eyes of seamen and their women turned Kydd's way. A full post-captain bursting in on a sailors' taphouse – what did it mean?

Kydd hesitated, then took off his gold-laced hat, clapped

it under his arm and slowly went over to Doud, who put down his ale warily.

Conscious of the incomprehension and hostility about him, Kydd allowed a smile to surface. 'And I see you're still topping it the songbird, Ned.'

The man squinted, then started with sudden recognition. 'Be buggered, an' it's our Tom Kydd!' he blurted, then fell silent, unsure and defensive.

Kydd grinned and said heartily, 'Should you want it, there's a berth in m' frigate.'

Confronted with the young seaman of the past now un-accountably garbed in the awful majesty of a senior captain, Doud was speechless.

'Are you free t' volunteer?' Kydd asked neutrally.

'I'm quartermaster o' *Naiad*,' Doud answered carefully.

Kydd felt a pang for the long-ago days in the Caribbean when things had been so carefree and . . . different. 'We have young Luke Calloway aboard,' he said.

'Leave 'im be, Cap'n!' said one of the females, sharply. A hostile murmuring began behind him.

Kydd decided it was time to go. 'Then – then I'll bid you goodbye, and wish you every fair wind.'

'Aye, thank 'ee,' Doud muttered.

Kydd got as far as the door before he heard Doud call after him, 'I'll come if'n ye can square it wi' Cap'n Dundas – exchange, or somethin'.'

Kydd paused. 'I think it possible.'

'An' only if I gets to bring off m' particular friend.'

More memories.

'Pinto?' Kydd brought to mind the quick, fiery-eyed Portuguese, deadly with a knife.

'Aye. Quarter gunner.'

'It'll be done. We're fitting out. You're needed aboard just as soon—'

'Aye. We'll be there – Mr Kydd.'

It cost him not one but three prime hands to achieve the exchange, and when *L'Aurore*'s marines reported, there was still only a pitiful number of proper seamen on the books. They had a seasoned sergeant, Dodd, but only a green sub-altern as officer, Clinton – no captain of marines over just twenty-eight privates. 'Is this all?' Kydd snapped.

'Oh, I rather think it is, Captain,' Clinton replied uneasily, looking to Dodd for support.

'None more left in barracks f'r sea service, sir,' the sergeant confirmed.

'Very well. Get 'em kitted and ready for posting immediately.'

'Sah!'

Ruing that they were sadly under strength as well with the Royals, Kydd turned to go below and saw Renzi standing on the quay, looking up in wonder. 'Nicholas, ahoy there! Come aboard!'

Renzi mounted the brow slowly, taking in the sweep of the frigate, her teeming decks and bewildered new hands.

Kydd pumped his hand. 'Welcome – welcome, m' dear friend! Let's below and I'll tell you how she fares.'

After Renzi's warm approbation of Kydd's apartments, Kydd unburdened himself of his worries. 'But she's a prime frigate, Nicholas. We should have no trouble manning her, they hear we're shortly outward bound.'

'It would seem so, but I would think Portsmouth not your most favoured place. Have you considered the outports – Lymington, for instance?'

'Set up a rondy there?' A recruiting rendezvous was more usually to be found in the big merchant-shipping ports.

'Why not? Some rousing posters promising adventure and glory pasted up where young lads can see them on the way to their work in the morning . . .'

'Yes! Well said, Nicholas. And, o' course, you'll bear a fist in the writing, you being the prime article.'

A strange look passed over Renzi's face before he hurriedly went on, 'Be that as it may, brother. I rather think something like:

'"All true British heart of oak who are able and willing to serve their King and Country, and um –"'

'"– can carry a purse o' Spanish cobbs a mile,"' Kydd interjected.

'"Be it known there are only a few berths left aboard the saucy *L'Aurore* now lying in, er –"'

'"Lying at Spithead under orders from the King,"' Kydd added stoutly, then muttered, 'And that a lie – we've none yet.'

'"Under the command of the famed Captain Kydd whose prize money from his last voyage –"'

'Belay that, Nicholas, I won't have it this is a voyage o' plunder. It's Boney we're after.'

'"– whose valour against the foe any stout heart may read for himself in the *London Gazette*, etc. Do repair to the right Royal Portsmouth rendezvous at the, er, some notorious tavern wherever—"'

'That'll do. Make it up fair and find a jobbing printer and we'll have 'em up all over town – and Lymington too. I'll have Gilbey man the rondy. That's our second luff – you'll meet him tonight with the others. Tomorrow we shift berth to the gun-wharf and ship our twelve-pounders so I'm having a dinner at the George while we can.'

The meal passed off heavily: *L'Aurore*'s officers were little more than strangers at this point but the gesture had to be made.

Howlett was polite but thin-lipped. As administrative head of the ship, he had to make some sense of the few hands they possessed in terms of duties and it was an impossible job. Gilbey and Curzon had little to do until they had a full watch of the hands and were at sea, but their present idleness had its own tedium in a ship only half alive.

Renzi was taken warily after Kydd introduced him as his confidential secretary, but then accorded a civil respect when it was learned that he was a past naval officer in his own right before a near mortal fever. Clinton sat wide-eyed and silent before his superiors while Surgeon Peyton looked patently bored.

Kydd longed with all his heart to get to sea. It would throw them together in the age-old interdependence and brother-hood of the wardroom and their true character would then emerge. As it was, there was not much more he could do to bring the L'Aurores together.

In the morning a passage crew from the dockyard came aboard for the short tow to the gun-wharf close to the harbour entrance and, with sulphurous and imaginative cursing from Oakley, *L'Aurore* was brought alongside. Kydd left him and the gunner to sway aboard the twelve-pounders one by one, each with its matched carriage that would stay with it through all its service life.

Watching the main-deck being populated with *L'Aurore*'s

teeth of war, Kydd tried to console himself with the thought that, lesser in calibre though they were, these were one and the same as were carried by the mightiest first-rates – along their upper of three gun-decks.

Gunner's stores, pyramids of shot – but not yet powder, which would be last aboard – arrived and the remaining vestiges of dockyard occupation fell away as the artisans and riggers concluded their last labours and left.

Then it was the final move in the fitting out: *L'Aurore* was brought out into the broad naval anchorage of Spithead and moored in lonely splendour, the fleet away in close blockade and other strategic deployments.

Kydd sent for the rest of his hands, the pressed men. Tenders brought them from the receiving ships and holding cells ashore: a straggling, resentful and dispirited rabble looking to desert at the first opportunity. And so *few*!

'Sir, in all we've hardly half a watch aboard, counting the marines. Unless we—'

'There's some error, Mr Howlett. We'll never sail with this complement. Get 'em on the books and I'll step off and sort it out.'

The port-admiral listened courteously, but made it quite clear that the battleships of Britain's strategic defences took priority and if Kydd was facing difficulties in manning, well, he was never the first, and enterprising captains would always find tricks to complete a crew.

As he made to leave, the admiral smiled thinly and produced a pack of orders. 'As you've indicated to me that you're in all respects ready for sea, Mr Kydd, here are your orders, which you'll sign for in the usual way. Good luck in your commission, and if there's anything further I can do for you . . . ?'

Burning with the injustice of it all, Kydd returned to *L'Aurore* where he was met by Curzon, who bitterly complained that the first lieutenant had not addressed him in a manner to be expected of a gentleman. Kydd gave him short shrift and demanded to know what the bedlam was below. It seemed that grog had got aboard and there was fighting between decks. He glared at Howlett and stalked off to his cabin.

With pitifully few petty officers there was no real chain of command, let alone a cohesive structure with perceivable limits of behaviour. The ship was descending into chaos before even it had established a character. All it needed was *men* – to fill the empty spaces but, more than anything, to form a connected whole and begin the process of coalescing into a single instrument of purpose.

Kydd took out the orders. Unless they had a bare minimum to handle sail it was futile to think *L'Aurore* could even weigh anchor, let alone form a useful addition to the fleet. He knew that it was not unknown for a captain to be removed in favour of another for failing to get his ship to sea.

He paused. Why wasn't his confidential secretary present? At last Renzi had every right to be privy to ship's secrets and he was going to take full advantage of it.

Renzi was in the coach, the next compartment forward, which had evolved into something approaching a ship's office. There, also, the master was correcting his charts, the ship's clerk was about his business and later the young gentlemen would be there, painfully going through their 'workings'.

'I'm opening our orders, Nicholas. To see what we should be about if *L'Aurore* had a crew,' Kydd said. He tore off the wrapper and spread out the sheets in order.

And the first said it all – in cold words that blazed with meaning.

He was being instructed to join with all dispatch the fleet of Lord Nelson in the Mediterranean. The first prize of all the Service could offer! The foremost fighting admiral of the age placed in the very forefront for the cataclysmic fleet action that everyone said must come!

'Our Nel!' Kydd gasped, staring at the page. He snatched up another – this was a part-order signed by Nelson himself, the impatient left-hand scrawl unmistakable. Yet another listed vital stores to be carried out to the fleet when *L'Aurore* sailed, again with the same signature. And addressed to Captain Thomas Kydd!

Thrilled, he laid the paper down. He was now one of Nelson's captains. He was part of the most famous league of fighting captains in all of history. It was . . . incredible!

'Dear fellow, I'm sure you've noticed something quite singular, not to say suspicious . . . ?' Renzi's cool voice penetrated his racing thoughts.

He looked up sharply. 'I did not!'

'The date, old chap. Here we have His Eminence issuing orders to one Captain Kydd from before Toulon, at least a few weeks' sail away from England and the *Gazette* had not even the time to reach him so he might read of your promotion. If I was of a sceptical cast of mind, I'd believe those forgeries. Otherwise . . .'

It hit Kydd with all the force of a blow. 'You mean – you're suggesting it was he who . . .'

'I would suggest that for a peradventure our doughty commander-in-chief, sorely in need of frigates, on hearing of the capture of *L'Aurore* asked for it to be sent to him instantly, and for its captain, one of recent record – *Teazer*'s last fight was much talked about, you'll remember.'

'But, Nicholas, even so—'

Renzi smiled openly. 'Nelson always had a *tendre* for those of humble beginnings, as you'll know. Why, I've heard that he was not content until he had a first lieutenant of *Victory* herself who was once a pressed man.'

'And—'

'Quite so. In Minorca he's been quoted: "Aft the more honour – forward the better man!" and by this I'd conceive that your claiming no interest among the highest now no longer holds.'

Kydd sat rigid as the realisation flooded him. Nelson had not only made him post, given him his ship but now – it had to be faced – *needed* him! All the frustration of his situation beat in on him. He couldn't let his hero down. Men had to be found, *whatever* it took.

He leaped to his feet, strode to the door and, opening it, roared at the astonished clerk, 'Pass the word – all officers to lay aft this instant!'

He returned, pacing impatiently up and down his broad great cabin until all his lieutenants had arrived. 'Gentlemen, I won't waste words. We have our orders, and they're to clap on all sail – to join Admiral Lord Nelson in the Mediterranean.'

There were gasps of incredulity. A raw and untried frigate being sent to join the famed Nelson was a huge honour but a greater challenge. The ship and her men would be tried to the limit and if found wanting would be mercilessly cast aside by the fiery admiral.

'Men!' Kydd snapped. 'I need men and I'll get them no matter the cost. Mr Howlett, what's our ship's company number now?'

'Eighty-seven,' he growled.

Well over a hundred to find – petty officers, prime hands, all the varied skills needed in a man-o'-war, not the dregs of the seaports or useless farmers.

'Mr Gilbey. How's your feeling of the volunteering at the rendezvous?'

'Ah. Not s' good, Mr Kydd. They saw your posters but, beggin' your pardon, it's t' be your first frigate command and they're distrustful as you'll be able to show 'em how to lay a prize by the tail.' At Kydd's expression he hurriedly added, 'Besides, word's out that we're likely enough t' be sent to the blockade fleets, s' no chance at prize-taking.'

'I see. Mr Howlett, you spoke to the regulating captain. Did he give you a sense o' the prospects for more pressed men?'

'No, with *Ajax* and *Orion* 74's having prior claim and the port stripped clean he doesn't hold out any hope in the matter.'

'Then we're on our own. Any ideas, gentlemen?'

The discussion ebbed and flowed, but the outcome was indeterminate. In a bracket of days they had to find a full crew – or a cleverer captain with answers would replace him.

Kydd dismissed them and slumped into his chair, gazing stonily out of the stern windows. Unbelievably he had gained his heart's desire and to have it snatched away so easily would be painful beyond belief – was there nothing he could do to prevent it?

After a sleepless night he was no further forward. Then in the early dawn light an idea came to him, but one so shocking he was astonished that he had thought of it. It was vile, dishonourable, a scurvy trick to be loathed by any true sailor. But it had one, and one only, saving grace: it was guaranteed to work. He would have his men.

Precisely at morning gun he was at the port-admiral's office.

'Sir, I'm grieved to say I'm sadly under strength and with urgent sailing orders for Admiral Nelson. I have a request which I beg you'll consider . . .'

Two days later when *Alceste* frigate hove into Portsmouth harbour to pay off after three long years in the West Indies, her men were turned over into *L'Aurore* without once setting foot on English soil. Kydd stood well back as they came aboard. Whatever else, these men were the best – deeply tanned, fit and, after three years together in a crack frigate, were a known quantity and a priceless contribution to his ship.

But they also looked dazed and bewildered, massing protectively together by the main-mast, occasionally glancing aft bitterly.

He knew how they would be feeling. As they'd sailed back across the Atlantic their thoughts had been with homes, loved ones and the little gifts and curios they would present on their happy return. And as the ship made landfall on the Lizard and began that last beat up-Channel, even the most hardened shellback would have been caught up in the all-consuming excitement – 'Channel-fever', the last hours of the voyage passing in a dream-like delirium.

Instead there had been the unaccountable diversion to the Motherbank anchorage, quickly followed by the ship being surrounded by boats from the guard-ship and *L'Aurore*, together with press-tenders, hoys, launches full of marines. It would have been all over very quickly, the men given minutes to find their sea-bags and chests.

Just an hour or two ago they had thought their voyage had ended but, thanks to Kydd's cruel decision, it was not to be. He crushed the hot thoughts of injustice that rose, his face stony. There was no other way.

'Keep the guard-boats!' Kydd called to Curzon, at the gangway.

The ship had boarding nettings rigged under the line of gun-ports and all boats at the lower boom were kept at long stay. Their entire detachment of Royal Marines patrolled the upper decks and there were even discreet parties in the tops with swivel guns.

The most effective, however, were the boats rowing guard, slowly and endlessly circling the ship at a hundred yards distant, ready to intercept any daring enough to make a break by leaping from the yards or in other desperate moves.

The first lieutenant set up his table to rate the Alcestes and one by one they came up, strong faces, men with pride in their bearing and contempt in their voices. Howlett processed them swiftly for it had been agreed that it made sense to keep the men in the same position they had been in *Alceste* and fit the lesser number of L'Aurores around them.

'What are you about, Mr Curzon?' Kydd roared. 'My orders are t' let no boat approach whatsoever!' A slim Portsmouth wherry had slipped past the circling pinnaces and was hooking on at the main-chains.

The boat hailed *L'Aurore* – Curzon turned, and shouted back, 'Two to come aboard, sir – saw your poster and want to join,' he added incredulously.

The pair hauled themselves inboard, their dunnage thrown after them. It was Stirk and Poulden, survivors of *Teazer*. Kydd couldn't bring himself to speak to them; they'd find out what he'd done soon enough. 'Enter 'em in under their old rate, Mr Howlett,' he said gruffly, and left the deck.

His first lieutenant reported with jocular satisfaction: 'A fine haul, sir! She mans more than we, so I took the liberty of turning away any I didn't like the look of.' Kydd grimaced.

To those held aboard, the sight of the lucky few escaping to freedom would only make their own situation harder to bear.

'I want 'em in two watches and messed before the dog-watches, if y' please,' he snapped. 'Ship goes to routine after supper.'

It was asking a lot, but this would occupy them with the choosing of mess-mates for each six-to-eight-man mess-table, the stowing of their chests and ditty-bags, and settling the unwritten assumptions of the pecking order.

Howlett would have overnight to produce a watch and station bill for sailing; that for quarters could wait until later. Kydd would then himself take decisions on divisions. This was the partialling of the ship's company behind each officer so that, with a fair cross-section of skills in each, they could undertake risky tasks such as a cutting-out expedition – storming aboard an enemy ship in its own harbour, setting sail on a strange ship and getting it to sea.

Divisions was as well the Navy's way of ensuring the men were cared for, that there was his own particular officer a humble seaman could call on whenever things turned against him.

Then it was a matter of storing ship for foreign service and putting to sea, away from the continual sight of what the men could not have. Days only!

Kydd slept well and was up before dawn. Gilbey had nothing of significance to report overnight, but at first light a wretched sight unfolded. Word of *Alceste*'s turning over had leaked out and a number of boats bobbed beyond the watchful row-guard. From the ship Kydd could see the colours of the dresses of wives and sweethearts who had watched and waited so long for their men to come home from their far voyaging and now expected to be let on board.

A murmuring spread along the deck as men came up from

below to see. An occasional hopeful wave from the boats was returned with shouts, but Kydd was stony-hearted. It was asking for trouble to let some men have women and others not and, no doubt, they were bringing more spirituous than spiritual comforts – the ship would be in uproar in a very short time.

'Keep 'em away!' he told the officer-of-the-deck.

When hands were piped to muster for Howlett's watch and station bill to be handed out to the senior rates to acquaint every man with his duties, Kydd decided it was the right time for their captain to address the L'Aurores and tell them of their stern calling to Nelson's side.

The men assembled on the main-deck, chivvied by petty officers, looked down on by Clinton's marines from the gangways and hectored by the pig-eyed master-at-arms, Jolley, whom Kydd had inherited from *Alceste*. They were quiet and sullen.

'L'Aurores – I can call you that now, as we've finally our full company.' There was little movement, only a hard muteness. 'This I'll tell you, there's no greater service than we're about to do for our country: to join Admiral Lord Nelson and his fleet and throw ourselves athwart Napoleon's course for invasion.'

He could sense the officers behind him stirring at the words but it was the seamen he had to win over. 'I'm sorry this has been so – so difficult for you all, but at the same time you'll agree that England stands in greater peril now than at any time in her history.'

He paused, looking down on the mass of sailors. He saw strong-featured characters, long-service seamen with carefully maintained pig-tails, neatly stitched clothes, standing tall but scowling resentfully at him. Others had glassy expressions and the characteristic loose-limbed look of the old shellback.

He knew he wasn't getting through.

'We'll start storing as soon as you've got your parts-of-ship, and never forget, it's all England that will thank you.' He waited for reaction, and when it was obvious there wasn't one, he turned to Howlett and barked, 'We'll start taking 'em aboard by five bells, Mr Howlett.'

The lack of reaction disturbed him. Usually some kind of shout or cheer went up and the hostile reserve was disquieting.

When the storing began he tucked his hat ostentatiously under his arm and went about the ship. It was a mistake: on every hand he met contemptuous silence and flashing glances of naked hatred. Tension radiated from each group. They worked slowly, grudgingly, calling to each other in mocking tones, testing the limits. As he passed the fore-hatch there was a sudden squeal of a block and rushing slither of rope followed by a crash as a cask of dried peas smashed at the bottom of the hold. Harsh laughter broke out: when Kydd looked about him the eyes did not drop but caught his in open challenge. It was getting out of hand, and not helped by an outer ring of boats hopelessly waiting, expectant bum-boats irritated and frustrated.

He had noticed Stirk was with the gunner's party but when Kydd looked in his direction he pointedly turned his back.

A hot rush of resentment flooded him. This was not something he was proud of or that he had done without considering the implications. He had been at the Nile and remembered Nelson's heartfelt lament at the preceding chase that 'Were I to die this moment, want of frigates will be found engraved on my heart!'

Kydd had to keep faith with Nelson and bring *L'Aurore* to join his fleet when so much needed. He turned on his heel and stalked off.

Renzi held back, keeping out of his way while he sat down and attended to his growing pile of papers. A knock at the door heralded the quiet and courteous sailing master. 'Sir, I've passage charts f'r Biscay an' the strait. Do ye want others?'

'Mr Kendall, we sail as soon as we can. We've a fine crew but I don't like their temper. What's your taking on 'em?'

The master paused, then said carefully, 'Sooner we're outward bound the better, I'm thinking. But have ye thought the ship's untried, we don't know her handling? We might carry away our sticks or worse wi' an unwilling crew.'

'That could be so, Mr Kendall, but I've a mind to come down on 'em before then. Ask Mr Howlett to step along to see me when he's the time, please.'

The first lieutenant entered warily. 'Do sit, Mr Howlett. Wine?' He accepted a half-glass from Tysoe as Renzi gathered up his work and left.

'I mislike the way the Alcestes are shaping up,' Kydd said slowly. 'I want vigilance from everyone, nothing left to chance, but no provocations.'

'Aye aye, Mr Kydd.'

'What's your estimate of our readiness?'

'Storing will be soon complete per your instructions. We take on water, beer and greens at Plymouth for Gibraltar, a few ocean necessaries still to ship – we haven't your cabin stores, incidentally, sir.'

'I haven't had the time. Readiness?'

'We can sail more or less when you desire, sir.'

'Very well – shall we say the day after tomorrow? The ship's under sailing orders, Mr Howlett.'

'Sir.'

Howlett made no move to leave. 'Sir. The men – they're in as ugly a mood as ever I've seen.'

Kydd grimaced. 'They're not the first to be turned over, and never the last while Boney has any ambitions. There's no other way I can think on, and don't forget, while it's been three years they've been gone, the last I was in the Caribbee there were redcoats there who'd been seven years since last they'd clapped eyes on England – and not likely to do so again this age.'

'I know that, sir, but—'

'What are you saying I should do? Let 'em step ashore on the ran-tan for a month? We'd never get 'em back. No, they're to turn to as ordered or I'll make an example as will put a stop to their galley-skulking behaviour.'

Howlett hesitated. 'Our Jack Tar is sensible of his rights as the custom of the Service allows, Mr Kydd, and in this—'

'*L'Aurore* will put t' sea in two days and that's an end to it, sir! Advise the ship's company of the sailing orders and if they growl bring 'em before me.'

Kydd made a point of doing his rounds of the ship before hammocks were piped down and the hands were sent to supper. Grim-faced, he paced slowly ahead of his entourage of officers and master's mates while the boatswain led the way, pealing out the 'still' on his silver call as they entered each space.

There was almost palpable tension as they progressed, the glitter of hostile eyes in the shadows of the mess-deck, a barely audible muttering at the rear. He made a show of speaking amiably to every petty officer in charge, but there were only surly responses and barely concealed belligerence.

'Very good, Mr Howlett. The men to go to supper now.'

It was time, too, for an issue of grog – in home waters, beer – and if there was going to be trouble the hotheads would start it then, but he did not want to provoke the men by stopping it.

There was little more he could do – damn it, he would sail the next hour if he could, letting the keen salt winds of the open ocean scour the ship of its mood. There was no sign of the disaffection lifting – and it was destroying his joy at achieving a frigate command.

He ate alone; Renzi had the absent marine captain's cabin and would be a subscription-paying member of the gunroom by now and making acquaintance. In any case, he didn't feel like discussion.

Howlett reported apologetically. 'Four in bilboes, I'm sorry to say, sir.'

'They stay in irons until tomorrow forenoon. I'll deal with the rogues then. What's the charge?'

'Fighting. The Alcestes taking against the L'Aurores when—'

'Be damned to it! We're all L'Aurores now,' Kydd snapped in irritation. 'Tomorrow they'll learn—'

'Yes, sir. I'll bid you good night, then.'

Kydd could not face his meal. If he failed to crack down now he would be seen as weak and his authority fatally undermined. Little by little he was being pushed into the very tyranny he despised and could see no way out of the spiral – except to get to sea.

'Do I intrude, brother?'

'No, come in, Nicholas. How's the gunroom? Do join me in this passable claret.'

Renzi accepted a glass. 'Eminently to my satisfaction, and thank you.'

'You haven't come here for the conversation . . . ?'

Renzi sighed. 'No. My dear fellow, I'm here to tell you that whatever happens you have my quiet support.'

'Whatever *can* happen?' Kydd said, nettled.

Choosing his words carefully, Renzi said, 'Do not take this amiss, old chap, but granted your undoubted insights into the character of Jack Tar, won from your own experiences before the mast, I rather fancy you are on a different course from they.'

'And what is that, pray?' Kydd said sarcastically.

'Consider. When you were first a lieutenant, I can remember the joy and wonder you declared when obliged to study the professional publications of the strategical sort. Your discovery was that the seaman's view of his existence is happily circumscribed by his wooden world but an officer's must necessarily encompass the grievous complications, political and economic, that constitute the outer world.'

'You're saying—'

'Your fore-mast jack has simple but robust views. He sees the enemy vanquished time and again and hears of mighty victories from England's hearts of oak. In fine, he has the courage of a lion and an iron confidence in his cause and his ship.'

'He does, but—'

'Therefore, dear chap, he cannot see in the slightest whit why you're getting on your high horse about joining Nelson. In his sturdy view there's time to take a taste of liberty and beat the Crapauds too. You are privy to the dreadful secrets of the coming invasion. In mercy they are not. Therefore their conclusion is that they're to suffer for your impatience.'

Kydd glowered. 'This is all to no account. They've got their duty and I have mine, and that is to get this frigate to the Med with all dispatch. We take powder aboard tomorrow and then we sail, and there's an end to it.'

They talked of other things but shortly Renzi made his excuses and went below to turn in, leaving Kydd alone with his thoughts.

He heard the boatswain's mate pipe the silent hours and the master-at-arms and ship's corporal doing their turn about the ship, looking for unauthorised lights. Kydd duly took the report and began to prepare for bed, dismissing Tysoe.

Minutes later a subliminal rumble took him instantly back to an earlier time and place: the gunroom of quite another ship, one that was about to be caught up in the desperate and bloody mutiny at the Nore. What he knew he was hearing was the ominous sound of a cannon shot being rolled down the length of the ship in a timeless gesture of defiance.

Still in his shirtsleeves he burst out of his cabin and pushed past the astonished marine sentry. He bounded up the single ladder to the night air and tried to catch sight of what was going on, but in the sepulchral gloom of the moonless evening he could see nothing.

'The lookouts, ahoy!' he bellowed.

'Ho!' the two aft returned promptly.

'Did you see anything?'

'No, sir,' they replied instantly. He would get nothing out of them, of course, but it was of a certainty now that in the darkness of the bowels of the ship men were meeting, whispering – plotting?

This was deadly serious and could easily explode into something far worse unless . . . But what should he do? Stand the marines to and make search of the ship? No – they would find nothing and all it would achieve would be to demonstrate to the rest of the ship that he was frightened. Turn up the hands and harangue them? Equally useless.

The long night passed, and in the morning it was as if nothing had happened. The watch was changed, the men padding over to their stations without hesitation, standing mutely while muster was made.

When hammocks were piped up there was no show of hostility or defiance – they were lashed with their seven turns, proffered to the boatswain's mate with his ring to test their tightness, then neatly packed within the hammock nettings, all without fuss. Had a corner been turned?

Breakfast was unusually quiet, however.

At eight bells, when the beginning of the forenoon signalled that the day was to start, and with the entire ship's company mustered to be detailed off for their morning work, a midshipman noticed a scrap of paper smoothed out and placed precisely in the centre of the deck just abaft the main-mast bitts. He picked it up and took it to the first lieutenant, who turned white before hurriedly passing it to Kydd.

With a sickening lurch Kydd knew what it would contain and struggled to keep his face impassive while he inspected it gravely, knowing that he was under the watchful eyes of his entire crew.

'Carry on, Mr Howlett,' he snapped, whipping the paper behind his back. He stood grimly, waiting and glaring.

'Hands turn to, part-o'-ship,' Howlett ordered, in an unsteady voice.

The boatswain pealed out the high, falling notes of the 'carry on'. Quietly, with hardly a word spoken, the men obediently went to their tasks.

When they had all moved off, Kydd called his officers

down to his cabin. 'Gentlemen. I'm obliged to tell you that as of this hour the ship's company are in a state of mutiny.'

'S-sir! That cannot be!' Curzon gasped. 'They went to their stations!'

He stared at the paper Kydd pushed at him. At the bottom were a dozen names, written in a crude circle. 'A round robin, sir?' It was a way to ensure that no single name could be singled out as the ringleader.

'Read!'

It was straightforward enough:

God save the King! Bless our ship and oure officers who are sett above us too rule us and we meane no foule mutiny and will saile against the foe if they dare showe topsales over but pray considaration for our misrabel pligt. For 3 yeares in Alceste frigate wee have sayled the Caribee for our King and cuontry and now returne too find no libbertey to enjoy the friuts of oure labor as any Cristian desurve.

Sir, we ownly beg thatt we be given ower just rewarde as eny servante of the King do. This is nott much we aske and so we beleeve ower cuase is just and trust in yuor undrstandding wehn wee respekfully declyne too sayle onless we be payed on the barel head ower full duue.

'The damn rascals,' spluttered Howlett. 'They'll swing for it now!'

'Once in mut'ny, always t' be distrusted,' Gilbey growled. 'We'll have no truck wi' mutineers, I hope. I remember in 'ninety-seven when Black Dick Howe—'

Kydd cut in sharply. 'They're about their duties, we can't move against them.'

'They're a scrovy lot as will fall on us when our back's turned. Sir, we should—'

'No, Mr Gilbey. If they meant to rise, they wouldn't warn

us like this.' Uneasily, however, Kydd remembered *Hermione*: Captain Pigot, with all his officers, had died at the point of a cutlass in an insane mutiny in a similar-sized frigate.

Howlett cleared his throat. 'Sir. The situation is plain. They'll not bend sail unless it suits 'em and in anyone's book that's rank mutiny. We must send for troops, clear the ship and haul 'em ashore to answer for it. No other way.'

'Mr Clinton? What of the Royals?'

The young man started, his pale face set at the thought of two dozen marines facing more than two hundred desperate men. 'I – they'll do their duty, sir. Sar'nt Dodd is posting them about the ship agreeable to my orders.'

Kydd cleared his head to an icy coolness. Whatever happened to them depended on what he did next, and he had no wish to rush into a confrontation. 'Gentlemen. They're going about their duties in accordance with orders given. For now there is no offence.'

Howlett snorted, but Kydd went on quietly, 'Let 'em carry on. There's a good chance their nerve will fail before it's time to weigh.'

'Sir, I must protest! This note is an insult and an abomination – and under the Articles of War constitutes a treasonable communication. We have no alternative but overbearing force while we can.'

'I take mind of what you're saying, Mr Howlett, but it's my decision to wait it out for now.'

He looked gravely from one officer to the next. 'On no account will I allow hasty words or other provocation to spark a rising. Confine yourselves to calm and lawful orders. If you feel the need for a weapon, a pistol concealed in the pocket will serve – no swords or similar on display. Any questions?'

There were none and *L'Aurore*'s officers returned to the quarterdeck. There was an unnatural calm: the men went about their work steadily but in a stiff silence with glances flashed down the deck towards the captain.

Kydd paced slowly, outwardly dignified and calm but his thoughts whirled. Already, as Howlett had pointed out, he was technically in breach of the Articles of War and could be dismissed his ship. Yet if he finally gave orders to weigh anchor and they were obeyed that would be the end of it all, dissolved into the blessed release of making the open sea.

At the forefront of his mind was the one towering imperative: to get his frigate to Nelson. All else was secondary. If he called for soldiers and cleared the ship he would get sympathy but would be left as before, without the men to sail her, and Nelson would be deprived of a most valuable asset. It was a frightful dilemma.

The morning wore on. Powder arrived and was stowed without incident. More stores came aboard and found their way to the boatswain's and gunner's lockers on the orlop. There was nothing to suggest that *L'Aurore* was a ship in mutiny.

As noon approached there was again the question for Kydd: did he allow the customary grog ration or suspend it for fear of inflaming the situation further? If he stopped their grog it would be seen as vindictive or a punishment so he let it go ahead.

The midday meal passed and the seamen remained at their tables, stony-faced. Kydd ordered all officers and warrant officers out of the mess-deck to allow them privacy to talk, hopefully to see the futility and danger of the course they were taking.

As the hour for their meal drew to a close the master-at-arms sidled up to Kydd. 'I know 'oo it is, then, sir.'

'What do you mean?' Kydd had disliked Jolley on sight: sly and vicious, he was too like the first of his kind he had met as a raw pressed man.

'Why, it's Paddy Doyle, o' course. Seen 'im flogged f'r wry words in *Alceste* more'n once. He's forrard in the bay now, talkin' with his mates – and I'm standing by the bitt pins, I was, an' heard him bold as brass cry up a reg'lar-built mutiny.'

This Kydd could not ignore: it could be the spark that ignited the horrors of a full-scale rising.

'Mr Jolley,' he said heavily, 'arrest Doyle and hale him aft.'

Howlett came across. 'Trouble, sir?'

'Rash talk only, Mr Howlett.'

'That's as it may be, sir, but we have to consider—'

Suddenly a muffled angry uproar surged from below, died away, then renewed into a storm of cheers and catcalls. The officers looked at each other, then at the fore ladderway. Jolley and his corporal emerged with Doyle between them and dragged him aft, followed by an excited rabble. Kydd hurried down into the waist – and his worst fears were confirmed.

The master-at-arms's nose was streaming with blood but, with a smirk of triumph, he grated, 'Did strike me, his superior officer, Captain! An' before witnesses, sir.'

Kydd took one look at the wild-eyed Doyle and knew he had no choice. 'Double irons and a sentry, Mr Jolley. The rest o' these men – back to your duties!'

All around the deck men stood in shocked stillness. Others backed away in horrified expectation. Clinton hurried up and looked questioningly at Kydd.

'Draw up your men on the quarterdeck, sir, with ball and cartridge but, for God's sake, man, make it look like you were exercising 'em.'

There was no going back now. At the very least there would

be a court-martial and the stark sight of a corpse at the fore-yard before *L'Aurore* had sailed an inch. It would take weeks to convene, needing five post-captains to sit on the trial. Only then, and under a dark shadow of ignominy, could *L'Aurore* look to finally taking the seas.

'Send to the garrison, sir?' Howlett asked Kydd.

L'Aurore's captain paused. There would be hotheads among Doyle's friends who could turn the situation into bloodshed in an attempt to free him from certain death. It was on a knife-edge of spiralling chaos. The whole cursed thing had one and only one cause: his own act in turning over the Alcestes. If there was any moral element it was that Doyle was going to pay for his own impetuosity.

Was it too late? Once the incident and news of the mutiny were thus made public it would inevitably play out to the end like a Greek tragedy. Had he lost the game?

Kydd stepped to the ship's side, staring out over the deserted anchorage to the dark green verdancy of the land. He needed to think, for what he was now considering was a desperate move that could make him a byword for lunacy in the Navy.

But it might work. And might yet allow him to sail to Nelson.

He wheeled on Howlett: 'I'll deal with Doyle now. Pray clear the lower deck and muster all hands.'

Astonishment chased puzzlement on the first lieutenant's features but he touched his hat and summoned the boatswain to set in train the gravity of a captain's table. The die was cast. Feeling light-headed with the implications of what he proposed, Kydd went below.

Renzi looked at him strangely, but kept discreetly quiet. He had no role in this and knew it: Kydd would face the consequences of his own decision alone.

'Ship's company mustered, sir,' Howlett reported.

Gravely Kydd left his cabin for the wan sunlight of the main deck. A lectern stood next to a table where the waiting ship's clerk made much of arranging the books and inkwell. In front of him was a silent mass of seamen, the marines lining the gangways above.

He stepped up to the lectern. 'Off caps!' Jolley roared.

Then, when all was quiet, Kydd began: 'Master-at-arms?'

'Two bells this afternoon, Patrick Doyle did strike me, 'is lawful superior, contrary to—'

'Thank you, Mr Jolley. Doyle, is this true?' An admission would stop Kydd's plan in its track but, fortunately, the man stood doggedly mute.

'Come, sir, this is no time for silence. Master-at-arms, tell me what happened – in detail, if you please.'

'Well, sir, on bein' h'ordered to apprehend Doyle, I proceeded down t' the mess deck, where I saw the prisoner with his mates, like. When I—'

'Who were these mates, then, Mr Jolley?' Kydd said mildly.

'Oh, er, there was Smythe . . . an' McVitty and, er, others.'

'Carry on.'

'And then there was words, like. I goes t' seize Doyle when he tips me a souser on the chops, so I—'

'So Smythe and McVitty are your witnesses. Where were they standing, pray?'

'Standing? Why, I reckons in front o' the crowd somewheres.'

'Not good enough, Mr Jolley. Was Smythe to larb'd of the others, at the back – the front? Where was McVitty then?'

'Um, t' starb'd, I reckons, Smythe near 'im.'

'Call Smythe.' When the sailor arrived, nervously kneading his shapeless cap, Kydd asked him, with all the gravity he could muster, 'Now this is of vital importance – a man's life hangs on your answer. Where were you standing when – when this incident took place? Think now!'

'Abaft th' fore-mast, sir.'

'Upon which side?

'Er . . .'

'We'll have your oath on it – which?'

'I c-can't rightly recall.'

'Hmm. Call McVitty.' A slightly built man with darting eyes stood before him. 'Now, exactly where was Smythe during this time? Be very careful with your answer, sir!'

'I – I—'

'Well?'

'Couldn't be sure, sir . . .' The man tailed off.

'Can't be sure?' Kydd said, in exaggerated astonishment. 'This is a fine thing to set before a court-martial.' He found what he was looking for in the front row: a grey-haired seaman with steady eyes and a slight smile, as though he knew where Kydd was headed. 'You, sir! Step forward. Were you on the mess-decks forrard when the master-at-arms was struck?'

'I was, Mr Kydd,' the man said, in a firm voice.

'There, Mr Jolley. As your witnesses are unreliable I have found my own.'

'Thank 'ee, sir,' the master-at-arms said uncomfortably.

'Well, tell me, who was it that struck the master-at-arms?'

'I didn't rightly see, sir.' The expected answer came back instantly.

Kydd allowed disappointment to show, then called over another – with the same result. 'Tut, tut. This is very unsatisfactory.' He drew himself up and hailed the men. 'Any man who saw who struck the master-at-arms to come forward!'

A ripple of murmuring spread out – but, extraordinarily,

124

it seemed there was not one who had happened to be looking in that particular direction when the blow was struck.

'Then I rather fear we cannot proceed in this, Mr Jolley.'

'Sir? You can't – sir, it's Doyle, an' that's a—'

'The court-martial would think the L'Aurores a sad parcel o' loobies were we to present evidence like this. You're not thinking to see the ship shamed so publicly, surely, Mr Jolley?'

'It was Doyle! I'd stake m' life on't!'

'Not sufficient evidence presented. Case dismissed, Mr Howlett,' Kydd pronounced crisply.

The first lieutenant stood as though in doubt of his hearing. 'Why, sir – it's – we should question 'em individually, lay out the consequences, get the Articles o' War and—'

'No. Besides, I'm not finished yet.' He hid a smile at Howlett's agitation – this was only the opening act in what he had decided. 'I'm going to do something about our lamentable situation.'

Instead of concluding the proceedings and returning to his cabin, he waited for the restlessness in the men to settle into baffled curiosity, then theatrically addressed the stunned Doyle. 'I'd be beholden to you for your advice, sir, as pertaining to the situation in this frigate.'

Behind him, Kydd heard the gasps of his officers. The captain – asking a fore-mast hand for his views?

He smiled grimly. He knew precisely the feeling of the seamen for he had been one himself. 'Doyle, I know the Alcestes were sorely used – this doesn't need me to say it. The end of long voyaging, why, a sailor needs to blow out his gaff, raise the wind. I know this – that's why I'm minded to overlook our little troubles for now.'

He took a deep breath and continued lightly, 'In fact I'll go further. Doyle – I'd like to know your opinion of what the hands would say to a little bargain. They get their ran-tan, grog a-plenty, even their wives aboard for all of a day, two days – even three days on the frolic. In return they agree that when it's all over, we do our duty and put to sea, no questions asked.'

While the man visibly tried to grapple with what was being said, Kydd went on, 'That is, for three days the main-deck as far aft as my cabin and the entire lower-deck is out of bounds to all officers not passing through. No account will be given to grog brought aboard, nor wives and sweethearts for all of this time.'

A grin surfaced and Doyle shifted restlessly. 'Ah, but we don't have the rhino.'

'Out of my own purse I'll see to it no man goes short of a right good muzzler. It'll all be chalked down, never fear.'

'Why, sir, an' that's right handsome in ye,' Doyle said happily.

'No hurt to the ship, o' course.'

'No, y'r honour.'

'Then do talk it over with your mess-mates and let me know—'

'Sir, don't need to. Ye has y'r bargain.'

'Very well. Mr Howlett, dismiss the hands, if you please.'

As Kydd turned and marched smartly back to his cabin, the officers crowded anxiously after him.

'Sir!' Howlett exploded. 'Am I to understand you're seriously intending to turn this ship over to – to those false-hearted rogues in disgusting revelry and licentiousness for three entire days? Are you—'

'Hold your tongue, sir!' Kydd said, white with fury. Howlett and the others fell back, looking at him in shocked disbelief.

'We have one duty, and one only that transcends all others, and that is to go to our country's aid when its need is greatest.

And that means to provide Admiral Nelson with what he must have.

'I was at the Nile. Lack of frigates nearly did for us then – and there's going to be an even bigger battle soon when Bonaparte makes his move against England and no one knows when or where that'll be. One thing only is certain: it'll be frigates that'll be telling Nelson.'

'B-but—'

'Consider for one moment what we've achieved. The mutiny's been broke, we've a full crew and nothing to stop us sailing in three days. Isn't that worth a little time out of discipline?'

'Sir, are you prepared to take the word of those mutinous swabs?'

'Most certainly. Mr Curzon?'

'Sir, as I understand it, their complaint was that they're not paid. And you're . . . ?'

'This is an evasion. They know damn well that a ship going out of commission doesn't get a visit from the clerk o' the cheque until the books have been sent to the Admiralty for the payment to be cleared. No – take my word on't, it's your old-fashioned Western Ocean rollick they're wanting.'

'But there are surely practical difficulties,' Curzon came back.

'How so?'

'If you're proposing to confine 'em aboard, how are they going to get their, um, women and grog?'

'There's ways and means, sir, which you should not be too nice in the enquiring.'

'This is hard to take, sir!' Howlett blurted. 'Discipline subverted for common debauchery and—'

'Mr Howlett, how long have you been in the Navy?'

127

'Sir?'

Kydd sighed. 'In your experience, what is the state of a man-o'-war new returned from sea? A nest o' decorum, the men consulting their appearance, begging leave to give thanks for their deliverance?'

He smiled mirthlessly. 'No, sir! Portsmouth Poll and her sisters flock out to get aboard and with 'em they bring their gin, and then, sir, the lower-deck soon resembles a promiscuous bacchanalia. But we don't pay mind to it for, Mr Howlett, it's the immemorial custom of the Service.

'So you can see, gentlemen, all we're about is allowing our brave tars their spree at the beginning, not the end o' the voyage.'

Relieved murmurs echoed as the sense of where Kydd was leading penetrated. 'And the ship's log will show no more than it always does on these occasions – and this to be sent to the Admiralty only when we make port again.'

'I mislike what they'll say ashore when they hear of this,' Howlett said edgily.

Kydd rounded on him: 'And who's to tell 'em? If any wants to come aboard they stay the whole time, no going back to spread the word. After we've sailed, who cares? We're outward bound on the King's service, as so we should.'

'Er – the grog?' muttered Curzon. 'I think we should know . . .'

'If you must. Our only contact with the shore is the cutter with a picked crew o' trusties who'll know to keep their mouths brailed up and I dare to say will know where there's a decent haul of grog to be had. They come on board and there's no one at the gangway to enquire too closely. It'll serve.'

'And – and the women?'

'We first throw out a welcome to the wives yonder who'll set up on the main-deck, then the other, er, ladies on the lower deck.'

'B-but discipline, order?'

'We leave them to it! Any who steps too far will answer to his shipmates as fouling their hawse. There'll be grog a-swilling and lewd behaviour to set the devil himself to the blush – but none of us in witness, for bounds are set about it.'

Suddenly grinning at the appalled faces of his officers, Kydd said, 'I advise you make your arrangements, gentlemen – I mean to throw open the ship at eight bells.'

Kydd heaved the deepest sigh imaginable: he was at last out in the open sea, sinking Portsmouth astern and leaving behind the ignoble scenes that had enabled them to achieve it. True, there were men comatose in the lee scuppers, and the mess-deck was a bear pit, but that was as nothing compared to the feeling of at last being quit of the land.

They passed the Isle of Wight in a fluky easterly breeze, losing Kickergill Tower in the far distance and then shaping course outward bound with all sight of old Portsmouth dissolved into a blue haze as their bowsprit eagerly sought the freedom of the seas.

He was determined to reach Nelson as soon as he could, but this would not be at the cost of prudence. The first thing was to get the ship away and let the healing power of the sea do its work. When *L'Aurore*'s company was ready, there was the agreeable task of getting to know her, finding out her best points and, as well, the less endearing, a vital process if he was to throw his ship into battle with the confidence that was necessary in a commander.

It could not be hurried, for their very lives might depend

on his deeply knowing his ship. Besides, in the course of events the company would shake down into their new vessel and, in a similar way, each learn about the other and the strengths and weaknesses, quirks and eccentricities that gave a ship its character.

Finally there was the formal procedure of producing an Admiralty Sailing Qualities Report on the vessel's capabilities, required for all ships newly taken into service. Kydd's intention was to stand west under easy sail until the next day, then in the chops of the Channel take his new ship through her paces, ending with a visit to Plymouth to have any defects and changes required made good at the dockyard.

Then he would set sail for the Mediterranean. That was the plan – but he was uneasily aware that his move to lessen the injustice of the turning over was appreciated for now but solved nothing in the long term. *L'Aurore* must sail foreign in days with a ship's company having had no liberty ashore in England for years. Would this, over time, corrode their loyalty and fester into something worse? With a deep breath of salt-tangy sea air, he went below.

Once again he marvelled at the palatial splendour of his cabin – as spacious as a drawing room and intended for much the same purpose. Tonight he would have his officers to a leisurely dinner and try to ease the strains of the recent past.

'Ho there, Tysoe. See if Mr Renzi is at leisure and then bring alongside a pair o' gin toddies.'

It was deeply satisfying to be able to entertain his friend by right rather than the past subterfuge of pretending the ship's clerk was being constantly required. The affairs of a captain's confidential secretary were, of course, not to be questioned.

He greeted his friend while Tysoe occupied himself with

the drinks. 'I'm concerned you're comfortable. Is the gunroom to your liking at all?'

'A caution to all who've sailed in lesser breeds, I can assure you.'

'And your studies – you'll bless the opulence of your cabin, I'm thinking,' Kydd added warmly.

'Er, quite,' Renzi said distantly, avoiding Kydd's eye.

'Oh? You know you have as well the liberties of the coach, if you wish. It's in the nature of a public space I'll agree, quantities of midshipmen and clerks diligently at their workings, but they'll never dare bother you as they will answer to me.'

'Um, yes, thank you.'

Kydd frowned. 'I'm a mort puzzled, Nicholas. Is there anything amiss in your appointments? A prime scholar should not need for—'

'No, no, dear fellow. My establishment is of the first rank, I do declare. It's just – there's a matter that's of a particular distraction to me at the present time which . . . I must think on.'

'If it's anything you'd like to talk about, m' friend . . . ?'

Renzi glanced at him. 'Well . . . it's by way of an embarrassment, if you understand me.'

'We've no secrets, Nicholas. Clap on sail and fire away, man.'

'Very well. It's concerning my studies.'

'Carry on,' Kydd said, trying to look wise.

'Um, as things were proceeding so well I thought to consult a publisher about the book's prospects – how one comes to an arrangement for its printing and so forth. And, er, there would seem to be some difficulties attendant upon it.'

'Difficulties?'

'The eminent and worldly publisher I spoke to seems to

think that the public reader prefers more in the way of entertainment and less of pure theory, quite putting to the blush my strenuous efforts to adduce rigour to my hypotheses.'

'A strange notion, Nicholas.'

'And vexing. Without I include distracting and irrelevant details of cannibals and savage damsels disporting naked, his view is that the number of volumes sold will not be sufficient to pay for its printing.'

'What's that against such scholarship you are bringing to your work? Why, it—'

'Dear fellow,' Renzi said sadly, 'writing in these modern times must now be accounted a business, with all the attendant woes of want of treasure, wares to be displayed at the marketplace before the *hoi polloi* and like concerns. In fine, it would seem he's asking I amend its delivery, adapt the words to a more modish taste, and that, brother, I will not do.'

'So?'

'Those in academia need fear no frowning public, neither those celebrated in the public eye. And should I be desirous of a private publishing, why, this may only be readily accomplished by raising a subscription – not, I hasten to add, for pecuniary reasons, but by this means the attention of the great and good may be secured in advance. And that I'm as yet unknown in literary circles quite dishes any prospects remaining.'

Kydd saw his friend's face fall and the worry-lines deepen and his heart went out to him. 'There must be . . .'

'And that is not the worst of it,' Renzi said, in a voice so low that Kydd strained to hear. 'I vowed that when I laid my opus at your sister's feet, in the same hour I would seek her hand. So what now has become of me?'

'Nicholas, m' friend, I'm certain it's you in yourself she'd be satisfied with, not some old book.'

Renzi looked away and spoke in muffled tones: 'When I received your letter of recall it was a . . . a relief. You see, Cecilia and I had h-high words and she is now gone off to her world of the highest society and I rather fear she has tired of me.'

'Cec? Never!' Kydd said, in sincere disbelief.

'No? Then why did she not come – as she always has – to fare us well on our voyaging? And no fond gift? A letter, even?'

'She – she might be busy . . .'

Renzi pulled himself up stiffly. 'But this is no concern of yours, sir. I shall consider my position and before that time I'd be obliged should you refrain from mentioning it.'

The next morning dawned bright and clear and, unusually for the chops of the Channel, a subdued and calm seascape stretched out in a hard grey winter glitter with barely a swell to make things interesting, but Kydd was beside himself with impatience to make trial of his ship.

At last the men's breakfast was concluded and both watches were mustered for evolutions. 'Under all plain sail, full and bye on this board,' he ordered. This would require the topgallants to be bent on after their easy passage out, as good a test as any of his crew's mettle.

He watched with satisfaction as the long sausages of sails were hoisted aloft efficiently, the men working steadily under their boatswain. Kydd could have no complaint about the way Oakley swarmed aloft before even the topmen themselves, ready for them as they stretched along the sails and began passing the lines. He was as much a stranger to these men as Kydd was but he was getting the most out of them.

L'Aurore responded well, lengthening her stride like an

obedient thoroughbred, the swash of her prettily dappled wake now extending broadly on either side. He called over the senior master's mate. 'Mr Saxton? Take two midshipmen and teach 'em to cast a log. I want our speed whenever I call for it.'

He gazed up at the set of the sails, their complexity of lines, the sweet curve of full canvas, and smothered a sigh. The last time he had handled a fully ship-rigged vessel was as a lieutenant in the old 64 *Tenacious*, and his main worry then had been that he would do nothing foolish under the eye of the captain. And now . . .

'Log?' he called imperiously. This would be a baseline performance figure – presuming the wind held he would first ring the changes on trim and see how *L'Aurore* did.

'Nine knots and a whisker!' yelled Saxton. Not bad, but not good. Earlier he had heaved to and taken the draft fore and aft. Some ships liked to be down by the head so the forefoot would bite, more often by the stern to increase manoeuvrability. What he needed now was the effect of trim on speed under standard sail.

'Right, Mr Oakley, get those forward.' Trundling the twelve-pounder carriage guns along the main-deck as far as possible was a quick method of shifting weights to imitate a re-stowage of the hold. The effect was immediate – not so much on the speed but the surprising amount of spray and slop that came over the bows. In heavier weather this would translate not only into a wet ship forward but *L'Aurore* being shy of head seas.

The guns were returned and Kydd tried something else. This time it was to see how close-hauled to the wind *L'Aurore* could be held, a vital matter in either chase or flight. Without fuss or complaint she lay to the breeze as close as Kydd could recall any square-rigged ship of his acquaintance – five and a third points off the wind no less. Promising!

Next he had a cask thrown over the transom with a jaunty red flag atop it. As it slipped away into the distance astern Kydd sighted aft along the centreline. As the ship slashed along hard up to the wind, little by little the flag inched its way to windward – this was leeway, the ground lost under the side pressure of the wind. He continued until the flag was a tiny speck at about a cable and a half upwind of *L'Aurore*'s track. Not bad – that would be the Sané steep turn of bilge he'd noticed in dock.

He wore about and ran the cask down on the other tack with similar results. It was most satisfying; here was something to rely on. Now for going large, wind abaft the beam. 'Take us on a reach, wind four points free, Mr Kendall.'

This was a quartering breeze, for most ships their best point of sailing. Again, *L'Aurore* did not disappoint, her brisk motion turning to a canter. 'Speed?' called Kydd.

'Near thirteen!' yelled back Saxton. In this light breeze the figure was astonishing and gratifying, for there was the prospect of more if pushed harder. Surprised grins spread around the deck as word got out.

'Running free,' ordered Kydd, and the helm spun as the frigate was placed squarely before the wind. It was proverbial that a ship responding well by the wind did not relish going free – but then a ship that was good both by and large generally performed each of these manoeuvres as a compromise, an outstanding sailer on neither.

One thing became immediately noticeable. With the wind and waves dead aft *L'Aurore* rolled. Not a simple, regular heave but a nervous wallow with a sharp twitch before she began a slower return roll. They would have an uncomfortable time of it going large in heavier seas.

Without stunsails and other ornaments aloft, there was no point in chasing speed, which left manoeuvring, tacking and veering – through the wind's eye or the long way around. 'We wear first,' Kydd decided.

In fairness to a new company on a strange ship they wore slowly, carefully – but there was no need for concern: *L'Aurore* obeyed demurely and sweetly took up on her new tack, quickly settling on her course. Again, but this time in earnest. And again. Without fuss, she went round and lay back on her old track as if nothing had happened.

So far, so good: now to the complex manoeuvre of tacking about. The breeze was falling to a pleasant ruffling. Kydd knew the signs: there would be a relative calm soon and his exercising would have to come to an end.

'Hands to stations for staying,' he ordered. There would be quick work on the braces and sheets but they were ready. This time, however, *L'Aurore* seemed to object to being hurried: her slim length to breadth required a more measured pacing, a precision of manoeuvre that would be a hard thing to accomplish in the throes of battle.

They went through stays one more time but Kydd had her measure now, and with it came a growing respect. This was a proud lady who had all the graces and expected to be treated with consideration, but there was little to forgive.

The wind faded into a fluky breeze and their speed began to fall away. Yet *L'Aurore* stood on, even with her sails hanging loosely and flapping occasionally as if in lady-like impatience. She ghosted along at a walking pace and Kydd's satisfaction with his new ship swelled. This was a most valuable trait – no prey would escape in a calm with this fine-lined frigate.

So what did he have? A fast ship, that was certain. How fast would have to await the right conditions. Fine-lined but delicate, rather lighter in her scantlings than he would have liked, but if she was to be a flyer it had to be paid for. This would include staying with twelve-pounders for there was no arguing with metacentres that said too much weight too high was dangerous.

L'Aurore was a comfortable ship. His appointments were first-rate and from what he had seen of the gunroom his officers would be satisfied with their cabins. The seamen had good berths but he would suspend judgement on that until after the first real blow, with seas coming over the fo'c'sle.

All in all, then, a fine ship – and one to love, he admitted to himself in surprise. Behind his critical assessments lay a growing affection for her: that willing responding to his wishes, the old-fashioned charm of her fitments that gave her a warmth of appearance so different from the war-like demeanour of modern British frigates.

They were going to get along.

Chapter 6

'Sir, I do welcome you to the Admiralty,' the first lord said to Mr Pitt, the prime minister. Noting the features ravaged by cares and the stooped carriage of the man who had given the flower of his life in the service of his country, he added gently, 'Should you require refreshment at this hour . . . ?'

It was late at night and they had the board room to themselves. Pitt ignored the table and sat wearily in one of the two leather armchairs, the few candles casting harsh shadows on his face. 'Henry, I have an audience with the King in the morning,' he muttered to his old friend. 'Do see if you can find me something of cheer to lay before him.'

Melville drew up the other chair and pondered. 'The people are in good heart, no dread or uncertainty there.'

'It's ignorance of the situation only.'

'John Bull is no fool. He can see what stands against us. No, they've placed their trust in the Hero of the Nile, that while Nelson rules the waves no Frenchman dare venture an invasion of these islands. It's pathetic and noble at the same time, I'm persuaded, but then it means we need have no fear of popular resentments, you can tell him.'

Pitt sighed and sipped his port reflectively. 'That's of no account. His Majesty abhors the man since in defiance of society he's taken up with that Hamilton woman.' He pulled himself up in the chair. 'Henry, imagine me one of your northern ironmasters come to Town to discover why we fuss so over the Navy. Pray rehearse for me just what it is that's facing us as of tonight and I'll be the judge of what shall be said later to the King.'

'Yes. Well – since you ask, it could hardly be worse. The continent of Europe is in arms against us and its resources plundered by Bonaparte to one end – the destruction of our nation. He has an encampment of a hundred and seventy-five thousand veterans within twenty miles of the English shore, some three thousand invasion craft completed and the whole waiting for his word to be launched at our vitals.'

'I know all of that – I'm a colonel of militia at Deal, I'll remind you, Henry!'

'Er, yes. As it's known, he needs but hours – a day or so at most in control of the Channel – and we're done. Therefore whatever it takes, they must be prevented from setting forth.'

'There are those who point to Keith and the Downs Squadron.'

'As they are in daily battle outside Boulogne. This is true, but it's not why Napoleon refrains from a sally. The real reason is that if his mighty invasion flotilla sails, it stands to be crushed by any of our ships-of-the-line lying in wait, and thus he must protect them with larger numbers of his own sail-of-the-line. Therefore his entire strategics are devoted to the one object: to crowd the Channel with his battleships to ensure safe passage for the invasion fleet.'

'And all the world asks this: why do we not make concentration of our own squadrons in the Channel? They'd never stand against us! Why are our battle-fleets sent thousands of miles overseas while there's such deadly peril in home waters?'

'Because, sir, we would not necessarily win in such a contest.'

'Not win?' Pitt snapped.

'Not necessarily, I did say. Napoleon, since the Dons' recent declaration of war, and with the Dutch Navy in possession, has now an immense number of sail-of-the-line at his disposing, a damn sight more than we. Should these all at the one time be brought together in the Channel . . .'

'Well?'

'Our own strategics are very simple: to stop this happening. And to this end we have a tried and trusty weapon. Blockade. At Brest they have Ganteaume and his armada, Missiessy at Rochefort, Villeneuve at Toulon. The Spanish under Gravina at Ferrol, Vigo and Cadiz, fine deepwater ports. And outside every one of these lies a British battle squadron sternly denying them the open sea.

'The effect of this is decisive: if any enemy leaves port that part will inevitably be defeated before it has time to join with the others, of that you can be assured. So while they lie apart and divided we are safe. Conversely, if they manage to break out and combine we will be overwhelmed. Therefore the heroes of the hour are those ships and men that are now standing before the enemy in all weathers to this end.'

Pitt looked up sombrely. 'Incidentally, who have you on this duty at the moment?'

'Cornwallis at Brest with seventeen of-the-line, Orde off Cadiz with five, Calder at Ferrol with eight and Nelson before Toulon with twelve. Not so many to set against them, I will agree.'

'So if they do get out, what then?'

'The chiefest danger is Toulon, which is why we have our most feared admiral there. And it's there as well that the French have their commander-in-chief. If he can contrive to break free he sails west, adding battleships from Cartagena and forcing the strait of Gibraltar. Overwhelming Orde, he effects a conjunction with the Spanish in Cadiz. He then sails north, releasing others from Ferrol and Vigo and reaching Brest where Ganteaume comes out. The Combined Fleet is then in overwhelming force at the mouth of the Channel – and our worst nightmare is upon us.'

'Quite,' said Pitt. 'Knowing these plans, however, we make our dispositions.'

Melville shook his head slowly. 'No, sir, we do not know their plans. What I have outlined is the most obvious move for them and the most tempting. But there are other possibilities that would make nonsense of deployments based on it.

'For instance, there's always Ireland. A descent on its unprotected coast with the scale of forces Napoleon now commands would most probably succeed and this would place us in the impossible situation of facing two ways in defending our islands.

'Then again there is the East. Bonaparte has always resented his defeat at the Nile, which turned the command of the Mediterranean over to us. If he can effect a landing in the Middle East again, he has a royal road to India and even the Ottomans in Constantinople. He will then have achieved his most desired object, a limitless empire without ever getting his feet wet.

'He may well consider a feint – at Surinam, say, or Africa – and, while we're so engaged, descend on the Caribbean in crushing force, taking our sugar islands. I don't have to say that in this case we'd be bankrupted and suing for peace within the year.'

Pitt slumped back. 'This is all so hard to take, Henry.'

'Yes. We have world-wide commitments, sir. To maintain protection on our interests ranging from Botany Bay to Nova Scotia requires a colossal fleet to be dispersed about the planet. Napoleon may keep his own in concentration for whatever purpose he desires.'

Closing his eyes in weariness, Pitt sighed. 'Then what you are saying is that if the nation's hero, Nelson, fails us and the French get out, we're ruined.'

'Yes, sir, I am.'

L'Aurore ghosted in over a winter-bright sea, past the Mewstone to starboard, and came to single anchor among the scatter of ships in Cawsand Bay within Plymouth Sound. Her captain stood proudly, reflecting on the times he had brought his humble brig-sloop *Teazer* here.

Now in full-dress post-captain uniform, with a fine sword, on the quarterdeck of his own frigate, it was a world past, a more innocent time but one that seemed to have been in preparation for this culminating moment – when, incredibly, he was on his way to join Admiral Horatio Nelson.

His commissioning pennant dropped from the masthead at precisely the same time as the Union Jack rose on the jackstaff forward while aft the white ensign floated proudly free. As a naval visitor of significance Kydd would now be expected to pay his respects to the port-admiral, and in deep satisfaction he heard the first lieutenant call away his barge.

'Hands to harbour routine, Mr Howlett,' he ordered, but

added quietly, 'Row-guard and no liberty of any kind. We sail for Gibraltar just as soon as we've stored and watered.'

'Aye aye, sir,' Howlett said coldly. It would be some time before Kydd was forgiven, it seemed.

'I'm sending out the store-ships as soon as I can stir 'em up. Turn the hands to, the moment they've opened the hold.'

Kydd returned as quickly as he decently could. The new port-admiral had been effusive in his congratulations, the action with *Teazer* having taken place in his waters. Narrowly avoiding a formal invitation to dinner, Kydd had set in train the storing of a ship for foreign service, including the items he was to carry to his commander-in-chief.

With rising excitement he called his barge and headed back. From the outside *L'Aurore* looked quite perfect. Larger than any craft in view, she was at one and the same time both martial and beautiful, and his heart went out to her.

Oakley's pipe squealed, pure and clean in the cold, clear evening as Kydd mounted the side-steps and punctiliously raised his hat to the quarterdeck. He turned to go below and Howlett fell into step beside him. He said, with a note of smugness, 'It grieves me to tell you, sir, that I have to report deserters already.'

'Oh? To be expected, I suppose,' Kydd said, with irritation. 'I would have thought it foreseeable enough for my first lieutenant to take steps to prevent it.'

'Ah, but these are your precious volunteers who are running. The first boat of trusties. I'm told half the crew ran off as soon as they had a line ashore,' Howlett said primly.

Kydd's heart sank. If the volunteers thought it worth risking savage punishment for desertion then conditions below were much worse than he feared. 'What are their names? They'll be made example of, never doubt it, Mr Howlett.'

'Names? Why, Stirk, gunner's mate, Doud, quartermaster, Pinto, quarter gunner and some others. Not your usual worthless skulkers, you'd agree, sir.'

'I'll deal with it,' Kydd said heavily, and went to his cabin. Renzi looked up but on seeing Kydd's expression made his excuses.

Tysoe helped him out of his fine uniform and to a restorative brandy. He sat in his armchair, moodily looking out of the stern windows at the whole of Plymouth Hoe and Old Town spread before him.

Stirk, Doud – his former shipmates whom he'd thought he could trust. Now they would go down in the ship's books as 'R' – run. And they would be hunted men, looking over their shoulder at every turn, knowing that if the Navy caught them it was a court-martial and death – or, worse, the long-drawn-out agony of flogging around the fleet.

But he could not let them go. As volunteers they had taken the King's shilling and were under naval discipline. There was as well the difficult prospect of finding official explanations for his inaction, and last but not least, it would tell the crew that any successful desertion would be met with forgiveness. He had to take action and make it convincing, even if it ended in recapture and punishment without mercy.

Was there no middle path? He had a short time only to make his move. As he continued to look out at the scene ashore, an idea came to him and he summoned his senior off-watch lieutenant. 'Mr Gilbey, I want you to step ashore with a party of trusties and set up a rondy in Plymouth Dock, at the Five Bells or similar. Now this will be to another purpose – have your men quietly visit each tavern to see if they can find word of these deserters and then let you know.

You are then to seize them and bring them back on board in irons. Clear?'

He found plain clothes and announced to Howlett that he was going ashore on a social occasion for the evening. There was a risk that some in his boat party might desert but it would have to be taken.

They dropped him by the Citadel, the other side of Plymouth Hoe to Dock but conveniently near Old Town.

He headed up the hill towards the louring ramparts of the Citadel until he was out of sight, then dropped sharply to the waterfront to enter the maze of old Tudor buildings that marked Plymouth proper. He knew Toby Stirk would never be so foolish as to risk roystering in a Dock tavern but would nevertheless go to ground somewhere close, like the noisome stews of Cockside resorted to by the merchant sailors whose ships crowded Sutton Pool and the Cattedown.

Irony tugged at him: it was Stirk who had come for him when he had been so desolated after the death of his fiancée Rosalynd that he had wandered there to drown himself in drink among sailoring humanity.

He had deliberately sent Gilbey on a fool's errand to show he was taking the desertions seriously, and now he must work fast to find his men before it was too late. Cockside was a square-shaped huddle of buildings. In the dark of the evening it was thronged with waterfront folk and Kydd slipped among them along the passages linking the rickety, cramped dwellings and taphouses.

At each tavern he wandered innocently in, looking about as if to find a friend, then apologetically withdrew. It was a very long shot: an old fox like Stirk could disappear into the countryside and wait for *L'Aurore* to sail before emerging, even if this part of Plymouth was never the haunt of King's men.

But he knew Doud, too. It would be in keeping with his open-hearted character to feel the need to sink a pint or two before moving on and he was quite inseparable from his old mess-mate Pinto. There was a chance.

One by one he played his act in every alehouse and grog parlour, but without result. Suddenly Kydd stopped and cocked his ear.

He had taken a short cut in front of a dilapidated boat-builder's slip. In its shed there was a chink of light and he heard voices, one of which he could swear was Stirk's deep, masculine rasp.

As he tiptoed towards the building, a grog-roughened voice started up:

> *'Tis of a flash frigate, L'Aurore was her name,*
> *All in the West Indies she bore a great name;*
> *For cru-el bad using of every degree,*
> *Like slaves in the galley we ploughed the salt sea.*
> *So now, brother shipmates, where'er ye may be*
> *From all fancy frigates I'd have ye steer free . . .'*

Kydd reached the big double door. It was barred with a stout timber athwart it. He lifted it; it gave and he lifted further. Suddenly the door burst outward to reveal the deserters around a carpenter's bench with a single candle and bottles.

The men stumbled to their feet. 'Wha'—? Be buggered – it's Mr Kydd!'

In a rush for the door Kydd was knocked to one side by Stirk and Pinto but managed to hang on to Doud, who made a wild swing that sent him staggering. Enraged, he returned a blow to the stomach that knocked Doud to his knees, retching.

Out of the corner of his eye Kydd saw that Pinto had drawn a knife and was advancing on him with a deadly look.

'Stop! Let me speak! There's no one else, I swear it – I'm alone!' he said urgently.

Stirk now loomed behind Pinto, his fists loose.

'Hear me out!' Kydd pleaded, his head throbbing.

There was a tense silence.

'Drop it, Pinto,' Stirk finally growled. 'Let's hear what he's got t' say f'r himself.'

Kydd swallowed. 'Men – that's t' say, Toby an' Ned – I wouldn't be here 'less I had good reason, cared what happened t' ye.'

There was no response.

'I'll give ye th' true lay – an' it's not pretty. See, we—'

'Ye turned over the Alcestes. After three year sweatin' in the Caribbee. *You!*' Stirk grated.

So that was what it was all about, the moral affront to a sailor's rights, not a careless disinclination to serve in an unhappy ship. And it seemed it was common knowledge that Kydd's active intervention had brought it about.

He thought quickly. 'Aye, it was me.' He tried to ignore the naked contempt on their faces. 'So I'm going t' square wi' ye all. I'm t' tell just what it was made me do it, and God help me if ever any hear I've split on 'em in the Admiralty an' told ye.'

There was no change in the stony grimaces. 'Now, I'm trustin' that ye'll not blow th' gaff on this to the common folk as places their trust in the Navy t' save 'em.'

The contempt faded to blankness and Kydd continued, 'We's been at war more'n ten years since 'ninety-three, but now it's different. Boney wants t' invade an' he means it.'

'An' he'll never do it! One reg'lar-built English man-o'-war's worth two o' the Mongseers!' Stirk proclaimed harshly.

'Ha!' Kydd snarled. 'That's where y'r arithmeticals are on a lee shore t' the truth. I'll agree – we're better'n any two Frenchies but what if they've got double the ships? We're level! What if they've more still? We go down fightin' gloriously – but we go down.'

'Our Nel has twelve o'-the-line off Toulon. Since th' Spanish came in against us, Boney's above a *hundred* t' throw at us.'

Kydd looked from one to another. Then, in low, measured tones, he detailed the colossal odds against them: the three thousand ships of the invasion flotilla itself, the uncountable hordes of Napoleon's finest encamped above Boulogne, poised to fall on England.

He went on: the lonely ships somewhere in the oceans of the world, listing on his fingers the out-numbered battle squadrons off the major ports that were all that stood between Bonaparte and their homes and loved ones. He held back nothing of the desperate measures Pitt and the Admiralty were taking to hold together the one thing that would save the kingdom.

'An' the post of honour, where d' ye think that is?' he snapped. 'Why, it c'n only be where th' Frenchy admiral is – an' where Nelson is as well. He's called f'r us in his sore need, shipmates. Are we going t' hold back?'

'Y' turned over the Alcestes,' mumbled Doud, stubbornly.

'S' what else c'n I do, y' simkin?' Kydd flared. 'Let a fine frigate swing about her moorings till her crew give me leave t' sail? So what'll fadge, Ned? There's an accounting wi' Bonaparte very soon now, you tell me t' my face a better way t' get *L'Aurore* to Nelson. Come on, say away, m' squiddy cock.'

Doud looked back at the others, shame-faced. Stirk folded

his arms and regarded Kydd steadily. 'Then why d'ye come after us? You've a full crew, aught t' worry of?'

'Y' needs me to say it, Toby? Then I'll tell ye – we're a new frigate an' we'll be in every scrape God sends. An' if I can't trust m' old mess-mates . . .'

The tide was turning, he could feel it. ''Sides, once Johnny Crapaud's come out an' been beat, we're free t' go a-prize-takin' or similar, I wouldn't wonder. Of which I know a little . . .'

He had them. 'So – if ye sees y' course clear to return aboard, well, y' not th' first sailors to fetch up slewed t' the gills as couldn't grope their way back.'

The next day started with Kydd's orders for a convoy. Never one to waste a frigate's Gibraltar voyage, the admiral had thirty-three merchantmen and an army transport in Cawsand Bay waiting for an escort. It meant a rush of work preparing signals, sailing-orders folders and all the apparatus of an ocean convoy but, mercifully, Kydd could hand it all over in the time-honoured way to the most junior lieutenant, Curzon.

An army officer presented himself with orders for Gibraltar, and the dockyard desired to know where he wished stowed the spare spars allocated for the Mediterranean. The respectful commander of *Hasty* brig-sloop made himself known, as did the lieutenant-in-command of the dispatch cutter *Lapwing*, both destined for Gibraltar and under Kydd's command as additional escort.

A fine thing to be a post-captain, he thought happily, as they were seen over the side and he turned to discover what his first lieutenant wanted. 'Er, we've found the deserters, sir,' he said.

'Deserters? Where was this, then, Mr Howlett?'

'Um, waiting for our boat.'

'Then stragglers it is, sir, not deserters.' The Navy had a practical view of being adrift on liberty. If a seaman was found within the bounds of the port the stand was taken that, notwithstanding the manner of his absenting, an intention to desert could not be proven.

His spirits rose. There would now be other voices and other views on the mess-deck; if there was a way of making it up to his old shipmates without compromising his position he would find it.

It was Kydd's first commission outside home waters in this war of Napoleon and there was still much to be done to prepare for the open ocean.

Tysoe was dispatched ashore for cabin stores – he could be trusted to lay in sufficient for an extended deployment, sparing only the wine, which in the Mediterranean would not be hard to find. Preserves and delicacies of all kinds began coming aboard – from lean bacon, pickles, hams, cheeses, mustard and all necessary tracklements to sustain a fine table to anchovies, a barrel of oysters, pepper, dried fruit, molasses, jams, all carefully chosen to add variety and interest yet remain wholesome for months in foreign parts.

Recalling his experiences as a common sailor in a voyage to the Great South Sea, Kydd made certain that plenty of onions were taken aboard. Large, juicy and pungent, these were a sovereign cure for the monotony of salt beef and pork, and with these and the 'conveniences' of herbs and pepper to hand, a cunning mess-cook would take delight in conjuring a spirit-lifting sea pie with all the trimmings.

By degrees the excitement of the outward-bounder spread about the ship – the new midshipmen and boys a mix of apprehension and joy, old shellbacks ready with hair-raising yarns of exotic ports and cruel seas. It would be different for the Alcestes, of course, Kydd knew with a pang. Torn from the country they had cherished in their hearts for three years, they were heading out to sea once again. It was hard, but it was war. In weeks they would be part of Lord Nelson's fleet – he was utterly determined that by the time they reached Gibraltar they would be worthy of the honour.

Last-minute stores were loaded, including newspapers – a large selection of the latest editions in corded bundles, protectively sealed within sailcloth wrapping and stowed carefully. These would be minutely pored over by the Gibraltar garrison and in the wardrooms of Nelson's squadron, a grateful reminder of a previous existence. Finally, dispatches, the most precious cargo of all.

At *L'Aurore*'s masthead the Blue Peter floated free. This was the first time Kydd had flown the flag of readiness to sail in his own right, and with satisfaction he watched as, one by one, the other ships repeated the signal. He left it to the cutter to awaken the laggards to their duty.

Promptly at the top of the tide the Gibraltar convoy put to sea in a fine north-westerly. Kydd had the cutter and the sloop move out first to secure the assembly point while *L'Aurore* shepherded the merchantmen out from the rear. As they left the heights of Rame Head abeam, they met the full force of the cold north-westerly, *L'Aurore* plunging and bucking until sail could be taken off the fine-lined frigate. It made assembling the convoy a trial: merchant ships were unused to the discipline of sailing in formation and had no crew to spare for the backing and filling required to stay in place.

Gibraltar was a thousand miles to the south, past Ushant at the mouth of the Channel and across the Bay of Biscay, then the length of the Iberian Peninsula. But from Plymouth it was a more-or-less direct line so it could be reached on a single board.

The gaggle of shipping settled down at last, the sloop leading to windward and the cutter handily at the mid-point and *L'Aurore*, with her speed, overseeing from the rear. Kydd knew the routine, however: they would advance at the rate of the slowest.

He kept the deck until it was known which that was, for much hung on the outcome. A slow sailer could grievously hamper the convoy's progress and be a curse on them all. Unsurprisingly, it turned out to be the *Mahratta* army transport, a fat-bellied ship that was as leewardly as she was slow.

Calling *Lapwing* within hail, he ordered her to instruct the vessel to spread all sail conformable to the weather and keep as close by the wind as practicable, irrespective of their course. The westerly was holding but if they were to make it around Cape Finisterre in one board there was no point in taking chances.

Without being told, the loose convoy trimmed sail to conform and, tightening their formation, settled down for the long haul south. Kydd remained on deck, quietly observing the officer-of-the-watch, Gilbey, work out what combination of reefs and bracing would result in the steady pace needed to match speeds with their flock.

He seemed competent, and economical in his use of the hands. Kydd's eyes turned on the men themselves. In the next minute a strange sail could lift into sight and then they might be fighting for their lives. Would they follow him?

The party by the fore-brace bitts worked efficiently enough at the hanking and coiling, with the easy swing of prime seamen but without so much as a word between them.

When they finished they turned their backs and padded silently away.

Kydd knew the signs only too well. These men had lost heart. And if that was so, then as things now were, he could not depend on them in a fighting situation.

In the night the wind freshened; by morning the smaller ships were struggling, bucketing along under the streaming blast from out of the west. Kydd ordered sail shortened but this was a typical Atlantic snorter, flat and hard from its thousand-mile fetch, sheeting spume from the wave-crests of the Biscay rollers and making life aboard increasingly uncomfortable.

What it was like in the army transport with hundreds of men and scores of horses didn't bear thinking about, and even aboard *L'Aurore* men were beginning to stagger to the ship's side, the seas coming in directly on the beam in a massive, jerking roll.

Yet for Kydd it was satisfying: the frigate lay to the wind with ease, a whole point or two still in hand to windward, her press of canvas steadying the worst of the rolling. He eyed the conditions: if it came to a fight they could probably manage, but on the lee side their gun-ports must remain closed against the surging roll, and only a first-class set of seaman-gunners could cope with the capricious deck motion.

Another day, however, saw the situation Kydd had feared. The wind had not moderated and, in fact, was backing south-westerly. Shortly decisions would have to be made for at this rate they would not round Cape Finisterre, at worst to be carried on to the lee shore of hostile Spain.

There was no help for it: they were headed, and well before dark signals were made to prepare to tack. The thirty-seven ships carefully went about to take up on the larboard tack, heading out into the depths of the Atlantic with solid combers crashing against their bows.

It was slow going, *L'Aurore* pitching harshly, sending sluicing seas time and again over her fo'c'sle. Kydd took the trouble to look at conditions on the lower deck for himself and, as he had suspected, water was spurting in from everywhere as the bows submerged into the shock of the oncoming waves, the deck itself a-swim with a racing surge before it found its way into the bilge.

There was little that could be done: no caulking could stand against the pressures. It was the fault of *L'Aurore*'s fine entry – designed for speed rather than the blunter fore-part of a British ship built for sea-keeping – and he would have to get used to it.

Early next morning he knew he had to make a decision. How long to leave it before he made his move south once more? Each hour they were making useful ground to the west but at the same time it was taking them by degrees to the north. Too early a move and they would have to repeat their beat to the west but leaving it too long would cost them in so much more delay.

He compromised on three more days, dead time in their thrash south but several hundred miles safely further out from the coast, the leaden overcast preventing a sight of the sun and making all positions the product of dead-reckoning.

Keenly feeling the responsibility of his argosy, its value in cargo, the several thousand souls, he finally gave the orders that had the convoy wheeling about to resume its southward track.

As they passed the forty-three degrees north latitude of Cape Finisterre, invisible miles to leeward, the wind magically changed. Veering sharply north and moderating in a brisk quartering wind, it urged the convoy onward.

It was too good to last. Soon after a watery sun appeared, giving their position as some seventy miles to seaward of Cape St Vincent, the winds dropped and their speed fell away to a walking pace. It was intensely annoying – once past, they could shape course directly for Gibraltar on the last leg with an easy wind astern.

Sail blossomed from every yard but, again, they were constrained by the lumbering transport, which was making poor going in the light airs. At this season and latitude, on the fringe of the south-west trades, calms could occur without warning – and equally within hours a storm could threaten.

Eventually the legendary cape was passed and course was shaped for Gibraltar. The calm, however, lasted into the night, a blaze of stars near enough to touch doing little for Kydd's mood. In the morning the breeze dropped even further, a playful zephyr all that was left. At noon the transport hung out a signal but it was unreadable, the fluky breeze not enough to raise the flags to read them.

As much for something to do, Kydd sent away a boat to investigate. It was back before long and Curzon wasted no time in telling him the news. 'Captain Jevons sends his compliments and believes you should know that because of your extended leg to seaward he will soon be in distress for water.'

Kydd bit back his retort: this was a retired post-captain persuaded to take command of the transport and far senior to himself. No doubt he had underestimated the water needs of the cavalry horses and had now found his excuse.

The nearest watering would be somewhere in Iberia and he would not venture his convoy on such a mission. Gibraltar should be only one or two days' sail or so away – but in this calm? He had no idea how long horses could go without water but guessed it was not a great deal of time. And after seasickness crossing Biscay, the troops would have every incentive to clean themselves up – using their precious drinking water.

In exasperation he ordered the convoy to heave to, a long process with the merchantmen in the light airs strung out all over the ocean. Then it was sweaty heaving for his crew to sway up their last three full leaguers from the hold and lower them into the sea. Fresh water meant that they floated and he left them there wallowing for the transport to grapple and haul in.

'*Deck hoooo!*' The sudden hail from the fore-top took everyone by surprise. 'T' loo'ard – sail an' galleys.'

Suddenly apprehensive, Kydd jumped for the shrouds and stared into the band of pearly haze that was the horizon to the east, the Strait of Gibraltar itself. Then he saw a straggle of small craft, many oared, the lofty sweep of the lateen of a Moorish felucca or some such. There could be only one reason for their presence: word had been passed to Tarifa, or another Spanish nest of corsairs, of a convoy becalmed, ripe for the picking.

Given any kind of workable breeze a frigate would be soon among them to blow them out of the water, but with this – cats-paws prettily darkening the sea in long riffles and disappearing as fast as they came, canvas hanging and slatting aimlessly . . .

The cutter would have oars and the sloop awkward sweeps but, without the agility of the lighter enemy craft, they would easily be evaded. His ships and their valuable cargo would then be picked off one by one. Kydd might soon be known as the captain of a frigate whose entire convoy had been taken right from under his nose by a ragtag swarm of picaroons.

'Mr Oakley – every man you can get in the tops with buckets, the fire-engine with hoses,' he ordered urgently. 'Get those sails wet!'

There was no time for much else; stunsails had long been set and he was ready to try, with the only move he could make, to put himself between the beetling menace and the convoy.

It was hopeless. There was simply a contented gurgling as the helm was put over, long minutes of lazy turning while all the time the threat sharpened into focus. On the transport there were movements of red figures where the soldiers were lining the decks with muskets – but they were in no danger: it was the fat merchantmen they were after.

The cutter and sloop needed no orders – they were already swinging to meet the enemy but they were near helpless in the calm.

'We're makin' way, sir,' Kendall said, with something between surprise and awe. It was true – a small but regular ripple was spreading out from their forefoot. Kydd joined him in looking down the ship's side and tried to estimate – one, two knots?

'Does she answer the helm true?' he threw at the conn. The helmsman wound on four spokes of the wheel. The bowsprit obediently began stepping across and the man spun the helm back, meeting the swing. The bow stopped and came back. They had steerage way.

'Damn it – we've got a chance!' Kydd blurted. But first they had to overhaul the entire convoy from their post at the rear. The race was on.

One by one they slipped past the helpless ships, threading

their way around drifting vessels, *L'Aurore* catching every slight wafting breath of air to urge steadily on. Kydd couldn't keep the smile from his face – this was her true breeding, the ghosting in light airs that he had noticed before. And now it was going to save them all.

Around the deck there were grins and laughter – the spell was lifting. This was a ship a sailor could be proud to be in, one that had the promise of witchery, of feats that could be yarned about for years afterwards.

The Alcestes were starting to change to L'Aurores.

The enemy were suddenly presented with the dismaying picture of a frigate emerging from the crowd of frightened sail, and in the flat calm unaccountably bearing down on them. They huddled together – a fatal mistake, for *L'Aurore* took her time, then slewed about to open with a broadside on the concentrated group.

After the gun-smoke rolling down on their target had cleared it was very apparent they were not about to be troubled any further by the marauders. Making off as fast as they could to avoid the other broadside, they left three wrecks to be dealt with by the cutter, which was gamely trying to keep with *L'Aurore*.

Sensing the mood, Kydd sent word that instead of the other broadside he desired to see of what calibre his gun-captains really were. Until the targets were out of range each gun would have a chance to punish the enemy. With a steady gun-platform and perfect conditions in the mirrored seas, the strike of ball and subsequent skipping were plain, as was a distant flurry when one hit home to savage cheers.

It was valuable practice but even more pleasing was the spirit it was raising in his ship.

*　　*　　*

Once the convoy had arrived safely in Gibraltar and the troops landed, *L'Aurore* was fitted for her main role: the Toulon blockade. For this the watchword was endurance – on station there could be no returning the seven hundred miles for resupply. They must subsist on what they carried, and that included both sea stores and spare parts.

Kydd spent some time with the warrant officers, trying to foresee any situation and whether they would be self-sufficient enough to handle it, using what they carried. With *L'Aurore's* small hold, there was no margin for extras.

The next day she sailed from Rosia Bay with the tidal stream, in a decreasing northerly that Kydd recognised as the tail end of the notorious tramontane, an icy blast from the interior of France. It did, however, enable them to crack on at a pace.

With just three days before they raised Lord Nelson's squadron, Kydd determined to use every hour of it. Gun practice. Sail drill. Signals. From dawn to dusk they slaved, shaving seconds off their times, competing mast against mast, gun against gun – but that was never the point. In the smoke and chaos of action it would be the crew who stayed at their posts, serving their guns and their ship with the confidence of long practice, that would emerge the victors.

On the morning of the third day lookouts were doubled while *L'Aurore* was priddied aloft and alow as though for harbour inspection. According to the rendezvous he had been given, they should raise the battle squadron at midday, *Victory* and near a dozen of-the-line and frigates under easy sail.

As always, the rendezvous was a line of latitude rather than a point, running some fifty miles south of Toulon, but the grey expanse of wind-driven sea was empty in every direction. He ran the line down from one end to the other – nothing.

There was no question of the accuracy of the line and he was sure of their position, so where were they? Had Nelson got word that Villeneuve had sortied and flung his squadron at the French? Somewhere out there the deciding battle of the war might be raging.

Or was the fleet at Malta or another port revictualling? Should he go in chase or stay where he was? If the squadron returned from wherever it was and he was not here . . . He would give it one day . . .

But there was another way. Supposing he went north, closed with Toulon and spied into the port. If the French were still there, all urgency was removed and he could return with an easy heart. If they were out – that was another matter and he would fall back on Gibraltar for orders.

He turned to the master. 'Mr Kendall, we're to look into Toulon.' *L'Aurore* lay to the wind and sailed north in bursts of spray into the short, choppy seas.

Next morning the French coast lifted into view, a hard, darker grey. It was not difficult to make out the low cliffs of Cape Cepet, the protective outlying arm around the great harbour and, behind, the two-thousand-foot Mont Faron, which Napoleon had used to such effect to bombard and recapture the port long ago at the war's beginning.

There was little to show the true situation but Kydd had a map drawn up by Sir Sidney Smith during that dramatic episode and saw that if he stood on past the cape to the far shore the harbour would open up to his left.

He concentrated hard. This would be all too familiar in the months ahead but for now it was the lair of the enemy and had the chill of the unknown about it. After he had joined up he would have access to the accumulated wisdom of years of blockade but at the moment . . .

A low rumble and gun-smoke arose from the cliffs, but Kydd ignored it and pressed on towards the distant shore. Sure enough the harbour opened up to larboard – first the Grande Rade, the Great Roads, where fleets would assemble before sailing. It was deserted but for a single frigate deep within. Then he saw them: a dense-packed forest of bare masts well beyond in the Petite Rade where Villeneuve's fleet were safely packed, secured by the artillery on the heights. They had not sortied.

So where was Nelson? The frigate inside loosened sail and put down its helm, making directly for them. Kydd tensed: to fight or flee? This was the most dangerous location of all, and he had what he needed.

'Take us out, Mr Kendall.'

L'Aurore swung about until she ran before the wind, rolling fitfully and eager for the open sea. The other frigate, however, had expertly cut to the lee of the protecting arm of Cape Cepet and was fast making to intercept them in a fine show of seamanship and local knowledge.

Aware that this was not his ship's most favoured point of sailing, Kydd watched apprehensively as they converged at the low finality of the cape, *L'Aurore* in the lead by barely a quarter-mile.

Then there was the thud of a gun from the pursuing frigate and her colours streamed free. English colours.

A short time later, after an exchange of the private signal of the day, HM Frigate *Seahorse* heaved to and requested the pleasure of the acquaintance of the captain of HMS *L'Aurore*. Soon Kydd was in possession of the knowledge that Nelson's fleet was at that moment in winter quarters, 170 miles to the south-east and expecting him.

Chapter 7

'Dear Uncle,' Bowden wrote, wondering just how he should begin the letter, where to start telling of the cascade of impressions and experiences he had met with since he had joined *Victory*. It was always a good opener, however, to enquire after the health of various family notables and he did so industriously, not omitting Aunt Hester's megrims and Cousin Ann's tooth.

His uncle had taken responsibility for Bowden's upbringing after his father's death. He was a very senior captain and needed no lessons in naval strategy but here was a singular thing to pique his interest: Lord Nelson's hideaway for his fleet. Not for them the ceaseless battering by weather: the French would never put to sea in a storm, which left Nelson's ships to take welcome refuge among the sheltering islands here in La Maddelena in the very north of Sardinia. Only a day's sail from before Toulon, they were at anchor in perfect tranquillity and refitting after the winter's blows.

It is, Uncle, a species of secret base just a few leagues from the French where we recruit our strength and fettle our poor ships. It's the wonder of all that when the squadron stands down from its watching and returns to its lair, here is found waiting fresh beef, sea stores enough to delight our stout boatswain's heart and a regular mail from home.

It was discovered by *Agincourt* in the year '02, and so we call it Agincourt Sound. It's perfect for us. The native inhabitants are few and barbarous, the land mountainous and uncongenial so we're left to ourselves in as fine a harbour as ever I saw.

Just how secret the location was he wasn't sure so he did not specify it in case the mail was captured.

The Gulf of Genoa in winter I find disagreeable to a degree. Clammy fogs, calms, a heavy swell. I'd as soon take the tramontane blasts of Toulon than that misery.

His uncle, though, would not take kindly to complaints about sea conditions so he quickly turned to other matters:

I have a particular friend, he is Richard Bulkeley who messes with me in the gunroom. He's an American midshipman, his father was with Nelson when they were young officers in Nicaragua. He's a wag at dinner and a sharp hand at cards, knows tricks that have us in a roar. He's made Captain Hardy's aide, so you may believe he's a bright fellow.

Bowden paused in his writing. Thomas Masterman Hardy, a tall, disciplined officer, was a fearful figure for any midshipman.

And I've been taken up by Lieutenant Pasco to serve with him at signals.'

His uncle would know by this that he'd done well to achieve a post of such distinction – signals in a flagship were crucial in action and he would, of course, be witness to any battle as well as having privileged knowledge of what passed between the commander-in-chief and his fleet.

He comes from before the mast, as does the first lieutenant, Mr Quilliam, who takes fools not at all gladly. He's a fine fighting record and was called by Nelson to join him in *Victory* in '03.

Should he mention Mr Atkinson, the kindly sailing master who had been at the Nile and Copenhagen both and was likewise called for by Nelson? Or Mr Bunce, the jovial carpenter who never tired of proudly telling that Nelson had once described him as 'a man for whose abilities and good conduct I would pledge my head'?

Others – the dapper Captain Adair of the Royal Marines, who could be seen with his men at fife and drum, parading on the quarterdeck every evening; the well-read gunner, Rivers, who had once been ashore in an artillery duel with Napoleon, or even Scott, the scholarly chaplain, who, it was said, was privy to more secrets even than the ship's captain.

But, dear Uncle, the one whom we all revere, who has our hearts and devotion, he can only be our Nelson!

How to express the thrill of being addressed by the great admiral, the most famous of the age, in a manner that suggested his reply was considered of significance? To be part of a brotherhood of trust and honour that raised one to a higher plane that made defeat an impossibility, to know an expectation of courage and ardour in battle was shared by every man in the fleet!

Struggling for words he finished,

And *Victory*, this indomitable ark! She's a famous sailer on a bowline, and many's the time we've thrown out a signal bidding the fleet keep with us, to their mortification.

He sat back, the guttering lamp casting shadows about the quiet gunroom, others like him taking the opportunity to finish letters to home and family before the mail closed. Soon – everyone said it – there would be a grand battle that would decide the fate of nations. What would happen? What would it be like?

Oh, and P.S. Who do you think came aboard, captain of *L'Aurore* frigate? It was Mr Kydd, Uncle! Made post after his gallant action that lost him dear old *Teazer*. He was civil enough to notice me before he left . . .

Before the smoke from their salute had cleared Kydd's barge was in the water, stroking smartly for the stately bulk of the flagship of commander-in-chief Mediterranean, Vice Admiral Lord Nelson. In it was the captain of HMS *L'Aurore* in full-dress uniform to call upon him and receive his orders.

Poulden growled, 'Oars!' and the barge slowed to kiss the fat sides of *Victory* precisely at the side-steps. Kydd addressed himself to the task of mounting the side in a manner befitting the full majesty of a post-captain.

Pipes pealed out above him and he heard distant shouts from a Royal Marine guard brought to attention. It came to the present with a crash as he passed into the ornamented entry port and Kydd's heart was full.

Then came an impression of unimaginable size, sudden gloom after the open sky, the double line of the side-party – and at the inboard end among other officers a slight figure in gold lace, decorated with four stars, who advanced on him with a charming smile. Kydd snatched off his hat and bowed.

'Welcome aboard, sir! And it's a right welcome sight you and your ship are too, Captain,' Nelson said, with disarming warmth. 'We shall take a sherry together and be damned to the hour!'

'I'd be honoured, sir,' was all Kydd could find to say.

The admiral's day cabin was vast and, with the spread of stern windows right across, as light and airy as a country house. 'Dry, Mr Kydd?'

'Oh, er – yes, my lord,' Kydd stuttered, at the last moment realising his host was referring to the sherry.

They found chairs and raised glasses to each other. 'It must be . . . Was it not at our council of war in 'ninety-eight before the Nile when last we spoke? When we lost the French before we found 'em again in Aboukir Bay?' It would never be forgotten by Kydd, who murmured a polite agreement.

'Frigates! I *must* have frigates!' Nelson went on harshly, the charm suddenly replaced by deadly seriousness. 'If we'd had even a handful of 'em about me that day we would have taken Bonaparte at sea alive and the world a better place!'

'Sir.'

There was no doubt where this conversation was leading, but equally swiftly the hard glint softened and, almost gaily, Nelson added, 'Yet it must be accounted that if de Brueys had any notion of the employment of frigates he would have had them ranging seaward, not at moorings in the bay. We'd then find a very different reception waiting, don't you think?'

'Which would rob us of the completest victory that ever was!' Kydd replied stoutly.

'Quite!' Nelson said, and relaxed into his armchair, fixing Kydd with his one sound eye. 'Tell me, what is your understanding of the duties of a frigate, sir?'

'Why, in a grand action o' fleets they are to—'

'The least of their duties, Mr Kydd, as your battle orders will attest. And?'

'Um, protection of our trade, cruising against the enemy's, scouting ahead o' the fleet at sea, er, carriage of important dispatches and persons as must be trusted to make port, and, er—'

'Which do you conceive to be the most important, sir?'

'In course, intelligence of the enemy, sir.' He had remembered the hellish tensions before the Nile.

'Exactly, Mr Kydd. To this end you will be bold, ruthless, cunning, and spare nothing to get to your commander-in-chief the intelligence he most fervently desires. Neither vainglory nor considerations of honour must tempt you to stand where a prudent withdrawal will thereby secure me knowledge of the enemy's motions.'

'I understand, my lord.'

'Then understand also why we are before Toulon.'

'The blockade, sir?' Kydd said, puzzled.

'Do you term it so? When our sail-o'-the-line are fifty miles to the south and entirely out of their sight and knowledge? My hope and prayer is that Mr Villeneuve will feel emboldened enough to sally, seeing no English battleships in the

167

offing. Toulon is the very devil to blockade, the high ground at their backs giving them sight of our ships for leagues.'

'Yes, sir. I was l'tenant in *Tenacious* 64 off Toulon before the peace.'

'So now you are in a frigate as will close with the port like a terrier at a rat-hole, letting nothing move except you shall report it.'

'Sir.'

'Lay salt on their tail, entice 'em out for an easy victory!'

'I will, sir.'

'Very well.' He put down his glass, the sherry hardly touched. 'I shall see you provided with your pennant number for the signal books. My orders are specified in the Public Order Book and the captain of the fleet will acquaint you with our way of maintaining this squadron. Now, *L'Aurore* – your usual Frenchy frigate does not shine in sea-keeping, her hold space so meagre. Are you in want of any material at all?'

'No, sir.'

'Good. A first-rate place for a fleet, Agincourt Sound, do you not think? Malta is not to be countenanced, even if it has the dockyards, it being so ridiculously distant. Gibraltar cannot sustain a fleet of size, all supplies must needs come out from England, and I'll be damned if I can feel free to move, always under a Spaniard's eyes. Here we can supply ourselves privily, wood and water when we please, but at a cost.'

'A cost, sir?'

'Yes. Sardinia is neutral, but Vittorio Emanuele – who is King of Piedmont and rules through his brother the Duke of Genoa here in Cagliari – must by all means be flattered and caressed that he allows us our discreet anchoring.'

'Sir,' Kydd said, daring a comment, 'if Sardinia is neutral, would not his actions provoke Bonaparte?'

'Quite. However, the French were obliging enough once to threaten an assault on this island. I have undertaken to His Majesty in that event to place my fleet before the invaders, which has concentrated his mind wonderfully on our modest request.'

Kydd glowed. That he was now at an elevation to share confidences with the commander-in-chief, Admiral Lord Nelson!

'You'll want to return to your ship, Mr Kydd. Pray do not delay on my account.'

'Aye aye, sir.'

Nelson's features eased for a moment. 'And now you are made post – a remarkable elevation for one with so little interest to call upon. Do rejoice, sir, in your fortune while I will know I may always rely on your devotion to duty.'

'Th-thank you, my lord,' Kydd replied, inwardly exulting at this proof of to whom he owed his advancement.

'Your orders will be sent across presently. Good day to you, sir.'

'Nicholas, it was the damnedest thing to be talking away to my commander-in-chief and he the hero of the hour,' Kydd declared, recalling the moment with wonder. 'Spoke to me about how to deal with the King of Piedmont and why he chose La Maddalena and things. I'm to study my orders diligently, I believe.'

They were concise, strong-worded and very clear. When ready for sea, *L'Aurore* was to relieve *Seahorse* off Toulon. Conduct of frigate surveillance operations was detailed. There were to be at least two on station such that if the enemy sailed one would keep with them while the other would bring back word; Kydd would find *Active* waiting.

They would keep close with the port, with the dual object of ensuring no movements would be missed and offering themselves as tempting bait. In as wide a region as the Mediterranean there were, of course, other fleet rendezvous specified. Each would be referred to only by a code number but the main alternative to Toulon was at the south tip of Sardinia, perfectly astride the main east–west sea passage from Gibraltar to the Middle East.

There were extensive sections on signals: to a frigate bearing urgent news it was vital the meaning was clear. To this end not only the familiar signal book was to be employed but the new Popham telegraph code was to be adopted with its near infinite number of messages possible.

Further orders covered such mundane matters as the manner of victualling ship, observations on the health of seamen and the importance of weekly accounts. Nothing was left to chance and the overriding impression Kydd had was of swelling detail, all of which was a tribute to the care and worry the commander-in-chief was bringing to his task.

L'Aurore sailed for Toulon the next day in the teeth of yet another hard nor'-wester, her captain under no illusions as to the importance of his tasking. Bucking and plunging by long boards north through misty rain, they raised the darker band of the French coast in the early afternoon and by evening were off the Îles d'Hyères at the eastern reaches of the port.

Standing off and on through the hours of darkness, they sighted *Active* in the morning, cruising perilously close inshore. The two drew together and through a speaking trumpet Kydd was told that *Seahorse* would be found to the westward as the two endlessly criss-crossed in the offing, and that it might be prudent to shorten sail in the blow that was coming.

Then they were on their own: somewhere they would pass *Seahorse* but for the rest it was eagle-eyed vigilance in the worst weather, and all responsibility for keeping the enemy under watch. What if he suddenly spotted the regular procession of the enemy leaving? Did he go looking for *Seahorse* or instantly clap on all sail for Nelson – and thereby lose the vital knowledge of where the French were headed? It was a desperate worry, for Kydd knew that it was within his power to lose the battle for Nelson if he decided wrongly.

L'Aurore gave a sickening wallow to leeward, ending in a teeth-jarring crunch as a wave surged and exploded against her hull, sending sheets of ice-cold spray over the sodden watch.

A rounded and stern headland loomed darkly out of the driving rain. This must be Cape Bénat, as far east as he need go; beyond, the coast trended north-east, past the old wine port of St Tropez to Cannes, Monaco and the rest to the Italian border.

'Hands to wear ship!' In this bluster there was no need to stress spars and rigging by staying about and *L'Aurore* eased around to lie on the starboard tack for the long wet haul west back past Toulon. When they cleared the last of the Îles d'Hyères for the open sea, Kydd left the deck. At least this was not a continual, wearing lee shore, as Brest was, where a mishap with a mast or spar carrying away threatened headlong destruction on the bleak granite coast.

He pulled off his streaming foul-weather gear, grateful that he had ignored Tysoe's disapproval of his comfortable old grego, wedged himself into his chair and went over his orders once more. His duty was clear and, as far as signals went, he had every confidence in the master's mate Saxton, who had taken away the Popham to 'get it by heart'.

The real problem would be when—

There was confused shouting above and he snapped alert. Grabbing his grego, he found the companionway and swung up on deck to see Curzon talking urgently to Howlett and pointing off the bow. A hail came from the fore-top lookout and then he spotted a close-packed gaggle of sail emerging from the murk.

With a lurch of the heart he saw that these were no trivial coasters, or even frigates, but vessels displaying the ominous bulk of ships-of-the-line. Was this a feint, a sudden excursion to sea to exercise Villeneuve's fleet? Or the real thing – a mass sailing of the battleships in Toulon to outnumber and overwhelm Nelson?

L'Aurore heaved to in front of the advancing sail, and waited. Then the stream of ships parted and the larger division formed up in the outer roads in a massive show. Telescopes went up feverishly as yet more crowded out into the bay.

The time for decision was fast approaching: should Kydd follow or peel off to inform? A sharp-eyed youngster excitedly pointed out an admiral's pennant flying on a large eighty-gun vessel. There was now little doubt that this was a major eruption of force, which could well be the historic first move in Napoleon's grand invasion plan – and he *must* act!

But then Kydd saw what the smaller division was doing: while the main force was assembling in the Great Roads of Toulon it was continuing on in a wide pincer movement, led by a lone frigate leaning hard into the wind.

He quickly realised what it meant. They were a body of warships designed to brush aside the watchers to ensure that the main fleet made the open ocean and disappeared into it without trace. Without doubt now, this was the act for which Nelson had been yearning – a mighty clash of arms on the high seas that would decide the issue once and for all.

He forced his mind to a ferocious clarity. No matter the forces sent against him, his duty was to stay with the main fleet and dog their movements until it was known where they were headed.

The pincer sweep was beginning to reach out to them. Kydd raised his glass to the frigate out on its own ahead of them and saw it was *Seahorse*. In a trice matters had changed: virtually every post-captain was senior to Kydd, and if decisions were to be made they would be those of the captain of *Seahorse*.

Not sure whether to be relieved or sorry, he bore away to split the pursuers between them and shortly afterwards *L'Aurore* was signalled, 'Enemy in sight', followed by 'Conform to my movements'. Kydd saw that *Seahorse* was thrashing out along the coast to the eastwards under full sail, leading her pursuers at right angles to the course the main body must take to reach the open sea.

Realising the intent, he obediently braced in and *L'Aurore* made off to the westwards, further splitting the pack. The enemy commander must now choose which English frigate to drive after, at the risk of losing the main fleet in the worsening visibility, or return to stay with Villeneuve.

The distant *Seahorse* vanished momentarily into a rain squall, reappeared and then was lost completely. The pursuers between widened the separation while the rest of the main fleet streamed out, quickly swallowed up in driving rain-squalls.

Kydd understood what was being done and when the enemy abandoned their chase *L'Aurore* shaped course southwards on the long side of a triangle that would see them converging on both *Seahorse* and the enemy fleet.

In any other circumstances it would have been exhilarating work, for *L'Aurore* was probably the fastest ship on the scene, but this was in deadly earnest – and the north-north-westerly that was making the breakout possible meant the wind was astern, and this was not her best point of sailing. In fact, for sea-keeping it had to be her worst.

The motion was appalling. A vicious barrelling roll had all hands grabbing for support and the wrenching movement, coupled with a harsh pitching into the backs of rollers, was deeply unsettling.

In just an hour or two's sailing, however, the rear ships of Villeneuve's fleet became visible. Kydd smiled in grim satisfaction. They had been right – the French admiral had not risked evasive manoeuvres and had headed straight out to sea, hoping to lose himself before the English frigates found him again.

And now the biggest question of all was about to be answered. Would Villeneuve head west towards Gibraltar to join up with the Spanish in Cadiz before storming for the Channel to fulfil Bonaparte's destiny, or would he go east, to fall on Naples or even Alexandria in vengeful answer to the humiliation of the Nile?

Kydd hung on doggedly as the frigate rolled and bucketed crazily, knowing that the fate of England lay in his hands. There was no variation in Villeneuve's stubborn southward course, however, and soon *Seahorse* came up with him, lessening the frightful chance of losing the French.

The frigate eased up with him and the two pitched and heaved together. The figure of her captain lifted up a speaking trumpet. '*We – staaay – until we – knooow!*' he blared.

There was no need for discussion and Kydd acknowledged with a wave. The two frigates parted to take station on either quarter of the fleet; with wind astern they could deploy as they chose.

Another hour passed with no move to either east or west. Conditions were worsening to a fresh gale, wave-crests torn to spindrift and eyes reddening at the continual spray sheeting across. *L'Aurore* staggered now, the French barely in sight and *Seahorse* out on the beam taking punishment.

Kydd did what he could, rolling tackles to check the strain on plunging spars, preventers rigged – if anything carried away it would cost them more than the ship. The hours passed: no change. Day was turning into evening and then it would be the nightmare of a chase in darkness.

There was only one thing that they could do: stay closer – whatever it took, stay with them.

It seemed *Seahorse* was of the same mind and the two frigates closed in astern just as night lanthorns appeared in the tops of the enemy battleships, their betraying light a penalty for keeping the fleet together in darkness.

Three horizontal lights flickered and stayed in the main-top of *Seahorse*. Kydd did the same. The light faded and the storm-ridden night began, the white combers charging out of the blackness adding to the violence of the scene – but this was the critical time, the darkness when Villeneuve would surely douse the lanthorns and slip away on his planned course.

Another hour. The same southerly course. Hours more. It was inexplicable – why no move? Kydd was wet, chilled to the heart, but nothing would take him from the quarterdeck at that time.

The watch changed, clawing their way along the life-lines now rigged along the main-deck.

175

Midnight and still nothing.

A short time later there was a perceptible wan lightening of the violent seascape; an invisible moon rising above the storm wrack, which must have been known to Villeneuve. Now it was too late for him: he could no longer disappear into an ink-black night. Why?

The tempest was reaching its peak and Kydd knew that *L'Aurore* was now near her limit. They would soon have to take the agonising decision to break off and, in the face of desperate need, abandon the pursuit to carry their vital news to Nelson.

Another frantic hour went by and then, at about two, a blue flare sputtered on *Seahorse*. As he watched, the three lights in her main-top moved into line as she swung away to larboard.

Unbelieving, Kydd saw the frigate haul her wind for the south-east and begin to diverge, clearly intent on leaving, the blue light to draw *L'Aurore* away too. He flogged his tired and frozen brain to think why this should be so.

Then he had it. Well south by now, they must have passed to the westward of Corsica and Villeneuve was therefore blocked from a rapid move down Italy. Similarly, on this southward course they had missed the chance of a rapid passage to the west of the Balearics and on to Gibraltar. Whether in fear of constricted waters in this blow or for other reasons, Villeneuve was on his way to the grand cross-ways of the Mediterranean between Sardinia and North Africa and, if told in time, Nelson had a chance.

L'Aurore's helm spun over and she sheeted in for the south-east, falling in astern of *Seahorse*. Now, steadied by her sails and on a quartering reach, she came into her own and in the wild night the two frigates stretched away for Agincourt

Sound, the smaller quickly taking the lead and putting distance between her and *Seahorse*.

Kydd was in the race of his life to be the one to tell Nelson that the French were out.

L'Aurore flew into Agincourt Sound, signal guns cracking, and in a thunderous flogging of canvas rounding to at the flagship. Kydd's boat was in the water instantly, her crew stretching out heroically. He bounded up the side of *Victory* to be met at the top by the grim-faced commander-in-chief himself.

'The French are at sea, m' lord!' Kydd said immediately.

'My cabin,' Nelson snapped. It took minutes only to impart the gist of what had happened and just seconds for the order 'All captains' to be passed, followed instantly by 'Fleet will unmoor'. A gun crashed out to add urgency to the order.

One by one captains whose names were known even beyond the Navy arrived without ceremony and were welcomed gravely by Nelson. Keats of *Superb*, Pellew of *Conqueror*, Hallowell of *Tigre* – men whose deeds were the stuff of legend, all fighting captains who would be the edge of the blade Nelson would wield in the cataclysm to come.

What was known was that the French were out; what was not was where they were bound. Nelson was brief and passionate: 'It is essential to the nation to find, meet and destroy the Toulon armament before they have chance to join with the Spaniards in an unstoppable force.

'From Captain Kydd's hard-gotten information we know they're progressing down the west coast of Sardinia in a fresh blow under shortened sail. We have a chance! I desire that the fleet weighs immediately. Under full sail in the lee of the gale, we stand south on the *east* side of Sardinia. Gentlemen, the rendezvous is at its south tip, the Gulf of Palma. There the two fleets will converge and by God's good grace we shall return to England with news of a great victory.'

There were dutiful murmurs from the hard-faced men around the table who clearly needed no goading to action. 'Then I do wish you all good fortune in the engagement to come. The frigate captains to remain, I shall not detain you further.'

When Boyle of *Seahorse* had breathlessly joined them Nelson issued his orders. The frigates were to range ahead, to instantly fall back on the squadron when the enemy was sighted. Every ship, friendly or neutral, was to be stopped and questioned; all conceivable opportunities for intelligence were to be ruthlessly pursued. At all costs the French would be tracked down and the fleets brought into contact – this was their sole and only duty.

'*Phoebe* will sail west-about through Bonifacio strait, the others will scout ahead of the fleet. I'm to bring the French to battle in hours, I believe.'

In the dying storm *L'Aurore* was first to sea. Once clear of Cape Ferro the frigates took up a scouting line, each on the horizon to the next, with the four abreast able to comb sixty miles of sea. With specific signals designed for distant operation, intelligence of the presence of an enemy could reach *Victory* in minutes and the long-sought battle brought about.

With Villeneuve's topsails about to rise above the white-tossed line of the horizon at any moment, there was no alternative but to stand to, guns manned and ready. For Kydd's ship's company, keyed up for hours, it was nerve-racking and exhausting, but there was now no question that *L'Aurore* had found her spirit and would give of her best.

Nelson's fleet reached south as night fell, but there could be no ceasing of vigilance. When found, the lights of the enemy would be close and in Kydd's orders were provisions for the waging of war at night, a frightful hazard on the open sea. The men slept at the guns as, no doubt, was the case in *Victory* and the rest of the fleet, waiting for what the dawn would bring.

They found a clear sea, empty – even the fishermen had stayed snug in harbour in the keen winds that were the last of the tramontane. And this was now the southern tip of Sardinia; they had made good speed and there was every prospect that when they swept around past the steep rocky bluff of Cape Spartivento they would be in sight of Villeneuve's fleet coming down the west side.

The line of frigates re-formed and they moved out ahead – until the rendezvous at the south tip was reached. They could go no further and the French had not been sighted. Until they had further orders the search must stop.

'Dear Uncle,' Bowden began, and hesitated. How to convey the hours and days of fearful excitement just past? Begin at the beginning – *L'Aurore* frigate flying into Agincourt Sound, Captain Kydd coming instantly aboard to set the ship in a fever of elation. Their putting to sea within less than two hours, a masterpiece of fleet planning and execution, then flying before the gale into the night, the men at their guns primed for instant action, the cold dawn – and no French.

Conceive of it, Uncle. In all expectation of the enemy there were none! We heaved to at the rendezvous and a council of war was made and I cannot begin to imagine our noble hero's fret of mind at losing Villeneuve. Should he choose in the wrong, the world will condemn him as a looby and we are lost.

His uncle would have little patience with the energetic opinions of the gunroom, and as, to a lowly midshipman, higher strategies were not within reach, he contented himself with the facts.

His lordship then decided on the east, believing the French were up to mischief among the Ionians, or Boney still has his heart set on Alexandria and a passage to India.

So we set our bowsprit to the dawn and a thousand miles later we discovered no Frenchies worth a shot. This vexed us extremely as we had then to accept we were in error and they had descended on Cartagena and Gibraltar, and while we chased porpoises off Egypt, Villeneuve was joining with the Spanish in Cadiz for a descent on England.

He wrote lightly but the alternative – to tell of the anguish in every breast, the dread of what they would later find – was not what an officer of the Navy would describe to another. But one image was sure to stay in his memory for ever:

To see our little admiral, standing alone with his thoughts on our quarterdeck would wring the hardest heart but, Uncle, never is he cast down. I can but stand in admiration of him always.

And then the shocking truth waiting for them at Malta:

You may believe we stretched away under a press of sail back westwards until we called at Malta to revictual. And while we were in Valletta an *aviso* from Naples waited upon us with our first firm news of the French, which set fair to strike us speechless.

He sat back in his chair, reliving the consternation it had caused.

It was said that Villeneuve pressed south, as we know, but at the gale's fervour he put about and crept back to where he started. So, you see, we were chasing an enemy that never was, and here we are on Toulon blockade once more!

Renzi sat at Kydd's grand secretaire idly doodling, trying to coax as many words as was possible from 'ethnographical' and in a black mood. Here he was, with every convenience at hand to wait upon the throes of creativity, and he was becalmed in the doldrums of the imagination, the *fons et origo* of fertile originality perfectly empty.

Even a pristine Herder, the 'Humanität' letters, lay open and unread, for how could he conjure structured thought when so distracted? It had hit him hard that he had been so naïve as to imagine one simply handed a manuscript to a publisher to see it later as a treasured book.

Now it seemed less and less likely that he would ever find his conjectures discussed by the world, talked over by the literati – and this tore at the very heart of the bargain that Kydd and he had struck on that inconceivably remote shore in Van Diemen's Land. His friend had said he would provide lodging and sustenance aboard ship for the very purpose of affording him the space and time he needed to produce his *magnum opus*. If it was never going to see the light of day, then just what was he doing aboard *L'Aurore*?

Kydd's courage and skill had seen him advance in the sea service to the highest ranks entirely by his own qualities and talent and he seemed set fair to go further. Would he feel his kindness was wasted on a scholar dead in the water, no future course charted? It would become evident soon and then . . . Perhaps he should leave quietly, now, while he was still held in some regard.

And Cecilia? His ardent feelings for her still remained but the most honourable course would be to withdraw. He was sensible that she held a tender affection for him but, like Kydd, she was destined for higher things and would make a dazzling wife for a rising man of business in the City. A catch in his throat turned to a spreading grey desolation.

Could he still snatch at success with a fortunate engagement and prize money? He could then lay out the guineas that would pay for the printing and see his book at last in his hands. But he knew now how it worked. Without a worldly editor to polish and render his prose into a round, acceptable public style, and the tracery of connections to cry up the book in literary circles that would have them besieging the booksellers to stock his work, he might as well hawk it to passers-by for a pittance on a street corner.

In despair he reached for paper and began a letter to Cecilia.

'Ho, there, Nicholas!' Kydd hailed as he entered, shaking water over the deck and allowing Tysoe to divest him of his boat-cloak. 'I pray I'm not interrupting.'

Renzi hurriedly folded the paper and slipped it into his waistcoat. 'Why, nothing of consequence, dear fellow. You took boat for *Seahorse*?'

'I did. And a rousing good time I had too. A most obliging officer, Courtenay Boyle. We talked the best part of the first remove over what Our Nel expects from his frigate captains, and damned enlightening it was as well.'

'Do tell me, Tom,' Renzi said, as warmly as he could muster.

'Not now,' Kydd said, taking off his buckled shoes for sensible shipboard pumps. 'Er, Nicholas, I'd like a little talk with you – at your convenience, of course.'

Renzi noticed uneasily that he was avoiding his eye. 'Why, of course, brother. Er, what is it?'

Kydd flashed him a speculative look, then busied himself arranging papers on the table. 'Um, it's to be concerning your continued presence aboard.'

Alarmed, Renzi answered noncommittally, 'I'm sure I've the time to talk with my particular friend.' Was it that Kydd had been told of the workload to be expected of one of Nelson's frigates in a great fleet action and felt the need for a more . . . practical aide, perhaps more focused? Or was it simply that he'd been ordered to remove superfluous members of his ship's company before the expected major engagement? Either way—

Kydd dismissed Tysoe, then turned to Renzi. 'Nicholas. How are your studies? That is to say, may it be said you are happy aboard *L'Aurore*?'

There was more than a tinge of circumspection in his tone and Renzi's dismay grew. 'Er, yes.'

'Good.' He turned and stiffly assumed his armchair. 'It's – it's that I have to speak to you about your situation.'

'Oh.'

'When I spoke with Boyle we didn't merely touch on signals and manoeuvres. Not at all – this is Lord Nelson's own squadron as is known to be a fighting Tartar. His expectations are far above your common run of admirals and I own it would grieve me sorely to fall short in such wise.'

'Quite.'

'And it was opened to me that in the Med these do include duties not to be thought of in a Channel man-o'-war. In fine, Nicholas, he's acting the potentate, talking with princes and kings and deciding great matters as if he was Pitt himself – it taking so long to get a reply back from Whitehall.'

'Er, yes, I see.'

'Do you? He's a mort of worry on his mind, not just the fitness of our ships for battle but if Johnny Turk is still friends with the Albanians, that sort of thing.'

'Dear fellow – I thought we were talking about my place in—'

'Nicholas. I'm getting to it.' Kydd went on: 'He can't make his decisions without he has news and information, true facts as are not false rumour. For this he must rely on friends in foreign places, details from our consuls, neutral ships, merchants – anyone who can make report on the motions of the French.'

He paused significantly. 'In this, however, he's possessed of a splendid right hand, one who speaks the lingo, is not shy of a puzzle, can construe the meaning in what's found in a prize, will step ashore and brace the local pasha and steers small around a delicate situation when he sees one.'

'Who—'

'*Victory*'s chaplain.' Kydd paused. 'And Nelson's confidential secretary.'

'Ah.'

'An amazing cove, apparently. A gentleman o' letters, he's close to His Nibs and is privy to every matter of confidence and delicacy. Including that of intelligence.'

'Are you saying by this that you wish me to extend my role into that of—'

'Never! How can you think it? Nicholas, I know well how you abhor spying and so forth. No – that will never do!'

'Then?'

'My dear chap, the getting of intelligence is quite at a distance from spying, being as it is the noting of facts merely, the gathering of opinions and observations. You see, in this we frigates who are far-ranging up and down the Med are best placed of all to collect together morsels to present to our commander.

'What would be of prime service to me, Nicholas, is if you're able to turn your headpiece to how *L'Aurore* can pull her weight before Nelson in all this. If when we touch at a port you go ashore and put your ear to the ground, if you take my meaning. Buy a newspaper and see what's in it, help me persuade a Bey to his duty with iron words in honey, um, as we might say.'

Renzi was speechless with relief. Now he would have definite purpose and meaning in his life while he pondered the future. Naturally, he should first acquire a thorough grounding in the tortuous political currents in the Levant before even—

'That is, if it does not incommode your studies, Nicholas,' Kydd added anxiously.

'My dear chap, if you deem it of value to our functioning here, then you may rely upon my duty in the matter.'

Kydd beamed.

L'Aurore's orders arrived as they completed storing. And, true to his practice, the commander-in-chief had rotated *L'Aurore* away from the tedium of blockade for fresh tasking. 'So it's to be the Adriatic,' Kydd mused, as he finished absorbing the terse, vigorous instructions.

'Venice?' said Renzi, curiously.

'We go a-roaming. Trade protection our cardinal charge.'

'Convoys.'

'It would appear, but not neglecting any opportunity to distress the enemy wheresoever and so on. Now, here's a rum business, Nicholas. We're required first to make our number with a Russian cove on Corfu – I didn't know there were any in these parts.'

'For what it's worth, old trout, here's the fruit of my reading, insubstantial as it is. Corfu is the chiefest of the Ionian Islands, seven that belonged to the Venetians since olden times and of high value – they were the only part of Greece to hold out against the Ottomans. With Mr Bonaparte's seizing of Venice he thereby acquired them for their same strategic significance, but now the Ottoman Turks are our friends.'

'And the Russians?'

'Not so mysterious. Tsar Paul took against the French in 1798 after the Nile and sent Admiral Ushakov to assist our Nelson. He did so most nobly by ejecting Napoleon and his friends from the Ionians, which he then garrisoned for himself.'

'So we—'

'But the Tsar turned again, this time against us in armed neutrality in 1801. Not for nothing was he called the "Mad Tsar", I believe.'

'Oh.'

'And he was assassinated by his drunken officers not long after. We honour his son Alexander – who was present in the palace at the time – as the Tsar today. It might be said that he's a friend to England but in this we have to accept that these same Russians are known to covet the Morea, in which the French do intrigue for the same end.'

'The Morea?'

'A large island at the end of Greece, also known as the Peloponnesus,' Renzi said. 'While it may be of inestimable value in strategical terms it's nevertheless the sovereign territory of our allies the Ottomans.'

Kydd's brow furrowed. 'I do recall that when we took Malta from the French after the Nile we were supposed to hand it on to the Grand Master of the Knights of St John – and he your friend Tsar Paul. They were much miffed when we were hailed by the Maltese instead. I've a notion I shall need to watch my luff while there.'

'Indeed. Remembering, too, that it could be said Malta owes its continued existence to the grain fleet from Odessa, which the Russians could cut at a whim.'

'But I can see now that Nelson must rely on the Russians to make a presence in these waters to discourage the French from eastern adventures. Is this why we went east-about in the late alarm, they not altogether trusted to be staunch in this, I wonder?'

'No doubt.'

Kydd sighed. 'A carefree life on the bounding main is for me quite past, it seems. A frigate captain needs to hoist in a gallows sight more than how to reckon his position. Lend me some of your books, Nicholas, and let's see what we can make o' this'n.'

In the wan glitter of the enfolding calm of Corfu Roads HMS *L'Aurore* picked her way delicately past the two 74s and five heavy frigates displaying the blue diagonal on white of Imperial Russia, and dropped anchor.

While her thirteen-gun salute thudded out in respect to the commodore's pennant at the main of the largest, Kydd saw the low white Mediterranean sprawl flying the two-headed eagle standard of the Tsar. He nervously twitched his full-dress uniform into obedience, anxious to adhere scrupulously to the protocol attending the meeting of two powers.

His barge was swung out but remained suspended, the minutes ticking by. Then the thump of an answering salute began from the Russian flagship. The gunner, Redmond, importantly noted their number with a nod to each, then reported to Kydd.

Precisely the same had been returned. The next act was for his boat to be lowered and manned. In dignified motions he descended the side and boarded, an ensign instantly whipping up the little staff on the transom. 'Give way,' Kydd murmured.

Poulden crisply gave the orders that had the boat's crew pulling strongly for the shore. Damn it, Kydd thought, just as soon as he could he'd have them in some sort of uniform jacket and suchlike, even if he must pay for it himself.

'Eyes in the boat!' snapped Poulden, as some of the rowers gaped at the alien ships. Kydd kept rigidly facing forward, wishing that he'd been granted the mercy of a boat-cloak against the keen Adriatic wind but, of course, his uniform in all its splendour must be seen from the shore.

'Hold water st'b'd – oars.' The boat glided in to the jetty steps, Kydd conscious of the two rows of glittering soldiery drawn up and waiting above.

'Toss y'r oars!' Simultaneously every oar was smacked into a knee and brought vertical. With a flick of the tiller, Poulden had the boat alongside.

Kydd mounted the steps with his sword clutched loosely. When he reached the top, an incomprehensible order was screamed and the soldiers flourished and stamped. He duly raised his cocked hat and was saluted by a nervous young subaltern with an enormous silver sabre.

A carriage whisked him up through the immaculate gardens to the white building. In the entrance portico there were two men. The older, with a red sash and swirling moustache, Kydd assumed was the Russian governor.

The other had a dark Mediterranean intensity and introduced himself quietly. 'Spiridion Foresti, Captain, British resident minister – consul, if you will.' His English was barely accented.

'You are new to the Adriatic? You see, it is more usual in these matters to send first a discreet representative to acquaint the local power of your name, your quality . . . and other concerns such that a proper receiving may be effected.'

Kydd flushed. 'Captain Thomas Kydd, His Britannic Majesty's Frigate *L'Aurore* of thirty-two guns.' This was urbanely relayed while he swept low in a courtly bow.

'Sir, this is Comte Mocenigo, minister and plenipotentiary for His Imperial Majesty Tsar Alexander, by the Grace of God, Emperor and Autocrat of all the Russias, Tsar of Poland and so forth.'

The count gave a short bow and growled a sentence at Foresti. 'Sir, the Comte wishes to indicate his sensibility of the honour of a visit by a vessel bearing the flag of Lord Nelson.

'He's mortified to confess that a banquet of the usual form will not be possible in the circumstances.'

Kydd bowed again, then discovered that a modest reception in the evening for his officers was to be expected.

'I should be honoured to attend, sir,' he said graciously. The Russian nodded, then disappeared into the residence.

Foresti turned to Kydd. 'Captain, I think you and I should talk together. Your ship?'

Foresti sat in a frigid silence as they were rowed out to *L'Aurore* but clearly knew enough of naval etiquette to allow Kydd to leave the boat first to be piped aboard before he himself was escorted in.

In Kydd's great cabin Foresti ignored the grand appointments and waved aside Tysoe's offer of refreshments. He looked pointedly at Renzi.

'My confidential secretary of some years, Mr Renzi,' Kydd said firmly. 'His learning and linguistic accomplishments have been remarked at the highest level in England.'

'Renzi? You have the Italian?'

'*Si, abbastanza bene.*'

'And your Greek?'

'*Ίσως λίγο από τις παλαιότερες ελληνικές,*' Renzi added modestly.

'In the Ionians,' Foresti remarked acidly, 'your classical parlance is as donkey dung, sir.' He looked intently at Kydd. 'I come to beg that you will tread very lightly about your business in the Levant. All is not as it seems, and should you lose the confidence of the peoples . . .'

'Sir. You are known to us and I'm persuaded we are to be guided by your wisdom and sagacity,' Renzi said carefully. 'Is there perhaps something we should be particularly aware of that will help us in our dealings?'

Foresti gave a tight smile. 'The captain here will understand that merchant ships have a colourful notion of bearing fair documentation. False papers are more to be expected in every case. Neutral bottoms are where you will find your irregular cargoes – but all this is well known to your profession.

'What is important for you to understand is that you sons of Nelson believe you have driven the French from the Mediterranean. Nothing is more wrong. They are every-where, currying favours, intriguing against rulers who treat with the English, preparing for the time when they will return victoriously.'

He drew out a blue handkerchief and blew into it. 'Their agents are pointing to the success Bonaparte commands in Europe, that in only a short while England will be no more and that it would be well for the wise to be on the winning side.

'Your allies? Sultan Selim in Constantinople has no control over his satraps, who govern their petty kingdoms in corrup-tion and tyranny. Ali Pasha rules in the Morea – they call him "the butcher of Yannina" but the Russians and the French hasten to do him homage, as does your good Lord Nelson himself. And the Turkish Navy may be at sea, but it favours the French and will never fight for you.

'The Russians? Mocenigo, I happen to know, is in secret communication with the French and is entirely untrustworthy. The grand Tsar pronounces one thing and does another; their dearest wish is to possess a port that is free from ice the year around and for this they are prepared to fish in troubled waters.'

Kydd's face gave nothing away. 'Then what in your opinion is the greatest peril?'

Foresti paused for a moment. 'That depends. For us it must be the thirteen thousand French troops in Italy at Otranto, eight thousand at this moment marching to join them, sixty miles only across the strait from where we sit. They are waiting for when Napoleon launches his assault on England and they will be released to seize back the Ionians and—'

'Thank you, sir. You have made our position plain,' Kydd said, bringing the conversation to a close. 'We shall indeed step warily in these parts. Now, is there anything we can do for you, at all?'

Foresti sighed and indicated that his services as prize agent were always to be had and the safe custody of dispatches to Nelson on their departure would leave him more than satisfied.

'Then I shall see you to the boat,' Kydd said, rising, and added, 'Sir, being as you are British consul, you may be saluted with eleven guns on going ashore, if you so desire.'

'Save your powder, Captain. And remember – trust not a soul.'

'Sir, may I name my officers . . .' Noise and laughter filled the reception room. It was large and very hot with a vast fire at the end tended by ornately uniformed Cossacks; around the room ladies, dressed in a style not seen in London for an age, mingled in the greatest good humour.

Footmen in colourful sashes and headgear offered fine-cut glasses of a strange Russian potion called vodka. Kydd's nervousness at representing his country formally melted away, his senses heightened by the rhythms from a trio of players energetically strumming on peculiar triangular instruments and the utterly alien odours wafting about.

'Ze Ritter Kommodor Greig!' Kydd turned to meet a power-fully built man, with a genial smile, who bowed with a click of the heels. This was the flag-officer of the Russian Ionian Squadron and Kydd hastened to return the compliment.

'My name interests you?' the man said teasingly. In polite-ness Kydd had not questioned why the senior Russian commander had perfect English and affected a Scottish name.

'Er, yes.'

'My father Samuil Karlovich, our most distinguished admiral under the Tsarina Catherine, came from Inverkeithing. A Royal Navy lieutenant in the service of the Tsar. We have many such to ornament our navy, sir.'

'And we likewise, er, Kommodor. I had the honour to meet Captain Krusenstern as served at sea with us before he set forth to sail around the world in our *Leander* and *Thames* as was. Have you word at all?'

The talk eddied happily about him as the vodka was tossed back in the Russian way, and nearby he heard Howlett making hesitant talk with an impeccably dressed and decorated civilian. 'Er, I've heard your Greeks can be an unruly parcel to rule. How do you—'

'Ioannis Capodistrias. I'm Ionian but count myself Greek, sir, in this island which is nominally Turk, garrisoned by Russia and lately occupied by France. In the article of ruling therefore we naturally compromise on the laws and usages of Venice, which we do all accept.'

Kydd hid a smile and glanced to the aristocratic Curzon, languidly at home in surroundings such as these – 'Yes, well, you have a new Tsar, I understand. Alexander? All hail to His Imperial Majesty, of course, and I'm privileged to claim your Count Nikita Panin as one of my closer friends. He and I—'

'The *graf* Nikita Petrovich Panin, who was one of the assassins of His Imperial Majesty's father, the Tsar Paul?'

'Oh! Er, I had no idea—'

'And who, nevertheless, is now Chancellor of the Russian Empire?'

Kydd looked about to see how Renzi was coping but couldn't catch sight of him in the animated throng. He leaned forward politely to hear the laboured English of yet another young officer about to make acquaintance of one of the legendary Nelson's captains.

Renzi was enthralled to be hearing about the life of a Dnieper Cossack in passionate French from a heavily bearded cavalry-man and did not want to be distracted.

'Sir, this is of the utmost importance!' a man behind him whispered again, plucking at his sleeve. 'You must hear me.'

The burly officer seemed not to notice and rumbled on, a faraway look in his eyes. Renzi threw an angry glare at the little man in thick spectacles but it did not deter him. Renzi rounded on him and demanded to know what it was that could not wait.

'Sir – in private, if you understand,' the man said, shifting uncomfortably.

Renzi weighed the loss of the intriguing conversation against the possibility that some problem was affecting their presence. 'Very well, sir. One moment . . .' He made his apologies to the officer and reluctantly followed the man out into the garden.

'I do beg pardon for my intrusion, sir. Were it not a business so urgent . . .'

'What is it you want, sir?'

'I have heard you are the secretary of the English frigate?'

'I am Renzi, the captain's confidential secretary, sir.'

'Then it is in you I must trust. I am Gospodin Mikhail Orlov, a merchant venturer of Odessa. I have interests in . . . these parts and—'

'Sir, I fail to see how one of His Majesty's ships of war can possibly be of service to one of – to yourself, Mr Orlov.'

'You don't? Then answer me this, Mr Renzi – your grand

194

commander Nelson *pines* after timber and spars, tar and canvas, does he not?'

To one desperate to maintain a worn-out squadron at sea indefinitely in the worst of weathers, 'pines' would not be too strong a word, Renzi allowed without comment.

'And do you not consider he would be interested in a sizeable and reliable supply of such, and at a price half that of the best the Baltic offers?'

'Are you referring to Panormo in Crete, Mr Orlov?'

'No, sir,' Orlov said, with conviction, 'I talk real quantity, to fit out the greatest fleet there ever was.'

'And, er, where might this cornucopia be found, sir?'

'This is my difficulty,' Orlov said quietly. 'I am recently in possession of information of a . . . a sensitive nature, which will very shortly transform my country. I will not hide it from you – it will confer immense commercial advantage on any possessor who moves quickly and with sagacity.'

Renzi looked pointedly at his fob-watch. 'Sir, I cannot see how this can be of any—'

'It will in one stroke free your navy in Malta from any dependence on the Baltic trade, which you now daily risk past the Danes, the Swedes and others who would deny you.'

'Pray tell me, Mr Orlov, what is it you wish us to do?'

'A simple request, Mr Renzi. That I take immediate passage on your fine frigate to Smyrna.'

'That may not be possible, sir. I cannot speak for Captain Kydd but it would seem our business is in the Adriatic, not—'

'Sir, I feel you have not grasped fully the significance of what I offer. I have been open with you, that it will be of profit to myself, but this can only be if your great Nelson has his sea stores. There is no risk attached to yourselves.'

'Mr Orlov. I cannot recommend this to the captain unless the business is made clear. The motions of one of His Majesty's ships are not to be commanded by others.'

'We have so little time. I simply ask—'

'The business, sir!'

Orlov's face took on a hunted look. 'Very well. What I am about to tell you is in the strictest confidence. The information is not necessarily available to the Ionian administration, um, at the present time.'

'I understand, Mr Orlov. You have my word on it.'

'It is an internal matter, of interest to the Russian peoples alone, that His Imperial Majesty is shortly to open up the canal of Tsar Peter the Great between the Volga and Don rivers.' At Renzi's blank expression he explained, 'This will mean vessels may at last navigate from the Caspian to the Black Sea and then to the Mediterranean, opening up the whole interior. Unlimited resources of timber and flax, metals and tar – it is a prize of incalculable value, Mr Renzi.'

'And your interest in this?'

'The concessions. These are of two kinds – in Russia, trading rights from the *pokhodnii ataman* ruler, the other, right of passage from the Sublime Porte of Constantinople. Either is useless on its own. Securing both confers on the holder a monopoly of trade.'

'Naturally, you wish for this honour.'

Orlov looked up with a bitter smile. 'Sir, neither the *ataman* nor the Sultan cares for commerce. Their interest is in the regular exaction of cash from this same flowing trade, much more reliably acquired from a single source.

'Since you will ask it, I will tell you that the French will have heard of this opportunity and will be moving quickly to secure the rights and thereby exclude you. And, be assured, these will go to the first to make cause – your Sultan ally will never argue with ready gold.'

Renzi could see that if it was true they would be in a position to relieve Nelson of a great deal of worry in his task of keeping his fleet at sea. If it was a fantasy, their protective patrol would in any event include the rich Smyrna trading route and Orlov had asked for no other commitment. 'One thing, Mr Orlov. Why an *English* frigate?'

'That when we arrive in Smyrna, the Pasha may see that I have the trust of the British and that by this he may see as well you still rule the seas,' Orlov said.

'And in matters of discretion your movements will never be known to your countrymen.'

'Just so.'

'I will speak with the captain this night. How might we get word to you?'

Kydd listened gravely to Renzi. 'There's only one course open to us, Nicholas. We must speak with Foresti.'

'I've thought of that, dear fellow. Unfortunately he has left for Cephalonia and will not return these next few weeks.'

'And then it'll be too late. I do believe I'll take a chance with this gentleman, merchant or whoever. Put him down in the books as the captain's guest and we'll take a surprise cruise around the Morea to Smyrna. If nothing else it will tell our privateers that *L'Aurore* is about and hunting.'

Chapter 8

The crisp south-westerly could not have been more welcome for the voyage to the furthest corner of the Mediterranean. Kydd's conscience at this happy prospect was eased by the sight of suspicious sail scuttling out of sight at the sudden presence of such unchallengeable might in their waters.

Rounding Cythera at the tip of the Morea, *L'Aurore* stretched north into the Aegean, through the ancient sea full of islands whose names were enshrined in classical history – the Cyclades with Naxos and Thera, past the Dodecanese with Patmos and Rhodes and on to Chios, outpost to Smyrna.

The harbour was crowded with a vast concourse of shipping of all kinds and the frigate picked her way carefully through to her anchorage. 'My thanks for this, Captain,' Orlov said, 'I will not forget it.' His baggage was ready on deck, and as soon as *L'Aurore* had moored he prepared to board the cutter.

'I go now to greet my business agent and together we shall call on Ali Nuri Bey, the Pasha of Smyrna. Er, it would be of some convenience should you remain a day or two displaying your largest English flags, merely for the reason I mentioned before. You may trust that I shall detail the consequences of my mission in a letter after all is concluded. Good day, sir.'

The boat disappeared into the bustle of the harbour. Kydd turned to his first lieutenant. 'No liberty, Mr Howlett – we sail in two days.'

Here there were no flagships to acknowledge or prickly shore fortresses to notice and he would make the most of the short stay. Hands were turned to, part-of-ship, and set about fettling *L'Aurore*. Some captains were known for their devotion to beauty of appearance, others for the exactitude of the angle of spars across bare masts but for Kydd guns were what gave a man-o'-war purpose, their functioning, reliability, the devotion of the men serving them. The gunner's party could always be sure of hands for their routine tasks, from chipping shot to flinting gun-locks, and Redmond was proud of the rolling programme of maintenance of his iron charges.

Close behind for Kydd, however, was that which gave the floating castle its strategic significance – motility. This potent threat carrying more artillery than whole army regiments could be moved like a chess piece to menace the enemy – but only if its miles of rope and acres of canvas were in a sound condition.

The only time most of the rigging could be safely unreeved was at rest and the boatswain began his painstaking inspection as soon as the seamen had been stood down from sea watches. In a light-sparred ship, like *L'Aurore*, the need was that much the greater and there were few left unemployed.

Renzi came on deck and moved to the ship's side, gazing dreamily across the hard green waters to the rumpled, scrubby land. Kydd wandered over. 'Not as would stir the heart, Nicholas.'

'Dear fellow, this is not only the birthplace of Homer but may lay just claim to be the centre of the civilised world.'

'Well, we have Greece to the west'd and—'

'Think of it,' Renzi said, with passion. 'A bare hundred miles or so across this wine-dark sea are Athens, Sparta, the plains of Marathon! And close at our backs are the cities of the ancient world – Ephesus, Pergamon, Sardis.'

'And to the north?' Kydd prompted.

'Ah! Why, it's Byzantium – Constantinople as now is, the Golden Horn where Jason and the Argonauts sailed, and to go further, there we have the Black Sea, and on to Russia and the Cossack hosts. But strike south and we reach the Holy Land, the oldest and first of mankind, and—'

'And now we're at our anchor here,' Kydd said drily, 'and later it seems a hard beat back to the Adriatic will be required.'

'But consider, this very city has had a river of treasure flowing through it over the long centuries. Now we know it for its fruit, carpets, opium, yet in its day the grand Silk Route of Marco Polo stretched from Cathay thousands of miles across track-less desert and baking plain, the camel caravans three years on their journey to finish at the end of all land – here, in Smyrna.'

Kydd nodded. 'Yes, well, when you have had your fill of the sights it would be of service to me should you pen some kind of address to that Pasha fellow. A Turk he is but we have to be—'

The officer-of-the-watch, Curzon, came up hesitantly. 'A boat approaching, sir.'

It was a native watercraft, one of the many criss-crossing the broad roadstead and under a press of sail heading directly for them. A figure aboard waved violently.

'It's Orlov!' Kydd said. The man shouted something and Curzon motioned the boatman to come alongside.

'Thank God!' he spluttered, as he clambered over the rail. 'You stayed.'

'As requested,' Kydd said.

'Sir! The very worst!' he said, throwing his arms up. 'Er, your cabin?'

Leaving a startled and curious Curzon, Kydd led the way below.

'What is it, sir?'

Drawing a deep breath to steady himself, Orlov said dramatically, 'We have lost, Captain! Our concessions have been taken by another!'

'*You* have lost we must say,' Kydd replied.

'No, sir!' Orlov came back with conviction. '*We* have both suffered – for it's the French who now hold the concession.'

Kydd gulped. This was another matter entirely: a trade in naval stores not only lost to the British but flowing to a blockade-starved enemy.

Orlov went on, 'They've bribed the Bey and secured the document. They now need only the signature of the Russian minister in the Mediterranean and it will be over for us all.'

'Count Mocenigo.'

'Yes.'

Renzi nodded. 'Who favours the French – and this is what you yourself were undertaking in Corfu when you received word from your agent in Smyrna . . .'

'The devil played for time,' Orlov angrily agreed, 'knowing

what the French were obtaining. With his signature over that of the Pasha, the Kremlin will grant the concession.'

'Tell me, when did the French leave Smyrna? There's a possibility – a slim one – that we might overhaul them.'

'A day – no, closer to two.'

'Several hundred miles away by now at least. I'm sorry to say, Mr Orlov, that even with a flyer like *L'Aurore* we stand no chance.'

'None? I beg you, shall we try?'

Kydd sighed. 'Very well.' Word was passed for the master, and charts were produced. 'Now, do you have any idea what ship they took passage in?'

'It was a – how do you say? – a fast *tekne*, a Turkish coasting trader as will not be troubled by the English.'

'What rig is that, pray?'

'Rig?'

'Er, can you show me one?'

Orlov went up to the broad sweep of windows and scanned the busy scene. 'There!' he said, pointing to a ship with an exaggerated curving of the bow and stern, wonderfully ornamented, and square-rigged over an enormous main sprit on a single mast with a balancing flying jib.

Kydd noted the clever play of fore-and-aft and square sail, which had the craft bowling along and a bow-wave creaming from the swept-up stem. 'Yes – at least seven, eight knots. Mr Kendall, what's your guess?'

The master rubbed his chin. 'Aye, I'd reckon so. But if we're thinkin' of a chase up the Adriatic, with that jackass fore-and-aft rig, he'll have the legs of us on account o' the reignin' nor'-westerly wind in our face.'

'Well, I'm sorry to say, Mr Orlov, there's no answer to that. We'll have three, four knots at most over him and that calculates to four or five days before we haul him in sight. He'll be long arrived at the Ionians by then.'

Orlov crumpled into a chair.

'Er, it does cross my mind . . .' Renzi politely interjected, looking up from a chart of the eastern Mediterranean.

'Yes?' Kydd said.

'The great Aristophanes speaks of the tyrant Periander in – when was it? – about 600BC, that—'

'Not now, if you please, Nicholas.'

'Oh. I was about to mention that he caused a species of rail-way to be made over the isthmus of Corinth, here.'

'A what?'

'Rail-way,' Renzi said, in a pained tone. 'A form of track upon which a wheeled trolley is mounted and –'

'Might we leave this for a later time? I have to see Mr Orlov ashore, and—'

'– which he employed to pull ships across the isthmus to the other side to be re-floated and sent on their way. As you can readily see, it obviates the need to circumnavigate the Peloponnese completely – the Morea if you will – a saving of some hundreds of miles in the voyage.'

Kendall snatched a pair of dividers and wielded them on the chart.

'He wrote of it in *Thesmophoriazusae*, I think it was,' Renzi went on, 'as they say, "as fast as one from Corinth", referring to this very rail-way. Which was called the "Diolkos" in antiquity,' he added helpfully.

'I make it close t' three hundred miles saved, if this'n is true,' Kendall said, in awe, but added suspiciously, 'an' I've never heard of it afore.'

'Nicholas?'

'It's true. Sea-going triremes of thirty-eight tons were hauled across – Octavian surprising Marc Antony after Actium springs to mind – but the main use was to considerably shorten the trade route in marble and timber.'

'How long to get them over?' Kydd snapped.

'Four miles or so – about three hours with a hundred and eighty slaves at the lines.'

Kydd bellowed for Howlett. 'Get this barky to sea as soon as you like, sir,' he told the startled officer.

Renzi hesitated. 'Um, the reason we've not heard of this marvel is possibly the rail-way no longer exists. The emperor Nero conceived of a canal through Corinth and, himself turning the first sod, ruined the approaches beyond repair before he was murdered.'

'And there's a mort o' difference a'tween a forty-ton Greeky old-timer and a frigate,' Kendall muttered.

Kydd grinned at Renzi's discomfiture. 'Where your trireme went I dare to say a ship's launch can follow. I mean to set a boat or two of size a-swim the other side under sail with carronades as will wait for our *tekne* and give it a fright.'

Orlov leaped to his feet. 'I will help! Anything!'

On the deck above there was the squeal of a boatswain's call and a rushing thump of feet as *L'Aurore* readied for sea. 'No, Mr Orlov. It were best you were not seen. I fancy this is work for my first lieutenant.'

'And I,' Renzi offered.

'I can't allow—'

'I'd hazard that you've considered the impropriety of bringing to and making prize of a vessel under the flag of an ally of ours? Therefore we are in disguise, our challenge is in the *lingua franca* of these parts – and where is your Italian speaker, sir?'

* * *

With the noble ruins of Athens passing just out of sight on the starboard beam, *L'Aurore* made anchor in the stillness of the little bay. Kydd had the gig away instantly. It was not hard to spot the fold in terrain between the cliffs leading through to deeper clefts – but what remained of the Diolkos?

The boat grounded softly on a gently sloped rise from the modest beach into the interior where dressed stones suggestive of ancient works lay about.

Renzi could give no further information about the rail-way, and explained apologetically that his classics master had not seen fit to include details of its engineering but that 'rails' in the original Greek might very well construe in the archaic form to 'grooves' or 'tracks'.

Quick casting about showed only sand-heath, then low scrub over light-brown soil up and over a pass. Pressing up the slope, Kydd saw that it levelled and twisted through a gully leading on the left to a grander ravine. There were no major obstacles that he could see; if there had been any such trackway it was likely to have been along here.

'There's no time to lose,' he pronounced. 'The launch and cutter. We make our own rails: lay two spars lengthways as we do carry 'em on board, and having no slaves to hand we set fifty men on the lines.'

Nothing was more calculated to lift the spirits of Jack Tar than something novel, out of routine and fit for a yarn in later life. The two boats were fitted with their gear, men told off for crew or haulers, and in no time the little flotilla was pulling lustily for the shore.

Howlett set out ahead to survey the route while Gilbey followed with a party to hack at the scrub. The spars were laid lengthways several feet apart and a trial was made with the launch, the heavier of the two. With twenty-five on each trace and rollers thrown in over the spars the boat flew up the 'rails' and Kydd knew all was possible, even without the heavy tackles he had in reserve.

The scrubby bushes were no impediment and, with a hearty sailor's 'stamp 'n' go', the heavy boats were trundled rapidly up to the crest of the pass. Beyond, stretching out ahead past a series of lesser slopes, was the Gulf of Corinth.

At the sight the men gave a cheer and waved gaily to an astonished goat-herder on the skyline. Down-slope the boats merely needed restraining, not hauling, and well before dark they reached their goal.

The carronades arrived, six men on each sweating at the effort, others with three balls in a haversack, still more with powder. The craft were quickly rigged, and a bare four hours after setting out from *L'Aurore* there were two war-boats outfitted for cruising.

Kydd allowed a smile. The ancients had been right and that night on the mess-deck there would be grog tankards raised to those fellow mariners of so long ago. 'Mr Howlett, I will wish you good fortune. You have your orders and Mr Renzi to advise. Are you clear about your mission?'

'Sir. To make all possible speed to the island of Cephalonia, there to lie off to the nor'ard to await any *tekne* seen to be making for Corfu and then to—'

'Yes. You'll want to set sail now – I won't detain you.' There were further cheers and good-spirited horseplay as the boats were readied; sails were hoisted and sheeted in and, with a wave, they set out.

Kydd watched them until they were out of sight. With a twinge of doubt he knew they faced more than a hundred miles along the narrow gulf before Cephalonia was raised and then they had to intercept the unknown *tekne* among all the other innocent craft and board it – this was asking much, even for the Royal Navy.

He turned on his heel and returned to his ship. They weighed immediately to sail the long way around and later rendezvous with the expedition.

Renzi settled aft, content to let Howlett take charge. His mind roamed over the improbability of what they were doing and where they were. To the right the mainland of Greece and its burden of history – Athens, Thebes and the cradle of the philosophies of logic he held so dear; to the left the Peloponnesus of Sparta and the Delian League.

It was a moment of magic. For all his classical studies he had never visited here and now . . . a pity there were no romantic ruins nearby, marble pillars that had stood since Pericles had rallied Athens and—

'Cutter, ahoy!' bellowed Howlett to the boat bravely seething along out to larboard. 'I'll thank you to fall in astern and take better station!'

How petty – and how typical of the man to play the admiral when not a soul was there to witness it, Renzi thought. Then he brought to mind commanders like Cornwallis and his ceaseless blockade of Brest. He had insisted on immaculate station-keeping and, far out to sea, majestic battleships formed line and column by signal, tacked about in succession and manoeuvred as though at a fleet review, with only the seagulls to applaud.

In the worst sea conditions anywhere, these ships kept to a culture of excellence that would see them through anything the ocean or the enemy could set against them. Humbled, Renzi smiled at the first lieutenant, who blinked, puzzled.

Dusk drew in. The gulf was long and narrow, and with

only one direction to go for so many miles there would be no problem in nocturnal navigation. He watched the men arrange themselves for the night. The canny Stirk had appropriated the wedge shape abaft the stem, easing a sail-cover behind his back and pulling his stout coat around him. The forward lookout sat low for ease of sighting under the flying jib on the running bowsprit and Calloway made his way aft.

The dark hours passed, the towering black mass of the coast to larboard slipping by in ill-defined shapes that slowly came and went. A pannikin of two-water grog was issued and ship's biscuits were consumed or carefully tucked away for later.

One by one the still black figures dropped from sight below the gunwale as they sought warmth from the chill but steady northerly and Renzi was left alone with his thoughts.

If the winds held they would make Cephalonia by the evening of the next day in good time to be in position near the tip of the island to dart out across the bows of their quarry when it appeared.

If it appeared. There was no overpowering reason for it to stay close in with this, the largest of the Ionians, other than to take the most direct course for Corfu. Conceivably the Turkish master might feel uneasy so hard by Russian shores and keep an offing out of sight. Or perhaps he had even made better speed than estimated and the vessel was now long past.

Renzi shrugged off the night-time phantoms and tried to doze but another thought came to jolt him to wakefulness. That there was increasingly little chance of his ever becoming a man of letters was now approaching a certainty but there was *one* possible course that would bring the stability and respect which would enable him to recast his future with Cecilia.

He would rejoin the Navy as an officer. With rising feeling he savoured the thought. He was now quite recovered from the fever that had seen him invalided out, and as the ex-first lieutenant of a sixty-four-gun ship-of-the-line he was a valuable acquisition and should find no difficulty in securing a commission.

Lieutenant and Mrs Renzi! It would be a naval wedding, probably in one of the little country churches favoured by officers around Portsmouth. They would live in . . . A betraying anxiety that she might already be spoken for rushed in on his warm vision like a harsh north-westerly squall, leaving him shaken. What was wrong with his logic that he couldn't steer a safe course through the most elementary of life's quandaries? If he could not—

'Ummph.' Howlett's body slid sideways against his, jerking the man to full consciousness. 'I beg pardon,' he mumbled. 'I didn't mean to—'

Renzi grunted, then settled to a fitful doze.

A welcome dawn found them well down the gulf, just where they did not know, but like mariners of old, they needed only to follow the coastline to their destination – cabotage, as it was termed.

A cold breakfast was handed out and they settled to another day. At a point where the gulf kinked, Howlett ordered the boats to land at a sandy spit and the men stretched and cavorted there in grateful release.

The voyage resumed. Idly Renzi wondered just how the final act would play. He was not in command, of course, but what if he were a naval officer again, leading such a party? In the hard light of day the night's thoughts began to wilt. It would certainly be a congenial prospect, the equal fellowship of the brotherhood of the sea in the wardroom, but things had passed that had fundamentally changed him. He had scaled the heights of intellect and seen the world abstractedly as a rational sea of intertwined natural prescripts. How, then, could he now revert to being a hard, practical officer capable of sending men to their deaths?

Moodily, he let the thoughts come unchecked as he stared at the dark, broken land. For once he was not inclined to search eagerly for a striking ruin or alluring grotto.

Cephalonia was sighted towards evening, with a smaller mountainous island close off its inshore flank. Course was shaped to bring them unseen from the seaward into the narrow passage between the two; their voyaging was nearly over. Renzi glanced across to the precipitous sides of the island, in the winter cold seeming reproving and hostile.

A snatch of Homer crossed his mind, for improbably this brooding island was the famed Ithaca: 'Odysseus dwells in shining Ithaca. There a mountain doth dream, high Neriton, in night-dark forests is covered—'

'Brail up!' Howlett ordered brusquely, and pulled out his watch. 'Call the cutter alongside, Mr Calloway,' he told the midshipman.

'Stirk, load the carronade with ball, but ship an apron.' They were making their first war-like move, readying their gun for instant use but with a precautionary lead cover to protect the gun-lock.

The other boat came up and Howlett outlined the plan for action. During the night there would be little they could do, hopefully making the interception some time during daylight hours. On the hasty sketch map Orlov had provided, there was a tiny beach on the extreme north-western tip of Cephalonia accessible only from the sea. It was usefully positioned as a step-off point to intercept traffic coming up the seaward side from the south.

They would beach there until first light. A lookout would be posted on the highest ground and at the signal they would swoop. The two boats under sail would position one on each quarter of the vessel, the launch to fire its carronade to place a warning across the *tekne*'s bows, the cutter to stand off and threaten with its carronade while the launch boarded.

If their quarry failed to show up in these two days they would carry on to rendezvous with *L'Aurore*.

Resistance was thought unlikely against a boat armed with a heavy-calibre weapon trained on the little merchantman's unprotected stern-quarters but if necessary they would use force.

There were no questions, but Renzi had qualms. The most serious was the weather: if it came on to blow, the boats would quickly have to reef or even retire and watch their prey pass on untouched. Nonetheless he slept well, settled on the beach for the night under a sail; the tideless Mediterranean ensured the waves were kept at bay.

As soon as it was light two men were sent toiling up the steep slope, waving at the top to show they had view of the sea to the south. The boats were readied afloat with a kedge anchor to seaward and sail bent on ready for hoisting – and they waited.

There were a few craft taking the passage past, clearly hurrying on north to Corfu: feluccas, a stout brig in company with a waspish xebec and a number of brightly painted fishing caïques sailing together.

Noon came. Another cold meal. Renzi squatted next to Howlett. 'Sir, Mr Kydd's orders were for me to render such advice to you as might prove useful. Do you wish to hear it?'

'Very well, Renzi. What is it? I'll caution you that whether I take it or no is my decision.'

'Yes, quite. Er, it does cross my mind that we should recognise the opposed boarding of an ally and subsequent actions most certainly constitutes an incident with international consequences to our flag.'

'I know that. It can't be helped.'

'My advice to you, sir, is that we assume the character of Russians. Our men are in no sort of uniform, but yourself and Mr Gilbey may wish to keep wearing a foul-weather cloak or similar over yours. Seen to come from a Russian-held island, the inference is that we're a coast patrol.'

Howlett's eyes narrowed. 'Are you suggesting some sort of charade? As soon as I give my orders it'll be seen—'

'Sir, I shall be speaking Italian, as is the way at sea in these parts. The men know what to do and will be instructed not to utter a word of English. This way none on the *tekne* can testify later to any evidence as to our origin.'

'You will be speaking Italian? And what do you suppose I speak?'

'You are the Russian officer in charge, of course. I am merely the humble translator.'

'I can't speak Russian, damn it.'

Renzi held himself in check. 'Then, sir, may I put it to you that any mumbo-jumbo you can contrive will answer.' If there were any Russian speakers on this Turkish coaster or among the French themselves they would be seen through, of course, in which case there would be no help for it.

'Very well, we'll be Russians.'

Renzi relayed this to the boats' crews, who grinned delightedly at the conceit.

The afternoon passed slowly but as evening began to draw

in there were faint shouts from the lookouts on the skyline. At last!

'Into the boats!' bellowed Howlett.

Sails taut and straining, they rounded the headland – and there, startlingly close, was a *tekne*. They quickly took position off its absurdly curved and ornamented stern-quarters and Stirk loosed off their twelve-pounder carronade. The shot sent up a mighty plume ahead of the little vessel, which lost no time in dousing its sails.

Renzi tensed. It was now the testing time. This could be the one – or not. The French might be aboard or the documents sent by hand of an anonymous messenger. The vessel might contain soldiers or even French sailors – there were infinite reasons why they should fail.

'Lay us alongside,' growled Howlett, fiddling with his foul-weather coat. 'Silence in the boat!' he snapped.

'In Russian, if you please, sir,' Renzi murmured.

As they neared the low gunwale of the *tekne*, the midshipman stood and roared at the bowman, 'Wagga boo-boo ratty tails!'

'Ahrr, moonie blah blah,' the man replied, knuckling his forehead and obediently hooking on.

Red-faced, Howlett clambered over the gunwale and was confronted by a small group of men. One stepped forward and snarled some words angrily. Renzi felt a huge wash of relief. It was in French. And obviously these were not military men.

'*Mi dispiace, Signore, non capisco,*' he said mournfully, spreading his hands wide in the Italian gesture of incomprehension.

'The cretin doesn't know French,' the first man said openly in that language to the older standing next to him, then beckoned irritably to the florid Turkish master. 'Tell him to explain why he's stopped us – we're on urgent business.'

The message was passed. Renzi bowed politely and turned to Howlett. 'Moo-juice blitter foo-bah sing-song . . .' He fought down exultation – apparently there were no Russian-speakers at hand.

Howlett looked at the deck and mumbled, his very evident held-in anger perfectly suited to the performance. Blank-faced, Renzi replied in Italian to the cowed Turk, 'My officer has been advised of the activities of pirates in this area and wishes to know what is this matter that is so urgent.'

'Tell him it's none of his business.'

Renzi came back: 'He says your appearance is not the usual to be found in a Turkish trader. This close to Russian territory, my officer believes you to be spies, sir. Have you any evidence to the contrary?'

The Frenchman pulled back in dismay, saying to the other, 'The idiot Ivan thinks we're spies, Claude. What's to be done?'

The older muttered, 'Bluff it out . . .'

The first turned back and blustered, 'This is outrageous! We're on a mission to Count Mocenigo himself.'

The indignation faded as Stirk, summoned by Renzi's quick wink, came across with five men fingering cutlasses.

'My officer regrets that in the absence of such evidence you are to be arrested for questioning.'

Stirk tested the edge of his weapon with a horny thumb and gave an evil grin. 'Watchee gundiguts barso!'

'Think of something, Claude,' the first muttered, 'We could be choking for years in some stinking prison.'

Howlett leaned across to Renzi. 'What the devil's going on?' he whispered hoarsely. 'I demand to know.'

'Fidgety fee t' blarney,' Renzi answered gravely, and passed on, 'My officer says further that this vessel apparently without cargo is most suspicious and is to be confiscated as well.'

'It's intolerable, Claude!'

The older snapped, 'I'll show these *péquenades* something that'll set 'em by the ears!' He wheeled about and stormed off below, returning minutes later bearing an ornamented red box set about with golden tassels and an elaborate central cypher.

'You recognise this?' It was relayed on. 'It's from the Sublime Porte, Sultan Selim himself, who would take it personally should you further delay his friends.'

Howlett could hardly believe his eyes and spluttered with excitement.

Renzi bowed. 'The officer admits he is mistaken and asks to be forgiven. Further, he wishes to make amends by conveying your box under our guard to Count Mocenigo himself.' He firmly took the box from the dumbfounded Frenchman and handed it to Howlett with another bow. 'Leave instantly!' he whispered, and led the way over the side.

Back aboard *L'Aurore* the atmosphere changed markedly for the better after the success ashore and they continued their Adriatic duties with renewed purpose.

The gunroom became deferential to Renzi after it was glee-fully told how in heathen Italian he had had Johnny Crapaud well a-tremble before telling one of them to duck below and bring him up the required document to hand over. Renzi felt that it might be better, perhaps, to leave it to a later time to explain how the French themselves had simply produced it for effect. The French rights were useless to the British, of course, but at the least it meant the playing field was now level again.

For Kydd, there was immense satisfaction on his return to La Maddalena. Invited to a dinner of captains in *Victory*, he sat in the glow of warm laughter and congratulations following his recounting of the adventure, receiving an approving nod from Nelson himself.

L'Aurore gave her place in the Adriatic to *Phoebe* and resumed her watch with *Active* outside Toulon, a ceaseless beat across the wide bay overlooked by craggy mountains that ensured their every movement was known, regardless of how far offshore they sailed. However, the commander-in-chief's policy of open blockade – keeping the battle-fleet out of sight many leagues away to entice the French out – required the watching frigates to close with the port past Cape Cepet and its guns to look directly into the enfolding roads, which they did by turns.

On a fine day it was exhilarating but in the more usual cold bluster it was miserable work – and dangerous. In the past one frigate had heaved to for repairs and been taken in the night by a daring French sally. And there was no relaxing the watch as the winds chased the compass before the sudden rush of the mistral and prudent mariners sought the open sea.

In the deep abyssal waters off Toulon there was no anchoring as with Cadiz: ships on blockade here were continually under sail and therefore had no rest in any weather. And always there was the chill. The Mediterranean in winter was capable of a frigidity that put the dire winters of the north of England to shame. It was a mind-sapping almost liquid cold that penetrated until the body retreated to a last core of precious warmth and frozen hands fumbled the knots to be tied far aloft, out on a bucking yard.

At times like these Kydd did what he could for his men but his own experience told him that in rough weather with the galley fire out there was little they could look forward to except the comfort of a hammock in the heaving darkness of the lower deck. Yet something held the men's devotion to duty such that midnight had them turning out of that hammock yet again to the cold and spite in the same hateful stretch of sea for another watch.

For the ship's company the *something* that was driving them on was the belief that anything was tolerable other than letting Nelson and their shipmates down. This was how excellence was achieved – it was how England was facing Napoleon Bonaparte and his vaunted invasion, and for Kydd this was how they would win.

The days turned into weeks, the weeks ripened to spring. *L'Aurore* was sent for a cruise to the west, to Gibraltar and along the arid coast of North Africa, then up the length of Italy back to Agincourt Sound once more to refit and recover. In the sheltered waters *L'Aurore* received onions, lemons and greens from local gardens and even bullocks and sheep were waiting, along with that precious commodity – mail from home.

While there, Kydd made small improvements to his frigate. The ship's side below on the lower deck was whitewashed, immediately raising light levels in the enclosed space and therefore cheering the atmosphere below decks. A manger was built forward, right in the eyes of the ship, and a pair of Sardinian piglets and two goats were installed. A chicken coop was constructed abaft the fore ladderway and one of the quota men received aboard in Portsmouth found himself once more employed as he had been before: taking care of livestock.

As the weather improved, Kydd took the opportunity to cleanse the mess-deck. The men set to with a will for it was their own home that was being sweetened; scrubbed fore and aft, then dried with borrowed stoves, it was sluiced well and painstakingly cleaned. The cables were roused out and laid on deck while the cable tier itself was also attended to.

And the gunroom acquired small graces of living. Most welcome was the well-used library that was being built up, with exchanges between ships freshening the offerings. Renzi furthered his reputation by contributing some of his own treasured favourites – Wordsworth and a crudely printed Shakespeare vying with startling accounts of the inhabitants of distant parts.

Gilbey proved gifted in running the mess, the subscriptions laid out to good effect whenever the ship touched port. His choice of commensal wine in the cask for mealtimes was voted exceeding fine, and sharing the captain's cook, a chef from Guernsey called Missey, ensured that Gilbey's little extravagances were given due attention. With regular milk and eggs and the prospect of roast chicken and pork cutlets in the near future it was a congenial mess.

The captain was royally maintained by the good offices of Tysoe, who ruled his kingdom with dignity and adroitness, his hair now tinged with grey adding a touch of severity to his demeanour. Mason, the thin-faced captain's steward, knew better than to stand against Tysoe and was set to bringing the captain's meals while Tysoe himself performed the honours of the table.

Potts and Searle, the young volunteers first class, found duties under Tysoe also: attending at table when permitted and with the grave responsibility for the captain's bedplace, toilette and every piece of brightwork that could be found in his quarters. When they compared themselves to the two others, who served only the midshipmen, the honour was keenly felt.

Kydd now believed he had the measure of his ship, her strengths and foibles, the little quirks that had to be allowed for, no matter the stress of the situation. A good captain had to know a ship like a dancing partner – to detect and respond to intimate cues, to foresee and counter over-spirited steps and figures and become one together in the complex *pas de deux* that was sail and sea.

Each morning at six Kydd would rise, wash and go on deck informally to sniff the air, feel what the weather would bring that day and set himself to rights. The watch-on-deck would carefully not notice him.

At breakfast he liked to entertain the off-going officer-of-the-watch and sometimes to invite a midshipman or two while the ship geared up for the working day. And at the noon sight he made a point of attending with his octant and later working a position in the coach with the anxious young gentlemen, correcting and encouraging.

Thus the ship's routine became a mirror of life itself. As the weather warmed, the sea sparkling under blue skies in place of the hard glitter of winter, the rhythm quickened. The full panoply of a Sunday at sea now became possible with no fear of rain and biting cold.

Under easy sail eight miles out, under a promising sun with the seas slight and a pleasing royal blue, *L'Aurore* prepared for her special day.

It would be Kydd's first Divisions, the formal inspection of the ship's company. He looked forward to the ceremony: it would give him a chance to see every part of his own ship, a privilege paradoxically denied him as captain for it would never do for him to appear suddenly among the men working or off-watch.

As well it would give him a rare insight into the temper

of the company in so many small but significant ways. Most of all he was anxious to see if what he hoped for was coming to pass: that the Alcestes were now reconciled in body and spirit to their new ship.

It was vital that they were: the interdependence they had built up must now embrace the whole, new and old, and if it did, he would be very gratified. These were no raw crew, they were prime man-o'-war's men, stout fighters and mariners, each with an individuality formed and seasoned by years of seagoing.

No mere cyphers to order about at a whim, they would have their own expectations of their captain and officers. A first-class seaman was valued for his initiative, the ability to work far out on the yards on his own and make instant decisions without the need for orders. If properly led, this was what would happen, but if not, Kydd knew how they could retreat inside themselves to become, so easily, blank-faced mechanicals.

He drew on his white gloves. The marine trumpeter had called the men to Divisions an hour ago, with a bold flourish, but the captain must wait. Beyond his door the seamen were being mustered by division, one under each officer, and were even now being inspected by their lieutenant.

At length there was a polite knock. 'Ship's company mustered for Divisions, sir,' Howlett reported smartly. It was his competence above all that would be tested today: responsible for partialling the company not only into watch and station but divisions as well, he was also directly answerable to the captain for the day-to-day smooth running of the complex organisation that was a warship.

'Very good,' Kydd said, in the age-old way, and accompanied him out into the brightness of the day.

There was absolute quiet, the slight movement of the ship causing the lines of men to sway gently together. Clinton, resplendent in scarlet regimentals, threw him a dazzling salute. 'Royal Marines, sah! All present and correct, sah!'

Kydd assumed a grave and formal air and stepped forward to inspect the Royals. As expected, they presented faultlessly, glazed leather headgear, pipe-clayed cross-belts and gaiters against their red coats a splendid show. 'A fine body of men, very well turned out, Mr Clinton,' he pronounced, trying not to sound pompous, and was obliged to accept another energetic salute.

'Ah, Mr Curzon.'

'Sir, my division of the hands: all present and sober.'

And it was what he was hoping for. In their best rig, the men stood easily, fearlessly. He stopped to inspect one closely. A glossy tarpaulin hat with '*L'Aurore*' picked out on a black ribbon, a short blue jacket, with several rows of brass buttons and white seams on the sleeve and back, over a blue striped white shirt and set off with a red neck-cloth. Tight white duck trousers and gleaming long-quartered black shoes with buckles – the very picture of a deep-sea sailor. And the whole hand-made and lovingly embroidered – it sang of pride in himself and his ship, and Kydd was touched and humbled.

He passed man after man, each distinct and idiosyncratic in his dress and features. These were supreme professionals: the daring young topmen, the steady fo'c'slemen, the creased features of the old hands. With a word for one, an admiring comment to another, he advanced along the lines.

There was nothing to fault here, no frowsty evidence of a sailor lost to drink, no shabby carelessness from a man not one with his shipmates. They were a handsome division and Kydd told a pink-faced Curzon so.

He moved to the other divisions. The same strength and character, the same prideful appearance. Here was evidence of rivalry, the healthy expression of regard and comradeship. He nodded to a blank-faced Stirk, smiled to see Doud his cheerful self once more, and beside him Pinto, in an English sailor's rig intricate with Portuguese ornamentation.

His barge crew were distinctive with white ribbons sewn through the sleeve seams of their jackets and trousers; the gunner's crew each wore a blood-red kerchief; the fo'c'slemen sported large anchor buttons.

It had happened: the collection of individuals that were the Alcestes and the L'Aurores had come together and were now one.

After the inspection of the men, it was the turn of the ship. With his entourage of first lieutenant, boatswain and his mate and a Royal Marines escort, Kydd set off.

Galley, dispensary, stores – even the hold was not exempt. This was not an inspection of masts and spars, guns and carriages – those could be relied upon to be seen to on a daily basis. This was a tour of all the hundred and one places never regularly looked into; a hard grind of scouring and painting had necessarily preceded it.

The mess-deck he held until last. It would be the most revealing of all, for this was more than the usual sailors' dwelling place set among the hulking presence of the cannon with their gun-ports to the outer world. A frigate had no guns on the mess-deck and did not need to be cleared – the men's living space was their own.

Howlett looked at him meaningfully as they entered and Kydd dutifully sniffed. This deck was the next lowest in the ship and was ventilated and illumined only by the three hatchway gratings above; the effluvium of hundreds of men living together could be an overpowering fug but here there was only a pleasing sharp tang of the vinegar and lime used to sweeten the wood.

'Very good, Mr Howlett,' he said, moving a tub at the end of a table, but there was no tell-tale discolouring of the planking, evidence of a 'holiday' in the cleaning of the deck. Straightening, he looked about at the mess-tables up against the ship's side and saw what he had hoped for.

The vertical racks there were filled with mess kit as individual as the men who owned it. Crockery, small japanned boxes of herbs and, at the top corners, carved pieces and dainty pictures set about with miniature ropework. Their ditty-bags hung along with them, canvas with an opening near the top, each lovingly embroidered by its owner.

The seamen were showing that they had made *L'Aurore* their home. It meant therefore that when they went to battle this, too, was what they were defending. He could have fussed at searching out faults – and he knew where to look – but he was satisfied.

'Well done, Mr Howlett,' he pronounced. 'We'll rig for church, I believe.'

He affected not to notice the discreet sign given and, seconds later, a drum volleyed and rattled above. The men tumbled down the hatchways, seizing benches and stools in disciplined silence, and by the time Kydd had made the upper deck the bell in its belfry forward had begun its tolling for church.

On the colourfully beflagged quarterdeck a lectern awaited him, and above him the church pennant snapped in the wind for all to see – not that they risked being disturbed in their devotions by friendly vessels this close to the enemy but regulations must be observed.

He paused, looking out over his men. They seemed so many, both watches on deck sitting on their improvised pews, others standing by the rigging, and behind him, the officers on gunroom chairs, all in an expectant hush.

In the absence of a chaplain he could choose to speak himself or, more usually, make use of the bracing strictures of the Articles of War. Today, feeling closer to his ship's company, he preferred something more personal, uplifting and resonant with the services now being conducted in ancient churches all over England.

He took the Bible from his clerk and opened it at Psalm the Third.

'Lord, how are they increased that trouble me! Many are they that rise up against me. Many there be which say of my soul, "There is no help for him in God." But thou, O Lord, art a shield for me; my glory and the lifter up of mine head . . .'

Raising his eyes when the ancient words were done, in strong, robust tones he told the L'Aurores that they must do their duty and trust that God would uphold them and give them the victory.

Then he told them sincerely of his satisfaction at the state of the ship and stepped back. 'Shall we raise our voices? "O for a thousand tongues to sing . . ."'

The words came lusty and strong, and to Kydd was pleasing confirmation of the harmony that now prevailed in *L'Aurore*. He joined in happily.

Then it was, 'Down all stools!' followed by the welcome 'Up spirits!' and the sanctity of the occasion dissolved into rest-day jollity.

Kydd accepted the traditional captain's invitation to a gunroom dinner and went below to join his officers.

* * *

March was turning into April; the weather improved but there was no let-up in the watch and ward over Napoleon's invasion fleet. *L'Aurore* retired with Nelson's squadron to the southern rendezvous of Pula Bay to water and replenish. While there, she took her turn with the entertainments.

For weeks beforehand *L'Aurore* had been abuzz with expectation and planning for the big day aboard *Victory* when they must perform before the glittering assembly of the commander-in-chief and visiting captains. Doud was tasked for several spots, and a shy, sensitive marine who turned out to be a natural flute-player was discovered. One of the older fo'c'slemen was persuaded to accompany on his violin a pair of startlingly agile topmen in their hornpipe, while Kydd himself was remembered as a fine voice: he would render 'Spanish Ladies' and sing in a duet with Curzon.

On the night it was a great success and the musical numbers were enthusiastically applauded, but what had the company in a roar was the theatricals that followed: a rousing interpretation in costume of the Frenchmen meeting the 'Russians' on the *tekne*, with hilarious gobbledegook and misunderstandings deployed to best effect and a grand climax with an extravagantly spoken 'Renzi' triumphantly carrying off an enormous treasure box.

Kydd returned to his ship enfolded in the warmth of the evening, reflecting that it would be difficult to recall a time of greater contentment. When the morning came, with a warm sun climbing to a blue heaven, the feeling remained.

Then at ten everything changed. Around the point a frigate under full sail burst into sight. It was *Phoebe* and she had a signal flying: 'Enemy fleet at sea'. Villeneuve had sailed.

Within an hour the flagship had summoned all captains and

Kydd found himself sitting with other grim-faced officers at the commander-in-chief's table hearing the news.

'Villeneuve sailed with a fine nor'-easterly on the thirtieth last,' Nelson said brusquely. 'Eleven sail-of-the-line, seven frigates and several sloops. It's reported he's embarked some three thousand troops – for what purpose we cannot know. His last course was sou'-sou'-westerly but Villeneuve's invariable practice is to stand out to sea until he loses our frigates and only then bears away on his true heading. I pray *Active* will stay with them, but with these moonless nights I'm not sanguine she will.'

Murmuring around the table showed the implication was not lost on them. Was this going to be a repetition of the breakout several months before when they had chased rumours and suppositions to the ends of the Mediterranean?

'I think it right you should understand the elements of the decision I now face.' He stood and moved to the chart. 'The enemy is loose in the Mediterranean with a substantial body of soldiers. So where are they going? To the west – to join with the Dons in Cartagena? If this is so, why the troops? The same applies to a general exit past Gibraltar, for in joining with the Spanish at Cadiz or the French at Brest why the soldiers? A singular number, inconsequential for an invasion force and not needed in a conjunction with the other squadrons.'

He gazed at the chart for long moments. 'To the east? Possibly. Egypt still remains as it always has been, a highway to India, as does Syria, and we can rely on neither the Turks nor the Russians. Our entire interests including Malta therefore lie helpless before a battle-fleet of such force.'

The lines deepened in his face. 'And once a landing is achieved neither Satan nor all his demons will serve to remove them.'

'Sir – the Morea?'

'Thank you, Captain Keats, and your point is well taken. Should the Morea or any of the Ionians be taken we shall be hard put to defend our trade both in the Adriatic and further south. As to a motion towards Constantinople I feel it unlikely but not impossible.'

Kydd felt the tension: there could be no commander in history faced with such a decision and his heart went out to the stooped figure.

'I conceive there to be one object open to Villeneuve that is consistent with the facts to hand. The gesture east is a feint.'

'Gibraltar and the Channel!'

The final move to link up the enemy fleets – it was happening . . . or was it?

'I think not. I believe it to be an attempt to draw my squadron the thousand miles to Egypt – so leaving Naples and Sicily unguarded.'

'If Sicily is taken, it will cut the Mediterranean in two!'

'Quite.'

'And Naples lost – with no other friend in these parts we'll have to give up Malta!'

'The mischief is incalculable. Therefore my dispositions are this: the fleet will deploy in the central Mediterranean between Sardinia and Tunis, which will cover the route eastwards yet be available if they be sighted to the west. My precious frigates—' his twisted smile was at Kydd '—will cover the inshore runs to the north of Africa and the south of Sardinia, the final remaining to look into the eastern passage by Italy.'

The decision made, Nelson's features eased. 'But, gentlemen, I do account this the greatest news this age. After two years the French are finally out. In a short while I shall have the ineffable happiness of meeting Monsieur Villeneuve on the open sea where we shall put an end to this nonsense.'

Growls of agreement rose pugnaciously about the table.

'So. Will history later celebrate the battle of Santo Pietro – or is it to be the famous battle of Minorca?'

Chapter 9

'So kind in you, old chap,' Colonel Crawford said, easing into the plush leather chair, one of a pair discreetly off to the side in the reception room at Boodles.

'How are you, Charles?' Captain Boyd took the other, his expression of concern sincere. His wife's brother had just returned from India for his health.

'As to be expected,' Crawford said. 'I'm to thank you for seeing me with such alacrity, Edward.'

'Not at all. Er, how may I be of help? Anything I can do, old fellow . . .'

The colonel gave a tight smile. 'I'm new come to England, as you know, and I confess myself aghast at what I'm hearing of our friend Boney. Is it at all as dire a situation as it's painted to be or . . . ?'

'Pick up a newspaper, old fellow, it's all there in as much detail as you'd like,' Boyd said, nodding politely to the club waiter who had brought the sherry.

'Come, come, Edward, that won't do – it won't do at all! You'll grant I'm an officer of some distinction yet I find myself without any clear idea of the present danger. In Calcutta it's quite a different story we're hearing, so, dear fellow, from your eminence do tell me truly what we're facing – no flam, the unvarnished truth, and I'd be much obliged to you.'

'The truth?' Boyd was flag-captain to the first lord of the Admiralty and as such privy to confidential strategy at the highest level. Yet his sister's husband could not be denied and it were better he heard it from him at the first hand than rumours at Horse Guards.

'Very well. Please forgive if I labour the point in regard to some matters – I find the Army has a whimsical notion at times of a sea battlefield.'

'Please do. Fire a broadside of 'em, should you wish.'

Boyd leaned forward. 'And this for your ears alone, my friend.'

'I understand.'

'Then this is your situation. Napoleon Bonaparte does not really desire to invade England.'

'Oh?' said Crawford, in surprise.

'His eyes are set much higher than these few islands. His ambitions are for a world empire, the seizing of far territories, the planting of colonies and so forth. It so happens that we stand in his way in this, barring the seas which are the highway to empire.

'He's impatient to be done with us, sweep us aside and, with the power of an emperor, he's devoted the nation's resources to the invasion of England, which he's determined upon. The Austrians have concluded a species of peace with him – there'll be no hostilities on the Rhine to distract him from his purpose, and while the Third Coalition drags its feet he need not fear Russia or Sweden either. Now is the time. Depend upon it, Charles, he cannot maintain his troops and equipment at readiness for ever – he must invade in this season or not at all.'

'So why does he not do so?' Crawford asked.

'Because if he tried, his horde would be massacred by our battleships.'

'And if they protect their invasion flotilla with their own in sufficient numbers?'

'Ah. There you have it. Our instinct has always been to blockade – to lay siege to their ports. Bonaparte's strategy must be to raise it so that all his ships-of-the-line may combine together in numbers over which we cannot prevail. And with the Spanish come in on his side he may count on no less than a hundred sail-of-the-line to this end,' he added.

'This is successful?'

'We are sore pressed, that's the very real truth, Charles. Our ships keep the seas constantly and wear out yet we have not only this blockade but must protect our interests in all the rest of the world.'

'Can you tell me something of the odds at all?'

'In a general sense only. The number of ships available to the commander of a squadron does vary with their readiness, for there will always be numbers away watering, victualling and repairing. I will tell you the gist of it.

'Around France, in their best ports, lie their battle-fleets. The main ones are at Brest under Admiral Ganteaume and in Rochefort under Missiessy, with now Ferrol and Cadiz to be added and, of course, the biggest being Toulon with Villeneuve. There are others lying in Cherbourg, Cartagena and so forth.

'Now if you consider the hostile coastline that we must blockade, then it is from Toulon in the Mediterranean in an unbroken line of some three thousand miles around Spain,

France and then in the Channel to the Netherlands. At the moment we're containing them – Nelson off Toulon for the entire Mediterranean, Orde at Cadiz, Calder at Ferrol and Cornwallis at Brest, each with about a dozen of-the-line and, of course, Keith with the Downs Squadron to watch the invasion flotilla itself.

'If Villeneuve sorties, joins with the Spaniards at Cadiz and Ferrol, then the French at Rochefort, and finally combines with the Brest squadron, we are quite overwhelmed. We know this, which is why we place our battle squadrons outside these ports in blockade to stop them.

'But this is too simple. Napoleon is always to be trusted . . . to surprise and terrify. He knows we will crush his battle-fleet before it has time to come together. He will want therefore to deceive us, send us after a false scent and thereby split our forces.'

'Do we – have we intelligence as will reveal Bonaparte's intentions?'

'Yes. In fact we do.'

'May I be allowed—'

'Our good fortune has been to intercept the very orders Napoleon dispatched to Ganteaume in Brest, detailing his strategic intent and plans for the invasion itself.'

'Good God!'

'Do you wish to know what was contained in them?'

'Of course!'

'Then I will tell you. This is how England is to be invaded. Villeneuve sails from Toulon with a powerful force including soldiers. He leaves the Mediterranean, brushing aside Orde's squadron outside Cadiz and collects the battleships waiting there.

'Instead of making a dash for Brest and the Channel,

Napoleon seeks to outfox us. He tells Villeneuve to sail right across the Atlantic – to Surinam. There he lands his troops and joins with Missiessy, who has come from Rochefort with his own potent forces, which are then used to cause mayhem in the Caribbean.

'A smaller force sails from Toulon, this time to strike south after Gibraltar, taking St Helena and reinforcing Senegal before attacking our young settlements on the African coast and grievously distracting us. That's not all – when Villeneuve and Missiessy return they release the Brest fleet and together they converge on Boulogne to protect the invasion flotilla as it finally sails – three thousand vessels conveying several hundred thousand first-class troops, horses and guns.'

'And our own forces? What do they—'

'Again, Bonaparte is far from lacking in imagination. You see, before this deadly scene is acted out, Ganteaume in Brest has already sailed – he begins to put ashore eighteen thousand men in Lough Swilly in the north of Ireland, to be reinforced by twenty-five thousand Dutch and French from the Netherlands. These are ordered to march directly on Dublin, an intolerable strategic situation for us that demands we send our fleets to prevent it – but we are too late. Having landed his men Ganteaume is even now sailing to join Villeneuve and Missiessy in the grand finale, a total of nearly fifty battleships. And when you reflect that even Admiral Nelson at this moment commands no more than eleven of-the-line and then only if all are present . . .'

Crawford remained silent.

'This then is Napoleon's plan. Will it succeed? I have my doubts. He's treating his naval forces as though they were a regiment of cavalry, no understanding of what problems the sea can throw at his commanders that can send his best-laid plans awry. Possibly his next plan will be more reasonable.'

'Next plan?'

'He knows we've captured his orders, he needs must make others. And this is our dilemma. I put it to you, Charles, how in heaven's name will we know if a sudden move in this chess game is the opening of a grand strategy that ends with the enemy in triumph at our gates, or if it is in fact merely a derisory side-show? Only time will tell, and then it'll be too late.'

'A vexing conundrum.'

'Quite so. And I'll confide to you this hour that it has already begun. Missiessy has sortied from Rochefort. Our best information is that this is a voyage to the Caribbean, as provided for in the previous plan. He has a powerful fleet and our islands are probably under assault as we talk here together.

'We must consider carefully. Is this an attempt to draw us away from our blockade so he may make his move on England? Or is it a full-scale onslaught on our colonies? Could it be that this serves as well to be a point of concentration for all his squadrons, which then descend together on the Channel? Or even . . . is this all a bluff of colossal proportions, that it is never the intention to go there, keeping a powerful fleet hidden in the ocean wastes ready to fall on us unaware?'

Crawford shifted uncomfortably. 'We must be prepared for all eventualities.'

'So we should. But know that our lines of communication at sea are long – very long. To send orders to Lord Nelson in the Mediterranean and receive his acknowledgement is a matter of six weeks and more. How, then, should we in the

Admiralty respond when we have urgent news of the enemy's motions? Immediately send details and orders to the admiral concerned? I rather think not, for by the time he receives them our event is history, and the orders an impertinence.'

'But – but how then can you . . . ?'

'We must trust our admirals, is the only course. Provide them with the best means to make a decision and step back to allow them to act entirely as they see fit at the time. No other will answer.'

'This I perceive, Edward. Knowing the grand situation you will dispatch intelligence pertaining and principles of action and hope mightily that your man plays his cards well, that he is not trumped by the enemy.' He remained thoughtful. 'If you'll allow me to say it, old fellow, it does strike me as a frightful burden on your Admiralty. All responsibility for the defence of the realm and, blindfolded, they must turn over the means of action to others.'

'It is,' Boyd said, with feeling. 'What shall we do with Missiessy in the Caribbean? Of course, any orders to the Leeward Islands station will reach there only after the Frenchman is on his way back.'

'I do pity with all my heart your first lord – Melville, isn't it? Such cares and woes and naught he might do . . .'

Boyd gave him a wry look. 'Do save your feelings, Charles. In this case they'll be wasted.'

'Why, surely—'

'Yesterday afternoon at three, my lords assembled in Parliament did carry a vote of impeachment against the first lord, who had no other alternative than to resign immediately.'

'Impeachment!'

'A foolish affair. His private and public accounts became entangled some years ago. The Speaker's casting vote in the event became necessary, but the result is the same. As of this moment, when the kingdom is under the greatest threat it has ever seen, the first lord of the Admiralty is gone and no one in his place.'

'This is monstrous! It's unthinkable!'

'I myself am without employment: there's no one authorised to sign for expenditures, promotions – or may take operational decisions. The Admiralty is rudderless – paralysed. I really can't think but that, whether we like it or no, we are now entirely in the hands of Lord Nelson and his band of brothers.'

From the perspective of *L'Aurore*, the Mediterranean fleet a few cables off her lee in line ahead was a stirring sight. Through Kydd's glass he could see *Victory*'s quarterdeck and one still and lonely figure, upon whom so much depended.

Kydd's orders were quickly collected. 'Proceed with the utmost expedition in His Majesty's Ship *L'Aurore* under your Command to round the Isles of Galita, keeping with the coast until you shall fall in with His Majesty's Ship *Ambuscade* before Tunis and thence to me at Rendezvous Number 38 as expeditiously as possible.'

Nelson wanted the inshore passage up against the North African coast reconnoitred for an attempt to slip past to the eastern Mediterranean – to the Ionians, Egypt, even Turkey. Nothing was to be left to chance. The secret rendezvous number was north of Palermo in Sicily, well placed for the fleet to intercept a move through either of the only two routes to the east.

'Loose courses, Mr Kendall,' Kydd told the master, and in short order *L'Aurore* spread her wings for the south.

Close in to the Barbary coast the dull ochre landscape stretched away in both directions from the scrubby islets, and the acrid scent of parched desert wafted out to them, taking him back immediately to those times before in dear *Teazer* that now seemed so uncomplicated.

Then it had been the scene of a vanquished Napoleon scuttling back to a divided France; now it was the infinitely more dangerous preventing of an all-powerful emperor combining his forces and falling on England.

The easterly was making progress difficult but Kydd knew that close inshore the desert winds coming out would be enough to see them along and with bowlines to courses and topsails the frigate seethed through the water, prepared at every low point and headland for the dread sight ahead of Villeneuve's battle fleet.

There were Arab fishing craft aplenty but without the lingo it was futile to stop and question them and no other square-rigged vessel was in sight. At the point where the coastline fell away they were in the Gulf of Tunis and their task was over. *Ambuscade* was duly sighted and they both bore away for the rendezvous.

They were received courteously enough but their lack of news was clearly a blow. Must they cast further into the thousand-mile expanse to the east – or had Villeneuve, as before, returned to Toulon? A sense of desperation gripped the fleet and a despondent Howlett muttered darkly that it were better that Lord Nelson had kept a conventional close blockade than fall back to allow an escape.

New orders came. Precious frigates were sent to the Ionians, to Tripoli, another north towards Corsica – and *L'Aurore* to the west, to round the Balearics and then look into Toulon before heading back to another rendezvous north of Sicily.

The easterly was veering and the frigate thrashed along at

her best speed, every man aboard conscious of time passing by, and the enemy slipping away from a climactic confrontation. Then at dawn, with Ibiza a smudge on the horizon, the lookout hailed the deck: '*Deck hooo!* Topsails over, fine on the larb'd bow!'

Kydd leaped for the weather shrouds. From the cross-trees he saw that the faded sails belonged to no self-respecting man-o'-war, but even a merchantman had eyes.

'Lay us athwart his course, if you please,' he said briskly, when he regained the quarterdeck. The master glanced up to the lookout, who threw out an arm, and before long a boat was in the water crossing to a sea-darkened Ragusan barque.

Kydd hauled himself up the sides. A characterful stench rose from the hold as a surly master presented himself. Experienced from countless boardings, Kydd knew the neutral was ruing the hours that would be lost to a search and examination of his cargo, so drew himself up and instructed Renzi, 'Tell him I'm not examining his freighting or his papers. It's where the enemy fleet is that's most important to me.'

Renzi began in his Italian but the master waved it aside and answered, in stumbling French, 'I know of no fleet, Mr Englishman, but I tell you, *les vauriens* are no friends of mine.'

'Have you seen any in the last month?'

'A month? Why, yes. In fact, many together.'

Kydd tensed. 'When?'

'Let me see. It was ten – no, eleven days ago. Off Cape Gatto and standing to the west in a fresh easterly, they were.'

'How many?' Kydd rapped.

'I remember well – they were so great in number. Twelve big two- and three-deckers, and four others under a press o' sail. They weren't like your fleets, all in a nice line, these were in a jumble, *hein?*'

238

After more questions about flags and pennants it was beyond question: Villeneuve had been spotted. Kydd raced back into the boat. 'Stretch out for your lives, y' rogues!' he gasped.

The French had been found – but it was the worst possible news he was bringing Nelson. Cape Gatto was near the choke point where the Mediterranean narrowed to Gibraltar and it was now very clear that Villeneuve had achieved what all had feared – a breakout.

L'Aurore raised the fleet after a furious sail. Her signals caused the flagship to instantly heave to the entire squadron. Kydd was summoned to report, only too aware of the consternation his news would bring.

He was back as quickly. Seeing his grave expression, Renzi put down his work and said quietly, 'A hard thing for Our Nel indeed. I'd believe that others might forgive should he be caught in a melancholy at our discovery.'

Kydd took off his coat and gazed out of the stern windows at *Victory* still lying to. 'It was a cruel blow, that I could tell, Nicholas. He's been waiting for two years to have an accounting with the French and now they're out and who knows where? What wrings his heart is that he thinks he's failed – they're out of our grasp and Villeneuve is following his master's orders and stretching out for England, joining with others in Ferrol and so on.'

'A frightful thing,' Renzi said, in a low voice.

'Or they'll be challenged on their way north by Orde's squadron off Cadiz! Nelson's much out of countenance that the deciding battle will not be his to command, for you'll know that Admiral Orde is his senior and no friend.'

'Then it's too late,' Renzi said gravely. 'We must say it's out of our hands now. Villeneuve two weeks ahead of us, the issue will be settled by others before we can come to help them.'

It was finally happening: the growing avalanche of joining enemy ships even now converging on the Channel, sweeping aside the Brest blockade and at last allowing the vast invasion fleet to put to sea. There would be heroic sacrifices by Keith's Downs Squadron as the juggernaut advanced until inevitably tens of thousands of Napoleon Bonaparte's best troops came flooding ashore in England.

It would be all over within weeks, the pitiful numbers of Britain's army swept aside in a victorious push on London and a falling back on the last strongholds of the ancient kingdom. The land they would eventually return to would be a very different place.

'If Nelson is not to be cast down, then neither shall I,' Kydd said firmly. 'The people will be unsettled – this is understandable. The Mediterranean Squadron is to fall back on Gibraltar for news, I'm told, but *L'Aurore* will stand resolute whatever this is.'

With deliberate calm, Kydd went out on deck, sniffed the wind and saw a signal fly up *Victory*'s mizzen halliards. It was the instruction to press westward on the long haul to Gibraltar and he lost no time in giving the orders for taking up their scouting position ahead of the fleet.

Once settled after the flurry of activity, the men showed little inclination to go below, standing in knots and looking back towards the quarterdeck. They would have worked out the implications for themselves.

Should he call them aft for a bracing talk? What was there to say?

Instead he crossed to the helm, looking at the binnacle deliberately as though checking their course. Then, nodding to himself as though satisfied, he stood back with arms folded and gazed thoughtfully ahead.

As he hoped, the officer-of-the-watch, Gilbey, came up hesitantly beside him. 'A rum do, sir.'

'What do you mean, sir?' Kydd came back mildly.

'Why, the Crapauds having escaped Lord Nelson out o' the Med.'

Behind him by the helmsman were the silent figures of the quartermaster and his mate, two hands and a midshipman.

'Not at all,' Kydd returned coolly, in a voice above the usual conversational level. 'I'm in no doubt it's part of the plan – have you not considered, Mr Gilbey, that this is why Admiral Orde has been placed off Cadiz for just this happening? He's to confront the French and in the delay we will join him, as will Admiral Calder from Ferrol, and we'll have a famous battle.'

He chuckled. 'I do pity Villeneuve – he'll wish mightily he'd stayed safe and snug in Toulon.'

'But—'

Kydd allowed a frown to appear. 'Have you any doubt of the outcome, sir? When I saw him Lord Nelson was vastly content that the French have at last showed themselves and longs for a conclusion. We couldn't find them – now we know where they are. Is this not a cause for joy?'

'Aye, sir,' Gilbey answered carefully.

It was all Kydd could do: the rumours would fly, he had no control over that, but if the men on watch, overhearing their captain, could take away the observation that to him all was going to plan then it was something they could hold on to.

Gibraltar. Eight hundred miles to the west: less than a week's sailing with a fair wind – but the veering easterly had gone through south and was now firming from the west. Dead foul for the Rock.

Day after day the Mediterranean Squadron tacked in long boards ever westwards, the staying about at the end of each a mechanical routine, their advance pricked off on the chart a dispiriting procession. And day after day the winds held steady from the west, always in their face, always foul for Gibraltar.

They finally clawed their way into the narrowing passage between Africa and Europe that would end in the Strait of Gibraltar. The winds had fallen to a balmy serenity – and with the notorious current through the strait driving in from the Atlantic the squadron was now threatened with being 'back-strapped' – unable to make progress in the light winds and therefore remorselessly carried back whence they had come.

The weary fight ended temporarily almost within sight of their goal when the squadron was diverted to Tetuan to take on fresh water and supplies.

Tetuan was well known to all nations for its good watering and it was not remarkable to see a Portuguese ship-of-the-line laying to its task when the squadron dropped anchor. What was not expected was the hurried departure of a boat containing a senior officer, which made its way to *Victory*. Even less expected was the result: *L'Aurore*'s pennants and the summoning of her captain.

The commander-in-chief was furiously busy, a stream of clerks, captains, officers and others demanding audience, seen and sent on their way with his secretary at the tall side-desk steadily documenting the activity. But when Kydd appeared they were banished and Nelson quickly sat him down at the vast table.

'News,' he said, a marked animation in his tired, worn features. 'I have a service for you this hour, Mr Kydd, but first I will tell you this that you might understand the task.

'The Portuguee is commanded by an Englishman who knows his duty and he has some startling information. While heading here, he sighted Villeneuve on a bowline north of Cadiz but – mark this – on a course west-nor'-west until out of sight.'

'The – the West Indies?' hazarded Kydd.

'As I could be persuaded,' Nelson growled, but fiddled with his pencil. 'Yet he has troops and the Spanish. To me, this seems to speak less of Brazil or the Caribbean and more of a pass north to raise the blockade of Ferrol and then a strike at Ireland.'

'My lord, if he sailed north, surely he must have encountered Admiral Orde and the Cadiz squadron.'

'He did.'

'Sir?'

'Villeneuve and his squadron sailed *through* Admiral Orde's force to enter Cadiz,' Nelson said bitterly, not hiding his contempt. 'Not a shot fired, he lets them pass.'

Kydd held a wary silence. It had been talked about that once one of Nelson's invaluable frigates in passing had been intercepted by the senior Orde and taken into local service out of apparent spite and there was little love lost between them.

'Not that you'll sight him – the Portuguee says he immediately retired northward, no doubt falling back on the Channel and not thinking to send a cutter to tell me of his motions or those of the French.'

'Sir.'

'I'm sanguine he'll answer for it later, but it leaves me with a decision. I can't dismiss that Villeneuve is making for the West Indies as in Bonaparte's old plan, but on the other hand I can't take the unsupported word of this officer in foreign service.

'In the face of all these rumours I've so little intelligence and I must remedy it. You're to sail for Lisbon this hour, Captain, find out what you can about Villeneuve and tell me.'

Bowden was not the only one busy with pen and paper: nearly all the gunroom was so occupied, for the chance here in Gibraltar to get a letter away to England, home and family was too good to miss. Ignoring the crushing weariness – they had been frantically storing ship in Rosia Bay until darkness put an end to it – he tested the quill nib and began.

Dear Uncle

I hardly know how to start this letter to you, for there's every expectation that by the time you receive it there'll have been that great clash of arms so devoutly prayed for by our dear commander, the pity of it all being he shall not be part of it.

What am I saying? As I write this, while we stay idle Napoleon's vile hordes may well be unleashed on you and all England to suffer the final reckoning. We cannot know, and Our Nel is beside himself with vexation, for he dare not move for want of intelligence of the enemy which is scant and full of question – but I shall start from the beginning from what we know at this moment . . .

He sucked the feathered end of the quill distractedly and continued with an account of the sudden irruption of the enemy and their extreme frustrations in following.

Conceive of the scene, Uncle, the fleet watering at Tetuan, a neutral Portuguese advising that the Frenchy fleet was sighted spreading sail for the open Atlantic. Is it to be the

West Indies, or is it a ruse to send us off on a wild-goose chase while they double back to join up in the Channel? We cannot know and what is worse is that while these light airs keep in the west we're prisoners.

Not one to weep over what can't be helped, our commander-in-chief orders us to water and take on greens and dispatches *Superb* to round up beef for the fleet. He sends a frigate to Lisbon for news. She's *L'Aurore*, a famous sailer in a breeze whom we haven't heard from yet. Then the wind shifts just enough to the sou'-west and we sail all of a sudden, even leaving *Superb*'s bullocks standing on the beach!

And so we make Gibraltar. Uncle, if you could hear the rumours fly, it would stand your hair on end. We've stopped every ship, but none with a whisper of where Villeneuve is or has been. It's as if the devil is concealing his own. The ship thinks to a man, however, that the Frenchies after emptying Cadiz simply carried on north and even now are raising Cain and disputing with Admiral Cornwallis for the Channel.

He paused, reviewing what he knew and ended:

What is certain is that as the Mediterranean Squadron this cannot be our concern but, dear Uncle, how long can a fire-brand like Our Nel lie idle while matters are decided by others?

There was little more to say so he carefully creased the paper but paused before the wafer was affixed, thinking that it might be wiser to leave it to the last minute, just in case.

Some five days later his forethought was rewarded. In furious haste he set up on the table and scribbled rapidly in pencil:

Uncle – I write in a rush. There's a dispatch cutter returning in one hour and I must give you this news, which I'll wager will set you a-gasp – Lord Nelson has broken out of station!

It was a crime beyond forgiveness for a commander-in-chief to abandon his station without the knowledge of the Admiralty. There, plans were formulated on the premise that on the world chessboard fleets were expected to be in readiness in known areas for the moves and counter-moves that constituted high strategy. It was without doubt that such a one absenting himself and his fleet would answer for it at a court-martial.

In idleness beyond enduring, Uncle, he took it on himself to exit the Mediterranean and go north to seek Villeneuve on his own account, taking the entire fleet. We sailed helter-skelter north past Cadiz, Huelva, and saw nothing. Then met with Capt Sutton, *Amphion* frigate. Oh, I forgot to say the French got past Admiral Orde to enter Cadiz, then he sailed away to the north. *Amphion* was in his command and left to guard his squadron's storeships as were left behind, north in Lagos Bay.

Anyway, Capt Sutton was sure no enemy sail had sailed by him and said the Portuguee must be right, that the Frenchies were away to the Caribbean, but Nelson said it was no proof, simply to say *he* hadn't seen them go by. Oh, my, can you imagine the discussions on the quarterdeck? Then out of the rain pops *L'Aurore* south from Lisbon. Captain Kydd comes aboard in a rush with the news that there was no news – everyone positive that no French sail had ever come this far north.

Well, that was enough for Our Nel! He has his proof – for

if Villeneuve did not go north or to the south then he is off out to sea, to the West Indies, and claims that as Admiral Orde is absent it'll be us as'll pursue him there. So here we are, the Mediterranean Squadron turned Atlantic, and we're off in a grand chase across the ocean! Thirty-one days astern of our quarry we do calculate.

He grinned and added,

In course, in his last orders before we set sail he claims *Amphion* as his own and sets the squadron loose on Adm Orde's store-ships to strip as they please. It'll be some months before their lordships hear of this sally and by then we'll be the other side of the Atlantic and there Nelson trusts we'll have our due accounting with Mr Villeneuve. In haste, Uncle – do give my duty to Aunt . . .

Chapter 10

The last the squadron saw of Europe was Cape St Vincent, a long, flat finger of land pointing out into the infinity of the Atlantic Ocean as if to urge them on towards their destiny. As it softened into a blue-grey haze and slowly faded into an empty horizon, aboard every ship there came the age-old contraction of their world into that bounded by the ship's side.

For a fleet, the consciousness extended out to the line of ships that were in company, but each world was its own, self-contained and complete. With flags alone to communicate, there could be no casual gossip or civil exchange of pleas-antries, no domestic scandals to discuss, no wistful hopes expressed.

And ahead was the enemy. At any moment a lookout's cry could signal the first far glimpse of Villeneuve's Combined Fleet and then somewhere in the midst of the ocean would come the climactic battle that would decide the fate of peoples thousands of miles distant.

Deep into the Atlantic the squadron heaved to, the onward

march of the broad searching ships in line abreast coming to a stop. *L'Aurore* was ordered to pass within hail of the flagship in the centre. Knowing he was under eye, Kydd ensured his approach was impeccable. The unmistakable figure of the commander-in-chief himself raised a speaking trumpet from *Victory*'s quarterdeck.

'Do you take these instructions to every vessel in my command, Mr Kydd – and know that even minutes lost waiting here in idleness takes the French further from my grasp.'

'Aye, aye, my lord!' Kydd bellowed back. Seeing the quick-witted Curzon sending men to the jolly-boat at the stern davits to prepare for launching, he added: 'Then I'd be obliged should you order the fleet to be under way directly, sir.'

After a moment's hesitation Nelson turned to Captain Hardy and said something. *L'Aurore*'s boat came alongside below the entry port and a small chest containing the orders was swayed aboard. It shoved off, and instantly a signal broke out at *Victory*'s mizzen – 'Squadron to resume course'. If Kydd was wrong that he could distribute the orders while all the vessels were under full sail, it would be at the cost of fleet-wide amusement.

The boat returned to *L'Aurore* as the line of ships ponderously caught the wind and continued on their way. Kydd peered over the side. Nelson's instructions were in individually labelled sailcloth packages and, from the way the men hefted them, properly weighted with musket balls.

'Ah, Poulden,' he said, as his coxswain hurried up to report. 'To every ship, beginning with *Tigre*. And mark well how it's to be done!' His plan required a frigate of outstanding sailing qualities but he knew he had that. With satisfaction he saw Stirk tumble down into the boat: his manoeuvres also required the hand and eye of a true seaman.

Tigre was the windward ship-of-the-line. With her boat towing astern *L'Aurore* shook out a reef and caught up with, then passed her, for the fleet was progressing at the speed of the slowest, the barnacled *Superb* at some six knots only.

The tow-line was thrown off and with the last of the headway Poulden closed with the massive blunt bows of the 74 as it foamed along, heedless. At a dozen feet distant Stirk's heave was unerring. The boat-rope shot up into the fore-chains and seamen aboard quickly took a turn, the boat now in an exaggerated bucketing as she was pulled along.

Then Stirk's messenger line sailed over the bulwarks and the seamen hauled in the commander-in-chief's instructions. Both lines were then cast off and thrown into the boat, which fended off and wallowed in the mid-ocean swell as *Tigre*'s massive bulk hissed past.

Miraculously *L'Aurore* was there for the boat: Kydd had brailed up his courses to fall back as *Tigre* passed and now quickly took up the tow and loosed sail for the next, *Leviathan*. One by one he did the same for the rest, and when it was done he resumed his position at the wing of the line.

'From Flag, sir. "Manoeuvre well executed".' Kydd tried to affect disinterest at the signal midshipman's report.

Day after day, mile after mile, the seas got brighter and warmer with sightings of tropical seabirds and flying fish. In any other time and place it would have been a sea idyll but soon there would be fighting and death. Daily gun-drill was regular and long; boarders were exercised, small-arms were practised. Somewhere ahead, in the open ocean or among the islands of the Caribbean, they would overhaul the French and force them to the battle that had been so long denied them.

Thirty, twenty, fifteen degrees latitude – the trade winds

bore the squadron on at a pace. The chills of winter were a fading memory: hauling seamen had naked backs and bare feet, and windsails were rigged over the hatch gratings to send cool airs into the lower-deck.

Still no urgent cry came; *L'Aurore*, like the other frigates, was far out on the wings of the extended line, a width of near sixty miles being combed by the ongoing ships. Every new dawn saw each ship silently at quarters, doubled lookouts in their lofty eyrie straining to see as light began to steal over the grey sea, turning it by degrees to a deep blue – and always with the line of the horizon gradually firming and innocent of threat.

And after four thousand miles and three weeks at sea an undistinguished and tiny intrusion into the far blue rim: Barbados. What would they find there? That Nelson had been comprehensively fooled into a wild-goose chase across the whole Atlantic? Or that the French had come and gone, leaving a smoking ruin where once had been the richest of England's possessions?

The squadron fleet came to anchor in Carlisle Bay – and, praise be, the cannon of Fort Charles thudded their salute. Smoke wreathed slowly about the Union Flag hanging limply above it in the tropical heat.

In minutes the bay was alive with watercraft heading out: bum-boats, with limes, bananas and illicit rum hidden inside coconuts, mixing with official vessels and store-ships.

Without warning guns began to open up around the whole fleet throwing the craft into confusion – but it was only another salute, the twenty-one for the King's Birthday.

Shortly after, a boat brought an excitable army lieutenant to *L'Aurore*. He had alarming and thrilling news: the French had been sighted! They had caused destruction and consternation everywhere – at St Kitts, Nevis, Montserrat – and everyone was on edge at where they would strike next. The arrival of Nelson's squadron was not a moment too soon.

Kydd realised that to have achieved such damage already, this could only have been Missiessy's Rochefort squadron, which had sortied earlier. This was a double setback: not simply the devastation caused but that it was not Villeneuve – had they chased across the Atlantic after a phantom?

A peremptory gun banged out from *Victory*, drawing attention to the 'all captains' signal. Within two hours of anchoring, after a desperate chase across the ocean, Nelson was summoning a council-of-war.

Kydd wondered how he would take the latest news but the answer came as his barge neared the flagship. The Blue Peter broke at the masthead – the order for the fleet to make ready to sail.

Kydd entered the great cabin with several others at once. Nelson stood in much good humour, welcoming them in, exchanging gossip of the voyage, asking after ailments. When all had arrived he bade them be seated.

'Gentlemen, you'll be as elated as I to know that not only was I right in my surmise that Villeneuve was bound to the Indies but that he's within a day or so's reach of me. We've word here from General Brereton on St Lucia that he's arrived in Martinique this past two weeks or so.' He looked about the assembled group with beaming satisfaction.

'Not only that . . . but he's since sailed and cannot be far distant.'

Kydd's pulse quickened. It sounded like an action was imminent. The clash of fleets would be in the Caribbean, much as Rodney's great victory at the Saintes a generation before, just north beyond Martinique. Could it be . . . ?

'I'm told as well that Missiessy's Rochefort squadron of five of-the-line and four frigates is returning to join him and, further, that Admiral Magon with more sail-of-the-line has but yesterday reached here.' Stirring among the captains showed the point was well taken – that now they were gravely outnumbered.

'The God of Battles has delivered them to me!' Nelson's eyes glowed with conviction. 'We now have a noble chance to meet and destroy them!' Growls of agreement rose from around the table, Kydd's enthusiastically among them. Who could possibly doubt that, with Nelson at the fore, a victory was certain?

'To business. General Brereton's information is that the French are headed south and our only colony of consequence there is Trinidad, which it is supposed is now taken by Villeneuve's armament. Now, do mark that Port of Spain, which is sheltered around the inner side of the Gulf of Paria, may only be approached by one channel, here – the Dragon's Mouth.'

This was the narrow passage between the island and South America, shallows and rocky islets on every hand. 'A grim place for an encounter, my lord,' came a low mutter.

'Possibly,' Nelson snapped. 'Once through, I'd believe we'll find the French and Spaniards at anchor off the town, and then – and then it will be the glorious Nile once again.' It was there that Nelson had impetuously thrown his fleet at the French at anchor and achieved the most complete victory in naval history so far.

'And we'll trounce 'em once again!' Kydd found himself saying.

'God willing. The Barbados military are insisting we ship troops for the recovery of the island, and while I have my

253

doubts of soldiers afloat I cannot refuse this handsome offer in such a laudable endeavour.

'I have dispatched a schooner south. It will signal confirmation of the presence of the enemy, which shall then be your call to clear for action. We sail as soon as the soldiers are embarked.'

So it was to be a titanic struggle set in the hellish conditions of a brackish mangrove-ridden inland sea, ferocious jungle heat and tormenting insects. The soldiers could not be allowed on the gun-decks and would suffer appallingly in the fearsome hot stink of the orlop until the battle was won, but it couldn't be helped.

The squadron weighed and stood south in the sultry easterly, the fleet that had endured a blockade in the depths of winter now sweltering in the blazing sun of the tropics in high summer. Ships and men had, without benefit of special storing or dockyard, made an immediate transition to full battle-readiness. This was the unsung glory of Nelson's leadership, a tribute to the minute attention he always gave to the details.

Within twenty-four hours Tobago lifted into view and they altered westward for Galleon's Passage keeping well out to sea for the last stretch before the Dragon's Mouth. As the afternoon wore on, in light winds they closed with the coast – Trinidad.

The leading frigate, *Amphion*, suddenly sheered out of position on seeing a schooner close inshore with a red pennant over black hoisted. It was the exact signal they had been waiting for and *Amphion*'s 'enemy are present' soared up eagerly.

The distant thunder of drums rolled over the water as the squadron prepared. Now there could be no more doubting, no more conjecture. They had chased Villeneuve and had him cornered.

As they neared the craggy, palm-girt beaches, the flames and smoke of destruction could be seen, forts and guard-posts ablaze in the steaming interior. Did this mean they were too late, that the enemy had landed and were victorious?

Grimly they stood to their guns as they neared the swirl of currents about Chacachacare, the first islet, sweating in the heat but keyed up for the fight to come. Once around the dark-green point in the violent red sunset, would they burst like an avenging thunderbolt on Villeneuve at anchor, just as they had at the Nile?

First one ship, then another glided past – and then Kydd himself saw beyond the point into the wide bay of Port of Spain.

It was utterly deserted of ships.

Gasps of disbelief turned to cursing as those with telescopes picked out the English colours hanging limply above the white residence ashore and passed on the sight to others. The island was never under threat and, in what could only be the working of the devil's magic, Villeneuve and the Spaniards had eluded them once again.

The next morning the Mediterranean Squadron put to sea for the return to Barbados. 'What did Nelson say?' Renzi asked quietly of Kydd.

Wiping his forehead, Kydd gave a lop-sided grin. 'Not, as who should say, cast down but . . .'

'How could it be? Everything pointed to . . .'

'A failing of information, is all.'

'Oh?'

'A villainous American merchantman swore that he'd been

stopped and boarded from a great French fleet that had then crowded on sail to the south. He was lying to deceive, of course, but when the signal post on St Lucia reported a host of ships bound southward as well, what else could be believed?'

'The lobsterbacks saw a convoy as would seem to them a mighty fleet, I'd wager. But the schooner – she signalled—'

'The schooner was a Bermudan who was innocently about her trade, signalling to her business agent ashore. That she chose the self-same flags is the greatest of coincidences – while ours was away still searching.'

'The destruction we saw ashore? If the French were not responsible then . . . ?'

'Ha! This is your local militia mistaking us for Villeneuve and being over-hasty to retreat and fire their defences.'

It was the damnedest luck, and now they were back where they had started. For the pity of it all, where were the French?

They had hardly cleared the Dragon's Mouth when they had their answer. A fast cutter made for *Victory* and soon its dispatches became general knowledge.

Villeneuve had shown his hand. He had not deployed his forces in laying waste to English possessions: instead he had spent precious time throwing his battle-fleet against a rock!

Two years previously, in an epic of courage and adventure, sailors from *Centaur* had scaled a near vertical monolith and hauled up guns and equipment, arming the rock like a ship. It was rated by the Navy as HM Sloop *Diamond Rock* and, located at the very entrance to Fort de France, the main harbour of Martinique, it dominated the approaches to the port. From its lofty heights they could spy on every sea movement.

Only after several days' bombardment and the failure of

their water supply did the little 'ship' capitulate. But their sacrifice would not be in vain. Nelson was galvanised and, abandoning Barbados, still with the soldiers aboard, set his fleet's course directly north to pass along the chain of islands that were the eastern limits of the Caribbean Sea and were among the richest in the world. Villeneuve would be sure to fall on them with the forces he commanded.

One by one the islands lifted above the horizon. Local craft were questioned about what they had seen before the ships sailed on to the next, Grenada, St Vincent, St Lucia. *Amphion* was sent to look into Martinique but found no fleet, Dominica, then Guadeloupe and on to Montserrat. A report there, however, had eighteen sail-of-the-line under French and Spanish colours slipping by not three days previously.

Was it to be Antigua, with the best dockyard in the Caribbean? Or had the enemy vanished into the blue as they had done so often before?

They raised Antigua at first light, the jaded gun-crews at their quarters in readiness – but yet again there was no word. If Villeneuve went much further there would be no more islands for him to assault. Unless he veered to the west and fell on Jamaica . . .

With the prospect of a cataclysmic battle at any moment against a foe with double his numbers, Nelson could not afford to send off his frigates on a thorough search and could therefore only piece together what could be gleaned from local report and rumour.

And this was building to a growing conviction – that Villeneuve's presence in the West Indies could no longer be assured. Spies in Guadeloupe had seen landed there all the troops and military stores that Villeneuve had carried across the Atlantic, which made it probable he had no longer any intention of invading and capturing territory. And a fleet of men-o'-war, however large, had no place in the Caribbean without an apparent adversary. So if it existed at all – and there was still no absolute proof – what the devil was it up to?

While the long-suffering soldiers aboard were released from their hell below-decks and sent ashore, Nelson called his captains. The tension and frustration were plain to see in the stooped figure but when he raised his head the fire was still in his eyes.

'It must be plain to you all that a decision must now be made. Do we move to the relief of Jamaica or . . . ?'

'Port Royal is eight hundred miles away, my lord,' Keats said slowly. 'If we meet with the same disappointment it will be . . . unfortunate.'

'And if in the pursuit we are able to forereach on the rogue and bring him to battle?'

In the stuffy heat it was hard to think constructively but the sight of their doughty commander fighting exhaustion drove them on. 'Then we sail for Jamaica? I fear I'll need to water first,' Bayntun of *Leviathan* said, fanning himself rapidly.

'Did I say that's where we set course? I rather think he's bound elsewhere.'

'My lord?'

'He comes to the Caribbean hoping to stir up mischief and then he learns to his dismay that Horatio Nelson is on his tail. Even with a score of battleships he knows he's no match for the British Fleet. I feel in my bones he's given up – that he's fleeing back across the Atlantic to Toulon again.'

'With not a thing achieved?' Keats rumbled, in open disbelief. 'My lord, with such an armament they may conjure such a mill in our waters as would be remembered for generations.'

The cooler tones of Hallowell of *Tigre* intervened: 'To come all this way to capture just one rock does seem a singular thing, sir.'

'Nevertheless, a return to France must be considered.' Nelson wiped his forehead and whispered, 'And be damned to General Brereton for his false information as sent us flying in the wrong direction.'

'Hear, hear!' murmured Hallowell, but they were interrupted by a loud knock at the door.

'My lord . . .' It was Hardy, ushering in an absurdly young lieutenant who looked about, abashed.

'This is scarcely the time for civilities, Captain,' Nelson said acidly.

'I conceive you'd be interested in what he has to report, my lord. Lieutenant Carr, *Netley* schooner.'

'Well?' Nelson snapped.

'Er, my lord. I'm lately escort with dispatches to a convoy out of St John's bound for England.'

'Yes, yes, get on with it!'

'Well, sir – my lord – three days out, which is to say two days ago only, we fell in with a French fleet of overwhelming force and—'

'What ships – how many? Speak up, sir!'

'I have a list here, my lord. Um, eighteen ships-of-the-line, six frigates, some—'

Nelson shot to his feet, his features animated. 'A day or two only! What followed?'

'I'm sorry to say, sir, the convoy of fourteen was largely taken, but I stayed with the main French fleet to determine their course, thinking my dispatches of less consequence.'

It was a remarkable act of moral courage by a junior officer to turn back to search out Nelson, thereby overriding his inviolable duty to deliver dispatches with all speed.

'And what course did they take?'

'North, sir. Of a certainty.'

Slowly Nelson sat down. 'We have them!' he hissed. 'One or two days ahead – what a race I've run after those fellows! But God is just and by this I'm repaid for all my anxiety.'

North – leaving the Caribbean and entering the stream of trade-winds that led back to Europe. After beginning the chase thirty-one days behind and sent after a false scent they were now almost within reach of their prey.

'My lord, notwithstanding they're but a day or so ahead, it does strike me that we're sadly outnumbered.' The hardy old Keats spoke for many and could never be thought shy of a fight.

'Prudence is not cowardliness, dear fellow, but in defiance of their two thousand great guns and ten thousand men, I would sooner be hoist at the fore than lose the chance to close accounts with Monsieur Villeneuve.'

Growls of satisfaction rose from around the table. 'Gentlemen!' Nelson said, with a tight smile. 'Fleet to unmoor immediately – course north!'

In the warm quartering south-easterly, stunsails were spread and, after laying Barbuda to starboard, they left the Caribbean, straining every stitch of canvas and nerve in the chase northward. Somewhere out there beyond the bowsprit was another fleet and when they converged . . .

Aboard *L'Aurore* the day passed into a tropic evening with no indication yet of the enemy. The comforting routine of the change of watches took place and the ship settled for the oncoming night. Kydd stood well back as the man at the helm was relieved and the quartermaster at the conn chalked Gilbey's night orders for course and sail on his slate. The watch mustered by the main-mast for the usual trimming before they could settle to yarn-spinning and quiet reflection.

As the red orb of the sun dipped below the horizon the world seemed quieter, more serene, and a defined night shadow moved steadily up the swaying masts – above, the poignant rose tinge on the sails of the very last of the day, below, the crepuscular draining of colour that would soon turn to the blackness of night.

Kydd enjoyed this time. Not especially a romantic soul, he could nevertheless respond to the timeless mystery of the evening, the clarity of nature's beauty here so far at sea beyond the land's dusty air and swirling odours. In a way his sturdy, four-square perspective kept him from the agonies of soul that seemed to haunt the dreamers but on the other hand he realised there were levels of the human experience he would never know as Renzi did.

His thoughts wandered to his friend. The man was gifted: he had found a purpose in life to direct his talents yet was clearly morbid, troubled. Was this a price to be paid for genius? In a short while, in the last of the light, Renzi would stir from his hiding place in the fore-top where he would have spent the previous hour or so in silent vigil. What went through his noble mind while in such rapt contemplation?

On cue, as the last tinting of rose lifted above the swell of the topgallant sail, a figure swung out of the top and descended slowly to the deck. Nothing was said and he and Kydd went below for supper and a little wine.

This night there was even less conversation than normal. At one point Kydd asked after his health and Renzi seemed not to hear, gazing past Kydd unseeingly, a frown of concentration on his sensitive features.

'A pretty problem, I'd wager,' Kydd chuckled, 'as is taxing a mind like yours, m' friend!'

Renzi gave a wan smile. 'I do ask pardon, dear chap, my mind's on quite another tack – a hard beat to wind'd, if you will.'

'Ah! You've seen a sight ashore as is testing your theories, I'd believe. Now, let me see – you've not stepped off since the Med, so it must be . . . the Ionians? Or can it be your Diolkos? But there's no humankind we saw there and your study is man and his response to life's challenges . . .'

Renzi winced. 'I'll grant you, Sardinia was of interest. I was gratified to find your Sard is the most nearly pure Latin of any tongue on earth, granted a forbearance of the barbarisms of Phoenicia within and . . . and . . .'

'Nicholas – there's something wrong, I'd believe,' Kydd said, in concern.

Renzi gave a half-smile. 'There is, brother. You'll recall our earlier conversation about the difficulties in the publishing of my work. I'm now, dear friend, utterly convinced that unless I cast it in the form of a purple traveller's tale or enter upon literary circles to cry up the piece then it will never attract the interest of a publisher.'

'If it's just a matter of the cobbs, Nicholas—'

'It is not. Without an academic tenure of some colour I will never be able to command the attention of a serious nature that it deserves.'

'Oh. So you're saying to me . . .'

'That my dabbling in natural philosophy is of no consequence in the larger sphere of learning and publishing. That it were better I accept this and cease my futile labouring.'

'No! Damn it, you've a right trim-rigged intellect as should set a course to—'

'But can you conceive of the *triste* and heavy burden it is to know that as you toil your striving is in vain?'

Unsure what to say, Kydd stayed silent.

'Never fear, dear fellow, I am reconciled, hoist by my own petard indeed, for is not this as a society unable to change its ways in the face of altered circumstances of nature? I must bring the ship of my soul about and lay over on another tack.'

'Er, then . . . ?'

'Quite. My *cursus vitae* is now without purpose. Whither shall I wander? is my constant cry.'

'Nicholas, it can't be quite so bad.'

'No? Then consider. Saving your kindness, I have no future. As your confidential secretary I am content – but this is a device only to allow me the felicity of space and time to bring forth my *magnum opus*. Without this . . .'

'Why, you're . . . that is, you have, um, every—'

'A woman is known by her marriage, a man by his occupation. What is it that I am, then? A failed word-grinder, a man of the sea who is not, a wretched—'

'That's it, m' friend – you are now quite cured of your fever as was. Shall you not petition the King to resume your lieutenancy and re-enter the Navy? A fine profession, your sea service – to be an undoubted gentleman with regular income and rattling good prospects.'

Renzi paused and reflected. 'This does attract, but has two flaws. One, that the eminence of officer is secured by a constant devotion to duty, which I would now find hard to bear, accustomed as I am to the freedom to reflect . . .'

'And the other?'

'The other – that . . . that we must necessarily part, and

being content with the ... civilities of friendship, for the present I would find that ... onerous.'

'You must allow, Nicholas, it'll give you the standing and income to ask for Cecilia's hand in marriage.'

'Possibly.'

'Or, if we're talking of hypotheticals, have you considered an atonement o' sorts, an approach to your father, which—'

'Never! There are matters of principle, of high moral standing, involved, which utterly forbids that course.'

'Then we are at a stand, Nicholas. I can't see how you—'

'We?'

'As Cecilia's brother, I have a mort of interest,' Kydd said evenly.

'Then allow me to put your fraternal concerns to rest,' Renzi said coldly. 'It may have escaped you that Cecilia has advanced in society beyond ordinary expectation and must now be accounted a beauty by any measure. She will have a field of ardent admirers – there's no reason to suppose she would place the attentions of a ... a penniless wanderer before those of a gentleman of means.'

'What? For a philosopher you make a fine juggins, Nicholas! I ... I happen to know she has feelings for you and unless you clap on more sail she'll think you a sad dog in pursuit who's not worthy of her.'

'You don't perceive it, do you? This saddens me. In your sight does it seem, then, an honourable thing to press my suit when she might aspire to a marriage of substance and style, without want?' He held up his hand at Kydd's protests. 'It's for her that I take this course. She may indeed harbour a sisterly affection for me but for her own sake I release her from any sense of obligation to wed whom she may. She'll now be in receipt of my letter to that effect.'

Kydd sat back in amazement. 'Good God! Don't you think her own feelings might be consulted at all? Does she not have a view on the matter you might discover if you asked her?'

'This is of no consequence,' Renzi bit off. 'She is a warm creature and her heart may well overbear her reason, which is precisely why it's my moral duty to withdraw and make the way clear for a more fortunate liaison.'

'Your logic will be the death of you one day, Nicholas!'

'Then you will perceive I die content in the knowledge that it will be in the rational cause.' He reached for the bottle. 'Now I'm to be used to the idea of her departing my existence, I believe.'

The days turned to weeks and their northerly course by degrees curved more easterly, tracking the great Atlantic wind system that had been followed by countless generations of seamen back to Europe.

The fine weather stayed with them, and in fifteen days their seventeen degrees of latitude had reached thirty-five. Ahead lay the Azores: an archipelago far out to sea, it nevertheless marked the parting of ways. Mediterranean-bound ships passed to the south; to the north was the Channel and England.

Why were they missing the French? The trade-wind route with its ocean-sized circulation of winds was the only practical means of crossing the Atlantic; to sail against the prevailing pattern was madness and very slow. Had they passed them in their eagerness to engage? It had occurred before, in the long pursuit before the Nile. Quite conceivably they had crossed wakes in the night, as had happened once to Nelson himself, actually sailing through the middle of the unsuspecting Spanish fleet.

And not a single clue had they on the vital question of

whether Villeneuve was returning to Toulon past Gibraltar or to the feared link-up with the fleet lying at Brest and then on to an invasion.

Nelson made up his mind: it was Toulon, as it had been before.

The misty blue islands of the Azores were left to the north, those gaunt rocks where Kydd had suffered a hellish ship-wreck in a frigate long years ago as a common seaman – he gave an involuntary shudder at the memory.

Gibraltar was days away only now, and the talk was all of what they would find. A galling report that Villeneuve had passed through the strait on his way to Toulon? Nothing could get past without being seen from the heights of the Rock. That he had entered Cadiz to join with the Spaniards? Or even that he lay in ambush with his great numbers in the restricted waters around Gibraltar?

All was speculation until they raised the giant fortress. Then the thousand-foot peaks of Cape Spartel resolved out of the luminous morning haze, the African outer sentinel at the entrance to the strait. They passed the thirty-odd miles through it at a tense readiness until the crouching-lion form of Gibraltar took shape ahead.

Into Algeciras Bay, and every telescope was up and fever-ishly scanning until one or two ships under English colours were seen peacefully at anchor in Rosia Bay. In light and fluky winds Nelson's fleet came to anchor, one by one. The glasses came up again, this time trained on the flagship.

And almost immediately a barge put off from *Victory*, its passenger conspicuous and unmistakable. It pulled quickly for Ragged Staff steps and then the figure was lost in the walls and bastions. In a fever of anticipation every ship waited for word in the close heat.

One hour passed – then two. Only when the barge slowly returned to *Victory* in another hour without Nelson aboard did it become all so painfully clear. He would not have stayed ashore if the hunt was still on.

After a legendary race of eight thousand miles across the entire breadth of the Atlantic Ocean and back, and coming from thirty-one days behind to within a day's grasp, they had returned to where they had started from, and with the same result.

Villeneuve and his fleet had eluded them yet again.

Chapter 11

'Do sit, sir!' The first secretary to the Admiralty, William Marsden, shocked by the shambling gait of the prime minister as he came into the board room, hurried to assist him.

'Where's Barham?' Pitt wheezed, then coughed into his handkerchief as he found a chair.

'He's been advised of your visit, sir, and will be with us shortly.' The new first lord of the Admiralty to replace the impeached Melville was the eighty-year-old Lord Barham, hastily recalled from ten years of retirement to assume the post that had been declared by the home secretary as second only in importance to that of the prime minister himself.

Marsden was well aware that others had declined it for the frightful responsibilities at this time but Lord Barham, despite his advanced years, was a safe pair of hands. With none of the political involvements that had bedevilled St Vincent and Melville, he could devote all his attention to the monumental task. And he was a sailor who could look back to starting service as an officer at sea in the 1740s, to that inconceivably distant age before the Seven Years' War, before empire, before the American war. He was already a post-captain when Nelson was born and had served in every war since. He had the coolness of a fighting sea officer plus a well-honed appreciation of higher matters.

'Refreshment, sir? We can offer—'

'No.' Pitt slumped forward in his chair, clearly in a state of exhaustion.

Marsden indeed hoped that Barham would arrive soon – his calm and ordered mind would set the prime minister's anxieties to rest, for the fragile Third Coalition could take no more reverses.

Footsteps echoed in the hallway. 'Ah – he's here now, Prime Minister.'

Pitt raised his head with an expression of hope – or was it supplication? 'My lord Barham,' he said, in a voice little above a whisper. 'You have news of Nelson, I've been told.' The whole nation had been breathless with apprehension this last month, craving news of the wild chase across the Atlantic. With the drama came the highest possible stakes, all reported in the newspapers to become the stuff of public horror and fascination.

'Sir. And this very morning. Admiral Nelson sent on ahead from Antigua the *Curieux*, a fast captured brig, to tell me all I need to know. The dispatches came after midnight but, in course, my wretched valet would not suffer me to be disturbed until the morning. I'd have the villain flogged if I still had a quarterdeck!' he added querulously.

'Have you had time to read the dispatches then, my lord?' Pitt asked heavily.

'Yes,' Barham said, but in quite a different tone, confident, energised. 'And I have decided what must be done and already made the necessary deployments.'

Pitt's weariness lifted a little. 'You've . . . Pray tell me what is now the situation, sir.'

Barham stumped over to the map rollers above the fireplace and pulled down the largest: the Atlantic Ocean and approaches to Britain. 'Bonaparte means to overwhelm our fleets and seize control of the Channel for his invasion. You'll allow he has as many tricks as a monkey and this is one – Nelson was correct that his biggest squadron was headed for the Caribbean and he was right to abandon his station in pursuit. He had devilish luck and failed to catch them, and now the French are cracking on sail for Europe ahead of him and may be expected to appear very soon.'

'Do we have knowledge of what they'll do then?' Pitt murmured.

'Sir, they have but to raise the siege of our blockade on Brest and Ferrol, and in the Channel we'll be faced with forty, fifty battleships and necessarily be overwhelmed.'

Barham let the point sink in but then added, '*If* we are supposing they are headed for the north. Nelson's dispatches state that the Mediterranean is the more likely destination, and that is where he is bound at this moment.'

'What is your view, my lord?' Pitt asked carefully.

'My view is not of consequence, sir. Unknown to Admiral Nelson, *Curieux* on its run here came upon the enemy fleet and stayed with it long enough to establish that it was undeniably bound to the north of the Azores and therefore the Channel.

'Sir, I do truly believe the climax is near. Villeneuve's twenty of-the-line are now free to join with Ganteaume's twenty-one in Brest and the Dons' fourteen in Ferrol to make an unchallengeable battle-fleet in Biscay somewhere. This must not happen.'

'How?' Pitt asked, in a low voice.

'Thanks to *Curieux*, we know what to do. The central issue is to stop the forces combining in the first place. Therefore I've taken what steps I can to prevent it – by intercepting Villeneuve before he has a chance to make a conjunction.'

'With what forces, sir?'

'I'm extracting our vessels from before Ferrol and rein-forcing them with those taken from Rochefort. These will cruise out in the Atlantic between Cape Finisterre and Ushant to challenge Villeneuve when he comes, while the Channel Fleet interposes to prevent Ganteaume reaching him.'

'Abandoning the blockade at two chief ports – this seems a risk.'

'Far worse, sir, to allow the French to combine.'

'Very well. When will this intercepting come to pass, do you think?'

'Within the week, sir.'

'And who is the admiral you've chosen to stand before the French at this crucial juncture?'

'Calder.'

The rock fortress of Gibraltar shimmered in the heat, the ships of the Mediterranean squadron at anchor in torpid tranquillity. A sultry night closed in, still without word of Villeneuve. Nelson remained ashore but no one begrudged him that: for some two years he had never stepped on to dry land and he was said to be nearing exhaustion with the nervous strain of the chase.

Another day – two, three. No word. The French did not materialise out of the bright westward haze; neither did coastal traders pass word of a great fleet somewhere in the Mediterranean. On the fourth day *Victory*'s Blue Peter was hoisted. Orders came: as a last forlorn move, the squadron would sail north on a vague rumour as well as to seek out the Channel Fleet for any intelligence – and perhaps a final desperate engagement with the enemy.

In full battle array the fleet sailed up the coast of Spain, then across Biscay, and a dozen leagues off Brest Nelson's ships fell in with the Channel Fleet of Admiral Cornwallis and all was revealed.

The new first lord of the Admiralty was Lord Barham, who apparently had a strong and decisive hand on the tiller. The invasion had not yet eventuated: England still remained staunch and ready.

And Villeneuve? Yes, the French were found. Admiral Calder and a picked fleet from the blockading squadrons had intercepted him inward-bound from the West Indies out at sea off Cape Finisterre before he was able to link up with the waiting ships-of-the-line in their harbours. An indecisive engagement had followed in near impossible conditions of fog and night.

Unnerved by the encounter, Villeneuve had run for safety to Vigo and now the situation was precisely as before: the French were still in scattered groups in ports and once more safely under British blockade. Napoleon's plan had failed.

In profound relief and fatigued beyond measure by the years of blockade and pursuit, Nelson begged the Admiralty for release and orders quickly came out granting the request. *Victory*, accompanied by the worn-out *Superb*, was to sail immediately for Portsmouth. There, Admiral Lord Nelson would haul down his flag as commander-in-chief of the Mediterranean Squadron and at last take rest. All other vessels of Nelson's command, however, would remain on station save the lightest of his frigates as escort.

The next morning *L'Aurore* led the two veteran ships into the Channel for their homeward journey after a chase of near ten thousand miles and without a single shot fired. That this was no fault of theirs was without question, but how would they be received by a frightened and demanding public in England?

Familiar coastlines came and went, a sweet sadness after a voyage that had ranged from the balmy Mediterranean to the mangroves of Trinidad with nothing to show for it at its end. In the hours of darkness they approached the Isle of Wight and in the first soft rays of morning they anchored at Spithead.

At ten the flag of St George slowly descended from the fore-mast of *Victory* and Kydd's barge fell in behind that of Nelson in escort as he was rowed ashore. A sea of people lined the ancient ramparts and towers of Old Portsmouth, stretching all the way to the grassy sward of Southsea.

As he returned on board his ship, Kydd's face was a picture of wonder. 'It's madness! They've taken Lord Nelson to their hearts and won't let him go. He's their god, they worship him.' He shook his head in disbelief. 'Nothing will do save it honours him.'

In his cabin he told Renzi about the seething crowds, the screaming women pressing forward – and the transformation it had wrought in the worn figure of their admiral. 'It set him up at once, the old fire and ardour, topping it the hero – it's not to m' taste, Nicholas, but by glory, I give him joy of it.'

He frowned. 'And now I, a simple captain, have a decision to make. Do the hands get liberty ashore or will I end with a ship and no crew?'

Without waiting for a response he made his way to the upper deck. The question had no easy answer: it was customary after a major cruise to grant liberty but would *L'Aurore* be paying off? If not, he was duty-bound to keep the frigate at sea readiness – but on the other hand his men had every moral reason to expect a riotous spree ashore, having been denied it after their Caribbean commission in another ship.

'Clear lower deck – hands to muster,' he ordered. Seamen tumbled up from below, wary looks betraying suspicion as to why they had been assembled.

Kydd advanced to the breast-rail. He took in the crowd in the waist and the petty officers along the gangways to the fo'c'sle. Then, loudly, he ordered the flanking marines to take position away behind him on the quarterdeck.

'L'Aurores, we've sailed together now thrice a thousand leagues. We've followed Lord Nelson in a chase the like o' which has never been seen and one to tell your grandchildren.' He watched the impassive faces for reaction. Oaken with sea and sun, their strong and open features spoke of self-reliance in times of testing, confidence in their skills and a bond between each other – and their ship.

Kydd made his decision. 'There's those who'd say I'd be pixie-led to give my ship's company liberty into that lunacy ashore – but I am! I've just returned on board after seeing our Lord Nelson to land and the people are crying out for their hero, because they trust in him and his tars to save them from Bonaparte.

'We've unfinished business with that tyrant, the time will be soon, and I'm putting you on your honour that when Our Nel calls you're there when he needs you.

'Mr Howlett, liberty ashore to both watches!'

The surprised stirring among the men turned to incredulous

delight. A shout went up. 'Huzza t' Lord Nelson! Another f'r Cap'n Kydd! An' three times three for th' old *Billy Roarer*!'

Kydd turned to Howlett and fought down a grin. 'Now, that's what I'd call a right oragious body o' men.' He left the man standing open-mouthed and went happily below.

'Well, Nicholas, it's done. I'm to Guildford for a few days, just to see my folk, settle their fears. It could be that Cecilia is at home. Do you like to come?'

'No. That is, it's inconvenient at this time, I find.'

Chapter 12

Mercifully, the wind was in the east and the Dublin packet was able to make good progress up the Thames to London. Cecilia patiently held the hand of the Marchioness of Bloomsbury who had ever been a martyr to sea-sickness; the Irish Sea had been days of misery and for her their arrival was not a moment too soon.

It was odd to be back in the capital. There was an uneasy touch of hysteria about the busy crowds, strangers and tradesmen only too ready to pass on the latest dreadful rumour and, above it all, the sense that some climactic thunderclap of history was about to burst upon them.

There was little conversation in the carriage back to the mansion; the marquess, called away suddenly by unrest in Ireland, had been delayed and would follow later while the marchioness wanted only blessed peace, a ceasing of motion.

'Cecilia, my dear,' she said weakly, 'I do so crave the solace of my bed and to be alone. If you would wish to spend a few days with your family . . . '

The nervous excitement of London was disturbing and

wearing, and Cecilia lost no time in taking coach to Guildford. The jolting sway of the vehicle was uncomfortable and her mood was bleak as she stared out at the passing countryside. At the front of her mind was the insistent thought that in the very near future she would have to take the decision she dreaded, for Captain Pakenham was making his intentions clear.

If only her brother were near! But Thomas was away in his new ship. She'd received a hurried note from him months ago telling of the great honour to be soon part of Lord Nelson's fleet and had had nothing since. Presumably he was in a distant ocean chasing after the French . . . and for some reason she did not feel able to broach the subject with her mother.

Jane Rodpole was happily, if boringly, married, with no imagination to speak of, which left Cecilia precisely no one in the world she could talk to. She was on her own in the biggest decision of her life.

The coach clattered through the charming village of Esher, then on to Cobham for a change of horses, but her eyes were unseeing. Everything was pointing inexorably to one overwhelming conclusion: that Nicholas Renzi was now part of her past and the sooner she was reconciled to the fact the quicker she could get on with her life before it was too late.

Then it was Abbotswood and Guildford high street. The coach swung into the Angel posting house and she was handed down by a respectful ostler. The town appeared strangely quiet, subdued and with few people on the street, but as unchanging as it always seemed to be.

She crossed to the Tunsgate and took the short walk to the little school run by her family. She stood for a while, hearing the chant of children in their classrooms and seeing not one but three ensigns – red, white and blue – proudly at the miniature topmast.

Why did life have to be so complicated? With the world in thrall to the terror to come, why must she be made to look into her heart with such anguish? She knocked at the door of the little schoolhouse and a startled maid curtsied and hurried to find her mother.

'Why, what a surprise! Walter, it's Cecilia come visitin', dear,' she called to her blind husband. 'Come in, come in, darlin'.'

Her mother fussed over her, getting her room ready and sending for her luggage at the Angel, then Cecilia sat cosily beside the fire as family events were caught up on.

'You've just missed Thomas, dear – he came up fr'm Portsmouth t' tell us of his voyagin' with Lord Nelson,' Mrs Kydd said excitedly. 'All over th' world they were. Did you hear of Nelson's grand chase a-tall?'

'No, Mama,' Cecilia said. The wild rumours in London didn't really count, and in the short period she'd been in England she had not found time for the newspapers.

But Mrs Kydd had. Proudly she told of the famous pursuit across the Atlantic from the breathless details she'd read, sparing none of the sensational elaboration. 'An' after all that, th' rascals are back safe in their harbours. Such a shame.'

'So where is Thomas's ship now, Mama?'

'Didn't y' notice, dear? The town is near empty wi' everyone going t' Portsmouth to see off Nelson. He's news o' Boney and he an' Thomas is sailin' to a grand fight to settle 'em for good an' all.'

Cecilia went pale. 'You're telling me Thomas and – and his ship are about to set sail against Bonaparte?'

'Well, he said as how they've got t' finish th' British Navy afore ever he c'n invade, and he says as now's the time.'

'Yes, Mama,' Cecilia said, in a low voice.

'Oh, I nearly forgot, darlin' – there's a letter f'r ye.' She rummaged about in the sewing basket. 'I didn't know when ye'd be home. Isn't it fr'm that nice Mr Renzi an' all?'

Cecilia took it – and her heart stopped. There was no mistaking the neat, elegant hand, yet a sixth sense warned her that this was no commonplace communication. She quickly slipped it into her pocket and excused herself in tiredness after her journey.

In the privacy of her bedroom she tore the letter open. It was too much: the words were kind and thoughtful but to the point. A lump rose in her throat and tears stung. As she read on, choking sobs overcame her.

Barham received the news calmly even if what was contained in Collingwood's dispatch was the worst that could be imagined. He took a deep breath and sat down slowly, still holding the dread lines. It had been urgently brought by one of the frigate captains, Blackwood, who had added personal detail of the shocking event, none of it calculated to lessen its severity.

Not only the first lord but other naval commanders, including Lord Nelson, had assumed that after his confused engagement with Calder off Finisterre, Villeneuve's turn aside into Ferrol would be a temporary setback only. Sooner or later he would emerge and join with Ganteaume's fleet in Brest across the bay.

Commanders further south had therefore been ordered to send reinforcements to Cornwallis at Brest, including Collingwood, still patiently watching Cadiz.

However, Villeneuve had sailed south and contemptuously forced aside Collingwood's three ships-of-the-line to enter Cadiz and join the Spanish waiting there. As frigates had then confirmed, there were at least thirty-three of the enemy massing in the port, more than enough to overwhelm any British squadron afloat.

The French had achieved their object: they were now in numbers sufficient to begin the process of storming north, picking up more and more ships as each blockaded port was passed, secure in the knowledge that their strength would ensure they could reach the Channel and sweep on to the invasion beaches.

'I conceive that unless we can stop Villeneuve, this is the last act, my lord.' Boyd, who had been retained as flag-captain to the new first lord, spoke softly, as if in thrall to the fearful news.

'It does appear so,' Barham said absently, staring intently at the chart. 'You've heard Napoleon is at this moment at Boulogne in readiness?'

'So I understand.'

'Yet there are complications for our Mr Bonaparte. The prime minister's efforts over the year to forge the Third Coalition look to have succeeded. The tyrant therefore now faces a foe assembling on his frontier to the east. He simply cannot afford to wait for this phase of the invasion plan to complete, and both rumours and intelligence suggest that before long he must strike camp and march east to meet the threat.'

'We're saved?' Boyd said, without conviction.

'No. The cynic in me is saying that with his usual deadly swiftness he will easily deal with the Austrians – after all, he has the largest army yet seen and one that has conquered most of Europe. The result will be defeat for the Coalition, undeniably. And that will mean the situation regarding invasion is even more perilous.'

'Sir?'

'Why, can you not see? His invasion flotilla remains unused and therefore ready. Presumably his battleships will wait it out in harbour and he will be able to return to the task in the spring, this time with no threat to his flank and able to take risks.

'No, sir, there is only one sure way to put a stop to the invasion – Villeneuve's fleet must be destroyed. Not simply a victorious battle but destruction, extermination. Then there'll no longer be the numbers available to Bonaparte to force the Channel. As plain as that!'

'Sir.'

'And I have an idea who I'll send for to achieve just that.'

'The Hero of the Nile.'

'Quite. We must match Villeneuve's numbers without depriving blockade squadrons at other ports but, within that, Lord Nelson is granted whatever forces he desires. I do so regret intruding upon his rest but the man knows his duty and will not decline. I will appoint him reigning commander-in-chief in the area – and he'll get *Victory*, of course.'

'And if they don't sail?'

Barham gave a grim smile. 'I've a notion Napoleon is out of temper with his admirals. If Villeneuve does not sail he will lose his last chance for redemption and glory. He'll fight, never doubt it.'

'Vice Admiral Nelson. Do step in, sir, and accept his lordship's thanks for your prompt arrival,' Boyd said, showing the great man to his chair. He looked strangely diminished in his old-fashioned civilian dress – drab-green breeches with square cocked hat, mustard waistcoat and a gold-headed stick.

Lord Barham came in with a smile and civil bows were exchanged. 'My deepest apologies for summoning you after such a short space, my lord, but—'

'Cadiz. I heard this from Captain Blackwood.'

'Yes. I would like to offer you your flag as commander-in-chief Mediterranean and Atlantic approaches to Cape St Vincent.'

'Thank you, my lord.'

Barham hesitated. 'I will not dwell on the danger that faces the realm. Instead I will ask, at this time, what forces do you consider you will require for this task?'

'To match the Combined Fleet's numbers would seem enough, my lord.'

'Then you shall have them – and every resource necessary, just as soon as they can be made available.' He looked meaningfully at Boyd, who frowned but kept his silence. It would be far from easy merely to locate and contact the ships concerned and only then to go on to make repairs and store them to a battle-worthy state – and time was very short.

The first lord picked up a well-thumbed copy of *Steele's Navy List* and held it out. 'This mission is of the utmost importance, sir. You may have whomsoever you wish to serve under you.'

Nelson did not take it. 'Choose yourself, my lord. The same spirit actuates the whole profession.' He smiled. 'Sir, you cannot choose wrong!'

When the weeping stopped, Cecilia steadied herself. The storm of emotion had shaken her in its intensity but one thing was very clear. She had utterly misunderstood Renzi.

. . . in the years since we have known each other . . . and it may not have escaped you that my feelings for you are not altogether to be described as those of a brother . . . thus I must accept that in the matter of publishing my hopes are quite dashed, no prospect of an income . . . if any sense of an implicit obligation can be said to exist, I do absolve you from it, in the warm trust that your marriage to another will provide the blessings of security and gratifications that are yours by right . . .

The poor, dear, hopeless and deeply honourable man! He believed it unprincipled even to imply matrimony while impecunious, demonstrating without any doubt that he cared about her more than he could say.

Tears sprang again, but were as quickly replaced by a rising tide of resolve. She had to talk to him! At last let him know her true feelings! Then she bit her lip. He was with Thomas, whose ship was in Portsmouth about to sail with Admiral Nelson.

Against the enemy! She nearly choked at the realisation: so consumed by her own concerns was she that it had not occurred to her that the two men she most cared about were sailing into mortal danger, into the climactic battle of the age that everyone was talking about.

Everything in her being urged her to go to them, to . . . to . . .

She stuffed a few things into a small bag and ran from the house. In a storm of feeling she hurried on to the high street towards the Angel, the waypoint for the Portsmouth stage, but as she neared it the coach emerged from the courtyard gate with a crashing of hoofs and jingling of harness, swerving around for the dash south.

She waved her arms madly. The coachman atop bellowed at her but hauled on the reins, the horses whinnying and jibbing at the treatment. The coach slewed and stopped.

'I must get to Portsmouth!' she shrieked. 'My – my brother sails with Nelson!'

Her tear-streaked features gave the man pause but he shouted gruffly down at her, 'An' we're full, lady – not a chance! Ever'one wants to see Nelson!'

'I'll – I'll ride outside – on top! *Please!*' she wailed.

A red-faced passenger leaned out of the window. 'Get going, y' wicked-lookin' rascal – never mind th' gooney woman!'

This served to make the coachman relent. 'Git out of it, Jarge,' he threw at the hornsman, who grinned and clambered over the baggage to join the postilion. He leaned over and hauled Cecilia up, her dress billowing until she made it on to the narrow seat next to him.

The whip cracked energetically, the big wheels clattered over the ancient cobblestones and what seemed to Cecilia to be the whole of Guildford gaped up at her. Thrilled and nervous by turns, she watched the road unfold before them and prayed she would be in time.

Working at his desk in *L'Aurore*'s great cabin Kydd suddenly looked up. They were peacefully at anchor at Spithead but he was aware of a commotion. Grateful for any excuse to take to the fresh air he joined a curious throng looking over to *Victory*.

It seemed her entire company was on the upper deck, their cheering carrying over the water.

'A peace?' suggested Curzon, doubtfully.

'Sailing orders cancelled an' liberty t' both watches, more like,' Gilbey grunted cynically.

Then *Euryalus*, next along, broke into a mad hysteria. This could be no frivolous occasion and *L'Aurore*'s officers looked at each other in consternation as a boat under a press of sail emerged from behind the ship-of-the-line on a direct course to themselves.

It passed under their lee and a lieutenant hailed them with cupped hands. 'A telegraph signal – from the Admiralty. Lord Nelson rejoins the fleet as commander-in-chief to lead against the Combined Fleet in Cadiz.'

Nelson was back! Like lightning the news spread about *L'Aurore* and then she, too, had crowded decks with elated seamen cheering in frenzied abandon. The victor of St Vincent, the Nile, Copenhagen – a fighting admiral like no other, sent to save England!

While the L'Aurores 'spliced the mainbrace' in celebration, Kydd and Renzi raised a quiet glass to each other. There was now no longer any question: the near future would see an encounter that would decide the fate of millions – conceivably the world itself. Would Nelson prevail or would Napoleon's hordes be free to fall upon England?

Within a day orders were received that had been sent on ahead by Nelson: *Victory* and others were to move out to St Helen's Roads in the lee of the Isle of Wight in preparation for an immediate departure.

On the day following Kydd watched surging crowds ashore; it took little guesswork to know that Lord Nelson had arrived.

No flag broke at *Victory*'s masthead – the commander-in-chief was still ashore. 'He'll be at the George,' Kydd said confidently. 'And I'm to make my number, I believe.'

'On shore on ship's business? Then it's only my duty that I do accompany the captain,' Renzi said primly, buttoning his waistcoat.

L'Aurore's barge joined others converging on the landing place near King Henry's round tower. There was a press of people in the streets and when they stepped on to the stone quay to walk the few hundred yards to the George it was all they could do to make their way through.

Cheered and jostled by turns, they finally arrived at the bow-windowed posting house where an impenetrable crush fell back reluctantly at Kydd's uniform. At the door a number of harassed-looking soldiers made a hurried lane for him and they entered a lower hall, if anything even more crowded.

Hailing a beefy gate-porter, they finally got up the stairs and into the presence of the great man. Nelson was standing quite at ease, dictating to a secretary and making pleasantries to a pair of well-dressed gentlemen, oblivious to the fawning of several others.

'Ah, Kydd!' he said, with evident pleasure. 'I do feel we can at last offer you some sport worthy of the name. Your *L'Aurore* is ready for sea?'

'Aye aye, sir,' he stuttered.

'Oh, this is Mr Canning, treasurer of the Navy and this Mr Rose, paymaster general. Without gentlemen like these, we would have no sea service.' He smiled genially. 'Do stay, sir – that's Hardy over there and we'll raise a glass to England together before we board.'

The coach swayed and slowed on the choked roads at the approaches to Portsmouth. The driver swore and snapped his whip over the heads of the mob streaming towards Landport gate but without effect. Cecilia pleaded to the uncaring mass to move. They whooped and shouted in return but did not give an inch.

'Never in m' life seen anythin' like this'n!' the coachman

said in amazement, fending off a tipsy would-be rider while trying to control the frightened horses. 'Like as not, we'm as far as we c'n get, lady.'

'Five guineas to get to the high street!'

He looked at her kindly. 'Can't see yez getting into Portsea without ye walks, miss. Help y' down?'

Cecilia began thrusting through the unruly crowd, giving as good as she got as she struggled on, but her despair mounted. Not knowing Portsmouth well, she turned down a side-street and hurried along, panting and desperate. She had no idea where to find her menfolk but instinct drove her on – towards the sea.

'Well, gentlemen, our destiny awaits. Shall we take boat now?' Nelson said at last. He went to the window to glance at the sky, provoking an instant roar from the crowd outside.

'The redcoats have been turned out, my lord,' his flag-captain said diffidently, 'but they don't appear to have it in hand.'

'Then I'll leave by the rear,' Nelson said crisply. 'I'll not embark from Sally Port. There's a bathing beach at Southsea further along the seafront, as I remember.'

'There is, sir,' the dockyard commissioner said. 'If we go by Penny Street and the church, there's a tunnel let through the wall.'

'Very well.' But as soon as Nelson emerged from the back door of the George there were frantic shouts and an instant surge, people pressing towards him to catch a glimpse of his face. A number were in tears or falling prostrate while others gawked or shouted.

As he stepped out into the street the crowd fell back as though mesmerised. Nelson himself was in the greatest good humour, continually raising his hat to the ladies, clasping a hand, acknowledging a knelt prayer. He seemed to move along in a bubble of silent rapture; then after he had passed came redoubled shouts and cheering.

To Kydd, a few paces behind, it was extraordinary, dream-like. He had no idea where Renzi was but the sea of faces pressing in was unnerving. Some reached out to touch him, paw his uniform, all clamouring for his attention.

They slowly crossed a green by high earth ramparts, hundreds pouring on to it as it became obvious where they were headed – a woman fell in a swoon and was overwhelmed by the crush. Then they were at a stone bastion by the sea with a small tunnel beneath.

Ahead of Cecilia there was a swelling roar; nearby people ran to see. She joined them and was carried along on to a greensward rimmed by the grey stone of a low fortification. It could only be Nelson ahead and she knew that nearby must be her brother and the man with whom she wished to spend the rest of her life. Then she saw high earthworks and scrambled to the top with the others to look down on history in the making – and there in a small group walking with Lord Nelson was her brother!

She screamed out at him but her voice was lost in the din and she saw them disappear into a tunnel – but with no sign of Nicholas. Then there was a rush over the stone fortifi-cation as sentries were jostled aside, helpless to stop the crowd. Cecilia found herself fighting for a place at the top of an outer redoubt that looked seaward and down on to a nearby small beach with bathing machines.

The group emerged from the tunnel on to the beach, Nelson stopping to acknowledge the adoring crowd with waves, his gold lace and four stars glittering in the autumn sunshine. His barge nosed in, and first two important-looking men boarded, with an officer she supposed was Captain Hardy. Nelson turned and took off his hat, waving it at the crowd, which burst into cheering. Then he entered his barge and it shoved off.

The cheering subsided and what sounded like a huge sigh spread out. Nelson twisted around, waved his hat once more and again the cheers went up. Then a breathy silence descended.

Kydd was last to embark. His waiting barge came in and, incredibly, there was Nicholas, standing in the sternsheets, while Kydd took his place. Cecilia froze with a mix of fear and exhilaration. Then, in a rising tide of helplessness and passion, she shrieked, 'Nicholas! Nicholas! I'll wait for you! I'll *waaait* for you! My darling – I'll *waaait*!'

Renzi's head snapped up, his eyes searching the crowd. She threw her arms about, signalling frantically, but the boat completed its turn and was now pulling strongly away. 'Nicholas! I'll *waaait*!' she screamed, but by then the boat had disappeared into the throng of small craft.

Chapter 13

Thre was a distinct touch of autumn about the unruly
bluster that met the men-o'-war under full sail down-
Channel on their way to confront the enemy. *L'Aurore* fared
worst. Needing to keep with the battleships in the fresh gale
she wore canvas that had her sore-pressed and her boatswain
worried.

But there was a fierce pride aboard to be part of the most
famous battle-fleet of the age. There would be yarns a-plenty
on their return, and if there was the historic clash-at-arms
everyone expected, then was this not their duty, the reason
for their being? There had been no desertions among the
men on liberty, the extraordinary scenes at Nelson's embarka-
tion witnessed by many of them. It was clear that they had
been affected, and Kydd felt that the ship's spirit was now
as exalted as his own.

He went below, allowing Tysoe to remove his streaming
oilskins and grateful for a hot negus. 'What's that you have,
Nicholas?' he asked, seeing Renzi absorbed in a handwritten
sheet.

'Oh, in the mail – from my worthy friend Mr Wordsworth. He's a poet of a wild and romantical nature, as you'll agree, but much given to self-reflection. In this he's asking my opinion on his musing about the present peril. Listen:

> *"'Yea, to this hour I cannot read a Tale*
> *Of two brave vessels matched in deadly fight,*
> *And fighting to the death, but I am pleased*
> *More than a wise man ought to be; I wish,*
> *Fret, burn, and struggle, and in soul am there.'"*

Renzi gave a half-smile. 'If you knew the fellow and the way he's changed his turbulent ways you'd find it a singular sentiment, my friend.'

Kydd snorted. 'Really? I defy anyone o' true heart to stand mumchance in these times – and wasn't he all for glorying in the Revolution?'

'As I indicated, his views have altered,' Renzi said defensively, and laid down the paper. 'On quite another subject,' he went on offhandedly, 'did you by chance notice your sister in Portsmouth at all?'

'Cecilia? When I was in Guildford she wasn't there, somewhere in Ireland, I thought. Er, why do you ask?'

'I'd swear I saw her on shore when we left, waving and calling out. I couldn't catch what she shouted in the hullabaloo.'

'I didn't see her,' Kydd said, then added slyly, 'Are you sure it wasn't just a wish-child?'

'I saw her well enough,' Renzi said abruptly and, for a fleeting moment, wondered if indeed he had dreamed it. Then again she might have just arrived in England and hurriedly come to see them both off. Or was it only for her brother?

A stab of longing pierced him – was it his name she had shouted? Did this mean . . . ?

But, then, it couldn't be – she would have received the letter of release by now. The hope died.

Two more ships-of-the-line, *Ajax* and *Thunderer*, joined the few hove-to off Plymouth and, without delay, the group got under way again. The weather moderated before dusk and a workmanlike north-westerly sent them foaming through the waves.

They sighted the well-known Rock of Lisbon and at dawn the next day Cape St Vincent. *L'Aurore* was detached to go ahead to reach Admiral Collingwood with orders to refrain from gun salutes when Lord Nelson joined: there was to be no indication to watchers ashore that Collingwood was being reinforced.

L'Aurore raised them cruising some fifteen miles to seaward of the old Spanish port. A beautiful and terrifying sight: sombre lines of battleships – twenty, thirty of them, the most powerful British fleet Kydd had ever seen, more than twice as many as had fought at the Nile, the most fearsome weapon ever wielded by one man.

He passed his message, and when Nelson joined towards evening there were no seventeen-gun salutes, no hoisting of colours, simply a general joy running throughout the fleet.

On the following day, one by one, the captains of the various ships were rowed to *Victory* and welcomed aboard. 'Ah, Mr Kydd,' Nelson said warmly, standing in glittering full-dress at the gold-leafed entry port, 'do enjoy our little birthday party, sir.'

In the splendour of the admiral's dining cabin, he found that the birthday was in fact Lord Nelson's own, his forty-seventh.

Remarkably therefore, Kydd realised, *Victory* must be herself close to fifty years old.

It was an evening to remember: the glitter of crystal and silver on the huge mahogany table, the blaze of gold lace and decorations, and the meeting of men whose names were already famous: Harvey of *Temeraire*, Fremantle of *Neptune*, Berry of *Agamemnon*, Duff of *Mars* – and the frigate captains: Blackwood of *Euryalus*, Prowse of *Sirius*, Dundas of *Naiad* and more, all standing with a glass and chatting amiably.

When Nelson entered he went up to Fremantle and teasingly held up a letter brought out by him from England. 'You're expecting a happy event, sir – what is your desire, a boy or girl?'

'A girl would gratify, my lord.'

'Then be content, dear fellow,' Nelson said, handing it over. 'And Betsey confides she would be in doubts of your health should we venture past the strait.'

He passed on to other captains and seemed to revel in the warmth and fellowship that filled the cabin. 'Shall we dine?' he announced, after a discreet prompt from his steward.

The meal was declared a great success and, mellowed by wine, Kydd relaxed back in his chair as the table was cleared.

Nelson, seated at the centre, called for attention. 'Now, gentlemen! As is my way I would have you in no doubt as to my strategicals. Let me be plain with you – we are now twenty-nine of-the-line. If the enemy delay, which I doubt, they bid fair to make increase to forty-six, even fifty, while in return it would be foolish of us to expect more than a dozen further.'

There was calm confidence in the faces as he continued: 'What I seek is not a victory. Not even a glorious triumph. Nothing short of *annihilating* the enemy will satisfy. All shall be devoted to such an end.'

He had their rapt attention now. 'My very greatest desire is to entice the enemy from port. Only when he is out in the open sea in his full numbers can I think to destroy him utterly. Therefore my fleet will lie fifty miles to the west and a token force only will remain in view of the port. The motions of the enemy, however, will be communicated to me in every detail by the watching inshore frigates and a line of repeating ships.'

There were nods of agreement: every encouragement was needed to ensure the enemy ventured out and was dealt with once and for all, or the threat would persist for many more months, years even.

'Now to your battle instructions. Gentlemen, let us assume the enemy ventures out in strength and he forms line-of-battle. No day is too long to arrange our line to be formed to oppose them, supposing we are thirty or forty sail.'

Kydd frowned: at a cable apart – a couple of hundred yards – forty ships amounted to a line six or seven miles long, an impossibly unwieldy thing to manoeuvre by the wind to bring up parallel to the enemy line.

'Therefore I propose to dispense with the old ways. We shall not form line-of-battle. Instead we will throw our force straight at 'em. Pierce their line and bring on a mêlée as will see our ships at their best.'

A murmur went about the table. Nelson was completely disregarding the hallowed Fighting Instructions issued by the Admiralty, which specified that to confront an enemy line it was necessary to form up in parallel and smash away in broadsides until they yielded.

Breaking the line had been done before, however: Rodney at the Saintes, Duncan at Camperdown, even Nelson himself at St Vincent, but always as a chance opportunity, never as a deliberate plan.

'This is how it will be accomplished. In the event we approach from the windward there will be two divisions, weather and lee. The weather shall attack ahead of the enemy flag in the centre, the lee on signal will bear up to fall severally upon their rear.

'The assault will be swift – under full sail to stuns'ls, the order of sailing to be the order for battle – for I wish a victory over the enemy flag and rear before their van are able to reverse their course to succour them. Is this clear?'

There was a hush as the implications of the novel strategy were digested, then admiring gasps as it penetrated. By throwing his fleet at the foe on sight, without the formality of juggling positions to form an opposing line, the enemy line was to be chopped into thirds.

The vanguard was effectively to be isolated from the fight when the line was broken at the centre by the weather division, turning it into a close-range free-for-all. The rear third would be dealt with in detail by the lee division, all before the leading enemy ships had time to put about and come to the aid of the others.

In essence, the stately line-of-battle and its exchanging of broadsides were to be replaced by a brawling, one-on-one fight, which Nelson determined to win.

It was daring, reckless even, for the oncoming British divisions would be under fire from the broadsides of the entire enemy line as they approached without the opportunity to fire back. But when they reached and broke the enemy line . . .

'A most marvellous plan, sir!' Keats said, in open admiration.

'Genius! Nothing less will serve to describe it!'

The comments were fulsome. Nelson's trust in the

resolution and capability of each captain was both tribute and compliment. And at its core – that the battle was to be transformed from a fleet action into a spectacular series of individual combats – the strategy tapped the very spirit of aggression that Nelson had inculcated.

He held up his hand. 'Something must be left to chance, for nothing is sure in a sea fight. In the smoke and confusion signals may be missed, but this I say to you – no captain can do very wrong if he places his ship alongside that of an enemy.'

'Pray God they sail, and soon!' cried Moorsom of *Revenge*, punching the air.

'And a leading wind as will see us close aboard 'em before they wake up!' another added.

Wine circulated again and, glasses charged, Nelson spoke for them all: 'I trust, gentlemen, in English valour. We are enough in England if true to ourselves!'

A roar of agreement arose – and Kydd knew what it was to be one of that band of brothers.

The following day was spent bringing together the fleet that the ships had joined. The men-o'-war lay to as orders crisscrossed by boat: there was much to arrange. This far into hostile waters it was not practical to hazard supply by store-ships and therefore the commander-in-chief had no option other than to send parts of his fleet to Gibraltar for provisions and Tetuan for water.

The first detachment set out, and with Rear Admiral Calder recalled to England, and five away on replenishment, an expectation of forty sail was looking less and less likely. However, this was Nelson's command and a rising charge of pride was bringing the fleet together in a way that mere orders could not. Almost immediately, those who had not done so began painting ship in the distinctive 'Nelson chequer', which had a warlike black hull with vivid yellow along the line of the guns, the gun-ports themselves deadly black squares.

Captain Blackwood called his frigate captains aboard *Euryalus*. A bluff, energetic officer, he wasted no time. 'We have our orders: the watch on Cadiz – others will get the observations to the admiral.'

He went on, 'An inshore squadron of three sail-of-the-line lies ten or twelve miles in the offing, there to tempt Villeneuve, and more are spaced along out to where the fleet cruises, fifty miles or more to the west. It's our duty to let Nelson know every movement of the enemy. For this we'll be using your usual Admiralty signals but as well, Captain Popham's telegraph code.'

It was nothing short of fantastical: Nelson was going to shape the battle in person but over lines of communication at the same distance as from London to Brighton, receiving priceless intelligence in minutes that would enable him to make his approach to the unsuspecting enemy precisely as he chose.

Other details concerned signals to be made at night or in fog, and Blackwood closed with handing a hastily sketched Pennant Board to each that detailed the distinguishing pennants of each ship in the fleet, necessary for the addressing of signals to individual vessels.

'Then to our station, gentlemen!'

L'Aurore left the fleet in company with the other frigates and, during the night, closed with the moon-cast Spanish coast. At dawn they began their watch, cruising slowly three or four miles offshore, the tiny handful of frigates endlessly passing each other off the ancient city.

Cadiz was well-known to English sailors: here it was that Francis Drake had 'singed the King of Spain's beard' more than two hundred years previously and blockades had been frequent since. The port was within a rocky peninsula on which stood a city of white stone, surrounded by vicious half-tide rocks but low enough to reveal an ominous forest of naked masts within the inner harbour.

Navigation was perilous in these shallow seas, which allowed entire blockading fleets to anchor offshore with impunity but at the same time hid a chain of sprawling reefs as much as three or four miles out to sea.

In the days that followed there was no sparing the ships, for missing the enemy putting to sea would be a catastrophe beyond imagination. Each morning, as the fragrance of the sun-kissed land came out to them, one or other of the frigates would close with the entrance at the fort of San Sebastian and look in. Oared gunboats once issued out to exchange shots but otherwise there was no disputing their presence.

This close, the tall, square Tavira Tower was in plain sight, the mirador that gave the Spaniards a sweeping vista some twenty miles out to sea.

Day by day the watch continued.

A blustery autumnal north-westerly forced the frigates seaward for a time, but also made it dead foul for leaving Cadiz. As the weather moderated they quickly closed again with the white-fringed shore.

A Swedish merchantman put to sea and was intercepted by *L'Aurore*. The affable master made no bones about what he had seen: deep within the harbour in the inner roads he had noted soldiers embarking in the Combined Fleet and talk alongshore had it that they were merely waiting for an easterly and would be putting to sea.

Kydd lost no time in setting in motion the communications line. They were equipped with monster signal flags fourteen feet across to be perceived a full ten miles distant. The new telegraph code proved its worth in detailing his intelligence but it took skill to handle the huge flags among the entangling lines of rigging.

It was becoming clear that a move was imminent: sharp eyes had spotted that sails had been bent to the yards and signal towers up and down the coast were unusually busy. Had they succeeded in deceiving Villeneuve that he faced only the handful of ships of the Inshore Squadron instead of Nelson, with his fleet being quietly reinforced out of sight? Were they misled by reports from Spanish watchers of Gibraltar that the five detached to store and water had, in fact, seriously weakened the British Fleet?

With thirty-five ships-of-the-line available to him, Villeneuve must have realised that if he was going to break out then it must be now – and when the north-westerly died and was replaced by the whisper of a variable easterly towards evening, even the humblest landman aboard *L'Aurore* knew what to expect the following day.

With the first delicate light of morning came the electrifying sight of the ships deep in the harbour rigged for sea. Sail to topgallants, fighting topsails, all were bent to the yards ready to set in a trice. And the dense pattern of masts was changing: they were opening up, separating. The ships were warping – the Combined Fleet was coming out.

Kydd's signal flags – the longed for number 370, 'Enemy's ships are leaving port' – soared up. Five miles away *Euryalus* acknowledged and relayed it on to the Inshore Squadron. Soon, fifty miles away, Lord Nelson would at long last be receiving the dramatic news he craved.

The winds were light but still in the east. It was taking a long time for Villeneuve's fleet to reach open water and tension grew. Everything now depended on the frigates: if the French disappeared into the vastness of the ocean once again, it would be a calamity beyond bearing.

Blackwood sent the sloop *Weazle* flying for Gibraltar to alert the storing battleships while the little schooner *Pickle* went north to spread the word. The first French frigates were emerging, their mission only too obvious – to destroy the impudent English watchers and allow the battle-fleet to slip away.

L'Aurore was long cleared for action; now she went to quarters, her men standing resolutely by her guns. Blackwood had divided his forces in the light winds, two luring the frigates away while the rest stood out ready to shadow the rest of the enemy.

L'Aurore was given new orders. It was vital that the commander-in-chief received negative intelligence – that the seas north and south did not contain an enemy squadron summoned by shore telegraph on its way to reinforce Villeneuve. Thus one of the precious frigates was dispatched north while *L'Aurore* hauled to the wind for the run south.

It would be the harshest of luck to miss the coming contest, but Kydd's mission was to go no further than the entrance to the Strait of Gibraltar and then return by the shortest possible route, assuming any reinforcements sent for from Cartagena would not delay.

They hugged the land up to the one promontory and turning point between Cadiz and the strait, a fearful journey with the scattered reefs. *L'Aurore* showed true breeding, though, and they raised the bleak sand-spit within a few hours; further inland there was a bluff cliff with a tower.

This was marked on the chart as Torre de Meca and the turning point – Cabo Taraf-al-Gar, Trafalgar on Kydd's chart.

He was struck with a sense of poignancy that reached out to him from the lonely place, in the light airs the sinister gurgling of a roiling counter-current adding to the sense of desolation. The chart had a neat entry noting the current, adding that this was known locally as the 'Risa de Cabo', the laughter of the cape.

There were no reinforcements; Kydd sighted Cape Spartel on the African side of the strait and his mission was accomplished. He lost no time in wearing round for the return, dreading what he might find.

The unpredictable weather had turned squally and wet; towards the end of the day he had made it back to Cadiz through the curtains of rain and ragged bluster – and the port was empty. The enemy had left, taking with it the shadowing British frigates.

Kydd was in a desperate quandary as to what to do next but then, to his vast relief, there was a hail from a lookout. To the westward, out of sight from the deck, a fleet had been sighted.

Whether it was Nelson or the French didn't matter: his duty was clear. As they bore down on the mass of ships an outlying frigate saw them, its challenge showing bright and clear against the dark grey of the clouds. It was the English *Sirius*.

Kydd closed with the vessel and, in a terse hail, was told developments. The enemy had been hampered in leaving by fluky winds and once to sea had suffered even further from the adverse winds. In all they were thirty-three of-the-line and five frigates and were heading south, towards the Strait of Gibraltar.

Lord Nelson, still in communication, was racing to intercept. Their immediate duty was to stay with the enemy fleet at all costs through the coming night, for it was now fast becoming a certainty that it would be the next day when that fateful clash would come.

Bowden had slept little during the dark hours of the middle watch – the irregular bass creaking at the rudder stock and endless shrill working of the steering tackle sheaves seemed more than usually intrusive. But he knew the real reason: as the day dawned it would unveil either an innocent, empty horizon or the dread sight of an enemy battle-fleet.

Unlike the majority aboard he had served under Lord Nelson in a major fleet action, the Nile, and knew at first hand of the chaos and injury, terror and fatigue – and the callous working of Fate that decreed this one go on to fame and glory and another be struck down.

He was not in a state of mortal fear of the new day for he had long ago concluded that his profession would always require he stand resolute in the face of personal danger, and if he was to aspire to higher things, an unreasoning terror would for ever be a millstone around the neck.

His problem was a sensitive and active imagination that had to be crushed in times of crisis, but now, lying in his hammock in the reeking blackness, it was galloping at full stretch, his restless mind reaching for certainties and assurance for the coming day.

It helped to serve under an unquestioned hero such as Nelson, whose only worry seemed to be that the enemy was not prepared to stand and fight. Now, there was a leader and an example! How could any fail to be inspired by his clarity of purpose, the single-minded objective of victory – and the warm humanity that underlay them?

And there was Captain Kydd, who had risen from fore-mast hand to frigate captain and was as much a natural seaman as Nelson. Bowden had seen *L'Aurore*'s name on the Pennant Board; at that very moment Kydd was somewhere out in the night, dogging Villeneuve, and whether or not the foe was there in the morning depended largely on whether he and the other frigate captains had done their job.

Or . . . during the night the French might very well have taken fright and returned to port as they had done so often before. Then all talk of a mighty clash would be so much vapour and dreams.

But then again . . . Villeneuve might have slipped his pursuers and was now ranging swiftly north to trigger the invasion.

Bowden tossed and turned restlessly until eventually a ship's corporal came with his lanthorn to call the watch. He dressed quickly and made his way up the hatchways through the gun-decks of stirring men.

It was a moonless night with the pale immensity of canvas above and the muffled plash of the wake below. The cosy warmth of his hammock was soon forgotten in the chill night breezes. After the usual muted jocularity of handover, his friend Bulkeley, clearly of a mind for rest as he went through the ritual, hurried below.

Lieutenant Pasco was having an irritable exchange with the quartermaster. The officer appeared disinclined to indulge in trivialities and Bowden had to pace the decks alone in the long hours before an imperceptible lightening hinted at the coming sunrise.

The light increased, wave by wave extending out, the

anonymity of early dawn slowly infused with colour until the technical requirement for daybreak was met – that a grey goose could be seen at a mile. Then the lookout's thrilling hail came nearly simultaneously from a half-dozen throats – the enemy fleet was sighted!

There was now no more speculation, no more questioning: the French had not fled back to port, they had not vanished into the vastness of the ocean. Somewhere, soon, there would be enacted the greatest sea battle the world had ever seen.

In the whisper-quiet morning breeze, it was a long hour before they could be seen from the deck but then, stark against the fast brightening eastern sky, the topgallants and upper rigging of countless men-o'-war stretched from one side of the horizon to the other.

By now *Victory*'s decks were alive with men gazing out over the placid sea. Some mounted the shrouds to get a better view, but in laughing, devil-may-care high spirits – as if they were at a village fair instead of readying to fight for their lives.

Bowden stood at ease next to the wheel, still on watch. Nelson came on deck, avidly taking in the spectacle he had yearned for over so long a time.

'A brave sight, my lord,' Pasco said diffidently, offering his officer-of-the-watch telescope.

Nelson seemed not to hear as he focused on the distant masts.

Captain Hardy appeared and stood next to him. 'I conceive they cannot escape us now, sir,' he said gravely. 'And we shall give them a drubbing such as all the world may notice.'

'I shall not be satisfied with less than twenty taken, Hardy.' He lifted his head to sniff at the wind. It was calm – barely enough to kick up more than wavelets that sparkled in the

misty sunshine, the picture of peace and serenity. Yet under-
neath, a long, heavy swell rolled in massively towards the
land, token of a great storm out in the Atlantic and certain
to be heading for them.

'A west-sou'-westerly,' he mused, and threw a light-hearted
smile at Hardy. 'It couldn't be bettered.'

There were knowing looks about the quarterdeck. For the
enemy it was going to be difficult. Heading south as they
were they had no choice – the shoals and rocks of Spain to
the east, and to the west the British Fleet advancing on them,
forcing them into a passive defence, the line-of-battle.

Nelson's plans, on the other hand, had given his fleet the
weather gage; upwind from his opponents he could choose
the manner and direction of his strike, and everyone knew
now how this was to develop.

'Let's be about our business then, gentlemen,' he said. 'Mr
Pasco, I'll trouble you to close up your signals crew – there's
a mort of work to be done.'

'I have the ship, then, Mr Pasco,' said Captain Hardy,
releasing the officer-of-the-watch, who wasted no time in
nodding to Bowden, transforming him in that instant from
lowly midshipman-of-the-watch to a far more important
signal midshipman.

Bowden mounted the ladder to his station – the poop-deck.
Higher even than the quarterdeck, it afforded a magnificent
all-round view of the ship forward to the bowsprit and on
either side out to the ships in company. He tried to put away
the thought that this was also probably the most exposed
position on board.

King, the yeoman of signals, was already at the flag lockers,
and the rest of the crew mustered quickly. The mizzen signal
halliards were cast off and shaken free, an able seaman sent to

verify others on the fore and main. The signals log was initialled and begun – and the first signal order of the day came from the quarterdeck: 'Form the order of sailing in two columns.'

Robins, the master's mate, flicked the pages of the Admiralty signal code expertly. 'Number seventy-two!' he called to the signals yeoman, who pulled out the two blue and white flags and thrust them at a pair of seamen to toggle on in the right order.

Robins pointed upwards immediately – this was not a difficult 'lift' to check. The seamen hauled lustily and the hoist soared up. Checking the expensive fob watch his father had presented to him, Bowden scrawled in the log that the signal had been made at six a.m. Then, glancing out to the fleet, he noted down the acknowledgements as they came.

This signal had essentially been to call the fleet to order after the loose formation of the night. Then, with a chill, Bowden remembered that the order of sailing was also the order of battle and, sure enough, it was closely followed by the order to bear up and sail east. Nelson's first signals of the day were to lunge at the foe.

The next made it formal – number thirteen, 'Prepare for battle', which put into effect a two-pronged charge into the very centre of the massed enemy fleet, the lee column to the right led by Admiral Collingwood in *Royal Sovereign* and tasked to cut through and envelop the rear. Sailing parallel, the weather column to Collingwood's left would be led by the commander-in-chief in *Victory*, seeking in one move to take on the enemy flagship and isolate his van.

It was becoming obvious, however, that unless the breeze picked up it would be many hours before they could hope to grapple and every sail possible was set, including the cumbersome stunsails, temporary extensions to the yardarms.

The sun rose above the horizon, strengthening and lifting a dreamy opalescent mist through which the stately progress of the Combined Fleet seemed a fairy argosy. Nelson ascended to the poop with Hardy to take advantage of its panorama of enemy and friend, the two staying in amiable conversation while the ship was piped to clear for action.

The well-practised evolution turned *Victory* into bedlam: teams of men stripped mess-decks and cabins of every comfort and piece of furniture that might be splintered by gunfire, struck them down into the hold or cast them overboard.

Next it was necessary to clear away some of the stanchions in the gun-decks with heavy mallets to provide more room to serve the guns, as well as unshipping inessential ladders until each of the three gun-decks was clear from stem to stern.

All hammocks were passed up and stowed, tightly rolled, in the nettings at the sides of the ship, protection against musket-balls. A net was stretched over the fo'c'sle and quarterdeck to catch falling wreckage from aloft while the two cutters at the davits aft were lowered and towed, other boats remaining on their skid beams.

The boatswain and his party were everywhere, laying out stores in strategic places for the repair of rigging torn by the French, notorious for firing high, together with preventer shrouds and braces, which duplicated vital lines. Where the tons weight of the lower yards was suspended at the mast, chain slings were secured. A lucky shot by the enemy at this point could end in unravelled rope and the heavy yard crashing down on the quarterdeck and men at the guns.

A spare tiller was brought and relieving tackles provided to work the steering from the tiller directly if the ship's wheel was damaged. The carpenter and his crew laid out their tools and ensured that the narrow passageway circling the orlop at the waterline was clear. In action his duty was to make his rounds to watch for the sudden bursting in of a shot strike and then to move fast to stem the inward rush of sea with shot plugs, lead sheeting and bracing.

And the great guns were readied: gun-captains collected their pouches from the store with their quill firing tubes, prickers and reamers, spare gun-flints and slow-match. A slung powder-horn completed their outfit. Each then went to his gun and ensured the great beast was able to do its duty. Were the ready-use shot garlands fully populated by balls? Was there a salt-box with two cartridges in place waiting? Wads in the overhead net? The gun-lock was fitted and tried, equipment mustered in the racks – worms, wad-hooks, crows. Side tackles were ranged along and a training tackle applied to the rear of the gun.

The gun-decks were provided with arms-chests: pistols, muskets and cutlasses. All that was needed to board the enemy – or to repel boarders. In the centre of the deck broached casks of water and vinegar were placed at regular intervals.

Meanwhile the gunner and his mates unlocked the Grand Magazine and the powder rooms, passing through fearnought flapped screens and moving along cramped, lead-lined passages in felt slippers to the most dangerous place aboard. The smallest spark here would mean instant destruction and death not only for the men inside but the entire ship.

Throughout the day's action they would be sweating here in the dimness using copper scoops to make up the cartridges to feed the guns, lit by specially sealed lanthorns and getting news only through the powder-monkey chain.

Finally, water was sluiced and sand scattered liberally along the gun-decks. In the bloody carnage of close-quarter fighting it would give much-needed grip to bare feet.

And quietly in the orlop, the lowest deck of all, Beatty the surgeon took charge of the cockpit, the space at the after end outside the midshipmen's berth. Chests were brought and he laid out his instruments: bullet extractors, fleams, forceps, ligatures – and the saws and knives to sever limbs. Tubs were placed nearby to take these 'wings and limbs' and carboys of oil of turpentine were opened to seal the stumps.

As far as it was possible, HMS *Victory* was now ready for the fight. The first lieutenant, Quilliam, reported to Captain Hardy that all was complete and the hands were stood down. The next time they would be called upon was when the ship beat to quarters.

'Sir, hands to breakfast?' suggested Quilliam.

'Make it so,' Hardy replied.

The men scrambled noisily below – with the galley fire out there would be no hot food but ship's biscuits, cheese and grog were acceptable fare with the enemy in sight, and there was much to contemplate and talk about over the mess tables. At the day's end, which places would be vacant, which cheery faces would never be seen again?

Pasco glanced at Bowden. 'You've been on watch, m' lad,' he said, with a smile. 'I'd advise you to duck below while you can, shift into your fighting rig and get a bite to eat. Come back in an hour.'

Grateful, Bowden made his way down to the gunroom, now bare and stark. His sea-chest, like the others, had been struck below and he wedged himself up against the massive transom knee to munch his rations.

Around him were his shipmates, some keeping to themselves in inner reflection, others conversing in low tones. He did not feel like talking and finished his meal with an orange that Pasco had slipped him from the wardroom, sipping sparingly on a tin cup of grog.

As for shifting into fighting rig, even if he wished it he could not – all his gear was in his sea-chest in the hold. This included his dirk, but earlier he had resolved that in the event of a boarding he'd snatch up a cutlass, a much more effective weapon, from an open arms-chest. There was therefore little he could do to pass the time before . . .

Except . . . He had a slate on a string. He balanced it on his knee, pulled out a signal form and his pencil and composed his thoughts.

'Dear Uncle,' he began, at a loss for words in the rush of impressions.

Villeneuve is sighted this morning at dawn ESE five leagues. Capt Hardy estimates 33 French and Spanish in line of battle to the S. And what a parcel of lubbers they look too! As would give apoplexy to Ad^m Cornwallis, I should think.

We've clear'd for action and the men are in great heart, as well they should with Ld Nelson in company.

He chewed his pencil, trying to think what to say, but it was too weighty an affair for small-talk and, besides, what exactly was he writing? A midshipman's dutiful letter to his benefactor – or his last words on earth to his family? Who knew when they would receive this? Others had begun their letters weeks before with the object of adding a last-minute postscript to go out in the mail with the dispatches that the commander-in-chief would be sending to the Admiralty just before battle was joined.

At this time, dear Uncle, I think of you and my family but, be assured, should it be by God's good grace I shall fall in this action then I die in a most noble cause, and know that I will not disgrace your love and name. Do not grieve – it will be to no purpose.

His eyes stung and he caught himself, finishing,

Remember me to my friends. I bid you all farewell and put my life into the hands of the One who made me. Amen.

When Bowden returned to the poop it seemed so crowded. Besides the signal crew, the Royal Marines were assembling there, nearly three dozen of them. Captain Adair flashed him a confident smile as he checked his men's equipment.

Bowden picked up the signal log. It had been fairly busy, mostly admonitions to individual ships to make more sail and take station. The two columns were now formed and heading for the waiting enemy line, but so slowly in the calm.

'I say, aren't the Crapauds sailing more than usually ahoo?' Adair remarked, shielding his eyes and gazing across the glittering sea where the aspect of the enemy masts and sails was slowly changing.

'Ha!' said Pasco in amazement. 'I do believe they're putting about and running back to Cadiz!'

'Be damned! Our Nel will be in a right taking if they get away,' Pollard, another signal midshipman sniffed, his glass up on the leaders.

Victory's bow, however, was resolutely tracking the new head of the enemy line, which was puzzling. From animated discussions the previous night, Bowden had understood that

Nelson's intention was to punch through the centre, and here he was, apparently abandoning his plan.

Then *Victory* beat to quarters – the martial thunder of the drummers at the hatchways started, the staccato rhythm of 'Heart of Oak'. Sailors scrambled up from below to man the guns.

A first-rate like *Victory* had the greatest fire-power of anything afloat: three decks of guns each ranged the entire length of the ship on both sides, the heaviest on the lowest – a broadside of half a ton of cold iron, more if double-shotted at close quarters. And there was the secondary armament: a fourth level of twelve-pounders on the quarterdeck, more on the fo'c'sle, including the giant sixty-eight-pounder carronades.

Already at his station for quarters, Bowden stood aside as the marines formed up with muskets, ready to be employed from this vantage-point. Most of the 140 of their number were below decks serving at the guns.

The great ship settled to a watchful expectancy as she closed slowly with the enemy. Out on the beam were the frigates, their last service for their commander-in-chief to act as repeaters for signals sent by the flagship in the thick of the fight. They would otherwise stay outside the conflict.

A flurry of signals caught Bowden's eye. They were from *Royal Sovereign* out on the lee column, instructing the line to sail on a larboard line of bearing. 'What does Collingwood mean?' Bowden asked Robins quietly, anxious not to show ignorance in front of Lieutenant Pasco, standing four-square at the front of the poop.

'Not for me t' say, but my guess is that Old Cuddy is giving leave to his ships to take on the enemy at will, not as a formed column. I dare to say he knows his business.'

Bowden nodded in understanding. The ships strung out

were now going to fall on the rear individually, to envelop it, and there was *Royal Sovereign* well ahead of the others, aimed like a lance at the last third of the line. Before long they would be the first under fire.

It was galling, the snail-pace approach made even worse by a further drop in the slight breeze. How ironic, he mused, this calm before the storm that was certainly coming, when they needed the breezes so much in order to close before they could be shot to pieces.

Their bow-wave now was barely a ripple, their speed that of the stolid pace of a rank of soldiers on the battlefield tramping towards the opposing lines. But theirs was not to face the crackle of muskets: ahead were the massed broad-sides of a wall of ships a whole five miles long, which they must endure head-on without firing a shot in return.

Over to starboard the lee division was nearing the enemy line. Villeneuve must open fire soon, but first his fleet had to hoist colours to accept battle – and thereby reveal which of the great ships was his flagship. It was nearing midday with the line a mile ahead when the colours broke free.

Instantly telescopes were up and searching. 'There! Near dead centre!' The pennants of a French commander-in-chief were at the main-mast head of an eighty-gun battleship next after the unmistakable bulk of the *Santissima Trinidad*, a four-decker and the largest ship in the world.

Then *Victory*'s band struck up – 'Britons Strike Home'! The lusty rhythm was taken up gleefully:

> *The Gallic fleet approaches us nigh, boys,*
> *Some now must conquer, some now must die, boys . . . !*

From another ship came 'Rule, Britannia', and 'Heart of Oak' thumped out from a third. In the stillness a defiance of the worst the foe could bring against them echoed across the water.

Bowden saw then that *Victory* had altered course. No longer stretching out for the van, she had thrown over her helm and was heading directly for Villeneuve's flagship. So the plan would stand as before: a concentrated drive at the very vitals of the enemy.

'How curious!' Robins murmured. 'Shall we ever know why?'

'Why what?' Bowden asked.

'Well, some would say that Nelson was waiting for Villeneuve to show himself before going straight at him. Others might believe that the entire purpose of his attack on the van was a feint to discourage 'em from turning back to rescue their centre.'

'And you think . . . ?'

'It might simply be,' drawled the signals master's mate, lowering his telescope, 'that he couldn't bear to see them return to Cadiz and made to fling himself before them, but when he could see that battle would be joined after all he fell back on his original design to cut out and destroy their commander. So, which is it to be?'

There was little time to ponder. With scattered flat thuds away to the right the opening shots of the battle were made at Collingwood in *Royal Sovereign*, heading his column. Bowden dared a quick move to the break of the poop to look down on the quarterdeck as though to check something but what he really wanted was a glimpse of the famous hero as he carried England's fleet into battle.

Nelson was standing with his secretary and others, Hardy at his side, all watching developments intensely. Men waiting silently at the guns followed his gaze. Then came a succession of dull thuds and the rear of the enemy disappeared in gun-smoke.

Bowden could feel the tension but the sight of the great man affected him powerfully – the tigerish confidence radiating out, the utter single-minded pursuit of victory. They simply could not fail!

He slipped back and stood tall before the seamen and marines, feeling the age-old battle-lust build. Then he heard behind him someone mount the poop ladder. It was Nelson, followed by Hardy.

Now able to see completely around the battlefield he minutely inspected the enemy position, the ships loyally in their wake and finally Collingwood's column, in action.

'Mr Pasco!' he called.

'My lord?'

'I wish to make a signal to the fleet. Be quick, for I have one more to make, which is for close action.'

'Sir?' said Pasco, poised to take the communication.

'You shall telegraph . . . let me see . . . "England confides . . . that every man will do his duty."'

'Aye aye, my lord,' Pasco said, and Robins hurried over with the telegraph code book. Pasco found the place, then stopped and said, 'If your lordship would permit me to substitute "expects" for "confides" the signal will soon be completed, because the word "expects" is in the vocabulary but "confides" must be spelt.'

Nelson, distracted, agreed. 'That will do, Pasco, make it directly.'

'Sir.'

After giving the order to first hoist the telegraph flag, the signals lieutenant found the first number and told it to Robins, who chalked it on the slate and shouted, 'Two-five-three!'

The yeoman of signals yanked out the flags from the locker and toggled them on to the halliards, spilling them clear for Pasco to check.

'Hoist!' The first lift of the signal soared up, and as it did so, Pasco found the next. 'Two-six-nine!' It was bent on to another halliard and one by one the hoists ascended. When it was completed Bowden noted the signal and time, then waited for the acknowledgements from the fleet.

While this was being done, Nelson was watching the lee column close in on the enemy, *Royal Sovereign* now nearly hidden in gun-smoke. 'See how that noble fellow Collingwood takes his ship into action! How I envy him!' he exclaimed to Hardy.

The first crump of shots sounded from ahead – *Victory* was now under fire herself. From this point on she would be the focus of aim for a hundred – two hundred – gun-captains and her ordeal was just beginning.

Another signal. 'Engage the enemy more closely' – 'Number sixteen!' This was the last that Nelson could be sure would be seen and was hoisted at the main-mast head, where it remained.

With barely suppressed emotion the admiral said, 'Now I can do no more. We must trust to the Great Disposer of All Events, and the justice of our cause.' He and Hardy descended to the quarterdeck and began a slow pacing up and down between the main-mast and the wheel.

Ahead, the enemy line was now a loose succession of ships, their details clear and forbidding, and it wasn't long until the first ball struck *Victory*, reaching out in violence and punching loudly through the main topgallant sail.

Soon after, several other enemy ships joined in, the sound of firing building as the deadly cannonade intensified. Strikes could now be heard forward, and the whirr and slam of invisible projectiles overhead were chilling.

A quick shriek came as a seaman paid with his life for doing his duty; other anonymous screams penetrated above the continuous fearful thunder of guns from now six or eight ships, furiously hammering at the oncoming column. It was a race that would turn on whether the ships now at their mercy were smashed to submission and stopped, or whether they could get inside the enemy firing arc, pierce the line and deliver a battle-winning raking of the stern and bow each side as they passed through.

On the poop Bowden's vitals froze at the awful feeling of exposure: at the ship's side there were only deal boarding and rolled hammocks to keep out the storm of shot and, with nothing to do but keep at his post, a rising feeling of helplessness threatened to engulf him.

One of the marines was knocked sprawling as if kicked by a horse and his musket slid across the deck. He sobbed, writhing, and Adair motioned to another two to take him below.

Imitating Pasco, Bowden began a regular calm pacing. A strange detachment stole over him, a feeling of unreality that separated him from the chaos and fear. Through his feet he sensed *Victory*'s own guns opening up, their heavy thump quite distinct from the sharp concussion of a shot-strike. Nothing now could be seen of the enemy except the upper masts above the smoke – but Villeneuve's pennons were still giving *Victory* her mark.

Bowden reached the poop rail and glanced down on the quarterdeck. One unfortunate had taken a ball squarely, his body flung grotesquely, its half-human features and an appalling amount of blood-soaked innards scattered widely. Nelson looked on sadly as it was dragged away.

Straightening, Bowden turned back, suddenly acutely aware of the whites of the eyes of the files of marines. Then, as if in a dream, the entire rank was torn down in a welter of blood and kicking limbs. Choking sobs were cut off and parts of half-clothed bodies were left lying on each other, like so many joints in a butcher's shop.

The carnage was indescribable but the remaining marines held firm until a breathless midshipman arrived from the quarterdeck, ordering Captain Adair to disperse his men about the ship. Eight men killed with one shot! It couldn't go on.

But it did: with the splinters still flying from a boat hit by a round-shot, *Victory's* wheel was smashed, the big first-rate now in an uncontrollable lurch towards the enemy line until emergency tackles on the tiller in the gunroom could be rigged – but the ship fought on with undiminished fury.

Bowden felt the wind buffet of a cannon-ball. Next to him a seaman turned, apparently with a question: his mouth opened, and as it did so, blood spurted in a gush of scarlet from where his arm had been – carried off invisibly and without warning. The man gave a piteous moan and sank to his knees.

Dispassionately Bowden recognised that the intensity of the slaughter was such that it was more reasonable not to expect to survive – at some point one of the invisible whirling scythes of death would seek him out and put an end to his existence. Strangely, he felt peace, the resolution of hope against fear, but a deep sadness that for him the future was now shut off.

A seaman beside him was suddenly spun around, falling without a sound, and as he was dragged to the side there was an ear-splitting crack aloft. When Bowden looked up to see, his world turned dark and he was savagely pressed down.

It was some seconds before he realised he was suffocating under a smother of canvas. Near panic with claustrophobia he struggled for his knife and in a frenzy sawed and hacked at the cloth until the smoky daylight emerged.

A seaman helped him out; the mizzen topmast had been shot away and hung along the side suspended by the upper rigging, the sail draped over the poop. 'Axes! Get this clear!' he roared. 'You, Clayton – on the lee side, Nicolson on the weather!'

He worked a bayonet free from a dead hand and began sawing at the tarred strands of a shroud. Panting, he stopped to look out – there was gun-smoke everywhere, a rain of splinters and stranded lines whipping down, but what froze him was the awesome sight of the enemy ships so very close.

Wreathed in smoke with livid gun-flash stabbing, they lay across *Victory*'s path but she was steering now for a gap astern of Villeneuve's flagship and its next in line. Mesmerised by the terrible sight, he saw other ships beyond the gap equally as big and quite untouched.

The noise was appalling – a crescendo of violence that paralysed his thoughts. Hacking away the remains of the fallen rigging in a demented fury, he was utterly unprepared for what happened next.

The guns were falling silent.

He stared forward – they had at long last passed inside the firing arcs of the enemy guns. These could no longer bear on their ship and the long agony of her approach was over. The ornamented stern of the flagship – the name *Bucentaure* in gilt across it – now lay quiet and unresisting as *Victory* glided inexorably forward into the gap.

A furious cheering began, for now a terrible revenge would be taken on the enemy. Her guns ceased their fire. Bowden knew that they were being reloaded with double shot and wicked canister for what was to come; the enemy must know it too – he felt a wash of pity, for in all conscience they were only doing their duty.

But war was a merciless dictator – he could see French boarders forlornly massing, but right forward on the fo'c'sle *Victory*'s boatswain was carefully sighting along the immense bulk of the sixty-eight-pounder carronade, the firing lanyard in his hand.

The distance narrowed; heroes stood in *Bucentaure*, still firing muskets, anything – aware of what Fate would bring they must know what was to happen in the next moments. The magnificent arch of stern windows loomed, a diamond-shaped tricolour escutcheon in its centre, the midday sun glinting on its interior appointments – and the boatswain yanked on the gun-lock lanyard.

The entire structure dissolved in a deadly blast of glass and splinters, a cloud of reeking dust and fragments bursting out to flutter down on *Victory*'s decks. Then, as they passed slowly, the three decks of guns below began their frightful rolling crash.

At point-blank range and double-shotted, they fired in succession into the length of the wounded ship, smashing their lethal iron balls into the holocaust of its gun-decks. Shrieks and screams came from the dense, acrid gun-smoke but the cannonade mercilessly went on and on until an entire fifty-gun broadside had crashed into Villeneuve's flagship.

Victory glided on beyond. Then her opposite broadside opened up to pound a vague shape in the drifting gun-smoke.

As Bowden saw the last rigging-entangled wreckage over the side he was knocked staggering by the sudden grinding lurch of a collision to starboard. He steadied himself and twisted round to see a French ship-of-the-line locked solid into *Victory*'s side. She appeared very ready for the encounter, her decks crowded with men; he could just make out her stern and the name *Redoutable* in gold.

Victory fought back: her marines levelled their muskets and blazed away at the swarming men assembling for boarding – but the ship's tumblehome, the inward curving of her side – formed an unbridgeable cleft between the two vessels.

Muffled blasts from below told of terrible gun duels fought in the blackness of the touching sides and then came a hail of French musket fire from the vessel's fighting tops. Grenades arced down causing dreadful injuries on *Victory*'s decks and the vicious *whuup* of musketry intensified.

Pasco appeared out of the smoke, his face working in agony before he crumpled, blood smearing the deck. But Bowden couldn't help him – he and King were frantically reloading muskets for Midshipman Pollard, who'd ransacked the marines' arms-chest for any remaining weapons.

As the wounded signal-lieutenant was dragged away they kept up a furious fire on *Redoutable* in a mechanical frenzy, aiming at the darting figures in the tops that were making a slaughter-house of *Victory*'s decks. This drew venomous fire in return, and as King handed over a loaded musket he was killed instantly with a bullet to the forehead.

The main-yard of the French ship jerked, teetered and then fell – hacked away by quick-thinking *matelots* who had made for themselves a perfect bridge across the chasm. With incredulous cheers the French swarmed up onto the yard and began racing across.

It was a complete about-face in fortunes: with so many of *Victory*'s upper-deck defenders brought down there was now the unthinkable possibility that the English flagship herself would be taken.

Captain Adair sprinted up with a file of marines and took position directly opposite to open fire. The leaders of the boarding fell into the yawning crevasse to a hideous death, crushed by the working together of the two hulls.

Those following hesitated – fatally. The boatswain had forced the starboard sixty-eight-pounder carronade around and blasted five hundred musket balls into their midst. They fell back, their triumphant battle-cries turning instantly to the screams of the dying. And at that moment Adair took a ball in the neck and pitched forward, dead.

Then a miracle came in the looming shape of *Temeraire*, which had been the next ship astern of *Victory* and now came up against the other side of *Redoutable* with a ponderous crash. Her carronades immediately took dreadful toll and then, together with *Victory*, her great guns in broadside smashed together into the vitals of the hapless ship.

It was a brutal slaughter but insanely the brave Frenchmen fought on until the blood-soaked hulk was in ruins – and her colours were struck.

A full-throated cheer roared out, redoubled when *Victory*'s men came to realise the perilous margin of their triumph. Bowden, stunned by the impact of the last hour, reeled over to the poop rail to watch Nelson taking the surrender. He couldn't see him in the cheering crowds so he turned back wearily to the three men remaining standing on the poop.

Then urgent shouts came from the fo'c'sle – bearing down on them was the van of the enemy, fresh ships that were at last turning back to come to the aid of their centre. Yet *Victory*'s sacrificing had successfully pierced the line and other British ships, *Neptune*, *Britannia*, *Leviathan*, all had crowded through and now steered to face them. There would be no rescue.

Another burst of wild cheering broke out – it was the *Bucentaure* hauling down her colours, the commander-in-chief Villeneuve now a prisoner. And ahead the giant *Santissima Trinidad*, mauled by three English battleships was battered into submission and capitulated.

A wide-eyed seaman hurried up the ladder and blurted breathlessly, 'L'tenant Pasco desires 'e should be told, how is y' signals crew?'

'He needs to know if we're able to work signals,' Robins said, looking about him. 'Er, I'm senior hand. We're still flag-ship and will need signals – I'll see he gets 'em.' He paused and added with gravity, 'Mr Bowden, I'd be obliged should you inform L'tenant Pasco as we shall close up a team directly.'

The poop was a ruin of draped ropes and wreckage from aloft but the flag locker was still intact and somewhere signal halliards not shot away would be found. Bowden clattered down the ladder to the quarterdeck. It was in name and appearance a battlefield – decks torn up, shattered guns, wreckage and sanded blood-stains everywhere, but the men were still serving their guns and in the rigging passing stoppers to hold together vital shot-torn lines.

It took cold courage of an exceptional quality to leave the relative safety of the deck and mount the shrouds to expose their bodies in full view of snipers, staying to work there while a tempest of lethal langrel and chain-shot ripped through in an attempt to disable their ship.

At the main-hatchway the only ladder left in action was slippery with blood – it was by this route that the unfortunates were carried below.

On the gun-deck there was a different kind of hell: in the

reeking, thunderous dimness it was the remorseless pain and labour of loading and heaving out the massive guns in a never-ending cycle. At any moment there could be the sudden eruption of a round-shot through the side in unstoppable killing violence.

In these acrid, smoke-filled confines the battle was being fought – and won – by the same gunners whose skill and tenacity had kept up a deadly fire the enemy could never match.

Bowden paused, awestruck at so much violence and noise in a confined space. The visceral rumble of the guns as they were run out, the squeals of their trucks as a counterpoint, their iron, now truly hot after hours of action, producing a violent recoil, some leaping insanely to strike the deckhead beams, their tons weight falling again with an appalling crash at extreme hazard to the tired men serving them.

The middle gun-deck was the same, a torment of clamour and darkness, and then to the lower gun-deck with the biggest guns of all, three-ton monsters chest-high to a man, bellowing out with a lightning flash and clap of thunder that hammered at the senses.

But nothing prepared Bowden for the Hades that was the orlop. No smoke hid the reality of suffering. The pitiless gleam of lanthorns played on the carpet of maimed bodies, the retching, moaning, bloody humanity waiting for their turn on stage – the concentration of light on the midshipmen's mess table, where Surgeon Beatty was working on a spread-eagled man, who writhed and shrieked.

He finished his task. Bowden saw a brief glimpse of a piece of limb tossed into a tub with a meaty thump while the raw, pulsing stump was dealt with and the body, mad with pain, carried off by the loblolly boys. Straightening, Beatty wiped his forehead with the back of his hand and moved off to select the next, resembling an angel of death in his black smock, caked with blood and body fluids.

Bowden gulped, and in the gloom began stepping over the wretches in every state of agony, from uncontrollable convulsions to a deadly pale stillness. One man lay panting, his hands over the obscenity of his entrails, patiently waiting to die; another was propped up, his brutally mangled face unrecognisable, sobbing quietly. Everywhere Bowden looked, others were heroically controlling their suffering.

The blast and thunder of the guns on deck above was mercifully drowning the inhuman screeches and tormented moaning, but it was a scene that would stay with him for ever.

'Er, L'tenant Pasco?' he asked weakly, of a passing surgeon's assistant.

'There,' the man said irritably, jerking his thumb over his shoulder. Bowden gingerly made his way over to the larboard side where a pair of lanthorns glimmered.

He saw Pasco by their light – but something about the tension in the group next to him caused him to hesitate. He made out Scott, the chaplain, and Burke, the purser, supporting someone against a broad knee at the ship's side, one in a lace shirt with no indication of rank.

It was Nelson. Bowden's gaze froze. Their cherished commander-in-chief was wounded. He couldn't look away from the slight form, clearly in agony but with his eyes closed, Scott rubbing his chest and others hovering.

Bowden remembered himself and moved to Pasco, lying full length on an old sail close by with his eyes shut. Crouching down, he said, 'L'tenant Pasco, sir. Sir – it's Bowden, come to report.'

Not sure if he'd been heard, he was about to repeat it when Pasco stirred and groaned, feeling tenderly for his right side and arm. 'Report then, Mr Bowden,' he said hoarsely. For some reason the guns above had just ceased their heavy rumble and thunderclap din.

'Mr Robins is certain he'll have a signals team together directly, sir.'

'As will serve a flagship?'

'He's confident it will be so, sir.'

In the cessation of noise a faint but clear burst of cheering could be heard from above. 'How goes the battle, then?'

'We've taken *Redoutable*, Villeneuve and his flagship, and – and others I can't name. We've won a famous victory, I believe, sir.'

Pasco slumped back with a smile. Bowden asked diffidently, 'You're wounded, sir?'

'A grape-shot in the starb'd side is all,' Pasco said, biting his lip. 'Nothing as will stop me coming on deck when the sawbones lets me.'

Lowering his voice, Bowden ventured, 'That's Lord Nelson, sir. Is he – does he fare well, at all?'

'I don't know to be sure. The medical gentlemen are looking very grave, so I suppose it's serious enough.'

Another muffled burst of cheering came down, longer than the first.

A peevish voice intervened: 'What is the cause of that?' It was Nelson, trying to rise.

Pasco levered himself up and told him, 'It seems yet another enemy ship has struck to us, my lord. I have it from Mr Bowden here.'

'That is good,' Nelson said, his voice weak and gasping, clearly gratified. Scott helped him to a sip of lemonade and continued rubbing, while Burke on the other side held his shoulders.

Bowden rose to go but felt Pasco's hand urgently on his ankle. 'Sir?'

'Hunker down, lad.' Doing as he was told he felt Pasco fiddle at his back. 'I thought so. Take off your coat.'

As Bowden tried to do so it stuck to him and a burning pain made him gasp.

'You've taken a knock yourself, did you not know? Something's laid open your back, younker.'

In the heat of the action he hadn't noticed, but now a dull throb underlay the sharp burn.

'Stay – sit down here. We'll get the doctor to look at it when he's able.'

'Sir, it's only a—'

'No sense in taking chances now the battle's won. Do as I say.'

Obediently he sat next to Pasco and tried to keep the horror of the infernal regions at bay. He was so close he couldn't help but hear Nelson's agitated plea. 'Hardy! Will no one bring Hardy to me?' he groaned. 'He must be killed. Surely he is destroyed.'

Time dragged, and for Bowden the sight of Nelson in such agony was trying beyond reason. Those caring for him continued to murmur that Hardy would come as soon as he could, but it did not seem to ease his anxiety.

At length a figure came cautiously down the ladder. 'Sir, I'm desired by Captain Hardy to assure you he is unharmed and will be down to see you presently.'

Nelson, his eyes closed and clearly semi-conscious, asked who it was brought the message. 'It's Mr Bulkeley, my lord,' the purser said loudly.

'It is his voice,' Nelson said, almost in surprise. Then, rising above his pain, he turned unseeing eyes to the midshipman and added, 'Remember me to your father, if you please.'

Later there was whispering among those who held him and the surgeon was sent for. 'Yes, my lord?'

'Ah, Beatty. I've sent for you to say that all power of motion below my breast is gone and you very well know I can live but for a short time.'

The surgeon carefully tested for feeling in Nelson's legs, but the commander-in-chief whispered, 'Ah, Beatty, I'm too certain of it. Scott and Burke have tried it already. *You know* I am gone.'

Beatty straightened slowly, finding the words with difficulty. 'My lord, unhappily for our country nothing can be done for you.' He turned his head away quickly, the glitter of tears caught in the lanthorn light.

Nelson subsided but said calmly, 'I know it. I feel something rising in my breast which tells me. God be praised, I have done my duty.'

Cold with horror, Bowden heard it all and sat unspeaking until *Victory*'s captain came below.

'Well, Hardy,' Nelson whispered, after he was told of his arrival, 'how goes the day with us?'

'Very well, my lord,' Hardy said softly, taking his hand. 'We've got twelve or fourteen of the enemy's ships in our possession but five of their van have tacked and show an intention of bearing down on *Victory*. I've therefore called two or three of our ships round us and have no doubt of giving them a drubbing.'

'That is well, but I bargained on twenty.' Nelson choked and recovered, a spasm of anxiety causing him to try to raise himself. '*Anchor*, Hardy, *anchor!*' he panted wretchedly.

The captain frowned. 'I suppose, my lord, Admiral Collingwood will now take upon himself the direction of affairs.'

'Not while I live, I hope, Hardy!' Nelson gasped forcefully. 'No, do *you* anchor, Hardy.'

'Shall we then make the signal, sir?'

'Yes – for if I live, I'll anchor!'

The spasm past, Nelson lay back but spoke once more. 'Don't throw me overboard, Hardy.'

Shocked, Hardy answered, 'Oh, sir, no – certainly not!'

After a few moments Nelson rallied and said, his weak voice charged with feeling, 'Take care of my dear Lady Hamilton, Hardy – do take care of poor Lady Hamilton.'

The effort seemed to exhaust him but he went on faintly, 'Kiss me, Hardy.'

His friend knelt and kissed him on the cheek, and Nelson murmured, 'Now I am satisfied. Thank God I have done my duty.'

Hardy stood for a minute or two, his face a mask, then knelt again and kissed him once more. 'Who is that?' Nelson whispered.

'It is Hardy, my lord.'

'God bless you, Hardy,' Nelson said feebly.

The captain of *Victory* then left.

Bowden could not tear his eyes away from the scene; he saw the faithful Scott lean down as Nelson said weakly, 'Doctor, I have not been a *great* sinner.' The chaplain, overcome, could not speak and Nelson went on, 'Remember, I leave Lady Hamilton and my daughter Horatia as a legacy to my country.'

Slipping in and out of consciousness he muttered, 'Never forget Horatia,' and again, 'Thank God I have done my duty.'

A little time passed, then Scott called out, distraught. Beatty was with his assistants but came immediately. He took Nelson's wrist and felt the forehead, then stiffly rose, shaking his head. He stood for a moment, looking down on the still figure. Then, collecting himself, he looked about him.

Catching sight of Bowden sitting against the side he stepped across. 'Sir, are you able to walk?'

Bowden nodded, speechless.

'Then you shall have the infinitely melancholy duty to inform the captain that his lordship is no more and, consequently, his flag needs must be hauled down.'

Chapter 14

The feeling of unreality deepened. It seemed the eyes of half London were on them as *L'Aurore* lost way, carefully and precisely ceasing to move, her bows into the swift current of the Thames. Her anchor plunged as she eased into position astern of the vessel they had escorted from the open sea to the heart of the capital.

It was the Honourable George Grey's yacht *Chatham*, on its most important mission ever: to take the body of Horatio, Lord Nelson, from *Victory* at the Nore to Greenwich, where it was to lie in state. Now, opposite the magnificence of Wren's buildings, the final act was to take place that would see Nelson return from the sea to the land that had given him birth.

Captain Kydd signalled discreetly and the boatswain pealed out his call. Instantly men leaped for the ratlines and by the beat of a drum mounted each mast in unison, spreading out along the yardarms in grave silence, every man with a black armband.

On *Chatham* Nelson's coffin was prepared for lowering

into the ceremonial barge alongside. Of great size and superbly ornamented, it was made from the main-mast of *L'Orient*, the French flagship that had exploded into fiery oblivion at the Nile.

As it was hoisted clear of the deck, Kydd whipped off his full-dress cocked hat. The rest of the little party on the quarterdeck followed suit, and out on the yards far above, every man did likewise. Into the awful silence came the flat thud of the first minute gun and a spreading murmur from the vast crowds lining the riverbank.

Next to Kydd, captured enemy officers were nobly paying their respects. Standing apart from them, however, was a tall, deathly pale individual whose greatest wish – to die in his flagship where so many others had done so – had been denied him. It was the French commander, Villeneuve.

Kydd glanced at him. What conceivably could he be thinking at this time? He had done his duty and more, but he had had the monumental misfortune to have Horatio Nelson as his opponent. When he had left Cadiz he must have known what was waiting, yet still he had sailed.

And it had been far worse for him than even the most pessimistic could have foreseen. A battle of annihilation that had left the Combined Fleet shattered, sunk, captured or fleeing. Ten times the casualties that the English had suffered and a psychological wound that would last far longer. It was defeat on a heroic scale to be talked about for all of time.

In his frigate Kydd had necessarily stayed clear of the carnage but from his vantage-point he had seen the dread grandeur of the conflict unfold through to its finality when, as if to signal an end to the cataclysm, *Achille* had taken fire and exploded.

He had also been witness to the shameful act of the

French van, appearing to be finally turning back in aid of the centre but instead careering on through the fighting, firing on friend and foe alike to flee the field. A dozen of the Spanish also had taken the opportunity to turn and run for Cadiz, no longer able to stand against the fury of the English guns.

But what he knew would for ever stay with him was what had followed after the guns had fallen silent, when he had closed with the mile square of wreck-strewn water off Cape Trafalgar: over there was *Victory*, no mizzen, her fore-mast and bowsprit a stump, trailing a tangle of stranded rigging and splintered spars. *Belleisle* was even worse: totally dismasted and a hulk, her sides appallingly battered by shot, yet her white ensign still gallantly flying, tied to the riven remains of her main-mast.

All told there were seventeen dismasted hulks from both sides drifting in the sea, along with the pathetic blobs of floating corpses, the stench of fire and the all-pervasive reek of powder-smoke. But for Kydd nothing was more poignant and shocking than the broken cry of a seaman noticing that Admiral Nelson's flag no longer flew in *Victory*.

The news had taken hold and, when confirmed by the commander-in-chief's flag rising first in Collingwood's crippled *Royal Sovereign* and then in *Euryalus*, a pall of mourning had descended that touched every man.

Now, at Greenwich, they were still in a haze of disbelief and bereavement, the joy of victory invisible behind a curtain of grief. They stood motionless as the coffin was gently lowered, the officers' heads bowed in the utmost solemnity.

Shortly after the barge had left, another arrived alongside *L'Aurore*. Villeneuve with great dignity bowed gravely, first to Kydd and then his officers, and entered the boat to be taken into captivity. For him it was a parole and gracious living, even an exchange to return to France; for the surviving seamen who had fought so heroically for him, it was the fetid hulks or prisons far inland – even the lonely desolation of the one being built on Dartmoor – to rot out their life, their only crime to have served their country faithfully.

Kydd had himself boarded and taken possession of a Spanish ship-of-the-line, and the cruel devastation that a raking pass had inflicted aboard had shaken him. More than a hundred and fifty seamen in one stroke killed or hideously wounded, their pain and suffering a living hell of unimaginable piteousness. Below decks they had found a charnel house of blood and remains, bodies still heaped by their guns, the racking groans of the maimed . . .

Yet the ship had fought on hopelessly until battered into helplessness by two British ships standing safely off.

'Mr Kydd – sir?' It was the anxious boatswain. 'Sir, you've made y'r arrangements wi' Sheerness dockyard about them larb'd fore-shrouds? Rare strained they was in the blow, an' we has t' renew 'em.'

'Oh, er, they've been advised, Mr Oakley . . .' The interchange sent his mind down another track to when the storm foretold by the heavy swell had finally struck.

The remainder of the day of the battle had been spent obeying Collingwood's instructions to bring the fleet to order and to secure the prizes, taking the helpless in tow and trying to shape course for Gibraltar. Kydd had men away as prize crew and, with the rest, had had to manhandle messengers and heavy hawsers in the rising sea.

The dead weight of the heavy battleship in tow was a sore trial for the delicate-lined *L'Aurore*, and as darkness fell, it had turned into a nightmare, the jerking and surging straining her bitts and the increasing swell now abeam making sheer existence a misery. What it must have been like for the helpless wounded in the bowels of the capture was beyond imagining.

By morning the barometer had dropped precipitously a whole two inches and driving squalls of heavy rain made working aloft a slippery death-trap, and then as the bluster intensified, reefs had to be taken in by the depleted and exhausted crew.

The day wore on and they struggled south, but an inshore current of some strength was setting relentlessly to the north, destroying their gains even as the long hours passed.

The wind increased, white combers on the back of the great swell crashing with force on the ship's side. In the afternoon breakers were sighted through the veils of rain – these were the treacherous sandbanks that ranged far out from the Spanish coast, exposed by the deep scend of the swell.

It got worse: a developing fresh gale, coupled with the relentless urging of the swell out of the west, was creating every mariner's dread – a dead lee shore. Now the struggle was for survival, a desperate clawing off from the shoreline against the wind.

Night drew in, and with it torrential rain and a raging whole gale that screamed and moaned in the rigging as if the souls of the slain were haunting them. Two seamen were swept from the lower shrouds in a particularly savage roll. They disappeared into the white torn murk with no possible hope of rescue. Another two suffered injury before the terrible night was over.

Kydd shuddered. That, with the piteous sight of *Fougueux* driving ashore and breaking up on the shoals, her pitiful cargo of helpless wounded to perish in the pounding surf, would stay in stark clarity in his mind for ever.

Yet incredibly their time of trial had not been over: the violent squalls backed to the south-west during the night, and when morning came it brought a sight that was as unexpected as it was unthinkable.

From Cadiz an enemy heavy squadron of six battleships and more frigates were clawing their way out into the wild weather to renew the fight.

Caught scattered over the sea in battle-damaged ships and others with prizes, the British were in no condition to face a fresh engagement – but they did. Collingwood signalled his dispositions: those with prizes under tow would continue on while any that were able would close on him and confront the squadron.

With scraps of sail, jury-rigged masts and men dropping with fatigue, they went for the enemy, and where their ships were in such desperate condition they made up for it by consummate seamanship and transparent resolution. The squadron turned about and retreated on Cadiz, their honour satisfied with the retaking of a couple of the worst-damaged prizes.

The weather clamped in yet again, intense white squalls under dark grey-green clouds slashed with lightning, visibility dangerously impaired time and again so close to the reefs and banks of Trafalgar. It hammered at the worn ships for days.

The prizes were now a liability – not only that but if the weather moderated there was every chance of an even bigger sortie by the emboldened Spanish. Reluctantly, Collingwood gave the order to abandon them, but this brought problems of its own for each prize had to be cleared of its pitiful cargo of wounded and others in numbers quite capable of a rising to seize a small frigate. It took adroit boatwork to transfer the prisoners and find somewhere for them.

When it was over *L'Aurore* was packed with suffering humanity and sullen captives – but they were now making headway south. Slowly but surely the victorious, grief-stricken, mutilated but ultimately triumphant fleet crept over the seas to Gibraltar.

There, the worst afflicted were brought alongside the mole and at last the casualties found rest – or burial in the little graveyard.

Kydd quietly went aboard *Victory*, her ship's company and the small dockyard labouring to fit her for the final voyage home. He was met by Bowden, who gravely took him to see the gaping wounds she had suffered, his own place of trial, and then below to where their commander-in-chief had breathed his last.

Admiral Collingwood had earlier sent his dispatches home in the little *Pickle* schooner but the Mediterranean Squadron would remain at its post. No glorious homecoming for the ships that had fought the greatest battle in all sea history, they would be repaired and ordered out again to stand once more as England's enduring shield.

Except HMS *Victory*. She would be sent home bearing the body of Lord Nelson – escorted by the smallest frigate that Collingwood could spare.

The tinny sound of a distant band intruded into Kydd's thoughts and brought him back to the present. The ceremonial barge had reached the embankment where Lord Hood was standing and, amid the melancholy strains of the Dead March from *Saul*, the coffin was prepared for lifting.

It was done. Kydd clapped his hat on and turned, meeting the solemn eyes of his officers. 'Carry on, please,' he said, and went below to his cabin.

It was over. The world was now a different place. The 'Great Fear' that had seized England since Bonaparte had set in motion his invasion plan was now lifted from northern sheep-herders, midland ironmasters and the powerful financiers in the City of London.

What lay ahead? Had the tide turned or were endless years of conflict still to come until one or the other triumphed?

And the Royal Navy without Horatio Nelson. It was beyond conceiving, the absence of such a figure at the summit of the profession beckoning each and every man to deeds of valour and standards of conduct that had forged a weapon of the sea that stood so far in advance of every other.

The pricking of a tear caught him unawares. He had seen common seamen weeping at the news, officers making their excuses, but he had known the man himself, the warmth, iron strength and utter devotion to duty, and to think . . .

He blinked furiously, trying to hold back. It was by Nelson's own act that he had been plucked as an unemployed commander and sent to the heights of glory that was post-captaincy. What had Nelson seen in him? Whatever it was, he had been sent for to join the illustrious band – he, Thomas Kydd, whose origins were as a pressed man, to know for ever that he had once been part of—

He couldn't help it. The tears coursed down and sobs

shook him. Then he felt an arm round his shoulders, tender, understanding. 'It's victory, Nicholas, but at *such* a cost . . .'

'Dear fellow, in truth my grief is as yours – but nothing is surer than that Horatio Nelson's memory will ever be immortal.'

Author's Note

Although I have written ten books in the Kydd series, I approached the writing of this one with a little trepidation. The battle of Trafalgar was, after all, the grandest spectacle in naval history and has been the subject of many hundreds of books. How could I bring a new and fresh treatment to readers? In the end I decided that my focus would come from two vantage-points – that of newly promoted frigate captain Thomas Kydd, and Charles Bowden, a midshipman aboard *Victory*, who had served with Kydd before. It seemed appropriate that the book was written in 2009, the 250th anniversary of the 'Year of Victories' and the laying down of this noble ship's keel.

As an aside, what struck me when I began my research was that so many Americans were fighting for King George III at the time: in the fleet as a whole there were some four hundred, and aboard *Victory*, twenty-two. It might appear puzzling that Americans were involved in the conflict, but it seems that before the United States Navy reached its full potential it was not uncommon for young sons of Uncle

Sam to be placed in the Royal Navy for the priceless experience it offered.

As I worked on the manuscript my respect for Horatio Nelson – already huge – if anything, increased. Often, in hindsight, the decisions of a battle commander can be questioned, but Nelson, on so many counts, either made the correct decision or took a sound calculated gamble. He was definitely right, for instance, to chase the French across the Atlantic. If he had not been lied to by a Yankee merchant ship there might have been a Trafalgar in the Caribbean and there, wildly outnumbered, even Nelson might not have prevailed. So perhaps England was unknowingly saved by an American.

I commend to all my readers at least one visit to *Victory*, now preserved in perpetuity in Portsmouth Historic Dockyard. Apart from admiring the sheer size and lofty grace of what was the eighteenth-century equivalent of a nuclear aircraft carrier today, do use your imagination to go back in time and think about the people who manned her at Trafalgar. What could it have been like for boys as young as eleven in that hellish battle? And how could men stand to their guns in hideous conditions for up to six hours and then, in the moment of triumph, cry like babies at the loss of their commander?

As usual, I owe a debt of gratitude to many people. Space precludes naming them all but I would particularly like to mention Peter Goodwin, keeper and curator of HMS *Victory*, who unstintingly gave of his time and knowledge during my week-long location research in Portsmouth, and granted me complete access to the iconic vessel; Dr Dennis Wheeler of the University of Sutherland, whose analysis of the meteorological conditions during October 1805 provided invaluable insights; and Gordon Simmonds, from the Historical Maritime Society, who painstakingly re-created just how *Victory*'s signals team must have worked. And, of course, a huge vote of thanks goes to my wife and literary partner, Kathy, my editor at Hodder & Stoughton, Anne Clarke, and my agent, Carole Blake.

Where will Kydd venture in the next books? Trafalgar destroyed Bonaparte's invasion plan for England, but in 1805 the war is by no means over. Now Britain is free to begin the race to Empire!